I0684938

Ice Blue Deception

A Trace Armstrong Mystery: Book Two

by John Scot

Meedeeah Publishing

Other Books by John Scot

Blood Red Picasso

By John W. Richardson

The Path of Consequence

Iron Rebel

Published by Meedeeah Press

To My Wife, Family, and Friends
Who Inspire Me To Keep Going
When The Writing Gets Tough.

Ice Blue Deception

PROLOGUE

Three bodies lay unconscious on the floor, one in each room. Accelerant applied. Propane tank seeping. Match lit. The knife came down into flesh, not once, not twice, but six separate times. As it was drawn out the last time, something became apparent. Something was wrong. Very wrong. Somebody would now have to die the hard way.

CHAPTER 1

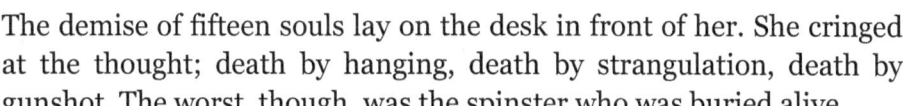

The demise of fifteen souls lay on the desk in front of her. She cringed at the thought; death by hanging, death by strangulation, death by gunshot. The worst, though, was the spinster who was buried alive.

Meg Lockhart glanced away, her eyes crossing the wood-paneled office to open framed windows, replete with white plaster buildings and the mindless escape of the Pacific Ocean. Late afternoon breezes brought the smell of eucalyptus and salt air.

She wasn't superstitious, at least not that she would admit. As curator of the San Diego History Museum, she needed to maintain an air of authority, always playing the part; blue silk skirt, white cotton blouse, regulation three-inch pumps. With her permed brown hair in a perfect do, she always had a smile.

Deep breath in, she refocused on the newly arrived royal blue silk sachet confronting her. It held a light blue diamond almost two inches in length, innocently called, 'Ice Blue.' Nothing about it would physically threaten her life, yet an intangible fear ran down her spine. The name gave no indication of the pain. After two ulcers and lots of antacids over the years, not much got to her anymore. This diamond was different. 15 people had lost their lives in the 100-year history of the stone. Ice Blue Demon was its nickname. It would be in a special exhibit for the next six months.

Bruno, the Bulgarian security guard, stood next to her desk, accompanied by another guard. His bald head sat directly on massive shoulders. "Construction guy needs to mount diamond in secure case for new display. Once set, cannot be removed."

Meg pulled the bag toward herself. "You mean the gemstone will be out of the safe?"

"Not problem. They hook wire to it."

"I don't like this one bit," she said.

"You come, I show."

Bruno slid the diamond back into the pouch. The guard duo led Meg from her upstairs office, down to the maintenance warehouse at the back of the building. Handing the pouch to the construction supervisor, Bruno said, "Ernie here needs to glue mounting in place. Light must be right."

Meg leaned against the skeleton of the large metal case. The lanky supervisor said, "The diamond must sit in a titanium holder, so the reflections match up to the case. Once set, we don't want to move it."

Meg shook her head. "Don't like it. Don't like it at all. This little gem is worth millions. With its bloody history, it's considered priceless. Can't we put it back in the safe when you're done?"

"Not without missing our deadline. We're behind schedule already. It was supposed to be here five days ago. We install the facade on the main floor over the Labor Day holiday. Only nine days to go."

"But why can't you put it away?"

"The showcase has multiple layers of security glass, and the lighting has to line accurately up. The diamond mounts internally, and then the viewports are installed. With our short timetable, we only have time to fit it once."

Meg frowned. "So what will keep someone from walking in here and taking it?"

Ernie smiled. "The case has motion security sensors and the warehouse has new electronic deadbolts on both doors, not to mention full-time video surveillance. The bolts come on at ten or if the motion sensors go off. Just about impossible for someone to get away. They would be locked in. Takes a supervisor code to unlock it. Bruno or one of the other security guys would then take care of our intruder. Not a pleasant experience."

Taking a deep breath, she said, "I'll be working in my office till nine tonight. Call me when it's complete. I need to sign off on this."

Diamond in hand, the supervisor replied, "Should be done before nine. I'll buzz you before I leave."

Meg left the warehouse and trudged up the stairs. After twenty years in the Balboa Park institution, the steps were getting harder, but she knew retirement was just a few years away. Soon there would be no more hair spray, saggy pantyhose, and painful high heels. Her stressful responsibility for three stories of priceless treasures would be a distant memory.

With the reddish glow of the sunset in the distance, Meg closed the window to the cool August breeze. Thoughts of a cat burglar climbing the outside wall made her laugh. She had watched way too many old movies. *Things like that didn't happen in real life. Certainly not in 1988. Not with modern technology.*

After three hours of paperwork at her desk, her phone rang. The diamond was mounted. Almost nine. Time to go home.

She locked her office and headed downstairs. The construction supervisor caught her at the bottom of the steps. "Take a look. It's secured, and the glass glued in place."

Entering the warehouse, a fiery glow came from the case. Peering inside, she said, "It's gorgeous, Ernie. A beautiful gemstone. I like how the reflection fills the display. Are you sure it's safe?"

"No problem, Mrs. Lockhart. See the wires coming out the back. If they lose connection, the whole room locks down. Notice the camera on the ceiling. 24-hour video. You can feel safe about this. Besides, Bruno is here until midnight. The overnight shift comes in after that. I'm leaving now; I'll walk you out."

Ernie closed the large door from the warehouse to the main floor and set the lock and the alarm.

Meg said, "I feel much better now that you showed me the setup. I may actually be able to sleep."

The two of them walked across the main floor and headed to a rear entrance corridor. Just as they were about to open the door, the lights went out, the room plunged into darkness. Deadbolts could be heard sliding into place.

Meg said, "I can't believe this, Ernie. You're going to give me a heart attack. This is absolutely crazy. The power is out again. You said we fixed that."

Ernie replied, "The electrician was just out last week. Installed a new breaker for our upcoming display."

"Our jobs are on the line. If something goes missing, guess who gets the blame. I'm tired of excuses. We spend thousands of dollars on this place, and they can't get the wiring reliable. Your elaborate electronic security is now worthless. The cameras are off, the case unarmed."

Ernie said, "That's why we have manual deadbolts. No worries. Those spring loaded deadbolts have locked us up tighter than a drum. Sorry to say though, we're stuck until it comes back on. "

Meg said, "No worries. How can you say that? Now everything is out of your control. You've got a priceless diamond that you can't secure, sitting in an open display that you can't even see on video. I'll tell you this. If that diamond is gone, you and your staff will be too."

The two of them found the stairway in the dark.

Ernie said, "Please don't worry, Meg. We've had power outages before. I know it's stressful, but that's why we have manual overrides. No one can get to the diamond. Take a seat on the stairs. The guards up front will get the power restored. Shouldn't take long."

Meg sat down on the stairway, her head in her hands. She was shaking with anger. Mumbling under her breath, she finally went quiet.

After a seeming eternity, the power finally came back on at 9:30. The sound of electromagnetic deadbolts retreating could be heard all over the first floor.

In the distance, Bruno came running in from the front security office. Seeing Meg and Ernie, he said, "You OK? Electrician come. Damn wires again. Can't believe, we get locked out like that."

"We're okay, but let's get to the diamond. I must know that it's secure," said Meg.

Bruno unlatched the warehouse door. The diamond glowed brightly in the case.

Bruno said. "All Good. You sleep better now."

Meg looked in. The light blue stone reflected brilliantly, but something seemed different. *What was it?*

"Anything look strange to you?" Meg said. "Seems different somehow."

Ernie glanced over the edge, "The reflection is off a little. Probably the glue hardening. I'll adjust it in the morning."

Meg said in a frustrated tone, "At least it's still here. I want all of you to check in with me tomorrow. We can't have this happen again."

Bruno looked at his watch, "We better get out. New deadbolt alarm sets at ten. The security cameras are back up. Don't want to be locked in all night."

The warehouse door was shut and alarmed again.

Bruno said, "I escort you to back door."

The three entered the rear corridor. As they came to the exit door, Bruno noticed a light on in the kitchen. "Darn cooks left light on." Through the small corridor window, he could see a lone knife on the counter. "Idiots left knife out. Their boss will kill if he knows. I'll put away."

Meg put her key card in the rear door, the brisk evening air greeting them as the latch was released. "Good night," she said in a stern voice. "We will deal with this tomorrow."

Headed to her car, she thought, *the diamond was still safe and secure. It survived a power failure. She still had a job. Hopefully, no more excitement while it is on display for the next six months.*

Little did she know how much mayhem the jewel of death would bring in the next few days.

CHAPTER 2

Guilty Pleasures. Saturday morning, six a.m., last week in August 1988. The tach was steady at a thousand RPM, my foot on the clutch. Sitting at a red signal light on Coast Highway—ocean on my left, grassy fields on my right—I put the Led Zeppelin cassette in the player. *Ramble On* filled the Bose speakers. I hit the gas and the engine revved nicely. The sun was rising over the hills behind me, and a bluish gray moon was prominent in my rear view mirror.

Looking to my right, a black Ford Mustang had pulled up. The driver glanced my way and shot me a rev. The four-lane road descended ahead of us into Cardiff by the Sea. It was vacant for at least a mile, a deserted strip of coastline, no entrances or exits. No cops. I looked over to the signal on the cross street, now yellow. My right foot pressed on the gas, engine revving, stick shift in first; stereo turned up high. It's time to Ramble On.

As the light ahead turned green, I let out the clutch, engine revving high and the tires smoking behind me, two loud chords of the song and then a shift to second, thrown back into the seat. Unfortunately, the Mustang was starting to pull away. Pedal mashed to the floor, engine screaming, then a quick shift to third, Mustang now two car lengths ahead. Speedo now at 60 mph. We were just getting started. The convertible felt light in the early morning mist, wind now blowing my hair back and flowing past my sunglasses. The tach rose again, this time, a little more slowly, but the race was now tilting in my direction, 70, 80, and now 90 miles per hour. I shifted to fourth as the Mustang started to run out of breath.

Glancing over, the other driver seemed a little paranoid of the speed, shaking his head. I kept the tach climbing. Four thousand, five thousand, then six. I shifted to fifth as the speedo crested 110. The Mustang was dropping back, but I wasn't finished yet. One hundred fifteen, 120, 125, and then the magic number, one hundred and thirty miles per hour. I smiled, the Mustang a distant memory, and I slowly dropped back to cruising speed.

A half mile later I pulled onto the access road that ran parallel to Coast Highway and led to numerous Cardiff businesses. The Lewellyn Bakery was my first stop. I pulled the beautiful blue Mercedes 280 SL into a parking slot across from the bakery entrance. Walking up, long time owner, Maxwell Thomas, signaled me with a wave. He was handing out samples of his signature blueberry donuts, steaming hot, to patrons waiting in line. Now in his seventies, sunburnt with patchy gray hair, he took a seat across from me on one of the outside patio tables, sliding the treats in my direction. Offering a napkin and a donut, I was in heaven.

Lewellyn's is located in Cardiff, an eclectic beach town 35 miles north of San Diego California, home to Pipes Beach and some of the best surfing on the West Coast. Dead center in an aging light blue strip mall, it's one of my favorite places to start the week. Long trays of amazing donuts meet you as you enter the door. All the seating is outside in an enclosed patio area. While the decadent gastric treasures mix well with the fresh ocean breezes, the beautiful topless automotive treasure sitting a few feet across the parking lot from me made this day unique. An old friend from the FBI, Bob Jordan, had lent me his gorgeous 1969 Horizon Blue Mercedes SL sports car. Two tan leather seats, chrome dash, convertible top, and six powerful direct injected cylinders, made for an exciting experience. The early morning sunlight reflected off the sky blue car with an explosion of brilliance from the sunlit blue ocean behind. Life was good.

"How's it going, Trace?" said Maxwell, as he took a bite from one of the steaming treats.

"Good today," I said. "I've got a friend's Mercedes for a week. One of my favorite models. It's a late 69, 280 SL in a real pretty blue. It's a third car for Bob. He retired recently from the FBI and has time now to spend puttering around the house and work on his cars. He wants me to tune it so it will go 130 mph again. He hasn't driven it much over the last few years, and it was sputtering badly when you step on the gas."

He laughed, "I could use a friend like that."

"I'll work on later in the week, but I wanted to run it through a new tank of premium gas first. This car needed to breathe. Made for the Autobahn in Germany, the best thing I can do is blow it out with a screaming trip down the road."

"Where's your office manager, Janet? She's usually tagging along with you."

"She's back in New York, starting the proceedings on a divorce. Since her deadbeat husband lives back there, she had to file and do the paperwork way across the country. She'll be gone most of the week."

"Last time I noticed, you guys seemed to be getting along well. I imagine you'll be happy if the divorce goes through."

"You have no idea, Max. She's had to put up with his infidelity bullshit for the last two years. We'll both be glad when this is over."

"So you've got to manage your affairs for a few days. Hey, at least you have something nice to drive."

"I'm taking this beautiful machine up inland later this morning. My cousin called yesterday. His dad passed away earlier in the week. My Uncle Paul. They live up in Fallbrook, about 50 miles north. He needs some help with the estate. He died under strange circumstances, and he wants me to check into it."

"Another case?" he asked.

"Might be, you never know."

He shook his head and then said, "Boy it's been a long time since I've been up that way. They built a new freeway since I've been up there. The 15 I think. Used to take half a day on old highway 395. Probably just over an hour now with the new road."

"Long time for me too. I've heard about a place over the hill passed Fallbrook called Rancho California where they are selling five acre lots pretty cheap. Might have to take a look while I'm up there."

"Where you stay'n?"

"In the old Fallbrook Hotel."

"Really. I heard it's haunted, but that was years ago. I'm surprised it's still standing."

"My cousin's house is nearby. That's the only reason I'm staying there."

"Creepy if you ask me. I heard someone died there not to long ago. Maybe multiple ghosts now?"

"Now there you go scaring me, Maxwell. You know I don't do well with invisible spirits."

"I remember you tell'n me you had trouble with the other kind of spirits--the liquid kind."

I laughed, "You know way too much about me. I promise I'm almost a tea-totaler now."

"How about some coffee in a to-go cup?"

"Sounds great. Black please."

As Maxwell went to fetch the coffee, the gleaming black Mustang I had raced a few minutes before pulled into the driveway and parked right next to the Mercedes. The door opened, and a tall, heavyset guy got out. He walked over to me, reached into his pocket and pulled out a shining object. He moved his hand over and opened his palm. His police badge shown bright in the early morning sun.

"I'm Captain Kirkpatrick of the North County Sheriff. You're under arrest..."

CHAPTER 3

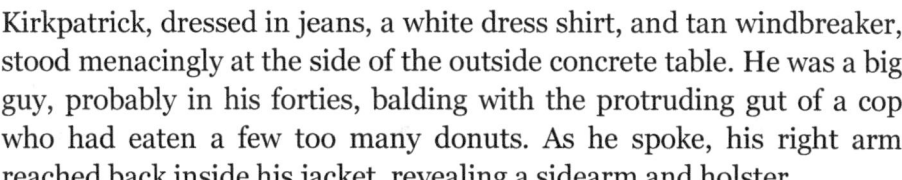

Kirkpatrick, dressed in jeans, a white dress shirt, and tan windbreaker, stood menacingly at the side of the outside concrete table. He was a big guy, probably in his forties, balding with the protruding gut of a cop who had eaten a few too many donuts. As he spoke, his right arm reached back inside his jacket, revealing a sidearm and holster.

"Let me see your license. You were doing well over a hundred miles an hour. That's automatic jail time."

I stood up and looked him in the eye, "So you show me a badge, but how do I know who you are? I'll be glad to show you some ID, but I need to see some from you."

He seemed annoyed, but he reached back for his wallet and pulled out a photo id for Captain Jake Kirkpatrick of the North County Sheriff's Department.

"Now show me your license, so I can call this in."

I pulled my wallet out and handed him my license. One that hadn't been updated since I came to California over four years ago. He pulled it briskly from my fingers and held it in the early morning light.

He read my name with an air of intimidation, "William T. Armstrong of Los Angeles. Forty-two years old, brown hair, blue eyes, five foot eleven, no restrictions." He paused, "So Mister Armstrong, down here in San Diego County we have a policy of taking speeders directly to jail. But it's early Monday morning, I don't have my patrol car, and I know that calling this in will waste half my day with paperwork and hassle. In fact, I don't even have my ticket book with me. So I tell you what, I can make a phone call, or I might be persuaded to get back in my car if you don't mind making a donation."

I laughed at the audacity of this guy, "So how much of a 'donation' do you need to go away."

His voice turned serious, "This is a real serious offense, Mr. Armstrong, which includes jail time, a court appearance and thousands of dollars in fines. However, this could be offset with a cash donation to the Sheriff's Benevolence Society for a couple of hundred dollars."

I sat back down at the table and pulled out my wallet, "Well Captain Kirkpatrick, I think you might be in luck. I think I can help your Benevolence Society today." With that, I pulled out a couple of hundred dollar bills which I had thanks to a pre-payment from Bob Jordan for working on his car. As I was getting ready to slide the money across the table, I found an old business card and put it on top of the money as I pushed it over.

Kirkpatrick, pulled the bills over and then froze as he saw the card that said, William T. Armstrong, Detective, California Highway Patrol.

I rose up, walked over and faced him in the eye. "Listen you son of a bitch. You might shake down the locals with your bullshit, but I'm not buying it. I'm down here in North County working with the FBI on a car theft ring which may just involve slimy cops like you," I lied, as I pulled my money back across the table. "I ought to arrest you for exhibition of speed, reckless driving, and involving me in a dangerous high-speed chase. However, if you will be so kind as to leave a twenty dollar tip for my coffee and donut I'll be glad to keep this to myself and not tell your boss, Lieutenant Fitch."

He stepped back and looked at me suspiciously, "Now I know who you are. I just recognized the face. You're that private dick from Sloan Beach involved with that double shooting a few months back. You ain't no Highway Patrol guy. I ought to call your ass in."

"You just go right ahead, Captain Kirk, but if I were you, I'd get back in my ugly Ford spaceship and fly to some galaxy far, far away. One phone call from me and you'll have a lot of explaining to do. My friends at the CHP would love to bust your ass for running a car race scam. Nice deal. Hell, I bet you make hundreds a week from the locals. Just show em your gun, and shake them down for cash."

He stared me down, "I think your name is Trace. Yea, that's right. I remember that name. You were following some lady a few months back that was abducted. Shot out a radiator on a van on the freeway. Then two guys end up dead. Caused us a paperwork nightmare." He reached into his wallet and pulled out a twenty, tossing it down on the table. "Listen, you just stay out of my way, and stay within the speed limit. If I catch you again, I won't be so lenient." With that he walked over to his car, got in and burned rubber out of the drive.

As a private detective, I run into all sorts of people. Most are hard working and live within the law. But there are always those that push the limits. Some, like Kirkpatrick, use their power positions to intimidate others. I really had to think hard about this guy. Yea, he caught me dead to rights, and he certainly could have arrested me, but once he pulled the 'bribe card,' he lost all credibility. Especially since he initiated the race. In court it would be called 'entrapment,' but I was just glad to get on with my day. I thought about calling Lieutenant Fitch and letting him know what went down, but I didn't want any trouble. As an outside investigator, I need law enforcement cooperation. If I ratted on this guy, that might go away. You never know the internal politics of these smaller departments. In North County San Diego, there is a hodgepodge of jurisdictions, which make things difficult at best and make me reluctant to call them in at times. Guys on the take like Jake Kirkpatrick just make it worse.

Suddenly I heard the door open behind me, and Maxwell appeared with a hot cup of Joe. He sat down again for a second. "What was that all about?"

I smiled, "Just one of the sheriff guys asking for a donation for their Benevolent Society."

"It looked a little tense there for a moment," he said.

"The guy tried to intimidate me into donating. They make a big percentage of what they collect. I just called him on it and persuaded him to donate to your cause with a big tip. After all, what's a cop without donuts."

"You're one hell of a good negotiator, Armstrong. I have no idea how you pulled that one off."

"Simple, Max. I just pulled out a bigger card than he had. The CHP is a much bigger outfit than the North County Sheriff. He didn't want to donate to them so I told him that giving to Maxwell can pay big and tasty dividends down the road. He seemed to think that $20 spent here was a great investment."

"I'll have to remember that if I see him again."

"Do me a favor Max. If you see that guy hassling customers would you let me know. I don't like pushy cops."

"Will do," he said as he collected the bill on the table. "Hey, I've got to get back to the counter. Thanks for the tip."

"See you soon. I'll let you know how Fallbrook goes. Hopefully no ghosts."

He smiled and walked back into the shop. I finished up the blueberry muffins and drank up the coffee. The sun was above the distant hills now and the day was warming up. Time to head north.

As I walked back to the car, sirens roared in the distance. Sounded like fire trucks and an ambulance. I started the German machine and went to pull out, when three sheriff cars roared into the drive, pulled up behind me, and three guys rolled out, guns drawn and aimed directly at my head.

CHAPTER 4

I froze, surprised as much as I was mad. The center cop yelled, "Freeze. Hands up."

He ambled over to the car; gun aimed directly at my head, "Get out of the car slowly. Keep your hands up."

I did as instructed. Standing, the other two guys came around the side, guns aimed directly at my chest. The lead guy said, "Put your hands behind your back."

As I complied, He slapped handcuffs on me and pushed me against the car. I snapped, "What's this all about?"

The lead cop said, "We have a stolen car matching this description. Someone stated that they saw you take it and that you were here in the strip mall."

I shook my head and murmured under my breath, "Captain Kirk strikes again." I wasn't sure if any of these three guys was in cahoots with Kirkpatrick so I decided to play it cool. Looking at the lead officer, I said calmly, "This is a friend's car. I'm doing some repair work on it. I'll be glad to give you the information, and you can call him. He works for the FBI. So who are you guys?"

"I'm officer Hanks of the North County Sheriff's Department; the other guys are Kelly and Serrano. We had a call from a Mr. Smith that his car was stolen from his driveway overnight and that he spotted it here. The license number and description match this vehicle."

"The owner's name is Robert Jordan. He works for the FBI. Take a look in the glove compartment, his registration is there. There can't be too many cars like this around here. 280 SL is a pretty rare model. I hope you got information from the person who called in. Sounds like a hoax."

He walked around and pulled the registration from the glove box.

"It's like you say, Robert Jordan up on Oceanview Drive in Cardiff."

"If you'll undo my hands, I'll be glad to give you his number."

With that, the guys lowered their weapons, and he undid the cuffs. I pulled my license and one of Bob's business cards out of my wallet and handed it to Officer Hanks. "Give him a call. He's recently retired so he should be home. I picked this up over the weekend, and he expects it back at the end of the week."

Hanks handed the card off to one of the other guys to call in. "So Mr. Armstrong, do you currently live in Los Angeles as it says on the license?"

"No, I recently moved to Sloan Beach. I haven't updated the license, sorry."

He looked at me quizzically, "You aren't Trace Armstrong the private detective are you? You look strangely familiar. Seems like I remember you from an abduction case a few months back."

"That's me," I said.

"I thought it was you. I was assigned to the case and remember seeing you at the old motel in Karden Beach. So if you are a private detective, what are you doing working on an old Mercedes?" he asked.

"Well I'll be honest with you, detective work is OK, but it doesn't always pay the bills. I was a foreign car mechanic for years back in Texas, before I moved to California. Worked on a lot of the exotic cars for the oilmen and others with money to spare. I just fill in my slow times now with a job or two. I especially like these older model Mercedes. The dealers won't touch them anymore, so I have almost Carte Blanche with a lot of my customers. I have a makeshift shop where I live, off of Stevens, in an old barn. Works for me."

One of the other guys walked over. "We put the call in Sir. It's like he said. He has permission to drive the car. It's on the up and up."

Hanks handed me back the registration. "It looks like you are free to go, Mr. Armstrong," he said.

I liked these guys, so I offered, "Hey while you are here, let me buy you guys a donut. My friend Maxwell owns the place, and he makes some of the best flour and sugar concoctions money can buy."

Hanks smiled, "We can't stay—too busy—but I will take you up on a to-go order. Any idea who might have called this in? Seems strange. I asked dispatch, and they don't have any name other than a Mr. Smith with a bogus call back number. You got any enemies who might do this?"

"I have a couple of ideas," I said. "I was thinking through, but no particular person comes to mind."

I called over to Maxwell who was watching the commotion from the outside door. "Hey Max, bring these guys a bag of your best, on me." I waved a ten dollar bill in his direction.

In a few minutes, Max came out with a large sack in hand. I passed him the ten and walked them over to the patrol guys who had moved their cars and were getting ready to leave. They were standing outside of Hank's car. They each took a donut. While they were eating, I asked, "Do you guys work with a guy named Kirkpatrick?"

They all nodded. Serrano said, "He's been around for a while, works the off shifts. Keeps to himself."

I said, "I ran into him the other morning. He hassled me about a parking place. Wanted to give me a ticket," I lied.

Officer Kelly spoke up, "He's a head case sometimes. Marches to his own drummer. Most of the guys don't care for him. If I were you, I'd just ignore him. If he writes you a ticket or something, let us know. We've heard some complaints, but he works graveyard so most guys wouldn't complain. He sometimes collaborates with a partner named Blanchard, but he's usually on his own."

"Thanks," I said. "Usually, you guys are top notch, but I was surprised at him." I let the conversation drop and said so long. All three men apologized and gave thanks for the donuts."

Now I had a little inside information. Captain Kirk was a night crawler, and he had a partner named Blanchard. Might be worth a little investigation sometime. If that idiot was out to get me, I had better watch my back, I thought.

Now the sun was getting high in the sky. As the officers drove out of the lot, Maxwell came running up. "More trouble, Trace? I thought those guys were going to kill you."

"I was a little apprehensive myself, Max. Somebody had called in a stolen car report for the Mercedes I'm driving. I have a hunch who it might be, but I'm not sure."

"Was it that big guy you were arguing with earlier?"

"Might be," I said. "Let me know if he comes in again. And please don't give him any info on me. I don't want that guy knowing where I live. As far as he knows now, I live in L.A. I want to leave it that way."

Maxwell nodded, "You said he was from the sheriff's department. I don't get many cops down here. We're off the beaten path, and this whole mall is closed at night except for the bar next door."

"Just let me know if you see him or if he hassles you. I doubt you'll be bothered with him again."

"What's your number?" he asked.

"Here's a card. It has my office number on it which is answered by a service. They have my home number and can forward a call."

Now I could move on with my day. I glanced at my watch. After eight already. I fired the engine of the convertible for the second time, put it in reverse and backed out of the narrow spot. The lot had filled up, and I was certainly ready to get out of Cardiff. As I clicked the shifter into first gear, I marveled at a huge formation of pelicans, flying low and in a V-shaped pattern just inland of the coast. They turned in my direction, and I noticed just how large they were. With a three to four foot wingspan, they filled the sky with a smooth flowing motion, gliding effortlessly in the slight morning breeze. They turned once more and now were directly overhead, reminding me in no uncertain terms how my day had started out. One plop on the windshield and one big one in my lap. Shit...

CHAPTER 5

There is something about a finely tuned automobile that instantly brings a smile to my face. A car that responds when you step on the accelerator, brakes when prompted and glides around curves as smooth as glass. That was the car I was driving. As bad as the morning was, I was determined to have a better second half. The Mercedes just purred as I drove south down coast highway through Cardiff, Sloan Beach and then a short pit stop at home to install the hard top. This model of Mercedes sports car was called a Pagoda in Germany, because of the unusual roof line. The back window curves in, giving the installed unit almost a greenhouse effect. I love the look.

As I pulled into my rented house in the industrial back part of Sloan, I drove over to the barn, which serves as a garage and workshop. I share the property with my good friend, Martino, a former motorcycle cop who had brought me to Sloan Beach just over two years ago. I had met him when I worked as an officer of the California Highway Patrol. He had helped me out when my partner was shot point blank during a routine traffic stop, that left him dead and my right leg shattered by a 9mm bullet. The result was six months of slow recovery, depression and my eventual departure from the CHP. If he hadn't been there for me, I probably would have killed myself or ended up on skid row.

I slid open the barn door, and pulled the Mercedes in, so I could pop on the top and do a little maintenance before my trip up the coast. Martino had retrofitted the barn with a concrete floor, car and motorcycle hoists, workbenches, and a good selection of tools along with an air compressor. Everything a mechanic could want in a 30 by 60 foot space. Pulling the car onto the lift, I noticed that Martino was at the other end of the barn, working on one of his police motorcycles.

"Hey man, how's it going?" I asked, with a wave.

"Not bad, just retrofitting a couple of bikes for one of the local police agencies. Adding new radios, light bars and louder sirens."

"Which city?"

"This one is for Karden Beach. Pretty cushy deal. I get to supply the parts, so I make a buck there, and this conversion pays eight hours flat rate. I end up making about $500 a bike for a day's work."

"How many you got lined up?"

"At least 20 this month. The sheriff's department has ten by themselves. Since the bikes are mostly the same model, I can get faster after I do the first one. Heck, last time I did this a few years back, I was doing two a day by myself."

"Pretty sweet deal, dude. That's ten grand this month."

"That's not to mention the additional service work they need. Hey, that's what allows me to go on long runs with the club. Got a big run up north next month. Fifty riders going to the bay area."

Martino is the leader of a local Christian Motorcycle Club. I'm not sure about his religious affiliation, but he gets to go riding on Sunday with his biker 'Church' service. That's a church I might want to attend.

I gave him a pat on the back, "Hey, speaking of the sheriff's department, do you know a guy named Kirkpatrick over there? He works the graveyard shift."

Martino nodded, "Yea, I've heard of him. He's a regular patrol guy. Doesn't have the best reputation. He's busted heads with a few of my riders pretty bad. A couple of the tougher guys in the club have mentioned him before. Why you ask?"

"I had a run in with him this morning. He's running a drag race scam. He raced me down Coast Highway in his own Mustang and then hit me up with a 'pay me cash or you go to jail deal' after the fact. Thankfully I still had one of my Highway Patrol business cards. That must have pissed him off because he then called in a stolen car report for this Mercedes I'm driving. Three Sheriff's cars pull in ten minutes later, guns drawn, and almost take my head off."

Martino laughed, "You raced him in that Benz? I bet he wiped you up and spit you out."

"This thing is a sleeper. He had me till about 100 mph; then the Mercedes just took off. He was at least 100 yards back when I hit 130."

"You hit a hundred and thirty in this little car, racing a cop?" He laughed again, this time, harder. "I can't believe you, Armstrong, you're lucky you aren't in jail, with the key thrown away. Not even I, with all my law enforcement connections, could have got you out of that one."

"The owner is ex-FBI. Bob could have made a call, but I'm glad I didn't have to pull that card. The only reason I raced him was that Bob wanted to ensure it would still do 130. That deserted part of Coast Highway down the hill and into Cardiff was the perfect place for a run."

Shaking his head, Martino said, "The real reason is that competitive streak of yours. You don't like to lose. Man, I've never seen you back down from a race. And to think you ran him with the top down. Thankfully he didn't run you off the road. No roll bar, flimsy windshield. You would have been a corpse without a head."

"Yea, you're probably right, but it was one hell of a ride. This car was smooth at speed with these Michelin tires. Hey, while you're standing there, slide the hoist arms under it. I got to change the oil and service it before I take off up north."

With that, I lifted the car in the air. Martino took a look underneath.

"Nice specimen, Trace. This guy takes good care of his cars. No corrosion. Most of these old German cars are rust buckets."

"Yea, he always keeps his cars covered in his four-car garage."

Martino walked around the back. "Pretty nice setup, fully independent suspension, dual exhaust, and fifteen-inch wheels. What is this little gizmo?"

I couldn't see what he was pointing to so I asked, "What gizmo are you talking about?"

"This little box here, under the right rear fender."

"What box?"

"Come here and look. It's got a little flashing light on it."

I put down the oil wrench and walked back. Up under the right fender was a little metal box with a small green light. I said, "Not sure man. Never seen anything like it before."

Martino reached up and grabbed the unit. Suddenly it popped off in his hand.

Holding out his palm, he said, "Do you know what this is?"

"No, not a clue."

He opened it up and inside was a battery and circuit board. Martino said, "This my friend is a radio bug. Someone is tracking your whereabouts."

"What? You can't be serious!"

"Serious as a heart attack. I've seen these before. A range of five miles. Metal box with a magnet on it. Takes two-seconds to attach it. Now the big question, who is tracking you?"

"Man, I have no idea. Maybe it was already there?"

"Might be," said Martino, "but the battery only lasts a few days. My guess is that your friend Bob is keeping track of you."

"I don't think so. I've known the guy for a long time. He trusts me, and this is his third car with full insurance."

"So, if not him, who else could it be?"

I had to think for a moment, "Not sure. Maybe that Kirkpatrick guy put it on, but I don't remember him loitering around the back of the car."

"It would only take him a second, Trace."

"I don't know for sure, but I certainly didn't see him do it."

"What would he have to gain following you?"

"I'm sure he was pissed this morning after he found out my CHP connection, but he didn't know that till he talked to me."

"You said he called in a stolen car report."

"There again, I can't say for sure it was him, but it was too much of a coincidence, happening ten minutes after he left to be anyone else."

"Well," he said, "let's make sure they can't locate you now." With that, he pulled the battery out of the holder. "I'd watch your back if I were you. Someone is tracking this car. If it's someone after your FBI friend Bob, they could be very dangerous people. If it's Kirkpatrick, he may want to beat your head in to keep you quiet about his racing shakedown."

I shrugged. "Man this is a mystery. I picked the car up Thursday night, brought it here and parked it by the house, messed with it yesterday and drove it out this morning."

Martino laughed. "Maybe it's your girlfriend Janet, keeping tabs on you."

"I don't think so. She's back in New York. Left yesterday. Flying back to do all the paperwork for a divorce."

"Really?" Martino said, "She has to go all the way back there?"

"Unfortunately, the house and all the marriage stuff were set up by her cheating husband back in the state of New York."

"So how do you feel about this? Do you trust her to do the right thing?"

"I tell you, Martino, I trust Janet a lot. She manages my business, and we have grown a lot closer over the past few months. We've talked about getting married in the future. However, I don't trust her husband. That guy sleeps with a different woman every night, and he works for the IRS. He's got a lot of power and knows a lot of people. I just don't see this going down without a big fight."

"You're probably right Trace. The question is, will she go through with it if the guy has full ownership of her bungalow in Sloan. She may want to stay married to keep the house. If he can talk all these different women into sleeping with him, he can probably talk her into staying put. It would totally be a power play."

"You're scaring me man. I'm going to call her tonight. I hope she's strong. Man, I love that woman. I can't imagine losing her, or worse yet, having her go back with that two-timing asshole."

"As I tell my guys, hope for the best, plan for the worst. You need a contingency plan in case the guy pulls a fast one."

"What do you suggest?"

"The main thing is to let her know you care and that you're prepared to be there for her and her two kids. I'm sure she has no feelings for the husband, other than wanting to kill him, but convenience, security, and kids are a whole different thing. You need to provide her an out."

"I've got some money in the bank, I work hard, but I live here in a little 800 SQ Foot rental house on the back of the property. Certainly no room for her and her kids."

"Have you looked at apartments or rental houses in town? Options may help at this point."

"Given this is a beach town, they are hard to come by and expensive, but I hadn't thought about looking into renting one."

"What about that dream of buying property someday. I remember you talking about that. Could that be an option?"

"Not for a few years. Got to save for the down payment and then we'd have to build some kind of house."

Martino shrugged, "I'm not sure what to tell you, Trace, but you better get something lined up. I've known Janet for over three years now. She likes order and her ducks in a row."

"I know man. She can be very impulsive too."

Martino walked over to the workbench and picked up the bug and the battery, and inspected them carefully. Suddenly he let out a gasp, "Oh man, we got trouble here. Look at this cell."

I picked it up and rolled it in my hand, "What? I don't see anything. Just an ordinary Energizer Double-A."

"Look at where it is from..."

"Oh shit... South America."

CHAPTER 6

Finding a battery from South America was not good news. Alkaline batteries usually come from the U.S. or Japan. The bug unit itself was a cheap sheet metal box with a magnet and little circuit board. Could have been made almost anywhere.

I glanced over at Martino, who was looking at the bug with a magnifying glass. "Japanese circuit board," he said, "but the South American battery is almost a dead giveaway that we are dealing with someone from Columbia or Brazil."

Martino has quite a few connections in law enforcement since he does a lot of maintenance and motorcycle work with them. A few months back Janet and I had been involved with a brother and sister team from Columbia, both of who were now in jail, awaiting trial or deportation. Part of one of the Cordone drug cartels. Martino had been able to get background information and helped us stay one step ahead of them.

"I can't believe we are dealing with the Colombians again," I said.

Martino put the battery back in. The little green light lit up dimly. He put it up to his nose. "This looks like a cattle tracker that would hang around an animal's neck. Smells sour like a cow. Look at how someone added a magnet with a sheet metal screw. Boxes like these are pretty prevalent in the third world countries to keep an eye on cattle on some of the big ranchos. I think you are probably right Trace. Appears to be a device you would find on Columbian Cartel property."

"Damn, so now what do we do?"

"I need you to call your FBI friend and tell him what we found. This light is pretty dim. Hard to say how long it has been on the car."

I walked over to the wall and put in a call to Bob Jordan at his house. Thankfully he was home and picked up.

"Hey Bob, this is Trace. Glad to find you home."

Bob replied, "The wife and I were just headed out for a few days. What's up? Is the car OK?"

"The car is fine, but we found a strange electronic unit on the inside of the rear fender just now. Small transmitter with a South American battery in it. Any idea when and where it might have come from?"

"Oh man, that's scary. The car has been locked in the garage for the last few months, which is alarmed with a motion sensor. It hasn't been out since you picked it up on Thursday. I can't imagine it happening here. What about you?"

"I parked it behind my house last night and drove it to Cardiff this morning. We have a locked gate on our property at night. Not out of my sight today. The little green light is dim, which indicates the battery is probably a week or so old."

His voice picked up, "Watch your back and your property. With the Cordone's still in jail, one of their accomplices may have come across the border. Not sure where the contact point might have been. Those bastards shoot first and ask questions later. I'll alert the office."

"Will do. You too. At least we found it before someone got hurt."

He gave a bitter laugh, "Not hurt, if they get to us, someone will be dead."

"We removed the bug. I'll call you if anything comes up. Otherwise, I'll have the car back to you next weekend." I hung up.

Walking over to Martino, I said, "Been in a secure locked garage for the last month. Hasn't been out of my sight today. Parked by the house last night. Man, I don't know."

His eyes lit up, "Something is not right here. Either your FBI friend is tracking you, the cop put it on today, or somehow the Colombians got to us. That battery is what bothers me. That had to come from South America. I tell you what. I'm going to put a new battery in it and plant it on that abandoned car in the field down the street. If I see anyone looking at that car, I'll call it in. If nothing else, it will detour anyone from coming here."

After an hour, I finished the maintenance and tuning on the car and backed it off the hoist. The old MB was purring like a kitten. I had Martino help me lift on the hardtop and fasten it in place.

"I'm headed up to Fallbrook. I'll be up there all week. Staying at the old Fallbrook hotel. Call me there if anything comes up."

"Will do, Kemosabe. I'm stuck here most of the week with these cop bike upgrades. Seems to be a rush on for the new lights and sirens. I'll put a call in downtown to see if there is anything on the wires about the Cartels, but I haven't heard much lately. The usually keep a low profile." Walking over to the workbench Martino turned on a small monitor on the upper shelf. "I haven't used this security system for a while. I'm not sure it even works anymore. It's got three cameras; one for the barn, one for the main property with a view of the houses, and one for the street. It hooks up to this VCR under the bench. Does a 10-second sweep of each camera in a sequence. One tape will last a full day. I'll put a new tape in daily while you're gone. The remote camera has a view down the street that covers that old car. We'll see if we get any interest."

"Sounds good. Maybe our chicken will come home to roost." As I drove out, I stopped by the house and picked up a suitcase that I'd packed with a weeks clothes. It barely fit in the small trunk of the MB. It's a good thing Janet wasn't coming along. There wouldn't have been room for her luggage anywhere. I was feeling more like a bachelor now, almost a playboy. Beautiful sports car, casual sports clothes, and even clean fingernails topped off with some aviator sunglasses. I felt like a West Coast Don Johnson. My normal car is a black Corvette, which draws the eye, but this Mercedes was different. Maybe it was the three-pointed star on the hood and deck lid, or the horizon blue paint, but I definitely noticed more smiles from women in the adjacent cars as I headed up coast highway and got on the 5 freeway.

It's funny how a car makes a man. This one certainly brought the looks, especially from the female gender. For a minute I felt much younger, maybe in my early thirties again, headed to the country club for a round of tennis or a golf game. I rolled up the sleeves of my white dress shirt, pretending my Timex was a Rolex. Opening the center console, I found a stash of cassette tapes from the Rat Pack, which found their way into the cassette player one after the other, but I focused on one from Sinatra with it's audacious lyrics.

I've got the world on a string,
sittin' on a rainbow,
Got the string around my finger,
What a world, what a life, I'm in love.

I was certainly in love with the feeling. A warm summer day, heading north. The blue Pacific Ocean on my left, the green coastal trees with a stunning backdrop of flower fields to my right. The purr of the finely tuned engine, along with the balmy sea breezes and the feel of soft leather, completed the experience. After a quick jaunt fifteen miles up the 5 freeway, I turned inland onto the 76 highway in the town of Oceanview, which was the last coastal town before the huge expanse of the Camp Pendleton Marine Base.

Fallbrook, the little inland resort town, affectionately called the Avocado Capital of the World is nestled twenty miles from the coast in some high foothills and is long time home of my Uncle Paul and Cousin Mike. I had reservations for the historic Fallbrook Hotel, where movie stars, famous politicians, and rowdy cowboy types had made visits over the decades. Built in the late eighteen hundreds, its Victorian elegance had probably seen better days, but it was near my cousin's house, and the price was right.

The 76 narrowed down as it wound out of Oceanview into two lanes, and the heat seemed to rise with each mile away from the ocean. The coast had been in the seventies, but the inland temperatures crept into the high eighties as I turned left off the highway, onto Mission Avenue, which wound for ten miles up through dry brown foothills filled with scrub brush and majestic oak trees. The two-lane crested a hill, and the little town opened up in a vista of older homes, a shopping mall, and rows of small shops along the main street. After a mile, I could see the huge faded blue two-story monstrosity of the Fallbrook hotel to my right, down a small incline. It appeared that the original town was built around the structure, with the old post office, library, and even a little cemetery laid out in a half-mile square adjacent to the building. As the town grew through the years, newer buildings and homes spread out over the area. Most of the original buildings were updated, but the hotel looked about as dead as the inhabitants of the adjacent cemetery.

The faded blue facade of the old two-story wooden building was dry and peeling, and one whole wing at the back of the building was closed for repairs. My visit didn't look promising. Once the pride of this little agricultural town, where it was a centerpiece for decades, this hotel originally had 60 rooms, bereft with 12-foot ceilings, huge porches and featured a gourmet restaurant. Now with one wing completely closed down, it looked ready for a wrecking ball. When I called for reservations, the woman on the phone was pleasant enough, and for $50 a night seemed like a bargain. Seeing it in person was a whole different story. The closed wing had graffiti on it, and a large looming real estate for sale sign didn't instill confidence. There were, however, twenty or thirty cars in the parking lot and most looked relatively new. At least, it didn't look like a drug infested welfare motel.

I parked the car to the side of the grand front entrance, near a large street lamp. Removing my one large suitcase, I headed into the lobby, where I was greeted by a lovely woman, probably in her late fifties, who had shoulder length dark brown hair, deep midnight blue eyes, and the palest skin one could imagine. She was mid height, probably five six, and didn't look like she had ever seen the sun. The reception area of the hotel was clean and well kept. The inside of the place looked much nicer than the outside would indicate. Decorated with tan and lavender wallpaper the entrance was magnificent with a huge chandelier overhead, polished hardwood floors and a large dark wood counter. All of the furniture, paintings and equipment looked to be from the

Victorian era.

Walking up to the desk, I said, "I'm Trace Armstrong, I have a reservation."

She smiled, revealing a beautiful mouth and pearly white teeth. "We've been expecting you, Mr. Armstrong. I'm Madeline, the owner. We welcome you to Fallbrook." She motioned to someone in the back as she passed me over a registration book.

With her porcelain complexion, high cheek bones, and sharp eyes, she looked almost like royalty. Wearing a long flowing black dress, highlighted with white lace, the contrast of colors was spectacular. Pushing the registration book back towards her, she turned it around. Just then two younger women came out from behind the dark velvet curtain which separated the front desk from an office behind. They stood on each side of her. Madeline said, "These are my daughters Rose and Alice. They handle room service and work in our restaurant. Be sure to check out our excellent menu in your room. If you have any needs during your stay, please let one of us know.

As the three women stood there, it was uncanny. Dressed in corresponding period clothing, they all had similar hair, facial features, deep mascara and dark foreboding eyes. All three were the same height, with pure white skin, and smiles so compelling I completely changed my attitude about my week long stay. Mother and daughters looking almost identical, yet something was unnerving about them. It was like I had been transported back in time and staring at a trio of ghostly spirits. Little did I know how correct my intuition would be.

CHAPTER 7

Madeline pushed a room key across the desk. "I'll have Alice show you to your room, Mr. Armstrong. You'll be staying in one of our nicer suites on the first floor, with high ceilings and a modern bathroom. You may have noticed the back wing of the building. We currently have it closed, waiting for the city to approve a restoration plan. It's a historic structure, and the older rooms were lacking modern plumbing. Hopefully, the upgrade program passes the city council this month so we can move forward. In the meantime, I ask you to pardon the mess out back. If you use the front door, you'll see our beautiful hotel as we intend for you to see it."

Smiling, I said, "I can't believe the difference between the inside and the out. The room is much nicer than I thought it would be."

"We take a lot of pride in our hotel, Mr. Armstrong. It's been in our family for three decades. Unfortunately, there are some people in town and on the council that would like to see it torn down. The underlying property is worth a fortune, but we feel the historic value is much greater than tearing it down and building condos."

"I can see why you care. They don't build places like this anymore. By the way, do the rooms have phones?"

"Yes, they do. You can use a phone card if you need to call long distance."

"Good to know," I said. "I do have to arrange to meet up with my relatives this week."

Madeline edged closer and said in a soft voice, "Are you by chance related to the Armstrong family over on Third?"

"Yes, Mark Armstrong is my cousin and Paul Armstrong was my uncle."

She reached out and clasped my arm. "I've been acquainted with them in the past. Sure a strange mystery about Paul's death."

"Really? I just heard he had died last week. I don't know much more than that."

She leaned in even more, "The rumor was Paul had a drinking problem. It was kept quiet, but there were a couple of people in uniform here over a week ago looking for him. When they found the body in one of our cordoned off rooms last Wednesday, we were very concerned. The police say it looked like he fell and hit his head. Booze bottles with him, and alcohol on his clothes and breath. They are calling it an accidental death."

"Who found him?"

"I did. I noticed the door was ajar when I did my nightly rounds. Sprawled on the floor, Paul had an enormous welt on the back of his head. Dirty and looking horrible, I figured he was hit over the head or beaten to death. Swollen and bruised, the coroner said he had been dead for hours. I don't believe that, to tell you the truth. The door was smashed in. Way too much force and violence for a drunk."

"Wow, I had no idea. I'm headed over to see Mark in the morning. I'll have to get to the bottom of this. Do you know who the people were that were looking for him?"

"Not sure, a couple of guys. Military. Probably in their fifties. Said they were old friends. Never seen them before. Can't figure out why they would come here."

"I'll let you know if I hear something," I said. With that, she stepped back and motioned Alice to take my suitcase."

I nodded a goodbye gesture and followed Alice down the hall as she rolled my suitcase. "You sure have great service here."

Alice nodded and in a slight voice said, "We try, but it is getting harder to run this place year by year. It's so old that things break faster than we can fix them some days. My family bought the place thirty years ago. Did a complete restoration at the time. But time takes its toll, especially on wooden buildings like this. Thankfully the bottom floor of the main building was updated about five years ago, before the city council changed. The historical society helped us secure funding for thirty rooms. The back ends of the rooms were gutted and new bathrooms with modern plumbing were added along with new heater vents. I think you'll like it Mr. Armstrong."

"You can call me Trace," I said. We stopped in front of room seven. Alice pulled a key from her pocket and opened the tall wooden door. As I stepped in from the dark hallway, I was blown away how big the room seemed. The twelve-foot ceilings gave the room an enormous feel. Alice pulled out a suitcase rack and put my case on top of it, next to a wooden dresser. The room had Victorian wallpaper in a tan hue with dark lavender insets along with thick carpeting, full-length drapes, and a large king size bed. The bedspread was a deep maroon color with full plush pillows at the back. The room had a faint smell of rose water, probably from the flower arrangement on the bureau next to the bed. Alice showed me the bathroom which was spotless and newly updated with reproduction sink, toilet, and tub.

Shaking my head, I said, "How can you offer this room for $50 a night. I'm impressed. Worth at least $100 or more a night."

Alice shrugged, "Until we get the OK for the complete restoration, we have to offer discount rates. Years past, it was a resort destination. Now with the faded paint and boarded up rooms, it looks more like a haunted house than a hotel. The only thing keeping us going is the restaurant and patrons who know how beautiful this wing is. Most people aren't aware that this hotel was designed and built by the same architect who built the famous Hotel Del on Coronado Island in San Diego. That one goes for $150 to $500 a night, depending on the season."

"I hope things come through for you," I replied.

She handed me the large metal key and a paper brochure while a beautiful smile crossed her face. "To show you how great our restaurant is, Trace, pick something from this menu, dial zero on the phone, and I'll bring it up for you. Once you've tried our food, I think you'll spend a lot of time in our restaurant."

With her kind ways, she seemed like an old friend. She definitely had the gift of hospitality. As she turned to go, I pulled a few dollars out of my pocket for a tip. She took it with her right hand and brushed my arm with her left. Her momentary touch was soft, yet cold as ice. Her smile bright in the dim light, she said, "I'm glad you're here Mr. Armstrong. Remember to order something. The apple pie is to die for." She closed the door behind her, and I was alone in the room. The whole experience so far had been strange yet somewhat exhilarating. I was now in what would be a high-end hotel at any other location, in a large room with expensive furnishings, with a beautiful trio of women managing the place.

As I sat on the side of the luxurious bed, my uncle's death was top of mind. When my cousin had called, he said nothing about a disappearance or possible foul play. He just mentioned that he had died, and there were some unusual circumstances. He needed some help putting things in order. Given that some of the relatives lived back east, he said the funeral would be delayed for a while. I was going to meet him on Sunday morning at nine at his house a couple of blocks away.

Feeling a little hungry from the long drive, I picked up the phone, dialed zero for room service, and ordered a hamburger and some of the Apple pie that Alice had mentioned. Margaret said it would arrive within the half hour.

My watch said it was 3:30. That would make it 6:30 on the east coast. I pulled out my calling card and dialed the Metropolitan Hotel in New York City, where Janet was staying. The front desk answered and quickly transferred me to Janet's room on the third floor. After five rings, Janet picked up.

"Hello," she said, in a somewhat irritated tone.

"Hey, this is Trace. How did your day go?" I asked.

"You don't want to know. Harold has got my life all jacked up. The bastard has most all the cards and a superb lawyer."

"What happened?"

"I went to court for a preliminary hearing. I hired an attorney that one of my friends recommended, but we were outgunned immediately. Since we got married in New York, we are working under their jurisdiction. I'm having to familiarize myself with the rulebook."

"How about your house in Sloan?"

"That's the worst of it. He's got it tied up in a lousy trust. The kids are listed, but I'm on the outside. Unless I'm willing to jump through a whole bunch of hoops, he can restrict access and set a really high rent. It's not fair, but it doesn't look good. He's got some sweetheart deal with this high-powered divorce lawyer. Probably a trade for looking the other way on tax fraud or some other charge."

Sighing, I said, "I was afraid the son of a bitch would pull something like this. What's next?"

"Tomorrow, we talk about custody. On that front, I have a pretty good leg to stand on. I don't think he wants the girls back there, and they have been out in Sloan Beach for years."

"Don't forget, Janet, he's on a power trip. I don't put anything past him."

"The good news is, Sarah is an adult, so he can't control her, but Julie is only 16. If he pushes for custody, I don't know what I will do. I'm afraid he might push for New York residency."

"Can he do that?"

"We lived back there when the girls were little. It's a gray area, but my lawyer says he may be able to limit her living arrangements to New York State for adequate visitation.

"Man, that sucks."

"You're not kidding. I hate New York, the cold, and especially him. I'm not having him pull Julie out of my arms."

"But the guy is a total slime-bag. Sleeping around every night. Doesn't that count for anything?"

"I've got to brush up on divorce law in New York. In California, the judges usually side with the woman in custody disputes, but I was totally unprepared for the onslaught he brought today. Lies and more lies."

"So if he pulls the custody card, what will you do?"

"I'm going to fight like crazy, but I may have to move back here."

"WHAT... but what about us?"

"I don't know at this point. I'm not giving up my daughter." She paused, "Listen, Trace, I've got to go. It's been a really long day, and I'm meeting with my lawyer at 7:30. Call me tomorrow when I know more." With that, she hung up.

Just like that, our future together was on the line. She was obviously stressed. Martino was right. Kids take priority, and that husband of hers was on a massive power trip. With a trust, her house in Sloan was probably in jeopardy, and now with a custody issue, she might have to move to New York. Her focus now didn't include me at all. At least it seemed that way. I slammed the phone back on the side bureau and pounded my fist on the bed. I honestly wanted to kill that son of a bitch, but like Janet said, at this point he held most of the cards.

I laid back on the bed, covering my eyes with my hands. Shit, what was I going to do now? I certainly wasn't going to move to New York. No way in hell. I could see the love of my life slipping away fast. Boyfriends just don't rate much when kids are on the line. I closed my eyes for a few minutes, trying to calm my nerves. I was boiling inside.

Just then came a knock. Opening my eyes slowly, I sat up and walked slowly over to the door. When I opened it, Alice smiled and entered the room with a large plate containing a hamburger and a large piece of apple pie. She walked across the room and put it on the dresser top. As delicious as the food looked, I wasn't prepared for what I saw next. Alice was wearing a tight, short black dress, her eyes surrounded with deep mascara. She turned and walked up to me, the aroma of exotic perfume filling the air. She looked so completely different than before; dark eyes, intensely painted lips, her dark brown hair brushed back from her face. Stopping inches in front of me, she said, "If you get lonely Mr. Armstrong, the bar opens at eight." She reached out for my hand and put something hard and cold in my palm. As she turned to leave, I looked down to see a large blue gemstone shining in the dim light, as she opened the door and left.

CHAPTER 8

Contrasting emotions. Vastly different feelings. Sometimes I think my head will explode. Here I was, standing inside my hotel room, just off the phone with my girlfriend, who let me know that she might have to move back to New York to be with her kids. A divorce she planned on her end that may not go through. Her asshole husband playing the power card.

My blood was boiling.

Contrasted with the engaging daughter of the hotel owner, whose eyes, smile, and personality were pulling on my heart strings. Who had invited me in slightly uncertain terms, to join her in the bar at 8 pm.

Usually, I wouldn't consider such a thing. I pride myself as a pretty loyal guy. But now I had a war going on inside my head. Those nattering nabobs of light and dark were warring inside. Should I go down at eight?

My mind said yes, but my heart was telling me something different. Janet and I had been through so much over the past few months. Both of us almost died, with bullets flying, planes crashing, and rare paintings leading us half way around the world. To tell you the truth, I'm crazy about her, but I've always felt slightly on the outside. Her deadbeat husband, half a continent away always seemed to control her life to a certain extent. Janet finally decided on the divorce, but now things appear to have crumbled. I could see our relationship failing quickly.

Now there was a young woman, Alice, probably in her early thirties, inviting me for a drink. Looking down, I could see a large blue jewel, over an inch long in my hand. What was this all about? Why had she handed it to me? Looking closer, it appeared to be a large topaz or other stone, blue in color, just like her eyes.

Walking over to the lamp next to the bed, I looked at it closer. It was cleanly cut and looked almost flawless. It had to be worth hundreds of dollars, if not more. Why would she hand me something this valuable? What would keep me from walking away with it? It didn't make sense, but maybe an ulterior motive.

Indeed, I would return it, and what better time than eight at night, when she would be in the bar. Maybe something else here. Was there some significance about a blue jewel? I remembered that my Uncle Paul had been in the gemstone business, with a small house and shop in the back hills of Fallbrook, but that didn't seem like a connection. Questions... questions.

The room clock clicked over to 5 pm. Time to wash away some of the anger with a hot shower and a change of clothes. The new bathroom had expensive looking faucets and elegant porcelain sink and tub. As the hot water ran, the tension and anger washed slowly away down the drain. I must have stood there for ten minutes, trying to decide what to do for the evening. As I got out and dressed, I knew I had to find out more. If nothing else, I would return the jewel. Dressing in slacks, dress shirt and sports coat, I looked at myself in the mirror. Combing back my dark hair, I shaved again. Heck, I didn't want to seem like a bum. Some gray had started to creep into my sideburns, but Janet told me that it made me more attractive. I'm not sure about that, but I certainly didn't look thirty anymore.

My mind drifted off into a daydream, playing different scenarios. I could see myself with Alice in the bar, my tanned complexion completely contrasting with her ivory white skin, the blue topaz sitting on the table in front of us. For some crazy reason, I dropped the jewel into a martini glass where it dissolved into an azure blue explosion of bubbles and smoke, engulfing Alice in a transparent cloud from whence she gradually disappeared. Shaking my head, I came quickly back to reality, my blue eyes staring directly back at me in the mirror. I turned on the faucet and splashed cold water on my face.

Wow, that was strange.

It was time for a walk, I picked up the large jewel and slipped it into the side pocket of my sports jacket. I closed and locked the door behind me. Walking down the hallway towards the back of the hotel, I passed a number of rooms before coming to a large wooden exit door at the end of the corridor. It was unlocked. Exiting out into the bright sun, I shielded my eyes from the sun, wishing that I had brought along some sunglasses.

The back end of the building led out to a small asphalt area, separating the main building from the boarded up rear wing. A small walkway led up to Second Street. Walking down the old sidewalk, I turned left on Second Street and walked up a minor incline toward Main Street. Historic buildings expressed old facades on the left side. One housed the post office, another an office building. Each of these structures was two stories high, built of wood, restored from the original. Across the street were a row of post-war bungalows each fenced in with white picket fences. To the right of these, just across from the hotel was a small, old graveyard.

The bold gray headstones, with family names from the early settlement, were surrounded by weeds, decay, peeling paint and general misery. In the midst of the depression, was a single vase, full of fresh, bright flowers—yellows, blues, reds—sitting on the headstone of one Robert Whittaker. According to the markings, he had died some years ago at the age of sixty, yet someone had kept his memory alive. The rest of the small cemetery was so overgrown that most names could not be discerned. I walked further in, the baked adobe dirt producing a small cloud of dust as I proceeded. The whole area was no bigger that a couple of garages and held about fifty adjacent graves.

It seemed strange that the graveyard was so close to the main square, yet in the early days of Fallbrook, everything was adjacent and within walking distance to the railroad and the town square. The rest of the homes and buildings in the surrounding streets didn't exist at the time.

I picked up a weird vibe passing a marker with the name Armstrong on it. Could this be a long-lost relative? Augustus Armstrong died 1909. Not my grandfather but maybe his brother or cousin? Strange feeling to end up in a weed-infested plot like this. So far this town was on the verge of freaking me out. I'm not very superstitious, and I don't usually believe in the supernatural, but having a cemetery so close to a strange old hotel was somewhat disconcerting. I could just visualize ghosts or vampires raising up at night, coming to roost in my room. I knew it was nonsense, but it felt strange all the same. After all, there are no such things as ghosts. Are there?

For the next hour, I walked for blocks through the old streets. The further distance from the hotel, the newer the buildings were. The summer evening was pleasant, with diners eating outside of restaurants along Main Street, along with the hustle and bustle of townsfolk walking home from work or out shopping.

I headed back, and ended up in my room a little after seven, deciding to take a short nap. As I awoke in a slight stupor, I looked down at my watch. It had just clicked over to eight. The daylight creeping through the sheers between the thick curtains had dimmed to an eerie darkness. Feeling in my pocket for the blue gemstone, I proceeded out of my room, down the hall and took a seat in the bar area of the hotel restaurant. From the back, Alice turned and headed my way with a smile. In the darkness of the restaurant, the backlight illuminated her silhouette, giving off a translucent glow, her flawless skin and sharp features highlighting her beauty. She came up behind the bar and said, "I thought you would come."

Pulling the blue gemstone from my pocket, I replied, "This stone has me curious. Where did it come from?"

She reached out and took the stone in her hand and held it up to the light. "It's a beauty, isn't it? Almost perfect Blue Topaz."

"But what does this have to do with me?"

She came closer, "It matches your eyes, Mister Armstrong."

"But why give it to me?"

"Because you'll find it has particular significance."

I shook my head quizzically, "Particular significance?"

"Yes Trace, family significance."

"Now you have me completely baffled. Family significance? I don't get it?"

Taking my hand, she said in a slight whisper, "We found it in your Uncle Paul's pocket when he died."

CHAPTER 9

My head spun. Here I was in a strange old Victorian hotel in the little town of Fallbrook, sitting in the bar, talking with one of the palest but most striking woman I had ever met. In my hand, I had a blue gemstone, which she described as a diamond cut blue Topaz. She inferred that this impressive jewel was discovered in the pants pocket of my dead uncle, who just happened to be found a few days before, sprawled on the floor of one of the abandoned old rooms in the back section of the hotel.

Alice walked around the end of the bar and placed two wine glasses on the bar in front of me. She took a seat on the stool next to me. The bar was off to one side of the restaurant entrance, set in dim light. Alice and I were he only ones in the room. Off in the restaurant, a few patrons were having a late dinner, but overall the area was quiet and private. Her cold hand brushed mine as she lifted one of the glasses.

"Would you care for some wine, Trace? My family has had their own vineyard for years, and I would love for you to try one of our Estate wines," she said. "It's a special selection called a Rosato. It's 60% Grenache and 40% Sangiovese."

Looking at her deep azure blue eyes, I nodded. "So what makes your wine special?"

"We crush the grapes early in the morning to maintain cool temperatures prior to fermentation. It has a wonderfully rich and tropical character. Almost like being on a Caribbean island."

"Sounds delicious," I said as I passed over my glass.

Taking both glasses, she walked down a short aisle and disappeared into the darkness behind a dark curtain, returning in a few moments with each glass full of the deep red beverage. She took the seat on the other side of me, towards the darker part of the bar.

Passing me a glass, she held hers up for a toast. "To a wonderful stay at the premier hotel in Fallbrook."

We clinked glasses, and I took a sip. The deep oak flavor of the wine highlighted its estate heritage.

"Wow, this is wonderful," I said.

"Only the best for our customers," she said with a wink.

"So tell me about this gemstone. You say it is a diamond cut, blue topaz. I'm not familiar with that term."

She took the stone in her hand. "We used to have a gift store in the hotel during its heyday, so I'm a little bit familiar with jewelry. Here in Fallbrook, we have a history of mining, from back in the last century. Most were tiny mines, specializing in Quartz or other common minerals. There were a few that produced Topaz of varying colors, and on very rare occasions more exotic stones like sapphire or ruby would be located. Most Topaz from this area is either amber or clear, which makes nice costume or low-cost jewelry. A few of the gem dealers would send off their clear topaz to be irradiated with radiation, which would, in turn, change the large jewels differing shades of blue, depending on the strength and length of time the topaz was processed. With the proper radioactive recipe and subsequent cutting, the originally cheap gemstone would end up looking similar to the famous Ice Blue, one of the rarest and most expensive blue diamonds in the world. The one you have in your hand is a good example, but unfortunately, the color is too deep to be an exact match. While the blue topaz looks like a diamond, it certainly isn't as hard, so it's easy to tell just by trying to scratch glass or a mirror with it."

I shook my head, "So you are telling me my uncle died with a gemstone in his pocket that was almost an exact copy of the Ice Blue. I've heard it is worth millions."

"Certainly strange that it was there. Stones like this would appraise in the thousands. It adds to the mystery of his death. Obviously, if the motive was robbery, the thief missed quite a haul."

"Do the police know about it?"

"We set it aside before they came. I know the Armstrong family, and I also know the local Fallbrook Police. If the family was to have any chance of recovering it, it needed to stay clear of the Fallbrook jurisdiction. Just put it this way, living in this town all my life, I don't trust certain individuals in that station. Too many strange things have happened recently. I talked with Mark Armstrong after the body was discovered and he said his detective cousin from Sloan Beach was coming up to help. When I heard that, it seemed like you would be a much better choice to discuss its discovery than the old guard at the police station. As far as they are concerned, your Uncle Paul was a drunk, and he hit his head while trying to find a place to sleep off a late night drinking binge."

I took her hand, "So Alice, are you the person in charge at the hotel? You seem to assume a rather important leadership role."

"Well thank you for the compliment, Mr. Armstrong. I handle a lot of the day to day activities. Now that dad is gone, my sister and I help mom with almost everything. I have a business degree, so I take care of most items having to do with money, the bar, and the vineyard. My sister helps mom in the restaurant and with room service. Mom spends most of her time cooking and running the desk. She has been there for so many years it is a complete habit to her."

"For so big a place, everything seems well run by the three of you."

"That's the problem, Trace," she said almost tearing up. "I literally haven't been away from this hotel for over two years, since dad had his accident. I would like to have a social life, but the only people that I get a chance to talk with are bar clients like you. This hotel is like a huge yoke around our necks. We had to let most of the help go when the back wing of twenty rooms was condemned by the city for inadequate plumbing. Now it just sits and rots, filling up with drunks, bums, and graffiti. Unfortunately, the three of us are rotting away with it."

"What happened to your dad?"

"That's another strange tale, Trace. Dad worked a lot with the family vineyard, just outside of town. Our wine business was on the upswing two years ago, even though we just had thirty acres, helping to cover our bottom line. The climate here is just perfect for a couple of specialty wines that are hard to find anywhere else. Even with our small volume, the quality was over the top. Dad was a wine connoisseur and a stickler for original methods and equipment like they had in the old country. He hand built the oak barrels himself, and we all got involved during crush time. What you are drinking now was the last vintage before he died. It won many competitions around the country and brought in top dollar."

"So what killed him?" I asked.

"He was running a small tractor on one of the fields, turning over the hard dirt. It appears that he had a heart attack, fell off the tractor and was run over by the sharp tines on the plow, which cut him to shreds."

"How awful for your family."

"It was a hard time for a few months, and I tell you Trace, to this day, I don't believe the conventional police wisdom. I think he was murdered."

"What makes you think that?"

"The fact that there were another set of footprints on the freshly plowed dirt leading away from the tractor and that something of incredible value was missing from his desk in the barn."

"What was that?"

"His book of contacts."

CHAPTER 10

There is something about a smooth glass of wine; cool, crisp and refreshing, that relaxes the soul and calms the spirit. Sitting at the bar with Alice, my mind wandered, thinking back to what she had said earlier in the evening. My Uncle Paul had been found dead in the abandoned back quarter of the Fallbrook hotel, yet had a large gemstone in his front pocket that to the uninitiated would be taken for an impossibly expensive diamond. Yet, no one had taken it. Questions were racing through my brain. Was he killed because of it? Was it planted on his body? If so, was it exchanged for a real stone?

Answers to those questions were fleeting, and might never be answered, but were intriguing, none the less. I had never been close to my uncle, having lived most of my life in Texas, over a thousand miles away, seeing him only a few times when my family had come to California when I was a child. He always had a mystique about him. He drove expensive European cars, dressed well, and lived in a remote ranch house, full of expensive furniture, and fantastic art. His second wife, Catarina, when she was alive, was a beautiful woman. Tall and of Portuguese descent, she had flowing black hair and a deep olive complexion. When I saw her last, she wore incredible jewelry. Much of it was turquoise or topaz. It had been over 20 years since I had seen her, but I still remember how exotic she was. During that visit, she had worn a white cotton dress adorning her thin frame, surrounded by a thin leather belt fashioned with gold and turquoise jewels. A red poinsettia flower was in her hair, and when she kissed me hello, her perfume was like mangoes and cinnamon. I was in my early twenties at the time, and she was in her late forties, but I swear there was almost instant chemistry. She was a stark contrast to my Uncle Paul, who had a pale white complexion, gray hair and had gone partially bald.

Even though my uncle was an ordinary looking middle-aged guy, his wife, house, and cars belied someone with a lot of money and importance. We always figured that he had made a lot of money with his avocado grove or possibly with the jewelry that he sold, but no one in my family seemed to know for sure. Catarina had disappeared tragically in a boating accident in Mexico, just over two years ago. My cousin Mark had said Paul was never the same since.

Alice walked behind the bar again and retrieved the bottle of wine.

"Let me top you up," she said with a smile.

"This wine is impressively smooth." I said, glancing back. "I love it, and I'm not usually much of a wine drinker."

"I tell you, Trace, I would love to get out of this hotel once and for all and just spend my time at the winery. I enjoy that business. Currently, we don't have a tasting room, since dad died. There is no one to run it. I coordinate with the harvesters, and we have a part-time vintner, but our production is way down. Our family is going to have to make a decision soon how we are going to move forward. This old hotel is like an albatross around our necks. Either the winery or the hotel has got to go. For everyone's sake, I hope it's the hotel."

"So why not sell it. I'm sure this centrally located property is worth a fortune."

"It's a little thing called the California Historical Property Commission. Since this has major historical significance, we are locked into a preservation requirement."

"Sounds like a bureaucratic nightmare."

"This building is so big and so old; it can't be moved. And the state doesn't currently have the budget to help us with restoration. So basically, we are stuck. I'd be the first to light the match to burn this to the ground, but our fire insurance is very restricted on this old tinderbox. If it burned, we'd walk away with nothing since the state has the title tied up. We wouldn't be able to sell the property for at least five years because of the red tape."

"Are there interested parties?"

"Actually quite a few. Mostly developers looking to build downtown condos."

"Isn't there anything you can do?"

"If we could get the city council to rezone the area, we would be free and clear. But there are two people on the city council that are part of the Fallbrook Historical Society that won't budge."

"Have you offered incentives?"

"These two guys are almost as old as the hotel. We've offered to offset things by providing funds to restore other old properties, but they won't even consider it."

"I'm sorry. What a mess. I can only imagine how you feel."

She reached out and lifted my right hand, "We'll Mr. Armstrong, I don't see a ring on your finger. My only hope is that a good looking guy like you comes and takes me away." With a sly laugh, she said, "You married or have a girlfriend?"

I took her hand, "I actually have both."

"What? You sound like an opportunist; most men wouldn't admit that."

"I went through a divorce a few years back. My wife ran off with the youth pastor at her church. But I technically haven't signed the final papers. The minute I do, she'll be out of a job as the church secretary. Call me a nice guy, but that day is coming soon. My girlfriend, Janet, on the other hand, is back in New York trying to get divorced from her cheating husband. I talked with her earlier today, and it's not going well. So, Ms. Alice, I don't know where I stand."

A big grin came across her face, "So there is hope, after all?"

"With wine like this, there just might be," I said with a wink. "But to be real truthful with you, Janet and I have been through hell and back over the past few months. I was shot at numerous times, she was abducted, and we both ended up in a centuries-old hotel in France, looking for some historical paintings from the second world war. What we found almost got us both killed."

"So you are an adventurer as well as an opportunist. Sounds like it may be dangerous to hang around someone like you."

"If you ask Janet, I'm sure would agree with that statement."

"So, the big question is, do you love her?"

"More than anything, Alice. But her husband is a conniving asshole. She has two kids and lives in a little bungalow in Sloan Beach. He lives in New York, works for the IRS, and sleeps around almost every night. Janet is no more than a long distant babysitter and a tax deduction."

Alice shook her head, "Sounds like a real problem, Trace. Maybe you need some counseling?" With that, she walked around the bar, refilled our glasses. She held hers up for a toast. "To long distant divorces and burning hotels."

We clinked glasses.

I held mine back up and said, "To a great wine harvest and a blue diamond on your finger, someday."

She stood next to me and gave me a hug. Smiling, she said, "Two lonely hearts and one bottle of wine. Maybe someday will be divine."

We stood for a few minutes, silent as the night. "Finally, she looked me in the eye, "I need to close up. Goodnight Mr. Armstrong." With that, she handed me a card. It just said, The Fallbrook Hotel. The place where magic happens.

If only I realized then, what that really meant.

CHAPTER 11

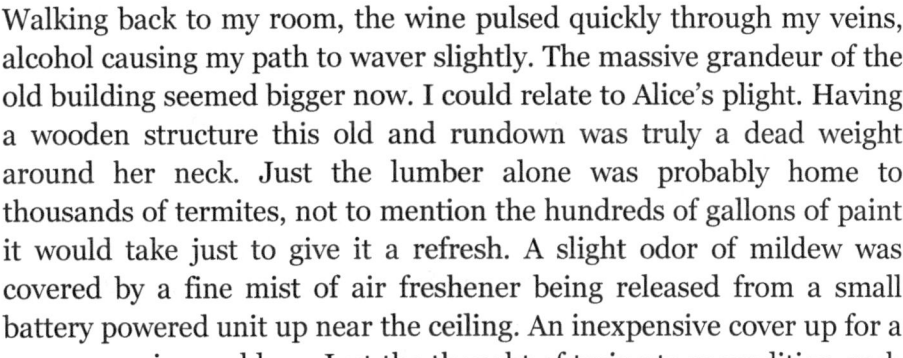

Walking back to my room, the wine pulsed quickly through my veins, alcohol causing my path to waver slightly. The massive grandeur of the old building seemed bigger now. I could relate to Alice's plight. Having a wooden structure this old and rundown was truly a dead weight around her neck. Just the lumber alone was probably home to thousands of termites, not to mention the hundreds of gallons of paint it would take just to give it a refresh. A slight odor of mildew was covered by a fine mist of air freshener being released from a small battery powered unit up near the ceiling. An inexpensive cover up for a very expensive problem. Just the thought of trying to recondition such a place made my head hurt.

I continued along the old corridor until I came to my room. Removing the large key from my pocket, I turned the large tumbler and entered the room. Stale heated air greeted me, and I left the door open for a few minutes to refresh the room. Walking over to the back wall, I opened the heavy muslin curtain and found old leaded glass windows, which had been affixed in place so they wouldn't open. Probably to keep people out, when the rooms were empty.

Air conditioning was missing from the window or under it as is the case with many hotels, which I imagine would add significantly to the cost of operation. Fallbrook can hit a hundred degrees in the summer, but the room was tolerable. A couple of large swamp cooler units were noticeable when I had walked in on the upper roof, which probably cooled the central area, and probably added the moisture that was causing that slight mildew smell. Thankfully, the bathroom had been upgraded.

I figured I might as well make the most of the place, since I booked it through the end of the week, and even in its run-down condition was better than staying with grieving relatives that I hardly knew. Unfolding the covers on the four poster bed, I plumped the pillows and pushed down gently with one hand. The old mattress still had some spring in it. Maybe this wouldn't be so bad after all.

I undressed down to my boxers, laying my pants and shirt on top of my suitcase, over on the side of the room. If there is one thing I've learned over the years, being a cop and now a private investigator, is to keep my clothes and shoes easily available in case I have to move fast. An old habit, I guess, but one that has saved my bacon a few times. I will say, I've never been caught outside my room naked, which has happened to some of my law enforcement friends over the years. When a gun fires or a fire starts, you don't want to have to search for pants and shoes. I was hoping that nothing like that would happen. After a long day and having consumed a half bottle of wine, I just wanted to go to sleep. Who knew what the next day would bring at my uncle's house?

Walking into the bathroom, I brushed my teeth and wiped down my face with a washcloth. Bloodshot eyes greeted me in the mirror. It was time for lights out. I extinguished the bathroom light and crept through the dim light seeping through the edges of the main curtain and from the faint red glow of digital clock numbers to the rather tall bed. I crawled in and sucked in a deep breath. The pleasant smell of clean sheets greeted me. This bed was comfortable. Very comfortable.

Since it was still warm, I just pulled up the top sheet and stared in the dimness at the large wooden ceiling tiles about twelve feet over my head. I ran the day's activities through my mind, from the drag race with the cop to the guns drawn encounter at the donut shop. I ran different scenarios about the transmitter we found on the Mercedes. Crazy day.

My senses started to settle in. It was dark and warm, with a distant rumble from the swamp coolers on the roof. My eyes began to close. Soon I was sound asleep.

Crazy dreams rambled through my brain, but suddenly I found myself awake.

I didn't know at first what had made me wake with a start. Was it a noise, or just a nightmare, I wasn't sure. I lifted my head and then sat up in bed. My eyes slowly adjusted to the darkness. The clock said 1:30 am, and the rumble from the roof was gone.

My senses were on high alert. My ears perked up. I could sense something. Maybe it was a mouse, or heaven forbid, a rat. I listened, but nothing was apparent.

It was like something was in the room. Senses again on alert. I could sense movement. Maybe it was a slight noise or just some innate sense, but something was in my room.

I pulled back the top sheet and hung my legs over the side of the mattress. Touching the floor, I moved my head from side to side. The dim light from the digital clock glowed on the side table, but something else was going on. I stood up but remained perfectly still. I listened and looked. There it was again. Almost like something breathing.

Taking a step away from the bed, I turned towards the back wall, my eyes adjusting. There was something there. I couldn't see it, but I could sense it. I took another step away from the bed and turned to face the curtain area on the back wall. A dim glow from the side of the window curtains crept in. I was now about ten feet from the back wall. Taking a step closer to the curtains, I could make out something in the very dim light. I almost seemed like smoke. It was very wispy, very dark. I took a step forward, eyes adjusting. It seemed to move.

Was the room on fire? I took in a breath, but I didn't smell smoke. Instead, there was another odor. Very faint. I took another step forward on bare feet. The very dim shape seemed to move again. It was about six feet ahead of me now, moving slightly from side to side. Like smoke or a wave or something.

Creepy feelings engulfed me. I knew I couldn't turn my back, but I had no idea what in the hell it was. I took another half step forward.

FLASH... a huge blinding light hit me squarely in the face. Temporarily blinded, what I saw in that flash of intense white light scared the crap out of me. Right in front of me was a wispy, almost transparent human form, with glowing red eyes. My eyes closed for a second with the flash, and when I reopened them, whatever the hell it was had disappeared. Now I could sense smoke, but the presence that was just in front of me had vanished. I took a few steps toward the bathroom door and cautiously viewed the dark room. The door was partially open. Was this a trap?

SHIT... I didn't know what to do. My gun was out in the car, but whatever this was, I had a good idea that a gun would not be effective. Shaking from almost panic, I decided to reach in and hit the light switch. One step, then a second.

Bam.. The light came on, and I quickly looked around. The bathroom was empty, and the light spilled out into the back area of the main room. A vapor that looked like smoke hung in the air, but the form I had seen just seconds earlier was now gone.

What in the hell was it? The eyes were human height, but the body was like a ghost or something. I tell you this, I have never believed in ghosts before, but this was clearly supernatural. How could this being or form or whatever it was, be there one second and gone the next? And now the presence of smoke or vapor, and the slight smell of something... I could hardly make it out. Yet it seemed familiar.

I felt fear as I walked closer to the curtain. Was someone or something hiding behind it? My eyes adjusted, the bright artifacts from the flash almost gone. I looked at the ground at the bottom of the curtain. There were no wrinkles or any sense of anything behind it. I stepped forward, fear completely enveloping me. I reached out to the center part of the curtain. Grasping it firmly, I ripped it back along its upper rod. It slid back, revealing a dim glow of moonlight through the old window. Nothing was there, and nothing could have escaped through the well-secured window.

Now I was getting paranoid. What was that smell? It was so slight, but I know I had experienced it before. I turned on the room light by the front door. Everything was as it was before. Walking around the room; everything seemed in place. I checked my clothes and decided to get dressed. I needed to check outside. Slipping my pants and shirt on, I reached in my pants for the door key.

That's when it hit me. The large blue jewel that was in my left front pocket was gone. Just then I realized what the smell was... rose water.

CHAPTER 12

In life, especially as a private investigator, when things don't make sense, you seek out a plausible reason. In the case of the "presence" in my room, my mind was on high alert. Certainly something was there. After all, the large blue jewel was missing from my front pants pocket. I remembered feeling it there when I replaced the large door key when entering the room.

So something or more likely, someone, had been in my room and removed it. I knew the time of the event because I noticed the clock as I arose. One thirty a.m. The creature or person who was in the room was about five six or five seven. Those glowing red eyes were about chin height on me. This person would have had to walk through the room and reach into the pocket of my pants which were lying on my suitcase, next to the dresser, against the wall.

I'm sure that movement is what awoke me. Law enforcement had taught me to be a light sleeper and a good listener. Things certainly didn't add up. How could someone disappear in a fraction of a second? How did they get in the room? The front door had a chain pulled across. It would have been near impossible for someone to enter that way. The rear window was screwed shut, and the curtains revealed a very solid wall surrounding it. Not a likely option.

The refurbished bathroom had only a small window about 10 feet off the floor. When I looked, it was closed. Given its size, a very unlikely, almost impossible option. The room had a newer claw tub with attached shower to one side. Its shower curtain was open. I could tell at a glance that no one was hiding there. There was a counter with a sink and faucet attached to the back wall of the bathroom, set on top of a standard wooden cabinet. Above the sink was a mirror, but given its size, would not be movable.

My mind was calculating, but nothing was even close to making sense. Now that I had my pants on, I grabbed my shirt, pulled on my shoes and decided to take a look around outside. The clock was at 1:55. Grabbing a small flashlight from my suitcase, I unbolted the front door, walked down the empty and dim hallway about 100 feet to the hallway back door. I opened it and saw that it had a handle on the inside but not the outside. It was a one-way door. Looking into the opening, I spied a door stop lying on the side of the small back cement slab. I propped the door open slightly, and fired up the little light.

A cement wall stood about ten feet from the back door which surrounded the back of the property. To the right, a short walkway ended in a shorter wall, which was about five feet out from the long side of the main building, leading from the back of the building to the front. The side of the building had gravel on the ground with shrubs growing between the rooms. The windows of the 15 rooms on this side started about four feet off the ground, just a little higher than the wall. I quietly prodded through the gravel for a few feet, but I was afraid the noise might wake the occupants. I quietly scaled the short four-foot perimeter fence and found a grassy area on the other side. This area had trees and larger bushes which gave me cover and an easier walk along the side of the old hotel. There were a few street lights, but all of the room lights along the side were out.

I counted down four places until I found my room. I jumped the fence again and looked at the exterior of my unit. There was a wooden extension about a foot or so deep that ran the length of the building. It appeared newer than the main hotel, probably added on when the bathrooms were upgraded to house plumbing and electrical. It was about three feet high. Then the window started and went up about six feet. At the top of the first story, there was a small overhang to divert the rain. The upper floors were dark. I couldn't see any sign of any disturbance or any indication of any entry into the building. The window was certainly secure, and the lower overhang was solid along the whole side of the building, covered with painted plywood sheathing. Dead end.

Extinguishing my light, I walked to the back of the building and re-entered the small back door, removing the door stop. The corridor was still quiet and dark. There was no sign of anyone as I walked back to the front lobby. The front parlor area had a light on but was uninhabited. I went back to my room, entered and looked around. Everything appeared to be undisturbed. Now I wasn't sure what to do. Should I go back to bed? Should I report a robbery? Should I look for Alice or her family? Everything was so quiet; I just decided to sit up for a while.

I sat on the side of the bed, mulling the supernatural options.

In the flash of the light, it certainly appeared to be a spirit. The red eyes still brought fear. It seemed to be vaporish and also disappear into a wisp of smoke. Nothing human about that.

As strange as it sounds, it appeared to be a ghost. Or at least, what I had heard about ghosts.

Which certainly meant that it could probably go through walls or door or cracks. Arrrgh... I didn't know what ghosts could do.

Could ghosts steal gemstones? That didn't seem plausible. At least not get them through solid walls. Could a ghost kill me? That seemed unlikely, but it might be able to scare me to death. Shit. Now what?

Maybe it was some kind of Poltergeist. Maybe like the movie, Nightmare on Elm Street. Now that thing could kill people. I could feel my hands shake a little. *Come on Trace, you know this thing ain't real.*

I laid back in bed and stared at the high ceiling. My mind was still freakn' out. I finally decided to turn on the bathroom light and close the door most of the way. If it did come back, maybe I could tell what it was. I laid quiet for a few moments, my eyes slowly closing. Ears on hyper alert. Sleep came fitfully a few minutes later. The next thing I knew, it was morning.

I took a hot shower and pulled out some clean clothes from my suitcase. It was a new day, Sunday. A day that I would see my cousin, and hope to figure out the story behind a diamond blue Topaz, that a ghost had heisted from my room, After dressing, I decided to go down the restaurant for breakfast. Locking the door behind me, I walked through the front area and took a seat in the small hotel restaurant. Walking in from behind the curtain was Madeline, Alice's mom. She was dressed smartly in a starched white uniform and gingham apron. She smiled as she approached. She had a small order pad in her hand and leaned in to take my order.

"What'll it be, Mr. Armstrong."

Quickly looking over the menu, I said, "Make it a number one, bacon and eggs with coffee."

"Coming right up." She said as she walked past me.

The sweet smell of rose water following her.

CHAPTER 13

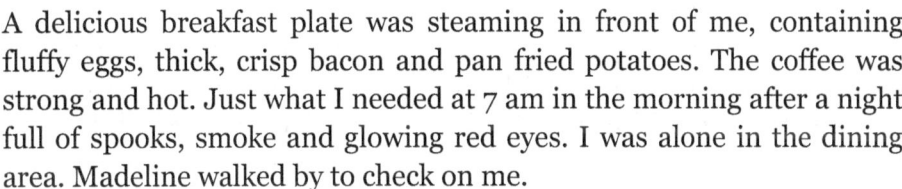

A delicious breakfast plate was steaming in front of me, containing fluffy eggs, thick, crisp bacon and pan fried potatoes. The coffee was strong and hot. Just what I needed at 7 am in the morning after a night full of spooks, smoke and glowing red eyes. I was alone in the dining area. Madeline walked by to check on me.

Looking up at her, I said, "Are you all alone this morning?"

She paused for a second, looking back over her shoulder. "Rose should be joining me soon."

"So how are things in the kitchen? You seem to wear many hats around here, Madeline."

"We don't do much breakfast business on the weekdays, Mr. Armstrong. The Main Street Cafe gets most of our patrons. They open early and have the best biscuits and gravy on the planet. Draw a crowd from all over North County and they are just down the street on the way to the freeway. I don't bother trying to compete with them. Not worth it. That's why I keep the menu here simple; bacon, eggs, pancakes. Basic staples."

"Well, everything is real good."

"Thanks, Trace. I learned a long time ago, that food can make or break a hotel. I get up early, get the eggs and potatoes going, and then

Rose takes over. I usually head back to bed for a few hours after the breakfast rush. In the good days, we used to have a whole crew. Now it's just family."

"Alice was telling me how tough it is now. How are you holding up?"

"To be real honest, this hotel has been almost my whole life. My husband and I bought the place thirty years ago. Completely refurbished it. Seen the good, seen the bad. This is the worst it has ever been. I hate it for my daughters, but with my husband gone, we don't have much choice. If we can get it rezoned, we can move on. Without that, we're stuck."

"I'll light a match..."

"I wish it was that easy, Trace. Believe me, it would have been embers years ago. As Alice probably mentioned, between the lousy insurance policy and the historical society, we would be out on the street dead broke if it burned. We'd lose everything, because we wouldn't be able to pay the property taxes on the land. With the historic designation, it would be five years minimum before we could sell the property. Taxes without income for that long would drain us dry. Believe me, we've run every scenario under the sun. In the meantime, I cook up the best meals in Fallbrook. Stop by for dinner. You'll see."

Looking up into her eyes, I asked, "I've heard rumors of ghosts in this building. Any truth to the stories?"

She took a quick seat across from me. "We've had reports over the years. Mainly noises in some of the timeworn rooms upstairs. Furniture moved, strange smells, things like that."

"Have you ever seen anything?"

"Why do you ask?"

"I heard a few things last night."

"What time was that?"

"About 1:30 in the morning."

"It was probably Bessie."

"Is that a ghost?"

"No, but some people think it is."

"What do you mean by that?"

"It's the vent flap on the top of the building. The coolers on the roof are set to go off at that time, and a massive metal door closes and reverberates through the main structure of the building. The spring and hydraulic shock that used to keep it from slamming down are broken. No one manufactures parts for the unit anymore. No money to fix it if they did. We just live with it. Most people sleep through it."

"That's not what I heard. There was something in my room. I'm almost certain."

"Don't know, Mr. Armstrong. Don't know." With that, she got up and said, "Rose is in the kitchen, I've got to get back to work."

"What do I do if I hear it again?"

She turned and shrugged. "I would pray, Mr. Armstrong, I would pray."

Not much reassurance from the owner, but I figured that was how she dealt with minor problems, especially ones of a supernatural origin. She probably thought I was nuts. I finished up breakfast and headed back to my room. I put in a call to my cousin Mark for walking directions to his house. He has a small bungalow to the north of town. Mark is a car salesman, and his wife Debbie is a real estate agent. Mark grew up in Fallbrook, moved away to San Diego for jobs and then came back a few years ago to settle down in a more rural atmosphere and have kids. He married Debbie about a year back. Last I heard, they hadn't gotten pregnant yet, but Debbie was enjoying her job selling real estate, primarily on weekends.

I arranged to meet them at nine at their house on Fig Street, just down from the hotel. I took another look around the room, under the bed, and in the bathroom. Everything seemed undisturbed. For safe keeping, I put everything back in my suitcase and took it with me as I exited out the back door. I stored it in the trunk of the Mercedes for safety, since I had no idea who had access to the room. After my ghost experience, I didn't want any other funny business.

Leaving the car in a secure spot, I headed out across the parking lot north until I reached Mission Blvd, which is the newer thoroughfare through town. Turning left, I went down one block until I reached Fig Street. Ten houses up the street on the right was Mark's Craftsman style bungalow. Large front porch, white picket fence, and a huge Elm tree gave it a down home small town look. Opening the small front gate I could see Debbie waving from the front door. She was tall, lanky and had straight dark brown hair that hit her mid back. Wearing jeans and a white tank top, she was tan and well kept. Her dark brown eyes had life to them. She smiled at me as we embraced on the front porch. I hadn't seen her since the wedding reception. It appeared that life was treating her well.

"Well, Trace, what has it been... nine months? Last time I remember you were with a blond gal. Janet, I think it was. Up from Sloan Beach. Mark told me you had been shot a few years back. You doing OK?"

"Hey Deb," I replied, "I think it was last October when we were out. Ten months to the day. Still with Janet, and yes, I did get shot a few years back. Lost my partner at the CHP in a shootout. Not a good couple of years. I'm pretty much back up to speed now. Slight limp, but most people don't notice. Doing the private investigator thing. I hear you're into real estate."

"Yep, I'm an agent with a broker in town. A lot of new construction coming to the area. Great job, but real tiring. Why don't you come in, Mark will be back in about ten minutes."

Walking through the small foyer, I sat on the overstuffed couch in the small living room. "So how you guys doing with funeral and all?"

"Mark's taking it pretty well. We knew his dad had a drinking problem, but never realized it was so bad. Hearing that he ended up at The Fallbrook Hotel was a shock. He used to drink at home, but over the last couple of years since his wife disappeared, it was all downhill for him. He'd disappear for days, and look real bad when he finally got back home. We never could figure out where he went. That's why Mark called you. We would sure like to know where he disappeared to, and what might have happened the night he died. Neither Mark or I think he passed away in that hotel. I'm sure he was dumped there."

"How are things at Uncle Paul's ranch?"

"That is the funny thing, Trace. We went over there once we got the news. Everything looked OK in the main house. Nothing out of place. Except for one thing. When we walked into his living room, one of the narrow floorboards was pried up. There appeared to be blood or some other kind of red stain on one side, like someone had tried to reach down with their arm, tearing it open from some of the attaching nails. We did a little snooping after we saw it. The dirt subfloor underneath was empty, but after placing a flashlight down in the opening, we could see where the soil had been disturbed about six feet away. Minor disturbance. It looked like someone had used a small broom to brush something away. We took a pry bar and lifted the boards in that area. Digging in the dirt uncovered a small metal box."

Shaking my head, I said, "Sounds like somebody missed the first time."

"That's what Mark thought."

"Anything in the chest?"

"Just a bunch of change and a few dollars. Looked like an old money box, that Paul probably used to keep the petty cash."

"Wow, It sounds like someone went through a lot of pain to get a few bucks. Vagrant or something?"

"That what we thought, until Mark got a hold of the box, pulled it through the opening, but tripped over the loose floorboard. The old money box flew out of his hand and crashed against the wall. The whole bottom of the small box came off, and suddenly there was an explosion of what looked like marbles. It wasn't until we turned the light on that we realized they were rubies, sapphires, and diamonds."

CHAPTER 14

"An explosion of gemstones. WOW! It's not every day that something like that happens," I said.

We couldn't believe our eyes," Debbie replied, "Most were small stones. Some of the rubies and sapphires were a little larger. We collected everything and took it over to the bank. Opened a safety deposit box. We didn't want anyone coming back for them here at the house. Just a guess but we are probably looking at tens of thousand dollars easy."

"I remember hearing that Uncle Paul used to deal in gemstones, but I thought they were the low-end stones like quartz and topaz. Stones that were mined locally."

"He has a whole workshop full of those. Mainly used for costume jewelry. Sure they're worth money, but we are talking hundreds of dollars for a whole box. When Mark gets back, we'll take a drive over to the ranch. The place is rather remote.

"Aren't you afraid that someone will break in?"

The house and workshop are locked up tight as a drum. A deep drainage ditch runs along the front of the property There is only one road in with a bridge and locked gate. No way to get a car or truck in otherwise. We considered getting a security guard, but there isn't much to steal. At least things you could get out without a truck."

Just then I heard a rumble out front. Glancing through the window, I could see the roof of an older Ford F150 pickup. Bright red in color. "Must be Mark," I said.

Deb nodded, "He's still driving the old 56 pickup his dad gave him for graduation. Can't part with the thing. He keeps it immaculate. I wish he'd keep my Mustang as nice."

Just then the door opened, and Mark walked in. He was just under six feet, solid build, sandy blond hair, surfer look. If you put the two of us together, you might mistake us for brothers. I got the dark brown hair and blue eyes, he got the blond hair with brown eyes, giving him an almost intense look. Mark and I were a year apart. He was a year older. My dad and Uncle Paul were brothers. In a similar fashion, they were also born a year apart.

Mark walked up and put out his hand, "Well if it isn't my little cousin Bill. How are ya? Has got to be almost a year since I seen your sorry ass. Have a seat."

Mark always had to rub in the fact that he was a year older and an inch taller. He called me Bill since that was the name I had as a kid.

Deb piped in, "He goes by Trace now."

Mark laughed, "Trace? What kind of name is that?"

"Short for Tracy, my middle name," I replied. I divorced the name Bill when I divorced my wife. But hey, old man, you can call me what you want."

"So your full name is William Tracy Armstrong? I always wondered what your middle name was. Trace ain't bad as a name, I guess. Fits in good with the private detective gig. My middle name is Victor. Ain't nobody gonna call me Vic, though. And don't think about calling me Marcus or some other wimpy name. The name is Mark. Always been, always will be."

"Shit, Mark, I wouldn't think of calling you anything else. Mark is such an old man's name; it fits well with your senior personality."

He countered, "Is that gray hair on those temples? Man, you ain't aging gracefully. More like straight to the grave."

I shot back, "Well if you had your leg blown to bits by a clown in a van, you'd have gray hair too."

"Sorry man," he said. "We didn't get much of a chance to talk when you and your girlfriend were up for the reception. I remember you saying something about being shot in the leg. How's it doing?"

"Better. The bone shattered when the bullet entered. I was laid up after an extensive surgery for months, but it healed pretty well. Unfortunately the desk jockey job with the Highway Patrol wasn't for me. Those two guys in the van ended my CHP career and my partner's life. Hit him right between the eyes."

"Shit, what a drag. Did they ever catch the guys?"

"That's the sad part. It was a routine traffic stop at one in the morning. A plain white panel van, with a magnetic sign on the side. Funtime Entertainment. We pulled them over because their taillights were out. My partner walked up to the side window, and the driver in a clown mask shot him point blank with a silenced 9mm. The driver reached out the side window, looked back and shot me as I was walking up. It happened so fast I didn't have time to react. Put me down on the ground instantly. I pulled my gun, but they took off. The vehicle looked totally legit. Didn't suspect a thing. Turned out they had robbed a very expensive estate earlier in the evening. They dumped the van across town and disappeared. Pro hit. As far as I know they are still out there. Got away with almost a million bucks in valuables. Paintings, jewels, cash."

"So have you investigated this case yourself? I imagine you'd like a little revenge."

I shook my head. "It's been too painful, too close to home. My partner Jack was a great guy. Ended everything for him and his family in a split second. Someday I will if the authorities don't get them first. Guys like that eventually screw up."

"So how big is the scar?"

I turned around and pulled my pants down past my boxers. "Big hole at the top of my left leg and a long scar down to the kneecap. Definitely ruins my beach time."

"Damn, that's one ugly son of a bitch," he grimaced.

"Won't win me any beauty contests, that's for sure. So how about you? How you getting' along now that your dad's gone?

"I'll be real honest Bill.. Er, I mean Trace. I wasn't entirely surprised. Ever since mom disappeared in Mexico a couple of years ago, things were never the same for dad. He started drinking a lot and would be gone for days at a time. I didn't expect to find him at the old hotel, though. I'm sure he was dumped there."

"Why do you say that?" I asked.

"Just the position of the body, and the fact that he'd been seen around town with some shady characters. I'd ask him about things, but he never let on. We weren't very close over the last couple of years. I was living down in San Diego when Catarina disappeared. Moved back up here soon after that. Met Deb at the dealer, started dating, and we got married soon after. Renting this old place so Deb can get a start in the local housing market. If things work out, we'll buy something else."

"Deb was telling me that you found a money box at your dad's place. Was that a surprise?"

"Not totally. Mom and dad liked beautiful things. Mom was an expensive date at times and dad always dealt in low-end jewelry since I was a kid. I figured he might have a few expensive pieces. Hell, he had a beautiful Mercedes and a fishing boat, not to mention the ranch. Those avocados bring in big bucks at harvest time."

I looked over at Deb and then back at Mark, "So what do you think happened to your dad?"

Mark glanced over at Deb, shaking his head. "We've been trying to figure that out. After seeing the floorboard removed at the house and finding the money box, I figure the motive might have been robbery. Somebody broke in, hit dad over the head and tried finding the money box. They probably didn't mean to kill him, so when he ended up dead, they got scared and just dumped the body at a location that wouldn't seem out of the question. A lot of transients come and go at the back part of that hotel. Pour a little whiskey in his mouth and put the bottle in his hand."

"What did the police say?"

"Dad was dressed in work clothes and appeared to be well intoxicated, bottle in hand. They called us and had us come claim the body. The coroner found a high blood alcohol count and blunt force trauma to the back of his head. Since the body was lying face up on a rock, it looked like he was just drunk, fell back and hit his head. Cut and dry they thought. They offered to do a further investigation, but dad had a recent history of public drunkenness. He frequented a local bar and got a little belligerent a couple of times. We didn't push it when they called. It wasn't till a day later that we discovered the floor board up when we went to his house."

"Did you call them back about that?"

Deb broke in, "I thought about calling them, but I remembered hearing that you were doing P.I. work. I told Mark we ought to call you. The police in town are not very helpful. They all but wrote it off. Hardly gave it the time of day."

"I'll be glad to give things a look," I said. "Trying to remember Mark, don't you have a younger half sister? Has she been contacted?"

"You remember my step mom Catarina. She was originally from Portugal, came to the States over twenty years ago. She had a daughter from a first marriage named Maria. After my mom died of cancer back in 68, Dad remarried Catarina. Maria was still living in Portugal at the time. She is close to our age, and has since moved to the Phoenix area. She'll be at the funeral on Friday."

"Is she part of the estate?"

"Not sure, Trace. Dad changed his will a while back according to his attorney. Right after Catarina disappeared in that boating accident down in Mexico. Maria is coming in Thursday morning, and we will be meeting with the attorney to go over the will later in the day."

"Sounds a little intense. Do you expect any surprises?"

"I don't think so. A month after Catarina went missing off the boat, some of her clothing and a shoe were found in a Fisherman's Net. Torn and shredded. The authorities ruled that she had drowned. There were traces of blood in the fibers. Sharks probably."

"Wow, that's gruesome."

Mark sighed, "Even though it was tough to look at, it was better than not knowing. The family got closure and a death certificate. Always so hard when there is a disappearance. It didn't help dad, though. He always blamed himself."

"What exactly happened?"

"It was an overnight deep sea fishing trip. Catarina and dad, along with four of their friends were partying hard on a Saturday night many miles off the coast of Ensenada. Everyone was pretty well drunk. Dad was piloting the boat. He slowed it down and fell asleep at the wheel. Weather came in overnight, and the seas got rough. When dad woke up, he couldn't find Catarina. The other four had gone down below to sleep. Last he had seen of her; she was in the pilot area with him. Best they could figure is that she fell overboard in the rough sea. Waves were crashing over the sides. Dad thinks he was passed out for an hour or so."

I shook my head, "I knew it was ruled an accident, but I wasn't sure what happened. Was your dad ever charged with anything?"

"The Mexican Coast Guard did a search. There was an investigation. The four other people on the boat were brought in to testify. Dad went through hell not knowing if he would be brought up on charges, all the while mourning the loss of his wife. Once the clothing was found, everything was ruled an accident."

"I bet your dad was relieved."

Mark shook his head, "I'm not sure. He just couldn't get over the guilt. He used to say he wished he was dead. I know he wished it was him that had fallen overboard."

Debbie put her hand on Mark's shoulder, "We ought to take Trace over to the ranch before it gets too hot."

Mark looked back over at me, "You up for a trip?"

"Sounds good, I'd love to see the place." I said. "By the way, have you ever heard of a Diamond Blue Topaz?"

"Sure, I've seen a few before. Cut to look like a large, expensive diamond. Why do you ask?"

"How much are they worth?"

"A good one might bring a few thousand dollars if it is an exact cut. I've seen a few that would fool a gemologist."

"Did your dad own one?"

"That was his specialty over the years. He had clear topaz stones

"Nuked" as he called it. He would send them down to a place in San Diego that exposed them to intense radiation that would turn them different shades of blue. They would have to "cook" for the proper amount of time to get them to be an exact match."

"You say they are good enough to fool someone?"

"Good enough he had to be careful."

"Really?"

"Why are you asking all these questions, Trace?"

"Because that may be why your dad was killed. He had one in his pocket when he died…"

CHAPTER 15

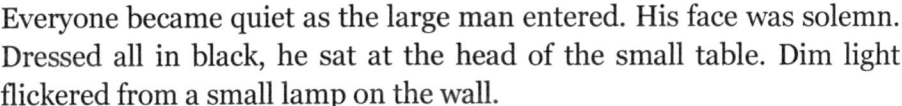

Everyone became quiet as the large man entered. His face was solemn. Dressed all in black, he sat at the head of the small table. Dim light flickered from a small lamp on the wall.

In a strong, deep voice, he said, "Our process is simple. We trade valuable goods all over the world. No border or security will stop delivery. Precise timing is a must. For years, the process has been flawless. Never a witness, never a problem. Now we have incompetence. First time."

Two men sat across the table in the darkness. The big one spoke, "That Armstrong guy gave us the box like you asked for. How did we know that the content was a fake? We went back, roughed him up. Unfortunately, he was drunk and hit his head. He didn't wake up. We went to his house and looked around. Found a box in the shed. Found another box under the house."

Handing them over, he asked, Is this what you want?"

The big man stood, opened the boxes, and then slammed his fist down hard on the table. "This is not what I want. Look at the labels. That is not the name I gave you. This is small change. Cheap rubbish. I must have delivery of the correct box by Thursday night. The delivery cannot be modified. I also need all loose ends handled. I pay for delivery. Failure means death."

The smaller of the two said, "We will handle this, Sir. You can count on us."

He replied coarsely, "If I have to have someone else take care of this, you imbeciles, you can be assured that your petty lives are the first thing he takes care of."

With that, the two men stood, and exited the room, their uniforms wet with perspiration.

CHAPTER 16

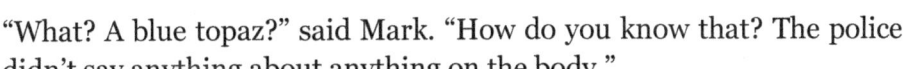

"What? A blue topaz?" said Mark. "How do you know that? The police didn't say anything about anything on the body."

I stood up, "One of the gals at the hotel gave it to me. They found it in your dad's front pocket when they discovered the body. Alice said they put it aside because of problems with the Fallbrook cops. I guess things routinely disappear."

Mark seemed incredulous, "Why would they do something like that? Do you have it with you?"

"No, it's back at the hotel," I lied. "It's over an inch long, but Alice said that the color was off. It was too dark to be authentic."

Deb interjected, "I have heard stories about the Fallbrook Police at work. A lot of good ol' boy stuff goes on. I guess it was for the best that they didn't find it. If the color is off, it probably isn't worth much. A few hundred at the most."

Mark spoke up, "So if he had a Diamond Blue Topaz in his pocket, do you think whoever killed him might have been after it?"

"It's possible," I said, "but why would it still be on the body? Unless somebody was after a real diamond, but even then, they would take the Topaz. It's still worth some money. At this point, it doesn't make a lot of sense."

"Maybe he brought it along to buy something else or pay someone off?"

"Anyone's guess at this point," I wagered. "We don't know how he got to the hotel or if someone actually killed him. It's possible he did fall back and hit his head."

"Well, that's why we invited you up, Trace. We hope you can dig into things a little," said Deb.

"You certainly have my curiosity up. Why don't we start over at the Ranch house? I'd like to see the scene of the crime, or at least where he lived."

With that, Mark led the way to the front door. Mark unlocked the truck, and Deb slid in the middle on the bench seat. With the three of us on the bench-seat it was a little cramped, but at least, I wasn't cramped against my cousin. Deb's perfume filled the cab, which offset some of the dusty smell of the old cab. We headed back up Oak Street to Mission and headed east. Staying straight at the intersection, we were soon on De Luz Rd which wound for about 20 miles on its way to the inland town of Temecula.

Uncle Paul's ranch house was just off De Luz about three miles out of the city. It was in a hilly section of grass covered ravines. The driveway had a locked gate. Mark got out and unlocked it, and we bumped our way down a winding gravel road for about a quarter mile. Coming around a short curve, the truck entered a small clearing. The old ranch house was on the right, and a vast grove of avocado trees was on the left. The clearing in the center was about a half acre, containing an old picket fence, a small lawn next to the house and a large garage style structure out back, which must be the workshop that Mark mentioned. Parking in front of the house we all got out. The old house was a sprawling ranch style affair with large paned windows, peaked roof, and pale green paint. While it was old, it appeared to be in good shape. A small muddy lawn separated the fence from the house, with a brick walkway leading to the front door.

Mark led the way, and he pulled a large keyring from his pocket and cracked open the wooden door. Dry musty air hit us as we walked in. The door led through a small foyer and then into a spacious living room. I could see where a couple of floor boards had been lifted. Otherwise, the room was furnished nicely with large overstuffed brown furniture and oak tables. The wall had expensive looking art of country cottages and the like. Over to one side was a small wooden desk and chair.

Overall, it looked well kept and probably way too much house for a bachelor.

Looking around, I asked "Did your dad have a housekeeper? Everything looks clean and well maintained. Not what I expected from someone with a drinking problem."

Mark picked up a small slip of paper from the desk, "Here is a receipt from the neighbor lady. She would come over every week and help dad out. Contessa is her name. She lives about a half mile up De Luz towards town. Sweet gal. Maybe you might like to talk with her. She knew my dad better than most anyone else."

"That might be a good idea," I said. Why don't you show me the rest of the house."

Deb led the way. To the left of the living room, the house had a functional kitchen with newer appliances. To the right were two well-furnished bedrooms. Out back, one of the original bedrooms had been modified into a screened in den appointed with some light colored wicker and soft plush pillows. It looked inviting, like a room you might see in the Caribbean.

"This is a beautiful room; I said, taking a seat in one of the wicker chairs."

Deb sat next to me in another chair, "I love this place. It has a lovely view out the sliding glass door to the back of the clearing and down into the valley. Fantastic view with the drapes open." Mark pulled a cord, and the curtains pulled back, revealing the view.

"Wow, you're not kidding. You can probably see at least five miles. What's down that way?"

"It's the river valley. If you look real carefully, you can see a little water there. It gets going pretty good in the winter."

"Nice place. I could camp out in this room for a while. Now all I need is a cold one."

"Comin' up, young fellow," said Mark. Remind me, are you old enough to drink?"

"Sure am, old man. Are you sure your doctor will let you drink? I've heard a lot of old guys have prostate problems. I don't want you to have problems peeing?"

He laughed and walked out into the kitchen. He returned in a minute with three tall bottles of Heineken which he distributed to Deb and me.

"Your dad had good taste in beer."

"Lot's more where that came from. A whole case next to the fridge."

"So when you lived here, where did you go to school?"

"An old wooden school house down near the river. Back in those days, there weren't many people out this way. The whole school only had a hundred kids. But I had some good friends, and we would hike into town on a regular basis. Back then, the train still came through. We used to hang out at the station. Sometimes we would make some extra money hauling bags and luggage over to the hotel. When I was 16, I got a precursor to the truck I have now. Used to drive, drive, drive. Fallbrook wasn't that bad. I used to give some of the Marines a lift over to the base and then turn down to Vista and Oceanview."

"Sounds like a great life. Most people complain about living in a small town."

"Once I got the truck I was free. Fallbrook has great weather and isn't too far from the beach in Oceanview. Bought me a surfboard, and spent a lot of time there. I think it's still out in the workroom. You want to take a gander out there. I haven't been in there for years."

"Sure," I said. "I'm surprised you haven't been out there already."

"It isn't much to see. A couple of workbenches, some tools and boxes of quartz and other stones. Let me see if I can find the key."

Mark rumbled in a closet at the back of the kitchen for a minute. "Here it is. Let's go out and take a look."

The three of us walked out the back door of the kitchen and followed a stone path for about fifty feet. The workroom was like a long rectangular garage. Probably used for storing farm equipment in the past. Sloped roof, wood siding, and a barn style sliding door on one end. We walked up to the side where there was a standard door. Mark fumbled with the key in the old rusted lock. It finally gave way. The door appeared to be stuck. He gave it a slight body slam, and it gave way. Mark walked in and let out a yell.

"Holy shit. Someone has been in here."

As I followed him in, I could see that everything in the room had been turned over and dumped on the floor. Cardboard boxes of stones dumped upside down. Tools were scattered, and the workbenches torn away from the wall and smashed to pieces. It appeared that nothing was left undisturbed. "Whoever was in here was looking for something," I said.

Deb stood in the doorway, peering from side to side. "Check this out," she said. "The side window latch is jimmied. That's how someone got in here. Certainly made a huge mess. With the look of the broken workbenches, they were certainly angry."

"Stand still," I said. Don't move. Look at these footprints in the dust. They are huge. You got a flashlight?"

Mark found one lying on the floor. Walking up behind me he shined the beam on the print on the floor. "Damn, that print is huge. One hell of a large person. Probably an 18 shoe size. Shit, who would wear a shoe that big?"

"I can tell you one thing, Mark. Whoever it was is probably the one who killed your dad."

Deb suddenly let out a scream. There on the floor was a huge rattlesnake. Coiled and ready to strike.

CHAPTER 17

I've been at gunpoint a few times, with my life on the line. Each time, everything seemed to stand still. It's a similar effect when you are staring into the eyes of a large coiled rattlesnake. I instinctively froze. Mark was standing right next to me, and I could see his hands shaking, but he didn't move from the spot he was standing.

Deb was behind the snake and put her finger up to her lips, signaling silence. Other than being startled, she didn't seem to have much fear. Stooping down behind it, she quickly thrust her hand behind its tongue jerking head. With a firm grip, she grasped it around the neck and took the writhing snake out of the workshop and walking briskly, took it to the back of the property and tossed it down one of the ravines. Within minutes, she was back brushing her hands off on her jeans.

"God, I hate those things," said Mark. I got bit by one as a kid, almost died. Deb is experienced with them. She used to volunteer with animal control. In fact, that is how we met. She had come out to my dad's house on a call about a year ago. At the time, she used a long pole to get one out of one of the avocado trees."

I replied, "I hate them too. I can't believe she just grabbed it with her bare hands. That sucker was big. At least five feet long."

Deb shook her head as she walked up, "All clear. You weren't scared were you Trace?"

"Those things scare the crap out of me." I sighed, "You don't think that might have been planted there do you?"

"Nah, the side window was left open," she said. "It probably crawled in here to get out of the noonday sun."

"So what do you guys make of the large footprints? Do you know anyone that might have feet that big?"

Mark looked for a second over at Deb. "Not that I am aware. The person would have to be almost seven feet tall to have feet that big. With the looks of the benches, this person, I assume a man, must be unyielding. Look at the nails pulled out from the wall. Shit, he could rip your head off without much trouble."

"Agreed," I said. "Whoever it was broke the latch on that side window and reached around inside to undo the door. At first, I thought someone must have climbed in. After seeing the footprint leading in from the entrance, it appears that the perp must have had long arms."

Mark walked towards the back of the shop with the flashlight. "Look at this Trace. The prints are clearer back here where the dust and dirt are deeper. There appears to be some type of logo in the center of the print." He knelt down. "Can you make this out?"
I knelt down on one knee and took a close look. "Got a pen? Here it is … Meindl… Sounds European."

"German brand," said Mark. "A lot of different armies use them around the world. Famous for their Stormtrooper boots. Both the French and British use them."

Nodding, I said, "So now we are looking for a very tall European."

"More than likely," Mark said. I don't remember seeing them over here. "When I was stationed in Germany when I was in the army, they were popular there. Well made, heavy duty and waterproof. That's why the Germans were so tough to defeat in World War Two.

"So we have an enormous individual break the window latch, lift the window, stretch a long arm in the window and undo the lock. Following the prints, he walks in straight back, then turns to the right. The prints then scatter backward and then go into a circle near where the workbench attached to the wall. It appears that whoever it was spent some time there with all the blended prints in one area."

Mark thought to himself for a minute, "If I remember right," he said, "I think my dad's main toolbox was there on the lower shelf. He turned and scanned the far wall. If my guess is right, the perp looked through the toolbox for something, and not finding it, threw the box across the room, back towards the door. The toolbox is over there on the floor, with the tools scattered all over the area around it."

"I see what you mean. I wonder if he was looking for a particular tool, say to pry up the floor, or if he was looking for something more specific?"

Mark shrugged, "Not sure on that one."

"Let's think it through," I offered. "We can see the tracks led here on the left side of the bench, loitered in the area, and that the tool box was thrown across the room. If he just needed a screwdriver or pry bar, would he throw the box? Probably not. He would just take the tool and go into the house."

Mark stood back and looked at the area where the toolbox was originally. "Notice that there are a few tools on the ground here. So he looked through and didn't find what he was looking for. He got frustrated and threw the box."

"Right," I said. Look at where the prints go from there. They go across the front of the workbench area to the other side."

"That's where dad had a pegboard full of jewelry tools above the workbench. Most are spilled here on the ground."

I carefully walked across to the right side of the bench area, "Look at the way the nails pulled from the wall. The nails point to the left. This is where he ripped the worktop from. Where did you find the flashlight, Mark?"

"It was right near where you are standing."

"Now we are getting somewhere. Where did your dad usually keep the flashlight?"

"It was kept on a hook by the front door so you could get it when you walked in. The ceiling light isn't very good, so he kept it there when he came out at night."

"Yes. So now we can say with pretty good certainty that the perp was here at night. With that side window, he wouldn't have needed the flashlight to see the toolbox in the day time. He walks in, grabs the light, walks over to the toolkit. He doesn't find what he is looking for, throws the box and then comes down to the other tool area. Evidently he didn't find what he was looking for here either. He drops the light, rips out the bench and tears the place up."

Deb, who was following the conversation, said. "So Trace, do you mean the perp was looking for some kind of tool?"

"Probably," I said. "But I'm not sure what. There are all sorts of hand tools scattered. We know the board was torn up in the house, but almost any of these larger screwdrivers or pry bars would have done the trick. I think it was something else." With that, I walked over to where the toolbox was scattered on the floor. There were small hand tools that had been dumped out, an assortment of fasteners, old keys, pens, razor blades and a couple of scraps of paper. Nothing much of value. I picked up the main box and examined it. There were some significant scratches on the side, and someone had made some numerical markings inside the lid with a sharpie. Looked like measurements for a project. "Let's see what we have here. A regular Craftsman eighteen-inch tool box. The main tray is on the floor, contents spilled out, the rest of the box is empty." Picking it up, I realized something was amiss. "Wait a minute. Come here Mark. Pick this box up."

Mark lifted the box. "Whoa. This thing is heavy. What's weighing it down?"

We looked it over, but nothing seemed obvious at first. I said, "Looks just like my Sears Craftsman box at home. Grey sheet metal and a few welds." I held it up to the light. "Wait a minute. It looks like it has something here." I reached in and pulled a small metal tab on one end of the bottom... POP!

The suddenly loose false bottom slowly lifted out in my hand. "Jackpot!, I said. "Maybe this is what the perp was after."

Underneath was a taped in place Glock handgun.

CHAPTER 18

Mark went to reach for the handgun.

"Don't touch it," I shouted. "We may need to check it for fingerprints."

He got a serious look on his face, "So what do we do with it?"

"I'll take it with me if you don't mind. My roommate has connections with San Diego Law Enforcement. I'll take the toolbox and the gun. Whoever this huge perp was, has probably left a ton of fingerprints on the outside of the box. Who knows what we will find with the gun?"

Mark shrugged, "It's OK with me."

"So Mark, why would your dad hide a gun here?"

He shook his head, "I can't imagine why he would. He has numerous firearms in the house. They are all locked away in a gun safe. Maybe he didn't know it was there?"

"That's a possibility," I offered. "But it appears that our oversized perp knew it was there. So why would somebody want that particular gun? It appears to be an ordinary Glock 9mm."

Deb bent down and took a look at the gun. Picking up the tray she took a sniff of the barrel. "Definite powder smell. I don't think that has been there very long. Check out the duct tape holding it in place. Looks fresh."

"You're right," I said. "So why hide it?"

Mark shrugged, "Maybe it was used in a crime? But that would mean dad would have known about it. Doesn't add up. If he was involved, why not just put it in his gun safe? Much better place than an old toolbox."

"Maybe," I said. "But this would certainly be a better hiding place. After all, we almost missed it, and the perp certainly did."

"This just isn't making sense, Trace," Mark said. "I don't think the perp was after a gun. It seems like he would more than likely be after the jewels, which were in a box in the house."

Deb nodded, "That makes more sense. Probably came out here after missing the box in the house."

Standing up, I said, "Why don't we go back into the kitchen. We need to make up a timeline."

With that, I followed Mark and Deb back into the house. We pulled up some chairs around the kitchen table. Mark grabbed a spiral notebook and some pens. Deb walked out into the kitchen and in a few minutes came back with three large glasses of cold water. She sat across from me and passed them out. She smiled and said, "At least the refrigerator still works."

I took one of the glasses, "When I checked into the hotel, Madeline the owner said that your dad was found in the abandoned section of the hotel on Wednesday night. The coroner said it appeared he had been dead a few hours. So that would make it last Wednesday that he was last alive."

Mark nodded, "That's what we heard too. Unfortunately, I hadn't talked to my dad for over two weeks. The last time was by phone on a Friday, two weeks ago."

"So we are missing a week. Did he ever have visitors here?"

"No, not that I know of. Not since mom died at least. He went to town a lot. Frequented a downtown bar."

"So, you were saying that a neighbor lady kept house for your dad. It still looks clean, so I imagine she was probably here recently."

Mark said, "Contessa comes over once a week. Been doing it for years. Almost always on Wednesdays."

"Can we talk with her?"

"Sure, she lives down De Luz. It's almost noon. I'm sure she is in the kitchen making lunch. If we hurry, we might get a bite to eat. She is a wonderful cook, and always enjoys the company. I'll lock up, and we can head over."

The three of us walked out of the house. Mark and Deb got in his truck, and I slid in from the passenger side. We took off down the long gravel driveway. The woman's house was about a mile down De Luz from the end of Paul's driveway. Within 10 minutes, we were on her doorstep.

Contessa was a pleasant-looking middle-aged woman of Latin descent. Medium height with a slim build, she had shoulder length dark hair and stunning blue eyes. Living in a post-war bungalow on a half acre lot, surrounded by fruit orchards; she was known throughout the valley for her excellent pies. She sold them in town, through a partnership with some of the restaurants. As the front door opened, she invited us in. The aroma of apple pie was in the air. We followed her through the direct entrance into a sprawling kitchen. Easily half the size of a garage, she had two large industrial ovens lined up against one wall.

Mark spoke up, "Contessa, this is my cousin Trace. He's in town to help me with the funeral and my dad's estate. It smells like you've got a batch of apple going?"

Contessa nodded and held out her hand to me, "Pleased to meet you, Trace. I'm making these up for the roadhouse in town. They usually sell four or five a night. Make up a dozen at a time. They stop by twice a week for delivery. Excellent customer. You know Apple was always your dad's favorite."

Mark smiled, "Contessa makes the best pies and desserts. My favorite is cherry, but she has dozens of recipes, some that are world famous."

Contessa reached out for Mark's arm, "Sorry to hear about your dad. Any idea what happened?"

"We aren't sure, but we thought we would check in with you. You were probably the last person to see him alive."

She shook her head, "Unfortunately, I'm not sure if I can give you much help. I went over last Tuesday night. My usual rounds. He wasn't there. The kitchen was somewhat of a mess. Multiple beer bottles, dirty plates, etc. But that was relatively normal. Since he had become a widower, he wasn't very good at picking up after himself."

"Any sign of forced entry?" I asked.

Turning around from the oven, she glanced my way and said, "Nothing out of the ordinary. He didn't have a lot of security. I just used my regular key to get in."

Deb asked, "Was the house stuffy, like it had been closed up?"

She smiled, "I can tell when he has been out for a while. The trash builds up in the house and gets real stinky. Didn't smell that way on Tuesday. My guess was he was probably there earlier in the week. The funny thing was, it looked like he had a guest, since there were plates and beer bottles on the table. He usually leaves a mess, but this was more than usual. Certainly looked like two or three people had been sitting at the kitchen table."

Glancing up, I said, "Did you ever see anyone hanging around his place? Maybe someone enormous?"

"We get our assortment of transients on De Luz Road, but they usually stay in the undeveloped areas. Many of them camp out. I don't remember seeing anyone at Paul's place. It's too far back from the road and it dead ends in the ravine. Not a place they would likely hang out. Why do you ask about someone big?"

"We saw some huge footprints out by the shed."

"Really?" she said, "Probably from a workman. He had guys working in the orchards at times. Trimming bushes, pruning, the like. Tree work usually means some pretty tough guys. But they would just pull into the orchard and work. Not usually up by the house."

Mark asked bluntly, "So do you have any idea, Contessa, what happened to dad? Best guess?"

"Well Mark," she said, "you know he loved to drink, and he was always carrying around those Topaz jewels that look real expensive. My guess is he showed the wrong person one of those in town, and they hit him over the head. He was at the Maverick Bar a lot, and often into the wee hours of the morning. I don't mean to be crass, but that end of town and some of those characters, seem like the logical suspects. Some of those guys might kill you for pocket change."

With that, she motioned us to sit down at the kitchen table where she passed around plates of her fresh apple pie.

Deb said, "This is amazing, Contessa. So much better than the frozen ones at the store." She pushed back her chair and asked, "Can I use your phone? I'm supposed to be holding an open house this afternoon on the other side of town. I'll need to get one of the other agents to cover for me."

Contessa smiled, "The life of a real estate agent. Always working on the weekends. The phone is on the little table in the hall. Help yourself."

Mark looked over at Contessa. "I forgot Deb was on today. She has been doing really well lately. The market is great during the summer, and she has some larger properties listed. It's always been hard to make a living in Fallbrook, but with a lot of new construction, the older homes are starting to move. We might actually be able to afford having kids someday."

Contessa offered some whipped cream. "Mark, you work at the Ford dealer in town, don't you? How's that gonna work out with Deb's schedule if you have kids?"

Mark replied, "Pretty well actually. I'm in fleet sales. Sell a lot of trucks to the ranchers. I have Sundays and Mondays off. Saturday is my big day. I can babysit on Sundays and we can enjoy the day off on Mondays."

I quipped, "Bout time we see some little Armstrong's in this town."

Mark replied, Soon. . . Real soon.

Talking with Mark about kids was always a touchy subject. I had married right out of high school and my daughter was in college. Mark had dated for years, but always ran when the word commitment came up. Figured he might be a lifelong bachelor. I was surprised when he married Deb. She was younger than he was, and now they were talking about kids. Being a newborn dad at 43 might be an adventure of its own.

Contessa walked around the table, offering seconds on the pie, but everyone was stuffed.

Looking up, I asked her, "These are really amazing paintings you have on the walls. Bright colors, ocean scenes. Where are they from?"

Contessa replied, "I'm from the country of Belize in the Caribbean. These depict some of the local activities, Surfing, sailing, and sightseeing. Painted by a local painter. Help remind me of my home country."

"Wow, they make you want to get on a plane and go,"

"I get homesick often, but these help bring my memories back. You ought to go someday, Trace."

"If the place is half as exciting as the action depicted in the paintings, I'm ready."

Contessa looked me in the eye, "Don't delay the fun in your life, Trace. Believe me, time passes all too fast."

With that, she picked up our dishes. We sat around for a few more minutes. It became obvious that she cared a lot about my Uncle Paul, but she lived far enough away that she hadn't seen or heard anything.

"Make sure to take some pie and fruit with you," she said, taking some items from the refrigerator.

The three of us got back in the truck and headed back to Mark's house. As we parked in the drive, Deb ran into the house to put the items in the refrigerator, and I followed Mark back out to the workroom.

"I want to look at those footprints again," I said. "Let's see if we can tell where they originated from."

Mark agreed. We spent a few minutes searching the dirt and pathways between the house and the workshop. The big prints seemed to come from the grass area near the house and followed the dirt path to the shed. But how they got to that area was a mystery.

Mark said, "I'm going to head in for a minute and get us a couple of beers. It's hot out here. Back in a minute."

He headed back up the path, and I went back to the workroom. The big footprints sure were a mystery. They seemed to appear out of nowhere on the grass outside the house. Then they led across the path to the workshop. Stopping outside, they entered the shop, moved around inside, but then ended by the front door. They weren't apparent leaving the work shed. But it was hard to tell outside since the wind and weather may have erased any evidence. But I could see ones coming in. Didn't make sense. I moved things around, but I didn't find anything of interest.

Looking down at my watch I realized it had been about 15 minutes since Mark had headed into the house. He must have forgotten about me. If I wanted a beer, I guess I'd have to get one myself. I headed over to the house, opened the screen door to the kitchen, and was startled to see Mark lying face down on the living room floor about ten feet away. I called out, but he didn't move. I went running over to him, but something massive hit me on the back of the neck. It stung for a moment and then everything blacked out.

CHAPTER 19

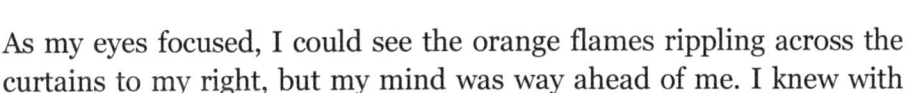

As my eyes focused, I could see the orange flames rippling across the curtains to my right, but my mind was way ahead of me. I knew with this much fire; I would soon be dead.

Reality swept across me; a strong tingling feeling poured back into my legs. They were hot, real hot. My jeans were smoking, yet the flames hadn't caught the fabric. As I lifted my head, I now knew what had saved me. The metal kitchen table had folded down as one of the flaming roof timbers had collapsed on it, but this flimsy table now covered my lower body, propped up by a half collapsed metal chair and one spindly leg which looked like it would further collapse any second. How I had survived this, I didn't know. I pulled my right leg back. It moved without issue, but as I went to pull my left leg, my shoe covered foot caught under the bottom edge of the table. Panic ensued, and I pulled harder. The table shuddered, but I couldn't budge it.

Thoughts of losing my foot caused me to pull harder, but the table just clamped down harder, digging deeper into the flesh of my foot, just below my ankle. My senses veered back to the fire. Flames were all around me along with thick, acrid smoke. I didn't want to die this way, but I also couldn't fathom losing my foot. Sweat poured down my forehead and into smoke filled eyes, which burned like crazy.

Suddenly there was a loud crack, as the metal chair gave way. The red hot metal table dropping further on my jeans. An intense burning pain roared up my leg as the thin cloth gave way to the red hot heat of the metal. I screamed in total agony and without thinking just erupted in an upward push of arms, legs, and body. The table teetered and crushed down harder on my foot, trapping it with even more intensity. Everything in my lower body was now in incredible pain, either from the burning heat or the crushing weight of the wood timber.

As bad as my lower body was, it paled in comparison to the searing fire above my face. Another cross beam on the ceiling had dropped half way and looked ready to engulf me totally in flame. I cried out, half in pain and half to a God I didn't know. "Help me," I cried, but everything just got hotter.

Then it happened. The beam above my head snapped, dropping at an angle as it swung quickly down from the left. I half closed my eyes. I knew it was over.

The beam hit the side of the table, and the whole room exploded in a huge sheen of sparks, as the embers poured down on my arms, neck and face. My arms pushed upward, everything on fire. Suddenly the other end of the flaming beam fell, pivoting the table to the side. My foot felt like it was being ripped off, but it came loose for a split second. Long enough for me to pull it free, and slide backward. Pushing back with my hands on the linoleum floor, I pulled myself up. Turning quickly, I came up on my feet and started to run to the kitchen door, just as the last table leg gave way. A huge ball of flame covered the table and hit me from behind.

Thankfully the side kitchen door gave way as I hit it full force. Tripping on the doorstep, I tumbled head first on the cool, muddy ground outside. I still felt like I was on fire, so I instinctively rolled and rolled in the grass and mud away from the house. As everything came to a stop, I tried to stand, but my left ankle turned to the side. Burning pain covered me as I looked at the smoking spots from the ashes on my arms. I knew my face and leg weren't much better. Everything hurt like hell. Behind me, the house rumbled as the fire expanded. It appeared to be fully engulfed. If Mark and Deb were still in there, they would certainly be dead. The roof was collapsing and full of flames. I tried to go back in, but the soaring heat stopped my approach. No one could have survived this. I looked down the drive, but Mark's pickup was gone.

This was crazy. Who would have taken the truck? The last I knew, Mark was lying face down on the floor. Deb had gone in before him, so I wasn't certain about her. Propping myself up on my good foot, I stumbled my way to where the truck had been. I could see fresh tire tracks on the drive. Looking down on the damp ground was the huge footprints we had seen before, followed by lines in the dirt.

It looked like the huge guy must have dragged something through the dirt and took off in the truck. Were bodies pulled from the flames? If so, did he take one or both of them?

In the distance, I could hear sirens, and I had to make a decision. Should I stick around or should I disappear? As I rolled my options around in my head, I tried walking, but my left foot was not cooperating. Then it dawned on me. If there was a body found in the rubble, I might be held responsible.

Police and fire are notoriously slow in coming to conclusions. The thought of spending six months in jail made my mind up that hiding on the back of the property would be my best bet.

One other thing came to me. I needed the gun out of the work shed. Jumping slowly while dragging my bum foot, I made my way slowly over to the shed, which had caught fire on the right side, closest to the house. I opened the door and reached down for the toolbox. Acrid smoke filled my eyes. Finding the tool tray, I ripped the Glock out of the hidden compartment, and checked it for ammo. There was a partially full clip. Might come in handy if I needed to fight off the perp or defend against wild animals.

Sirens now were screaming close. The roof of the house had completely caved in while flames shot at least fifteen feet in the air. Smoke poured fearlessly into the afternoon sky. I hobbled to the back side of the shed and wound my way down the rocky ravine at the back of the property. As I kept my head above the tallest rock, I could see a couple of firemen running up the drive in the distance. They stopped in front of the house, looked at the clearing, and then walked back to the shed. I could hear them talking.

The tall guy said, "This thing is fully engulfed. We'll never get the pumper truck over the broken driveway bridge. With this much flat clearance, I say we just pull in some hoses and wet it down."

The shorter guy, wearing a fire helmet said, "Fine with me. This place looks abandoned. No cars or anyone around. Probably one of the vagrants started it with one of their campfires.

I'll call into the office and have them send out an inspector. By the time he gets here, this thing will probably be wet down to embers. The cops will probably want a once over. Why don't you call over and find out who owns the place."

With that, the tall guy pulled a walkie-talkie from his belt and barked some orders out. The other guy started walking around the perimeter of the burning structure. He stopped suddenly and picked something out of one of the bushes.

"Hey Bob, take a look at this. An empty five-gallon gas can. This was a torch job!"

CHAPTER 20

There are different levels of pain. A deep wound throbs, a cut hurts, but the pain from a deep burn is absolute overwhelming hell. As I propped myself on the side of the ravine, the significance of my injuries became apparent. My arms and face felt like someone had taken a cigarette to every inch of my exposed flesh, but that sensation paled in comparison to my left leg. The red hot table had seared its way through the lightweight protection of canvas that my Levi jeans had provided. I knew that I needed help. The burns certainly must be second or third degree. The burned flesh felt like it melted to the inside of the pant legs.

Options rolled around in my head. I so wanted just to rise up and stumble over to one of the firemen. Have them call an ambulance. Each heartbeat brought a new surge of pain, and the hot afternoon sun baked the intensity of each exposed burn. But I had been in law enforcement long enough to know what would happen. My explanations wouldn't go very far with a gas can screaming loud and clear that this was arson, or worse yet, a murder cover up. If they found a body in the rubble, I could go away for a long time.

I didn't have time for that. I needed to know who set the fire, and where my cousin and his wife were, if they were still alive. And most importantly, find out who wore size eighteen European storm-trooper boots. I looked at my watch. Two o'clock. I had about five hours of light to get somewhere. The back area of Fallbrook had one main road called De Luz, which wound like a snake for over twenty miles through rolling hills and large rock outcroppings from the north of Downtown Fallbrook over the semi-mountainous area to the inland town of Temecula.

My uncle's place was about five miles out from the Fallbrook Hotel. His property faced De Luz on the north and was a large flat clearing bulldozed out from between two of the rolling hills in the area. The avocado and fruit trees ran up the hills across the clearing. The back of the property dropped off steeply and sloped into a distant dry creek bed a quarter mile below. From where I was, I had three options. Somehow get past the firemen and get to De Luz or take my chances in the brush and hope to get somewhere before dark. The front option seemed impossible without detection. I would only be able to move slowly at best. I couldn't risk it. With my bad leg, climbing the hill with the fruit orchards was out of the question. Way too steep.

The back way was a primitive, almost wilderness area. At least it was downhill. The pain in my leg started to sear intensely again, reminding me that I had better do something quickly. I looked over the berm and saw that both of the fire guys had headed back to the truck to pull hoses. I had five minutes at best. I needed something to help me walk better. Using my right leg, I pushed myself up, the workshop shed about fifteen feet from me. Pulling myself over with the help of one of the outcropped boulders, I hobbled over to the shed. I set the safety on the Glock and put it in one of my back pockets. I glanced nervously around, hoping that no one would see me. Then I saw it... a roll of duct tape on the floor half way in the shed. Yes, this would work.

I picked up one of the medium size wrenches from the floor and made a quick splint for my left foot by taping the wrench to my shoe and then to the bottom of my leg by wrapping it tightly around my work sock. This kept my foot and ankle from turning under, but it hurt like hell as it rolled across my ankle bone. Hearing voices in the distance, I exited the shed, keeping close to the building, dropping behind it on the opposite side, hidden from front view by the house. I picked up a short 1x2 on the edge of the building from an old stack of lumber to use as a makeshift cane. Reaching the back of the property, I found the back ravine to be much steeper here. I would have to cross over the berm where I had come up. With the brace and a great grit on my teeth I broke into a semi run. I found the boulder marking the spot I had lifted myself up at, and dropped over the side.

I could hear one of the fire guys yelling in the distance, "Hey, is that a person behind that shed?"

The other guy replied, "Probably just a coyote. I don't see anything."

The other voice raised up, "I'm going to take a look."

The first guy yelled back, "Let's get this hose connected first so I can douse this thing. I don't want to be here all day."

I knew I had to get out of sight quick. Thankfully the brace helped my stability, but each step was agonizing. I half slid, half stumbled my way down the side of the ravine. There wasn't a path, just lots of flat brush, and dry grass. The thought occurred to me as I headed down. If this brush caught fire, I wouldn't have a chance. With the afternoon wind picking up that kind of fire would race down this hill.

That thought made me just go faster. The makeshift cane helped me take some of the pressure off my left leg. Looking back up the hill, I could see the giant arcs of water from the fire hoses as they started to pour down on the blazing house. I saw one of the fire guys glance over the edge, but he didn't seem to see me. Within minutes, I had reached the dry creek bed, which had some small trees along the bank. These would give me cover as I proceeded. The creek bed had a sand bottom with very few weeds. I headed ever so slowly back towards town, not having any idea where I was going.

The path leveled, and the shadows became very long. I knew the creek would eventually lead to a larger stream or river, but now I was entering a deeper valley where I had no view ahead. The broad walls of the canyon hid the sun and made going a little tougher. The creek wound through the hilly area, each upcoming turn hiding the creek bed ahead from view.

Limping steadily along, I was now losing sight of the burning house behind me. Suddenly there was a massive explosion in the distance, with flames shooting hundreds of feet into the air from the house. It was then that I remembered that there was a propane tank on the other side of the back wall at my uncles' house. As the fire rained down from the sky, the hills behind me caught fire like gasoline. Looking at the brush and scrub around me, I knew it would only be minutes before the afternoon wind pushed the fire through here. Dropping my makeshift cane, I started running, pain filling my eyes.

CHAPTER 21

The summer winds in California are usually onshore from the coast. The closer to the ocean, the cooler they are. Fallbrook is about 25 miles inland, but sits in a hilly valley, with some of the taller hills going up a thousand feet or so. In August the creek beds are dry, and the foliage has turned brown. Perfect conditions for a brush fire. The afternoon winds had picked up, increasing in intensity as the canyons narrowed, winding their way through the broad, shallow valley, which now would undoubtedly lead the fire my way.

Looking back at the burning house, the large arcs of water had disappeared, which meant the firefighters had been directly affected by the blast. I hoped they were OK, but from the size of the explosion, I knew they could have been hurt or even killed. I started back running the best I could, which was none too fast, with a splint and a bum ankle on a severely burned leg. Fires were erupting all over, and now edging down the back ravine, coming my way.

Visualizing the scene in my mind, I figured whoever set the fire must have run a trail of gasoline over to the tank since it was at least fifty feet from the side of the house. Somehow this whole thing felt like a setup. There had been no sign of Debbie and Mark. The truck was gone, with only some large footprints to consider. I was apparently left for dead, and the last time I had seen Mark, he was sprawled on the floor, ten feet in front of me. Deb had gone in before him, probably in the back room.

With footprints in the muddy dirt out front, it appeared that someone or something had been dragged to the truck. One body, maybe two? From the firemen, I knew that gasoline was involved. I knew that the person with the large shoes had been in the shed and must be unyielding to rip the benches from the walls. But what did this person want? Lots of questions, no answers.

As I kept running down the dry stream bed, it curved deep through a short canyon. I was now in total shadow, the view of the house behind me now completely hidden, except for the billowing smoke high in the sky. With the restricted canyon, the afternoon wind whipped even stronger. Scattered trees lined the banks.

I stopped for a minute to get my bearings when I heard something coming my way. I turned, just in time to see a pack of coyotes rounding the corner behind me. These were well-fed animals, with the pack leader being about the size of a large German Shepherd. Coyotes are usually afraid of people, except when in packs. I hobbled over to the side of the canyon wall, pulled the Glock from my belt, and tried to hide myself the best I could.

They came racing by, yelping loud, at least eight in total. The pack leader stopped as he must have caught me in his eye. The smaller animals settled in behind him, viewing me suspiciously. The large guy now took a few steps cautiously in my direction. They edged closer, eyes fiercely looking at me, snarls coming from their mouths. I pointed the Glock at the pack leader but knew I only had a few bullets and a whole load of trouble just a few feet away. I was certainly a toss up who might win if I shot the leader. I was in no shape to fight off a pack of crazed animals. Holding the gun in my left hand, I reached down and picked up a large rock. I held it high with my right hand. The big male stopped, looked at me and took a step back. I moved my arm to throw the rock, and the pack leader took off, the smaller animals following and just kept on going around the next curve. Putting the Glock back under my belt, I was relieved and kept on going.

As I pushed off from the wall, I now noticed the wind whipping through the canyon was filled with smoke. It burned my eyes and got thicker by the minute. I started back through the canyon, wishing I could run as fast as the coyotes. Looking back, the flames had entered the canyon walls in the distance. I started running again, but my strength and tolerance for pain were waining. I kept going, but now live embers were coasting along with the smoke. Some of the grass on the side of the canyon started to smolder. I kept going.

As I rounded the next turn in the canyon, the stream bed widened slightly. The walls were rocky and steep, with trees and brush everywhere. It was like a small oasis, with some stagnant water sitting in a small pond about fifty yards ahead. In the distance, on the other side of the pond was a small shack with my one hope of salvation. There was an old bicycle, propped up against the wall. It had fat tires and looked like someone might have been in the area recently. I yelled out, but there was no response.

Just then there was splashing in the small pond as the coyotes came out from behind the shack. My only hope was to get to the bike. I might survive by lying in the pond water, but I might die of an infection from the contaminated water on my burns. I picked up another rock and kept to the right of the pond. The smoke now thickened as I advanced. The coyotes were in the shallow water, not wanting to move. I kept to the right, walking slowly now. We seemed to be in a standoff. I kept the rock high in the air. Suddenly the tree on my left started smoking. The smoke and embers were now beginning to block the sunlight and turned everything in a grayish-brown haze.

Just then a flame raced through the dry leaves. I had to get the bike. Coyotes be damned; I had to get past them to get on that bike. I started running, and the dogs howled, but I soon had the bike in my hands. I went to pull it away from the wall...

Oh shit, someone had locked it to the shack with a chain and cheap combination lock. The tree across the pond was now fully engulfed. I could feel the heat as the flames roared upwards. It would soon be too hot to go on. The shack--made of dry wood--would indeed go up. The animals paced nervously in the pond. I pulled on the bike, but the cable restrained it. I threw the cable and lock on the ground. Putting the rock high in the air, I brought it down with a crash on the lock. The rock bounced, but the lock held tight. Now the tree over my head had caught fire from the wind. Embers were falling all over me again. I had to make a decision.

Looking at the green slime in the pond and the nervous animals, I picked up the rock again. Now with both hands, I brought it down again with a crashing blow. The lock held. The numerical face now beat in; I couldn't see some of the numbers. A flaming branch fell between me and the pond. The coyotes howled. Now the roof of the shack was smoldering. I picked up the rock again, stood up and put it high over my head and threw it crashing down on the lock again. It bounced off, the dial still intact. Now it was too late. The roof was now on fire, and the branch near the lake fully engulfed. Picking up the bike with two hands, I threw it against the shack in anger and kicked the useless lock with my right foot. It banged against the side of the wooden structure and fell to the side, the cable the only thing holding it up.

I turned to head to the pond, mingling with the snarling dogs my only chance for survival, when I heard it.

Clink...

The number dial had fallen out, and the lock was released. I turned, pulled the cable free, and pushed the bike past the shack and into a clearing farther up the canyon. The fire was all-encompassing now, but I was able to guide the bike around the next corner through the smoke and sparks. Standing on my bum leg, I put my right leg over the bicycle, straddled it, and put my right foot on the pedal. In a wobbly move, reminiscent of a child's first adventure on a bike, I started off. It was hard to push with my left foot, but I slowly began to make progress. The sand of the creek bed slowed my progress, so I veered over to the side of the stream bed. The brush along the canyon walls was all lighting up now. I stood up to pedal faster, but the jeans pulled on my burnt leg causing almost indescribable pain, but with flames behind me, the adrenaline pushed me forward.

I pedaled, and the bike picked up speed. Twisting through the canyon, the walls widened out. The sun appeared again, and there in front of me was a small driveway or road crossing the creek bed. In crazy pain, I pushed the bike up one side of the berm, remounted it and started to pedal like crazy in the direction of town. Now I was able to outdistance the fire. The canyon opened up into a larger open space. Behind me, there was smoke and fire everywhere.

I figured the road I was on would eventually end up crossing De Luz Road as it was the only main road in the area. Thinking ahead, I had two destination options. The easiest would be Contessa's house off of De Luz, or I could keep going and maybe make it back to my hotel. Contessas's would certainly be closer, but I didn't know for sure if she would believe me about what happened. She seemed level headed, but it was a gamble. The other thing might be that she evacuated, but she was far up the road from my Uncle's house. I just kept going. The only pain worse than pedaling with a severe burn was stopping with one. As I raced down the hill, I could see a tree lined road in the distance. It must be De Luz, I thought. The small road I was on took a few turns and then went though a significant dip. I knew I was almost there as I came around the last corner. Looking up, I saw the street sign for De Luz and two police officers standing right next to it. The both stepped out into the road, held their hands up and forced me to stop. I was dead meat now!

CHAPTER 22

An incredibly confined feeling overcame Mark as his brain began the journey back to consciousness. The back of his head felt like someone had hit him with a sledgehammer. He tried to move his arms and then his legs, but he was constrained in some convoluted position, legs and arms held tight. As the fogginess disappeared, he tried to open his eyes. They were covered with some kind of cloth that smelled deeply of smoke and grime.

His first thoughts were a hospital bed, yet as the sensations increased, he could feel something hard and hot underneath his left side. Certainly not a mattress. As he began to regain movement in his arms and legs, each little movement seemed to tear at his flesh. It was as if he was covered in glue and each movement pulled hair and skin with it.

Mind racing now, his senses started reporting danger. His body felt as if it was wrapped somehow, his legs restrained behind him, and his arms pinned behind his back. The temperature was hot and baking, yet he could feel a strong wind blowing all around him.

He tried to talk, to yell, or even scream, but his mouth was covered with what felt like tape. He started to wriggle and move, but each movement tugged viscously at exposed flesh, pulling hair and skin and causing intense pain.

This couldn't be explained away. This was no hospital or back of an ambulance. He tried to scream again, but he couldn't even suck air in his mouth. The cloth covering his face was restricting the air flow through his nose. The possibility of suffocation was real. Mind flashing all sorts of scenarios. He flailed again but was held tight. Heart racing and chest heaving, he realized that trying to fight his restraints was getting him nowhere. Relaxing his body, he tried to decipher the sensations he was feeling. Taking a slow deep breath, he noticed the smell of manure and eucalyptus trees, certainly not any hospital room he could imagine.

Muted light was apparent through the cloth around his face. It was still daylight, and it felt as though he was lying at least partially in the sun. Sounds were muted, but he could sense wind blowing in trees and the trickling sound of water in the distance. Birds were chirping in the distance, and he was almost sure that he was outside on some hard surface.

Suddenly, there was a sound of footsteps around him. He could sense movement, and then was viscously kicked in his side, and then pushed with a shoe against a wall or other hard surface. Pain exploded in his rib cage. He then felt movement around his face. Was he about to die? Thoughts of a large knife ran through his mind.

Instead, in a rapid movement, the tape covering his mouth was violently ripped away, and a deep, strange voice from above yelled harshly into his right ear, "Where is the blue diamond?"

Mark stammered, now able to speak, "What? What are you talking about?"

The voice increased, "Where is the large blue diamond that your father had?"

Mark's thoughts raced. Who was this? What did he want? What would he do with him if he answered? He thought again for a moment and then replied, "I don't know about any diamond. My father dealt in topaz and other cheap gemstones. If he had a diamond, it's news to me."

"It's not in the house, and you are the only one who would know where it is. Tell me now or you die."

Mark yelled back, "Who the hell are you? I don't know anything about a diamond."

Reality was coming quick to Mark. The strange sensations were now making sense. The smells, the heat and the hard, bumpy surface he was lying on could only be one thing. He was in the bed of a pickup truck, probably off the side of the road somewhere in a grove of eucalyptus. From the feeling on his skin, he was probably wrapped with duct tape and his head covered with a sack. Fear crept through him. This voice was probably the person with the huge storm trooper boots they had seen at the house. His mind clearing now, thinking back, he yelled aloud, "Where is my wife?"

The voice responded shrouded thick with sarcasm, "She was no use to me, she has been dealt with. The same fate awaits you if you don't tell me where the diamond is."

Mark screamed, "You better not have harmed her."

Just then another massive kick came to his side, "I don't have time to deal with you. Tell me where it is."

"I told you I don't know. He never kept any diamonds."

"One last time. Where is the diamond, or you die?"

Mark thought to himself, stall for time. He responded, "Untie me and I might be able to help you."

The deep voice sounded exasperated, "Just give me the location."

Marked tried to rise, throwing a stall he said, "It's under the floorboards of the house."

With that, he could feel hands around his neck as his tight wrapped body was lifted up. He figured the person would now untie him. However, the voice turned to a growl, "Wrong, you lying son-of-a-bitch. The house has been torn apart, and it wasn't there."

Mark knew his bluff was called. He said meekly, "It was under the floor."

The voice yelled back, "You lie!" Tape was wrapped back around his mouth and then in one swift motion, Mark was pushed out of the back of the truck. He landed hard and started rolling down what felt like a steep rocky cliff. Tumbling head over toe in a restrained darkness, he kept falling, hitting rock after rock, the sensation of a fall that would never end. Pain exploded all over his body. Rocks dug deep, flesh torn away. In what seemed like minutes, he finally came to rest in a soggy, leaf strewn patch of earth, extreme sensations radiating from all parts of his body. It felt like every bone in his body had become disjointed. The tape restraining his legs and arms behind him had contorted all movement in some bizarre back breaking freak way. He couldn't move his legs at all.

Thankfully his head was laying on his side so he could still breath. Water was running, and the stringent smell of eucalyptus filled his nostrils. He had a good idea where he was now. Must be down the long side of the De Luz Creek road at the bend of the Santa Margarita River. Very isolated, and almost impossible to access because of the steep cliff.

No one would find him here.

He would probably die from the elements.

But one thing had not come to Mark's mind until he laid still for a few moments. Ants in the pile of leaves that he was in loved one thing. The sweet sticky adhesive of the duct tape. As he laid hurting in the dim, damp darkness, he could feel them biting their way across his unwrapped skin. Then he could make out the ants crawling in front of his eyes on the inside of the cloth covering his head. Then the unthinkable happened. A cockroach ran in front of his eyes and across his face...

CHAPTER 23

Sitting on the bike, the older police officer took one look at me and asked in a worried tone, "Are you all right? Appears that you have burns all over. That fire got awful close to you."

I examined his badge. He was a Fallbrook cop. Name was Harry. Probably been around a long time. Good Ol' boy. I had to be careful here. Play it smart, by playing dumb.

Glancing up at him, I said, "I was visiting a friend up the road when I heard the massive explosion. Must have been a propane tank from one of the residences on the hill. The fire started raining down, and the wind carried it like an intense hurricane through the canyon."

Looking me over he said, "You up at the Smith place?"

I'm not good a lying on the spot, but I figured I might be able to get some info out of the cop with some well-directed questions. Thinking fast, I replied, "I think so, at least that was the name on the address that my friend gave me. I'm selling an old Ford truck. Red 56. My friend has wanted it for some time. He had taken it down to a shop in Fallbrook to have a mechanic look it over. Just after he left, the fire came through.

Once I saw the ember filled smoke, everything happened so fast, I just grabbed a bike near an old shed on the property and headed out as quickly as I could pedal. A tree broke into flame above me, showering me with sparks. Just needed to get away. Since Mark was in town, I figured they wouldn't let him back through the barricades. I imagine the roads are all blocked now. His out buildings I know have burned, not sure about his house. You haven't seen a truck like that have you?"

The officer shook his head and turned to his partner, a younger athletic guy, "Hey Paul, you haven't seen a red 56 Ford pickup today have you?"

The young man shook his head, "I just came on duty an hour ago, Harry, and they sent me up here to back you up. Ain't seen nothing vintage like that."

Harry turned back and said, "Sorry man, I'm sure he is still in town. We've got De Luz blocked at the city limits."

Just then the sound of a cadre of sirens could be heard as at least six department of forestry trucks headed my way up De Luz from Fallbrook. They turned at the little street that I was on and roared up the hill I had just come down.

Harry looked back at me. He seemed to have bought my story. Nodding, he asked, "If you can wait a half hour or so I can give you a ride."

I shook my head, "Naw, I'm hurting, but I need to find my truck. I'll just ride this old bike into town. The shop my friend went to is over on Main. I'm staying in town. He might have to bunk with me tonight. If you happen to see the truck, tell him I went to the Main Street Garage."

Harry put a call in on his walkie-talkie to the fire dispatcher. The dispatch guy barked back, "De Luz will be closed all night."

Harry smiled, "There you go, no use hanging around here. Your friend won't get through tonight. Sure you don't want a ride?"

"I'm OK," I lied.

With that, I pushed the pedals back around, so I could start off with my good leg. My burnt leg was still hurting like hell, but I didn't want to let on how bad it was. Thankfully old Harry was distracted. Staying to the side of De Luz Road, I pedaled slowly towards town. I would go by the road to Contessas in about a half mile, with the central town about two miles away. With the afternoon fading away, I decided to check in with her. Now that I had made it past the cops, my confidence had increased.

Turn after turn the old pedals squeaked away as I plodded along the slight uphill of the road, pushing against the scorching afternoon wind. Pushing with my right leg was easy, but I had no power on my left with the brace. I just pushed and then followed through with my left. Behind me, the sky was full of smoke and more sirens could be heard in the distance. The frontage road leading to Contessa's house came into view. I could feel my legs unconsciously speed up. As the bike bumped onto the side road, I saw her house on the left. It was the house closest to town in a row of old post-war bungalows, each lot separated with a fence, trees or hedges. As I reached the end of the frontage road, I pulled the bike into her driveway, where I could see her loading things into the back of her truck. She was dressed in jeans, a white top and tennis shoes. Evacuation for sure. Maybe she could give me a ride to the hotel? She would probably need a room if there were any left.

She turned slightly as the clanking pedals caught her attention. Looking into the afternoon glare she asked, "Is that you Trace?" With a bewildered stare, she said, "You look like you're hurt."

I stopped the bike and dismounted. Laying it on the ground, I walked her way with a decided limp and said, "I'm burnt really bad. There was a fire at Paul's house. Mark and Deb are missing. I'm not sure if they were in the house or if they escaped. Mark's truck is gone. I barely escaped out of the house."

"What?" Startled, she turned to face me. "How did the fire start?"

"Not sure. When we returned from your place, I walked out to the shed out back with Mark. Deb went in the house. A few minutes later Mark walked in to grab a couple of beers. He didn't come back for a while, so I got a little impatient and went over to the house. Walking in the kitchen door, I saw Mark sprawled on the floor at the end of the kitchen. That's when the lights went out for me. I felt something hit me on the back of the neck and the next thing I knew as I awoke that I was lying on the kitchen floor with the whole house on fire on top of me."

"Oh my God," she said. "How did you get out?"

"Thankfully the metal kitchen table was above me, as one of the roof timbers fell and almost crushed me. The table saved me, but the flames superheated the metal table and burned my leg real bad as the table legs gave way and it pressed down on my jeans. My left leg was trapped. Thankfully I escaped out the kitchen door before the rest of the roof came down."

"I can't imagine how you got out."

"It wasn't easy, but as the massive timber fell, it hit the table and bounced it for a second, and I was able to pull free."

"How about Deb and Mark?"

"I don't know. The whole house was engulfed by the time I got out. If they were in there, they would not have survived."

"Oh no, I can't believe this has happened."

Seeking to reassure her a little I responded, "The thing is, when I ran outside, Mark's truck was gone. I looked at the ground where it was parked, and I could see another set of those large footprints that we asked you about earlier. It appeared something or someone had been dragged out to the truck, as there were dark marks in the dirt next to the footprints in the muddy soil."

"This is almost unbelievable. Did you call the police?"

"You're going to have to believe me here, Contessa. After I got out of the house, I heard sirens and stumbled to the back of the property. I could hear the fire trucks rumbling in the distance. I wasn't sure what happened or what to do, but I didn't want to talk to anyone. From what I've heard about the local cops, I figured I would end up in jail as a suspect. I stayed at the back of the property, watching things unfold. The fire guys came and started to put out the fire. One of them found a gas can outside the house. Someone had set the house on fire."

"You mean someone tried to kill you?"

"It appears that way. I have no idea about Mark and Deb, but with the gas can, I would certainly be pulled in for questioning. I need to get to the bottom of this, and time is of the essence. I can't risk going to jail."

I looked at her not knowing what to expect.

She looked me in the eye and exclaimed, "I know one thing, Trace. You certainly wouldn't come back here if you had anything to do with it."

Pulling my arm, she said, "Let's get you inside and look at that leg. Tell me what else you know."

As I hobbled into the house, she had me sit down at the kitchen table and prop my burnt leg up on one of the chairs. She brought out some kitchen scissors, removed my shoe, and cut off the duct tape surrounding the makeshift splint. Then, starting at the bottom of the pant leg, she pulled the fabric away from my skin as best she could. The pain was intense.

"Don't worry Trace, I'm a nurse."

"I thought you were a chef?" I mumbled.

"I work as a nurse during the week at the Fallbrook Hospital. Do my cooking on the weekends. Now let's look at that leg."

She worked the scissors up the fabric, cutting the cloth an inch at a time. The pain was so intense; I looked away. Once she reached my knee, she started to cut on each side. Pulling the cloth back, she let out a gasp.

I looked down and almost passed out at what I saw.

CHAPTER 24

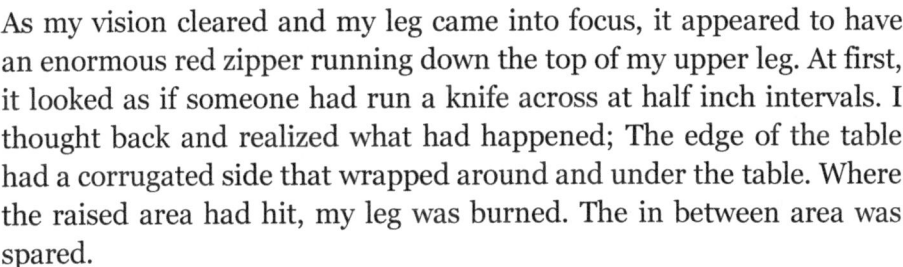

As my vision cleared and my leg came into focus, it appeared to have an enormous red zipper running down the top of my upper leg. At first, it looked as if someone had run a knife across at half inch intervals. I thought back and realized what had happened; The edge of the table had a corrugated side that wrapped around and under the table. Where the raised area had hit, my leg was burned. The in between area was spared.

Contessa spoke up, "You're going to have one funny scar when this is all said and done, but that's a lot better than full contact. Let's get this cleaned up and some salve on it."

She headed off, urgency in her step for the bathroom and returned minutes later with some antiseptic, bandages and hand towels. As she poured the disinfectant on a cloth, she said, "Turn your head and bite down on this wash rag. It's going to hurt more than you know, but we have to get it cleaned up."

She was correct. The fiery pain roared through my leg like a flaming arrow. It felt as if my skin was literally being torn away. I bit down so hard I thought my jaw might break.

Touching my shoulder lightly, she spoke in a reassuring tone, her incredible blue eyes communicating a nurses relief, "The painful part is over Trace, let me put on some of the soothing gel and a clean non-stick bandage." As she got out her medicine, she asked, "I noticed you have a previous scar on your leg. What's that all about?"

"I used to be a cop. Almost lost my leg in a shoot out. The bullet hole is a little higher up. Shattered the bone."

"I guess you got a thing about not walking on your left leg," she quipped.

"The first one hurt like hell, but this burn is worse. Thanks for fixing me up."

My jaw let up, and I could feel the cooling application of the menthol laden cream spread out across my parched skin of my thigh and upper leg. I looked over at her face. It was apparent that she was feeling better, just as I was.

With a serious look, she said, "I hate burns. They hurt more than almost any other type of wound and are so prone to infection. I think you'll be OK now, but I also noticed you had a splint on. You got something going on with your foot or ankle?"

Nodding, I said, "The table fell hard on my ankle, and it turned over as I ran from the house. I had to tape it in place to be able to walk, or more like hop and drag as the fire came my way."

"I'm going to slowly pull off your sock now. You can watch if you want to, but it may not be a pleasant sight."

I glared into her kind blue eyes as I could feel her hands untying my shoe. There is something about a woman caring for you that is endearing. Contessa was near my age, but right then the complement between her dark brown hair draping over her shoulders and her smooth dark skin, made her seem like an angel. I felt like hugging her, but as she pulled down my sock, another jolt of severe pain rocketed up my leg.

"You really messed yourself up, Mr. Armstrong. This ankle isn't going anywhere for a few days if you hope to walk normally again. I've got a proper metal splint and some gauze that will get you by, but you need to stay off it."

Within minutes, and several trips to her medical supplies in the other room, she had my ankle secured, gauze applied and my shoe back on.

"I want you to try standing Trace," she said, standing in front of me, hands extended to help me up. I raised up slowly, using my right leg to prop me up, then bringing my left leg down slowly to the floor.

"Take a step forward."

I lifted my left foot and brought it back down to the floor, but the repositioned ankle snapped upward, restrained suddenly by the metal brace. This contact sent a pain wave directly to my brain, causing me to fall forward, right into Contessa's arms.

She caught me as my arms flailed around her to stop my fall. I suddenly found myself in a very awkward position, my face buried in her shoulder, as my arms caressed her to keep myself upright. She smelled delightfully of apples and spice, her hair falling across her shoulders soft and smooth against my face. Embracing me slightly, she pulled me up to a standing position.

Smiling, she said, "We have to stop meeting like this, Trace. You need to try this again."

This time, she stood next to me on my left side, holding my arm as I took another step forward. This time, the brace kept snug, and I was able to complete the step without much discomfort. Over the next few minutes, I slowly got accustomed to the new splint and was able to walk without too much difficulty as she stayed by my side, guiding me forward.

Turning to her, and our eyes met again. For a few seconds, we just stood still, not knowing what to say. The reality of the day overcame us both. I spoke first, breaking the silence.

"Thank you for saving my leg and for believing in me, Contessa. I may not have made it without you. We have one hell of a mess outside. Fire, an explosion, people missing, my relatives possibly dead. Some crazy large footprints, a missing truck, and a crony police department probably looking for someone just like me to be accountable for the whole thing."

She took a step closer to me and replied, "I'm standing here with a stranger who just showed up on my doorstep, burnt beyond belief, who is very lucky to be alive. He just escaped a burning house a couple of hours ago, which may have taken the lives of his cousin and his wife. He tells me a wild story of evading police and wants me to believe somehow that his journey with a burnt and twisted leg led him through a burning canyon, filled with coyotes to my doorstep. My mind tells me this can't possibly be true. I must send him and his problems away, but my spirit feels different."

She caressed my shoulder and motioned for me to sit down, "I usually don't talk about myself, Trace, I'm a very private person, but I want you to know a little about me. I grew up in the small Caribbean country of Belize. It's located just below Mexico on the Atlantic side. Mom was of Latin descent; dad was European. You might have noticed my blue eyes. About the color of the bright blue ocean there. Belize is a rather poor country, but my parents got along OK. I married pretty young, moving to the coastal city of Placencia with my husband, Jorge. Ran a small tourist restaurant. We always wanted kids, but I was never able to have any. He got a job in Texas about five years ago. I came with him, but he died in a tragic accident. I haven't dated much since he died. Just never felt comfortable in the new country. Since I was living alone here in Fallbrook, I started doing odd jobs for some of the neighbors. That's where I met your uncle. Today I open the door to a burnt man from a house that exploded, being chased by police that no one can trust. I should send him away. But something tells me that we are here for a reason."

I stood up and looked at her. Her bright eyes were misty, probably from the sad memories of a long time ago.

"I'm sorry to hear about your husband. It must have been tough being in a strange country without him."

Nodding, she said, It was tough. I hold on to one memory of him. She pulled a simple necklace from around her neck. On it was a small blue stone. "Jorge gave it to me after we were married. He always called it a diamond, but we both knew it was just a cheap imitation. He said it matched my Caribbean eyes. Blue eyes are rare in my country. I wrote my mom a while back, and she kept asking if I was dating yet. I told her no. She wrote back and mentioned something really strange. She said she had a feeling that I would meet a man someday, with eyes just like mine. The letter said when he knocks on your door, be sure to let him in. Well here you are, Mister Blue Eyes...."

CHAPTER 25

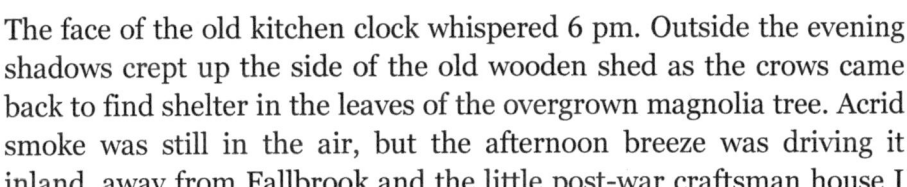

The face of the old kitchen clock whispered 6 pm. Outside the evening shadows crept up the side of the old wooden shed as the crows came back to find shelter in the leaves of the overgrown magnolia tree. Acrid smoke was still in the air, but the afternoon breeze was driving it inland, away from Fallbrook and the little post-war craftsman house I found myself in with Contessa.

I stumbled across the kitchen, peering out the window into the overgrown side yard. Contessa's Chevy truck was waiting, the back filled with a few boxes and essential belongings. My mind questioned my next move. Should I have Contessa take me back to the hotel, or should we do something different? One thing was for sure, if we went past the roadblock into town, we wouldn't be able to get back in until at least tomorrow afternoon. Not good. Too many things could happen. As I stood there, I felt the cool draft on the exposed part of my leg not covered with the bandage. My jeans were cut away, and my foot was in a splint. Not exactly a good way to be seen, especially by the police. What to do?

Contessa came up behind me, her hand finding a comfortable perch on my shoulder. She asked softly, "What are you thinking?"

I turned my head slightly, "I need some pants, and a map, along with the fact that I could use your help. I realize I've messed up your evening."

"Do you want me to drive you back to your hotel? I'm sure you probably have some pants there."

"Under normal circumstances, that would be helpful. Unfortunately, if we leave now and go past the road block, we can't get back in. I need to see if I can get back up to Paul's house if at all possible tonight. At least close enough to see if the firefighters are still there."

"What could you possibly hope to find tonight? It will be pitch dark out there, and most likely there will be fire and police on site. If they get sight of you, they will indeed give you a free trip to the station."

"I wish I knew Contessa. I just really want to know if Mark and Debbie died in the fire or if they escaped? The truck was gone. Who in the hell drove it away? Those stupid footprints make me think that there is some huge goon involved in all of this. But would that person want Mark and Debbie alive or dead? I saw what looked like drag marks in the mud outside the front door, right next to those prints."

Contessa motioned me to sit at the table, "I have a map of the area. Let me pull my truck in the garage, so if the police come by they will think I have left."

"Great idea. While you are doing that can I use your phone? I want to call my friend Martino who has connections with the San Diego police and the FBI. I need to put out an APB for Mark's old Ford pickup."

"Sure thing, it's on the wall by the stove."

I put a call into Martino, but I got his answering machine. He usually went out for dinner and then came back and worked into the evening in the barn. I left him a short, but detailed message about what had happened and gave him a description of Mark's truck for an all-points bulletin. Martino had all sorts of law enforcement contacts since he did a lot of mechanical work on many of the motorcycles and other vehicles for numerous police departments in Southern California. I left Contessa's number and hung up. Contessa was walking in the back door.

She said, "The truck is in the garage, and I turned on the porch light. As long as we stay in the kitchen out of sight of the side window, wc should be OK. When we have fire alerts out here, they have us leave the porch light on to notify them that we have left. If they drive by again, they will just keep on going. When I was outside the smoke had died down, and the wind has dissipated. They will probably get this contained tonight."

"Good news. Now all I need is some pants."

She laughed, "We'll Trace, I might be able to help you."

She walked out of the kitchen and returned in a few minutes with a large cardboard box. "I picked these up from your uncle a while back. Old clothes to take to Goodwill. Let's see what we might have in here."

She pulled out a wad of old shirts, a few pants and one pair of very worn and faded coveralls. I picked up the coveralls, "Just what the doctor ordered, I said. "I can pull these over my existing jeans and bandage, and no one will know the difference."

"You'll look like any other Fallbrook farmer, Trace. He's also got a baseball hat in here. San Diego Padres."

I pulled on the pants and slid on the hat.

"How do I look?"

"Just like a local."

"Good. Do you know if there is any other way up to Paul's property other than De Luz Road?"

She shook her head, "Nothing real good. There is the creek bed behind his property that I'm sure you discovered earlier. There will be fire guys all over that tonight. On the other side of De Luz, there is a dirt horse path that some of the locals use. Runs somewhat adjacent to De Luz for miles. That might be a way to get near the property without being on the road."

"Is it big enough for your truck to go down?"

"Not sure. We could try, but as I remember it has a lot of ruts."

"Can you show me on the map?"

For the next few minutes, we traced out a route on the local map that we might be able to take.

"We should wait until after dark to leave the house, Trace. The police and fire guys are sure to make another drive or two along De Luz to make sure everyone has left. It will probably be safe to go out after eight. They usually don't mess with things much after that. In the meantime, let me make some dinner. I've got some chicken to go with some of that pie you had earlier."

Contessa brought out some leftover fried chicken along with another two pieces of pastry. We ate quietly, talking through the events of the day. As the shadows turned into darkness, she dimmed the lights in the kitchen, and we headed out to the garage.

Walking around to the passenger side, she tossed me over the keys. "You drive. It's a 73 Chevy, automatic, half ton. Good ol' girl. I'll ride shotgun. If we get cops, let me do the talking."

With that, I started the old truck, pulled it out of the garage, and headed down her long drive. She said, "You can access that horse trail about a half mile down De Luz on the left. Probably best to keep the lights off. Still enough light to see the road."

I nodded my head, "I'll take care of old Betsy. Slow but sure."

We drove slowly in the dim light, turning down a small ravine onto the narrow horse trail. The area was extremely dark. I said, "I'm turning on the parking lights now that we're off the road. Hopefully, enough light to see a few feet ahead. The going was slow with large ruts and many bumps.

As we came to a clearing, the trail appeared to go down a rather steep hill. Contessa spoke up, "This is the tricky part, Trace, It's a pretty steep downhill, but the path looks wide enough for the truck. You'll want to take it real slow. There is a sharp turn at the bottom as I remember."

"I'll put it in low gear,"

For the next few minutes, we crept along in the almost total darkness, trees and brush on both sides. The truck rattled and creaked. Contessa locked her door and slid over on the seat next to me. The parking lights didn't give off much light, and I could only see inches in front of me. After what seemed like an hour, we appeared to reach the bottom of the hill. There was a tree directly ahead of me.

Contessa tugged at my arm. "This is the bottom. You'll need to turn sharply to the right."

"OK, It is really dark here. I'm going to back up and then turn."

With that, I put it in reverse, backed up a few feet, turned the wheel to the right and slowly gave it gas. There was a significant rise in the road. The truck struggled a little and then came over the hump. All of a sudden, in the darkness there was a loud cluck and a sound like metal on metal. I couldn't make out anything in the dim light.

"I'm turning on the headlights," I said.

Pulling the switch; Contessa screamed, and I quickly found out what the noise was. There on the left side of the trail was the back bumper of an old Ford Pickup, perched precariously off the edge of the path.

CHAPTER 26

Contessa gripped my arm tightly in the darkness, "What is that?" she asked, trembling.

"It appears to be a truck over the bank of the trail," I responded. "Probably came down from the road above. It's red. Might be Mark's truck."

Her grip intensified, "Do you think there is anyone in it?'

"One way to find out... Do you have a flashlight in your truck?"

She slid over and opened the glove box. "I have a four cell in here. Hopefully, the batteries are still good."

Handing it to me, I turned the lens, and a bright glow erupted.

"Sit tight. I'll go and check it out."

Her other hand now gripped my arm tight.

"Take me with you. I'm not sitting here alone. I've heard way to many scary stories about De Luz Road."

Putting the truck in park, I opened the driver's door slightly which immediately blinded us with an intense beam from the dome lights.

"Yow that's bright. Watch your step as you get down. The road is rutted and uneven."

I gingerly slid off the seat, landing on my right foot for comfort. Then I held her arm and helped her down. Taking a step, my burnt leg hurt badly as the rut jarred the brace into my ankle. I took a step back to clear the door while she held my shoulder tight. Closing the Chevy's door, we took a couple of steps forward, shining the beam on the back of the truck bed we could see over the edge of the road.

As we got closer, the light beam revealed the front of the old Ford had struck a rather large tree. The truck was stuck down the side at about a 45-degree angle. The hood popped up where it had hit the tree, suggesting that the truck had come down the hill with lots of speed. The rear axle was over the side of the road, but the bumper had dug into the berm. The tailgate was down and sitting on top of the dirt. I played the light down on the truck bed. There was a lot of leaves, some trash, but nothing of immediate importance. Moving the beam up to the back window, Contessa squirmed next to me.

"It doesn't appear that there is anyone in it, " I said with encouragement. "Maybe I can climb down and see it better."

Her grip intensified, "Not with that leg, you're not," she said. "There's no way that I would be able to drag up back up this hill. Give me the light. I'll slide down the bed and look."

It was apparent that Contessa's nurse profile was taking over. Her fear seemed to turn instantly to resolve.

"Are you sure?"

"Just give me the darn light and let's get this over with."

Like giving a reluctant patient a shot, she took the light, stepped onto the tailgate, and slowly worked her way down the floorboards, gripping the side of the bed as she went. The light beam splayed all over the place but then steadied as her Reebok's came up on the front edge of the truck bed. She steadied herself, and then aimed the light through the back window.

"No one in here," she yelled back. Gaining courage and her footing, she said, "I'm going to see if I can get into the cab."

With a quick lift of her leg over the side, her left foot rested on the running board of the old truck while her right leg held steady in the bed. Straddling the edge of the bed while holding the light with her right hand she reached around and tried to open the door. Pulling and pushing on the latch, she finally freed it. It creaked open, revealing the old dashboard with it's dim dome light. Bringing the flashlight over with her left hand, she examined the interior.

Yelling back in the darkness, she said, "There are all sorts of muddy footprints in here. The brake pedal is covered in mud. Looks like your giant with size eighteens was in here."

I yelled down, "Is there anything on the seat or the floor?"

"Just lots of dirt and a few leaves."

"Any sign of a struggle or anything?"

"Not really. Just a bunch of dirt and mud on the floor. The gearshift is in neutral, and the parking brake is off."

"Can you play the light over the bed again?"

"Let me close the door, so the battery doesn't run down" With that she pulled the heavy door closed and climbed back up into the bed.

Shining the light down she moved some of the leaves with her foot. "Your creeper guy was back here too. Large muddy prints at the front of the bed. Looks like something was possibly pushed out the back. Maybe a box or something. There are some sliding marks in the dirt and dust. They might have been here before. Not sure."

"Can you check the passenger side?"

She crept over to the right part of the bed. Widening out the beam of the light, she played it on the side. "Muddy prints on the running boards and some mud on the edge of the bed. Looks like creeper guy climbed in this way."

Propping myself against the front of the Chevy I asked, "Do you see anything else? Anything out of the ordinary? Mark had his truck pristine when I saw it before. A drivable classic."

She shined the light around some more, looking in the different corners.

"Mainly just leaves and dirt, most of which probably got here on the trip down the hill if it was clean before. Looks like somebody with muddy shoes climbed in the back and also drove the truck. Possibly something heavy in the bed. Maybe they took something out of the house and drove it away?"

"Why don't you come back up. Let's see if we can get over to the house tonight. This truck isn't going anywhere. I'll notify my friend

Martino when we get somewhere with a phone. They can run fingerprints. At least we know there isn't anyone in it."

Contessa pulled her way forward on the passenger side. All of a sudden she stopped, and shined the light down. "Trace, there is something sticky here on the edge of the truck. There are differences in the dust where it is sticky. It's rectangular like there was something taped here."

I limped on the right side of the tailgate, being careful to keep my balance, "Show me," I said.

"It looks like there were at least four strips that were applied and then pulled up. Maybe something was taped in place."

"Hand me the light. I want to take a closer look."

Shuffling over to the right side, I shone the light on the side truck bed. Sure enough there were four distinct rectangular areas on the top lip on the truck right side.

"Sure looks like something was taped here," I said. "Good sleuthing, Contessa."

I then ran the light across the truck floor bed and looked at the sliding marks Contessa had mentioned. They were uneven in the dust and came across the tailgate. Something heavy appeared to have been pushed out. It was just then that I noticed something else. On top of one of the rounded bolt heads that held the wooden boards of the truck bed in place, right near the tailgate was a small red substance…. Blood.

CHAPTER 27

———————— ～⁀～ ————————

Now things were getting serious. Blood on the truck bed gave a new urgency to the whole situation.

"We are going to need to bring the police in on this," I said. "We'll need forensics on this blood. Time may be of the essence."

As I looked up, I caught a concerned look on Contessa's face. She replied, "I agree. Something you may not know, Trace, is that this remote area is technically in the county jurisdiction. Sheriff's department out of Vista. Fallbrook has had an off and on police department over the years. Good budget years they have one, bad years they go with the North County Sheriff's Department. The Fallbrook guys will come if it is a house, but they usually don't like to get involved with open land or these wilderness areas.

"That's good news. I don't want to deal with the Fallbrook guys. We need to get to a phone. I left a message for Martino about the truck, but I need to update him. I know the leaves, dirt, and this blood wasn't there before."

"Whose blood do you think it is?

"My guess is that it would be from Mark or Debbi. Maybe both."

"I guess that might be good news," she said. "Maybe they escaped the fire."

"Hopefully not facing a worse experience. The footprints of that giant are not encouraging. Is there a phone anywhere near here?"

"This trail goes to an equestrian park up the road. There is a phone booth there I think."

"Can you describe to someone where this area is and how they could get to it via De Luz Road?"

"Sure. It's affectionately called dead man's curve on De Luz. It's a sharp left hander when you are heading to town. Fifteen miles an hour with a short wooden barrier at the curve to keep you from going down this steep ravine. Whoever sent the truck down here would have simply had to drive the truck next to the barrier and just push. They have been trying to get a proper guardrail there forever. There are a couple of other bad curves on the road, but this is the sharpest and most deadly. At least a hundred feet down. Lot's of accidents."

"How much further on this horse trail to the park where the phone is?"

"Probably a mile. The park butts up against the Santa Margarita River. Nice area to go riding. We can backtrack on De Luz from there to your Uncle's house."

"We need to get going. But before we do, can you shine that light up the hill. I think the blood may have come from someone who was in the truck bed when it was pushed over, and they bounced out."

"Good idea," she said. "I'll walk up the road a bit."

Contessa aimed the light up the hill and walked up the road a bit, shining it back and forth. I got back in the Chevy, put it in reverse, backed it up a bit to miss the old Ford and then drove forward along the dirt road. After a few minutes, Contessa got in the truck.

"Nothing up there that I could see. But there is a lot of brush. Thankfully the wind drove the fire in the other direction. This side would have gone up in a second."

We continued down the road. As we drove along slowly, a dull ache took over my stomach. Pangs of guilt maybe. The woulda shouldas. Mind questioning my actions. Should I have stayed at the house and talked with police? I knew that would have landed me in jail. At best it would have been hours till I got out. The gasoline can would have been the dead giveaway. Second guessing.

Contessa spoke up, "Probably a good thing you didn't go to the Fallbrook Police. Those guys certainly would have arrested you. Anyone from out of the area would be a prime suspect. They hate coming out here on De Luz. It would have been days before anyone found the truck."

"Thanks for the reassurance. I've been second guessing myself since we found the blood."

"Don't blame yourself Trace. I hate to say it, but those Fallbrook guys are lazy, and they hate working with other departments. Things usually stay in Fallbrook, good or bad."

"They sure didn't spend much time with my uncle. Just wrote him off as a drunk. No investigation or anything."

"They would have taken you in as an arsonist who used a little too much gasoline."

"Sounds like their M.O."

"Unless you had enough money to bribe your way out. Lots of stories in town. A couple of the guys are supposedly really dirty, but they got friends in high places. Best to avoid them altogether."

Rounding a narrow corner, the dirt road went up a short rise and exited on De Luz. I said, "Is that the park across the way?"

"That's it on the other side of De Luz. Just pull up next to the ranger station. There won't be anyone around tonight, but there should be a pay phone on the back wall."

I slowed the truck and pulled behind the building. There was a telephone line coming in from the power pole. On the side was a phone and dim light.

"Let me make a call," I said.

I pulled out my trusty phone card, dialed a few numbers and soon connected to Martino's line. The phone rang ten times and then the answering machine picked up. Not again, I thought. Halfway through the message, an out of breath Martino answered.

"Martino here," he said.

"Hey man, it's Trace. Thank God you are there."

"Hey, I got your message a minute ago. Just got back. Getting ready to call it in."

"I've got an update. We found the Ford truck a little while ago. Down the hill from dead man's curve on De Luz. Must have been pushed over the side. We found blood in the truck bed. Looks like something or someone was pushed out the back or maybe flew out when the truck went down the hill. It's crashed into a tree."

"Oh man, I know exactly where that is. De Luz is a favorite with motorcycle riders. That curve comes up fast and usually has a lot of sand and gravel. Treacherous. Some guys have gone over."

"Well, there is a 56 Red Ford pickup at the bottom now. With the blood, we looked around, but we didn't see any signs of anyone or heaven forbid, a body."

"I heard your message about the Fallbrook Police. I've had some run-ins with them before. Good thing you did what you did. I've had some biker friends cool their heels in their jail for days at a time. Real assholes. I'll call my friends at the Vista/Oceanview Sheriff's Station and get then out there tonight. How you doing Trace?"

"My uncle's housekeeper Contessa got me fixed up. My left leg is all burned to hell, and my ankle is junk, but she got me bandaged up and set a splint on my foot."

"Where are you going from here? Back to your hotel or do you want to meet the sheriff at the truck?"

"Tell you what, I'm going to head back and check out my Uncle's house. Not sure if the fire crew might still be there, but with the fire heading east, they have probably headed up the road. Then I'll double back to meet up with them. Then I'll have Contessa take me to my hotel. This whole area was evacuated so we probably can't get back in tonight."

"It's almost nine thirty. I'll tell the sheriff's guys you'll meet them after ten. Good luck."

With that, we exchanged some phone numbers, and I made sure he could get me later at the hotel. I got back in the truck and told Contessa what the plan was. We headed back down De Luz to my uncles' property.

The night was dark with smoke obscuring a small sliver of a moon. I kept to the side of the road, parking lights on, just in case one of the Fallbrook guys was still out. Within minutes, I saw the driveway to my uncles' house. As I went to turn in, Contessa screamed. "Look out Trace. The bridge is out."

I instantly slammed on the brakes in the dim light. I missed the drainage ditch by inches.

Throwing the truck in park, I hopped out with the four cell flashlight. Hobbling to the front fender of the vehicle, I could see that the small wooden bridge that usually ran across the six-foot deep drainage ditch on the side of the road had been broken off and now was just a bundle of boards at the bottom of the ditch.

"Plan B," I said. "Let's park the truck up the road where there is a cutout. We'll have to walk."

"You're going to have a hard time with that ditch, Trace." We'll have to walk down a ways where the ditch broadens out."

"OK, bring the flashlight and let's get going. We need to meet with the sheriff at ten or so."

After parking the truck we ambled along, my leg hurting somewhat. Once we got across the ditch, we headed back to the main driveway. Hobbling along in the dim moonlight, we walked the quarter mile around the hill until we got the clearing where the smoking remains of the house was. Thankfully, it appeared the fire guys had headed down the road. The whole dirt area was extremely muddy from the water from the fire hoses. There was some minor residual smoke coming from the ashes. It was an entirely different situation than when I had escaped. Everything appeared to have burned down to a few feet over the ground, but some of the larger timbers and some of the sections of the roof that had shingles still on them were elevated. I walked along the edge, shining the light into the smoldering mess. Moving the light back and forth everything was just black. Contessa said, "What's this?"

I moved my light down to where she was pointing. She reached down and went to lift a reflective glowing object up. All of a sudden she let out a massive scream. As my light caught the object she had lifted, I saw it was a square diamond ring on a human skeleton finger.

CHAPTER 28

A cold blooded scream of terror came from Contessa's lips as she dropped the burned hand back into the ashes.

"Trace... that must have been Debbi's hand. Oh my God, the square diamond ring, I can't believe that someone left her to die in this house." Tears streamed down her face, and I could see her visibly shaking.

I responded, "That damn giant, whoever he is has killed Debbi. We just saw her vibrant and alive earlier in the day. We have to get to the bottom of this."

Pangs of guilt overcame me. I felt responsible somehow for all of this. Running from the cops just didn't seem right. The thought of Debbi being burned alive sent shivers down my spine. I knew it was possible, but seeing the burned hand made it all too real. Seeing the distinctive square diamond ring that I had seen on her finger earlier in the day left no doubt who it was. I reached over and held Contessa. Her body was in shock as a spasm of tears filled her eyes. We stood silent for a minute just holding each other.

"We need to see if Mark's body is here," I said slowly. Not that I want to look, but I know exactly where he was when someone hit me over the head."

As I pulled slowly away from her, I reached down and picked up the flashlight. "I'm going to backtrack down the front of the house. As I remember, Mark was just outside the kitchen and in the living room. He was lying face down on the floor."

Contessa's voice steadied, "Where Debbi is would have been the small back bedroom near the end of the house. I can't imagine what must have happened to her. Hopefully, she was unconscious when the fire erupted."

"Let's hope so. I barely made it out, and she was much deeper in the house. There was no exit back there except one window."

Walking slowly at the edge of the burned structure, I could see where the entrance step to the living room was that would have been a few feet from where I had last seen Mark's body. The burnt remains of the main structural timbers and partial roof shingles were lying askew in the area. I slowly moved the beam over the debris, but all I could see was steaming ashes.

Pulling out on some of the unburned roof shingles, I was able to clear the area somewhat. The wooden floor boards had almost completely burned away in the middle of the house, leaving most of the debris a couple of feet below the main block foundation. Near the outside edge of the room, some of the floor was still intact. Inspecting it, I made out the floor area where I remembered Mark's body laying. Nothing but ashes there.

Waving over to Contessa, I said, "It doesn't look like his body is here. At least it isn't where I remember it being."

Contessa seemed somewhat relieved, "Maybe he was able to escape like you did."

"If he did, he was probably subdued by whoever set this. He was apparently dragged out of the house." Turning the flashlight towards the front yard, I said, "Look here, I'm standing on the concrete step that led to the living room. If you look in the mud as the front blocks lead through the front yard, you can see some of those large footprints and then a line where something dug into the ground. I bet it was Mark that was being pulled out."

Contessa took the flashlight and followed the large prints along.

"Look Trace, the old wooden picket fence has burned almost completely away, but there are prints visible. There are drag marks that end right next to some tire tracks, probably where the truck was parked earlier."

"Exactly. I bet he was taken away."

Contessa put her hand on my shoulder as we both stood up. She asked, "What is this was all about, Trace? Why would Mark be taken away, when you and Debbi were left to die?"

"My guess is, the giant probably was looking for something. It was pretty apparent that someone was trying to locate something here. The floor boards in the house were ripped up, and the entire workbench in the shed was torn away from the wall. Mark would be the likely person that might know where things were."

"Do you think this person would have known Mark or the family?"

"Not sure, but I bet they were hiding out in the back bedroom. Debbi must have stumbled on him—I'm guessing it is a guy with those giant shoes—and then was subdued. Then he KOed Mark when he walked in, and certainly gave me a headache as he knocked me out."

"Seems plausible, but where would he take Mark? Why wouldn't he just leave him here?"

"Good question," I said. "Let's head back to your truck. We need to meet up with the Sheriff at the overlook."

"I hate leaving Debbi here all alone, Trace. I know it's irrational, but even with all the things I've been through as a nurse. All the people who have died in my presence, I still can't get used to it. I can't imagine someone doing this."

"I know what you mean. I'm feeling guilty about this whole thing for some crazy reason. Leaving the scene seems now like a cowardly thing to do."

"You did what you had to do. Don't be so hard on yourself, Trace. With those Fallbrook idiots, you could easily be in jail right now. It's not like you had a phone here where you could have called someone. You might have died when that propane tank exploded. Let's see if we can locate Mark somehow."

We turned and started walking back down the drive, throwing ideas back and forth as we walked.

I said, "I know my uncle dealt with rare gems, jewelry, and had a large blue topaz in his pocket when he died. When I got here today, the floor boards in the living room had been pried up. Mark and Debbi said whoever did it missed a box of random gemstones left on the subfloor."

Contessa said, "Whoever did this was probably looking for something. My guess is it might be valuables, but maybe it's something different. Maybe information or even something like a photo. Maybe blackmail?"

"I hadn't thought about that," I said. "Whoever it was wasn't concerned with a minor box of gemstones. They must have seen them. The box was right there under the floorboards. Why would you leave stones worth thousands of dollars behind?"

"I've heard of blackmailers demanding hundreds of thousands of dollars."

I thought for a second, "Maybe you are on to something, Contessa. Blackmail might be an option, but I have no idea what that might mean. It just doesn't make sense to leave a box of valuables behind."

"Maybe it's the scale of things, Trace. Maybe it's an item much more valuable than a box of assorted gemstones."

"Something worth killing three people over?"

The conversation continued as we reached the truck.

"Why don't you drive, Contessa. You are much more familiar with De Luz than I am, and my leg is hurting like hell. It's after ten now so the sheriff guys should be there."

"Will do Trace. It's a few minutes over there."

She fired up the truck, and we headed down De Luz slowly on the way back to town. Winding through the curves with the headlights on, Contessa hit the brights and in the distance, I could see the deadman's' curve guardrail. We pulled up slowly and parked next to it. There was no sign of the sheriff's department. Putting the truck in park, but leaving the lights on we got out and looked over the side. In the darkness, I could just make out how steep and far down the old truck would be. Just then I heard some rustling and around from the back of Contessa's truck came a loud voice. "Freeze. Police. Put your hand's up!"

CHAPTER 29

With the lights of the truck shining past us, it was almost impossible to make out the faces of the officers that were now holding us at gunpoint. Two options rolled through my head. The first was these guys were sheriff deputies, making sure who we were. The other was not a pleasant thought. They might be Fallbrook guys, in which case it would be best to play dumb. Unfortunately, as one of them spoke, it was apparent they were a pair of good old Fallbrook boys, their old Ford squad car parked in the distance.

One of the guys stepped in front of the truck door, his gun aimed at my chest. He was heavyset and barely fit into his extra large uniform. It was evident that he had a ready supply of donuts and didn't get out of his chair much. He said, "So who do we have here? It looks like the pie lady and a Padres fan," referring to the San Diego baseball hat I was wearing.

"I hope both of you know you aren't supposed to be in the area. There was an evacuation earlier this evening. Now I happen to know that the pie lady had her porch light on, which indicated that she had evacuated her house. Now I find the pie lady here with this gentleman. So let's begin by having you sir come over to the hood of the truck and telling me your name.

I said rather loudly so Contessa could hear me, "The name is Bill Tracy."

The cop pulled me by the arm and slammed me up against the truck. Pulling my other arm around quickly, he slapped a zip tie on my wrists behind my back. Slick move. Not expecting that. He pulled it tighter. Luckily, though, I was able to bundle my fist in such a way that the zip tie felt uncomfortable but would give me some slack once I released my fist. In the light, I could see the other cop leading Contessa away in the opposite direction. Separate and interrogate. What the hell were these guys up to?

"Well Bill Tracy, you're going to jail with me," he said in a gruff voice as he body slammed me against the hood a second time.

"Watch it," I said with a moan. "What's the charge?"

"I don't know yet, but I don't like strangers in my town late at night. It's too late and too dark to deal with you out here." With that, he pulled me free of the hood and led me up the road to his black and white Crown Victoria. I looked back noticing his name badge said Patrick and saw Contessa and the other officer by the passenger door of her truck. I yelled loudly over to her, "Meet me up at the police station in the morning." Holding me by the collar, he opened the back door and went to shove me in. Having seen this move a thousand times, I lifted my knee and caught the latch of the door. It hurt like hell, but it stopped my forward movement and spun me around. The fat man didn't like that. He kicked the door open again and threw me into the back seat.

As I crashed into the stinky vinyl seat face first, I gathered myself and sat up somewhat. Loosening my fist, I gathered a little slack in the zip ties. Sliding across the rear seat, I inched towards the passenger door. I needed a good view of the driver. In a couple of minutes, the other cop got in, and the car started. As we pulled away, I slid hard against the passenger door. On these old Crown Vics, there is an inside door handle, but they use child locks to make them inoperative. That gave me a little margin of security.

The cops started a conversation and then tried to engage me by asking questions. One thing I learned long ago. When it comes to cops, it's best to say nothing. Keep quiet, stay out of trouble.

I knew if I ended up in jail it wasn't going to be good. It would only be a matter of time before they discovered the body at the fire. I certainly didn't need to face a murder charge. If I was going to act it must be quick. Offer a surprise.

The car was roaring down De Luz at least 60 miles per hour. In the lights ahead I could see one of the other hard turns coming up.

It was now or never. As the car squealed around the turn, I reached over and tried the rear door latch. I could feel it click. The old knee on the child lock trick worked. As the car started to slide, I pulled hard. The door flung open and centrifugal force threw me out into the darkness. I bounced on the berm of the road and then it seemed like minutes until I hit again. And when I did I realized just how steep the hill was. I started rolling; my hands still clutched behind my back. As I hit large bushes and other brush hard a couple of times, the force of the blows freed my hands from the zip ties. Now I was able to shield my face as I continued the roll, slide and tumble my way down a brush-covered dirt hill.

In what seemed like an eternity, I finally came to a stop in a leaf filled berm. Thankfully the old coveralls that I was wearing had long sleeves and protected my arms and legs from much of the abrasion of the roll. I slowly tried to stand in the darkness, but the splint on my foot was all jumbled up. Massive pain everywhere, especially my leg burns and twisted ankle. I had no idea where I was or how I might get out of here. I doubted that the cops would come for me tonight, but I had no idea what else might be out there. Peering up the long hill that I had come down, I could see two silhouettes standing in the distance at the top. Soon they disappeared, followed by the reflection of headlights taking off into the distance. I was right about the cops. I was all alone again. But this time, I had no weapon, no light, and no phone. Attempting to stand the best I could on my right leg, I rearranged the splint. That's when I heard it. The pack of coyotes howling at the moon just a few yards away.

CHAPTER 30

How long could a bad day be? This one seemed to go on forever, and just get worse as it went along. My leg was an absolute mess. Brace askew, bandage torn, every bone in my body hurting, not to mention the intense pain of the burns I had from the ripped gauze. Could I walk? Maybe, maybe not. At least, I wasn't dead... yet.

Thankfully the lazy Fallbrook cops wouldn't pursue me at night. No way would they hike down this steep hill after me. They hadn't pulled my ID, so they couldn't identify me. They would just leave me for dead. I wasn't sure what they might have instructed Contessa to do, but they probably had her head into town. They obviously didn't want any loose ends in their evacuated area.

Looking up into the dim moonlight, all I could view was the crazy overgrowth of Manzanita bushes, huge brush, and a variety of overgrown trees. As I tried to stand, I noticed the ground under me seemed soggy and treacherous. Not exactly something I wanted to traverse with a bum ankle.

Viewing an imaginary map of the area in my head, I pictured myself halfway between where my uncle's house was on De Luz and where we had seen the old red Ford truck. I was on the west side of the road, so I knew it wouldn't be too far to reach the horse trail Contessa and I had driven on earlier in the evening. Unfortunately, I was now in a soggy creek bed, full of every sort of vegetation and a howling pack of coyotes not far away.

What to do? I've always found it helpful to rule out options that are improbable or impossible. I knew I couldn't climb the 50-foot dirt hill I had just slid down to get back up to the road. Even with two good legs, it was too overgrown and too steep to make progress. One down. I could just sit on the soggy ground where I was, try to sleep, and wait until morning. With the pack of hungry coyotes nearby that would not be a smart idea. Two down.

I could climb one of the trees nearby and perch myself on one of the limbs. That would get me out of the reach of the coyotes. But then I remembered two facts about trees that made that improbable. One was black slithering tree snakes. I hate snakes. The other was ants. Most trees in a swamp like this are a haven for ants going after the sweet tree sap. I would be eaten alive, not to mention trying to climb a tree with a brace on. Three down.

Now for something a little more positive. I could try and cross the soggy creek and find the horse trail we had come down earlier. Possible, but certainly not comfortable in the dark. I could hear the sound of running water, so getting there would mean getting wet. The summer evening had turned chilly, with the coastal fog due to roll in at any time, further obstructing the dim moonlight. This whole area surrounding De Luz was mostly wilderness. Without the moon, I could end up hopelessly lost.

It's funny how life can turn bad in just the blink of an eye, or in my case the opening of a car door. I hate not having options, but I knew that I would need to take action... and fast. My feet were getting cold and soggy. The coyotes howled, I started to move.

I started off east, towards what I figured was the horse trail. The terrain was very uneven, and I found myself hobbling and almost crawling at times. The brush was so thick I had to crawl on my hands and knees to navigate under it. My left leg hurt so bad, I just kind of pulled it along. The terrain dropped, and I found myself in a shallow creek bed with a few inches of running water. I was able to cross it quickly and move forward.

After a few minutes, the area in front of me came to a small rise. It was the western bank of the small creek. Pulling myself up inches at a time, I found myself on the horse trail again. Now I had my bearings back. It was probably a half mile to where the old truck was and a mile and a half or so to the park clearing where the phone was. I stumbled along in the cold darkness, away from town and towards the old Ford.

My hope was that the sheriff's department would be out tonight and able to find the truck. If not, a long walk to the phone would be necessary. At least I was now moving.

Unfortunately, the clouds were thickening and the tree lined creek area was starting to develop a subtle fog. Step after step it got darker and darker until the moon completely disappeared into the gathering mist. No city lights, no moonlight, no street lights, nothing.

It's one thing to walk along a cold dark road in the dim moonlight. It's another altogether to walk along in almost total darkness. I don't scare easily, but total darkness is like the claustrophobia of a small space. I do OK for a few minutes, but then noises and natural things cause me to panic. In both cases, there is nowhere to run.

Thankfully I was on a dirt road with a berm on each side. I kept going in the same direction. Step after blind step. There was a slight breeze, a trickle of water running and a subtle rustling in the leaves; otherwise it was completely quiet. Suddenly I heard the yip of a coyote in the direction I was going, and then from behind I felt the presence of some coyotes running past me. They didn't stop but headed off after some distant prey. The yips got louder and in the very dim light I could make out the weak form of something in the distance far down the side of the road to the right.

Keeping my distance to the left side of the road, my eyes adjusted to fleeting glimpses of moonlight through the wispy fog. The coyotes had something. They were all yipping now surrounding some poor animal. It wouldn't be long now, I figured. Thankfully, their attention to this animal would keep their attention off of me.

A single coyote is usually not a problem, but a rabid pack makes them brave and sometimes they will attack humans. Step by step, I kept moving forward, trying to get a better look at what it was that they had captured. Whatever it was it seemed to be moving and struggling. It was down in the ravine next to the road where I couldn't see it. Probably a stray dog. On the one hand, I felt sorry for it, on the other, I was glad it wasn't me.

A few more steps and I could hear soft moaning in between the high pitched yelps of the coyotes. My curiosity drew me closer. Rustling, rolling, struggling. That's when I heard it. The moans got louder and then the muffled sounds... HELP Me.

Animals don't yell *help me...*

CHAPTER 31

Darkness, despair and an enormous sense of urgency. Someone was lying in the ravine next to the side of the road surrounded by yipping coyotes. I could make out the animals taking turns going in and attacking the prey. Yip, bite, run. Through it all, I could make out the muffled sounds of someone calling for help.

Courage is a strange thing. When it comes, it comes fast. But right then, I froze. My conscious mind stopped me dead. Seven or eight large hungry animals in almost absolute darkness. Whipped into a frenzy, like sharks with blood in the water.

What to do? I limped closer and felt in my front pocket. Car keys, pocket knife, one cell penlight. Not exactly a formidable arsenal. Nothing that would stop a pack of crazed coyotes. *Think damn it, Think.* I wished I had the gun from my uncle's workroom, but it was long gone, dropped on the side of the road hours before. I reached in my back pocket, pulled out my wallet. A few bills, some business cards, and a credit card or two. Could barely see any of it. I felt in the hidden pouches, found some emergency change. A couple of quarters. Nothing to put them in out here.

Found another hidden area under the credit cards. Something soft stuck deep inside. I fumbled for a minute, and then pulled out an old crumpled book of matches. Been there a long time. Since my days at the Highway Patrol. Used them to light emergency flares that didn't light by dragging them on the pavement. Soggy matches, years old. Maybe they would light; maybe they wouldn't. Worth a try.

In the darkness, I found a small tree branch with dried leaves on it. This would light up like a torch, but only if I could get a formidable flame to get it started.

I've often told others that I don't have money to burn, but right then, the small bills in my pocket seemed to be the most flammable items that I had. I bent down, took one of the bills and placed it on the dirt next to the branch. Opening the old matchbook, there was a half dozen deteriorated safety match sticks. I pulled one out, struck it against the coarse striking area of the matchbook. Sparks in the darkness and a wisp of smoke. No flame. One down. I pulled another and this time slid it faster. Sparks, smoke and a tiny little flame, which was instantly extinguished with the evening breeze.

I turned my body to block the wind, pulled another match across. This time, I had a flame. I held the back of the match up so the fire would grow. Shielding the match with my other hand, I lowered the flame and lit one end of a five dollar bill. It started to burn. I held it at the other end, folded it in a v lengthwise and grew the flame. Within seconds, the tree leaves were now going. The flames now provided a bright light in the extreme darkness. It took my eyes a second to adjust. Over on the side of the road, the coyotes stopped yipping, and they all stared at the light, their eyes glowing brightly with reflection. Holding the branch up, careful to not catch any trees and brush on fire, I took a step towards the animals. They each took a step backwards. Then I let loose. Yelling loudly, I raised the flames and ran towards them, courage infecting my spirit. They all took off and ran about twenty feet into the darkness. Coming to the side of the road, I saw what they had been attacking, but at first, it didn't make any sense. It looked like a huge ball of duct tape. As I saw the body move, I realized what I was seeing. It was a man completely wrapped in duct tape, moaning deeply, with a rag or handkerchief covering his head and eye area encircled in tape. His legs were folded and tied behind his back. The person's mouth was taped shut with three or four wraps of tape encircling his head.

What sadistic son of a bitch had done this, I wondered? At first, I thought it might be a homeless person, but the tan boots were a dead giveaway. I had just found my cousin Mark, still alive. Dumped in a deserted creek area in a thick part of the wilderness. The stream so deep, we didn't even see him earlier when we drove by. Left to die or be eaten alive.

Putting the branch down on the side berm of the road, I ran over to Mark. I reassured him that I would free him. In the flickering light, I pulled out my pocketknife.

"Mark, it's Trace. I'm going to cut through the tape around your head and mouth. Hold still."

Within seconds, I had the cloth removed from his head, and the sticky tape pulled from his mouth. Then I cut the tape holding his legs that were hog-tied behind him. He kneeled up, obviously in pain.

"Thank God, you came when you did, Trace," he said meekly. I could feel the coyotes nip at me. I was truly about to give up. I heard a truck go by earlier, but evidently they didn't see me in this soggy ditch. Whoever wrapped me up had me wrapped so tight I could barely move. My legs are completely jacked up from the fall. I don't know if I will be able to stand."

As I looked over, the branch was just about ready to go out. Scrambling, I found a couple more and put them on the side of the road safely in the dirt, creating a makeshift campfire. With the fire under control, I took the knife and slowly cutaway the tape that covered almost every inch of Mark's legs and body.

I remarked, "The sadistic son of a bitch who did this must have used a whole roll of tape. Any idea who it was?"

He rolled to his side and tried to stretch his legs out. He was in massive pain. He pulled his shirt off and then attempted to get his pants off as the tape was removed. He said, "I'm covered in ants. Shit... ahh... I've got to get these clothes off." Stripping down, he continued, "No idea who did this. Whoever it was had knocked me over the head as I walked into dad's house. When I woke up, I was tied up and blindfolded in the back of my truck. The asshole had a deep voice and wanted to know where a large diamond was. When I told him I didn't know he started kicking me with some very hard boots. Must of been the giant we had seen the prints from."

Then he looked up at me and asked in a very pained voice, "How is Debbi? Last time I saw her, she had gone in the back bedroom. I hope she is OK."

Realizing the situation, I played dumb. "I'm not sure. I had followed you into the house, saw you lying on the floor when someone hit me over the head from behind. When I woke up, your dad's house was on fire, and I was left for dead, the house completely engulfed in flames. Only by the grace of God and a falling timber that freed my trapped leg, was I able to get out. When I got out, the truck was gone, and the house had completely caved in on itself. Not sure what happened to Debbi, but you could see drag marks in the mud outside the walkway surrounded by those size 18 footprints. That's just before the propane tank exploded and caught everything on fire for miles. I barely escaped. I'm burnt bad, and my ankle is toast. Thank God you are still alive. Contessa and I drove through here earlier tonight, and we didn't see you. You were too far down in the creek bed. The only thing that saved you tonight was the coyotes. Without them trying to eat you alive, I would never have seen you."

Just then the area exploded in light, and five men came running at us, guns drawn.

CHAPTER 32

─────────────⌒────────────

"Freeze, Put your hands up." The cop with the large flashlight yelled as he ran my way. With the glaring light in my eyes, I had no choice but to comply. Glancing next to me, I noticed Mark struggling to stand. He had removed his shirt and was shaking it out. Another officer ran towards him and screamed out, "Drop that... now." Mark complied instantly.

Within seconds, we were surrounded by five tall police officers. It was hard to make out their faces or their badges with the extreme light in our faces. But a sigh of relief came over me as I made out North County Sheriff's Department on one of the badges.

"Boy am I glad to see you guys," I said, almost out of breath from being startled. "My partner Martino called sometime earlier this evening about a missing truck and also two missing people. I just found Mark, one of the lost friends and the owner of the red 56 truck."

The cop with the light in my face said, "Is your name Trace?"

"Yes, it's Trace Armstrong, I'm former Highway Patrol from L.A., now working as a detective out of Sloan Beach. The guy without a shirt is my cousin Mark Armstrong, who owns the vehicle."

"I'm Sergeant Hank Watson out of the sheriff's office in Vista/ Oceanview. We are responding to the call from Martino. Great guy.

Helped us a lot with our motorcycles. He filled me in a little over the phone. Said something about a fire, a truck, and finding blood in the truck bed."

Hank took a step back, lowered his weapon, and instructed his men to do the same. Widening the beam on his six cell light, he looked at us standing there on the dirt path. "You both look like you've been through hell. Is that duct tape on your pants, Mark?"

Mark nodded and moaned slowly, "I've been lying in that ditch there for the last six or seven hours, blindfolded, covered in ants, and completely hogtied with a full roll of some of the toughest duct tape known to man. Whoever did this hit me over the head at my dad's house on De Luz. I was passed out on the floor when he set the structure on fire, pulled me out and left my wife and my cousin to die in the flames. Trace escaped, but we don't know about my wife, Debbi," he said choking up. "I can't stand, and Trace is severely burned. I guess you could say we have both been through hell. A hell that is just starting if we don't find my wife alive." Mark fought back tears, but finally just let loose. The emotional pain was taking its toll, which I knew would get much worse when the body was discovered at the fire.

Hank replied, "Why don't we take a short statement tonight back at our car and then have you come into the station tomorrow to finish the paperwork. We'll put a bulletin out for your wife and the perp, but it doesn't sound like there is much to go on. We've got two cars up on De Luz. I'll arrange to get you home where you can get some sleep. Neither of you look like you can stand any more excitement today. I'll have my night shift guys start an investigation over at the De Luz house and arrange for a tow company to extract your truck."

"Sleep sounds splendid," I replied. "Just curious Hank, how did you find us?"

"Pretty easy to see your fire from up on De Luz. We just parked up top and hiked it down the ravine about a hundred yards back, out of sight to make sure who you were. Thankfully, you are the good guys. Neither of you look like you would be able to climb out in your condition. I'm having my driver up top backtrack and come down this horse trail and pick you up. We'll take your statement when he gets here."

Mark spoke up, "I'm so glad you don't want me to climb anything. I don't know if my legs will ever work right again. I can't even stand. Please excuse me while I shake out the rest of my clothes. I must have a million ant bites over most of my body. If I ever find the perp who did this, I want to put him in a cage with a bunch of ravenous snakes, rats and coyotes just to give him a taste of what he put me through today."

I put my hand on his shoulder and replied, "I want to be there to see that. Sleep will do you good, my friend."

Within minutes one of the squad cars pulled up on the dirt trail. We sat in the police car with Fred, the deputy in charge, and went over everything that happened during the past day, from each of our points of view. He put a call in on the radio to have one of the office personnel call Contessa at her home, but there was no answer. She must have gone into town. The clock on the dash said it was almost midnight. One hell of a long day.

Fred was then instructed to take us out of the area. Mark was in so much pain, and bleeding from coyote bites, it was decided to take him to the hospital, instead of taking him home. I waited a short time while they admitted him to the emergency ward for an overnight observation. He couldn't walk, and they pushed him in with a wheelchair. At least he would be able to get some sleep. There was no visitation that late so I told him not to worry. We would meet up the next day. Fred then dropped me off at my hotel. We would meet at the tiny Sheriff substation office at the Fallbrook Library at nine in the morning. Mark was not doing good the last I saw him, but he was in good hands. Unfortunately, tomorrow would be a brutal day for him once his wife's body was discovered. I was just glad the both of us were alive.

As I exited the police car, the hotel parking lot appeared entirely different than it was in the morning. A dichotomy that wasn't missed by my sleepy eyes. It was full of cars and work trucks. Everyone from the fire area was now in town. Probably good for the owners of the hotel, but also a lot more work. Walking with a decided limp by the blue Mercedes I was relieved that it looked undisturbed, even though it was surrounded by huge work vehicles. I opened the trunk and got my suitcase out. One less thing to worry about.

I stared at the old hotel, lights blazing brightly from the front foyer. The old girl wasn't sleeping yet, in fact, the music from the bar rocked through the midnight chill, indicating that the local townsfolk weren't about to call it a night before 2 am.

Passing the row of cars in front of the old Benz, I spied Contessa's Chevy truck. At least she had made it past the Fallbrook cops and hopefully was able to get a room, however, as the foyer opened up in front of me as I walked in, it was apparent from the cots lined up against the wall that the old hotel had reached capacity. Most of the overflow was in the bar, turning a lousy smoke filled day into a time to bury the problems with a drink or two.

Curious if I could spy Contessa, I shuffled around the back of the bar, looking past the throng at the tap, who were talking and carousing loudly. Now that the restaurant was closed, the hotel had pulled back the curtain that usually separated it from the bar. Assorted guests were sitting at some of the cafe tables, talking softly. Over at one of the back tables was Contessa, her dark hair contrasting against the reflection of the hotel sign shining through one of the old leaded windows.

Walking with a painful limp from behind, I put my suitcase down and rested my hand on her shoulder. She jumped slightly at my touch and said, "Whaaa, Trace, what are you doing here? I figured you were in jail. Sorry I jumped, some of these farm boys get a little rowdy when they get drunk. I've been trying to stay out of the way until it's lights out. Unfortunately, I didn't get a reservation, since I just got here about an hour ago. How about you? Do you still have a room?"

Pulling a key from my pocket, I said, "I sure do. Why don't you grab one of the cots and you can share my room; that is unless you snore or decide to attack me."

"You are a life saver, Trace. I figured I'd be shacked up with a bunch of old timers out it the parlor all night." Standing she said, "I promise not to attack you, but I am going to give you a huge hug. How the heck did you escape from Fallbrook's finest?"

I smiled, "It's amazing what you can accomplish when you fall out of the backseat of a police car at high speed on one of the scariest curves on De Luz Road."

"You fell out of the back seat? How did that happen? I saw them zip your hands behind you."

"It's an old police technique they taught us at the academy. They warned us that prisoners would often bump the child locks off on the rear doors with their knees, and then pull open the door from inside and roll out to freedom. I just used an old prisoner trick and waited for a steep drop off on one of the curves. Worked like a charm, other than the huge berm, brambles, and trees on the way down. I can't tell you how bad I hurt right now. My leg and ankle are toast. My right side has got to be one big bruise. Thankfully those ol' boys from Fallbrook were way too lazy to come down that steep hill after me in the dark. They just left me there tied up to die, or at least cavort with some hungry coyotes."

"It's dark in here, but I can see you are all scratched up. You must feel like crap?"

"Not as bad as my cousin Mark. I found him at the bottom of that hill hog-tied and blindfolded in a full roll of duct tape."

"You found Mark? How... What... Is he still alive?"

"I got to him just before a pack of coyotes was about to make him dinner. He can't walk and is covered in ant and insect bites. He certainly won't be doing well at all tomorrow when he finds out about Debbi. The police dropped him off at the emergency room at the hospital for observation. He could barely talk and had to be taken in by wheelchair. The creeper guy had tied him up and wanted to know about a large diamond before he pushed him out of the back of his truck. Some big shit is going on with my cousin's family."

Contessa shook her head, "I'm so glad to hear he is still alive. Good thing he's at the hospital. From what you said, he'll need lots of attention to keep him from getting an infection, not to mention his legs being bound up. Tomorrow will be hell for him once the reports come in." Standing, she said, "I can't believe what you have been through today, Trace. You must be part cat with nine lives. I hope tomorrow has a little less excitement. Let me get my suitcase out of my truck. What room are you in?"

"I'm in room seven down the hall. Just knock when you get back."

Contessa headed outside; Picking up my suitcase, I walked out of the bar and down the main hall to my room. Opening the door with the old brass key, I flicked on the dim yellow light. There on the middle of the bed was the large blue topaz on a silver tray.

CHAPTER 33

The deadly blue topaz had turned up again. This time it was displayed on a silver platter. What could be more appropriate than the jewel that had caused so much grief in the last two days sitting in the middle of my bed. Stepping closer in the dim light, I inspected the tray and looked for any note or notation where it had come from.

My room was locked all day, yet a maid and the whole hotel staff would have key access to place it there. At first thought, my mind turned to Alice, the older daughter. She was the one who had given it to me in the first place and had taken an interest in me. She might have discovered it somewhere and put it on display where I would find it. However, that didn't seem like her style. She wouldn't leave something that valuable out in the open, where a maid or other staff member would have access.

No, this was something different. This was meant to send a message. The jewel had disappeared initially from my room after I had seen the ghost or whatever it was in the middle of the night. A bright flash, some smoke, and the jewel was gone. Now it was sitting there right in my face. Right in my face, not on a dresser or table where I might have misplaced it. No, this was an in-your-face move by somebody, or something.

I sat my suitcase on the dresser and then sat on the side of the bed, pulling my one cell penlight from my pocket and carefully examining the tray. It had no fingerprints or other markings on it. The large jewel had been wiped clean of prints and was placed precisely at the center. The comforter on the bed was smoothed tight—no knee prints or other markings—it looked just like I had left it in the morning.

Slowly I walked around the room, careful not to disturb anything. I looked in the trash can—empty and in the same place it had been earlier in the day. I looked in the bathroom; nothing in the waste can, nothing on the sink. It didn't appear that anyone had been in my room except the maid to make the bed and replace some towels, but she had done that while I was at breakfast.

It was too late to try and talk with Alice. She was definitely in a bind trying to close down the bar and get all the overflow settled for the night. Nothing made much sense. While I was in the bathroom, I picked up a couple of tissues and used them to move the tray and the gem to the bedside table. Looking closer, everything seemed pristine. Then I remembered something. Bending down, I took a sniff of the plate and the jewel. There was a slight aroma of rose water. Just like there was after I had seen the apparition the previous night. Whoever had taken the Topaz had now returned it.

There was a quiet knock on the door. I arose, limped to the door, and looked through the peephole. It was Contessa holding a suitcase and a folded cot. Turning the heavy old latch, I invited her in.

Nodding, she said, "It's still a party out there. Glad you're down the hall a bit. Some of those boys are getting rowdy. Thanks for saving me, Trace."

"You're welcome. I know you're tired, but I can certainly use your help. My leg is all jacked up from that fall and roll. I'm terrified to look at it."

"No problem. Let's get you up on the bed and take a look."

I walked back to the bed, removed the old coveralls, sat down, then turned and rolled my legs onto the mattress. "Man, that bandage is all twisted up," I said looking down at my left calf. "The splint is about to fall off. Please tell me I haven't done permanent damage."

She turned on the side table lamp and glanced down, "What is this jewel doing here?"

"You tell me," I replied. "It was centered on the bedspread when I returned on that shiny silver tray. It certainly wasn't here this morning."

"I know you said it was missing. Who do you think put it here? Someone from the office?"

I sat up in bed and propped my head on a pillow and replied, "That's what I thought at first, but I don't believe it now. The oldest daughter Alice had originally given it to me, but she wouldn't leave it here like this. No, I think it might have been placed there by a ghost."

"What? Now I know you are delusional. You better get some sleep."

"There is something I haven't told you, Contessa. In fact I haven't told anyone about it. Last night, which seems so long ago, I woke up about one thirty A.M. There was a large crunching noise, which I think was the old metal vent on the roof for the swamp cooler. I had stood up on the side of the bed, staring at the ceiling trying to determine what the noise was. I walked a few steps toward the bathroom and in the real dim light, I saw the outline of something. Very faint."

At first I just thought it was my eyes playing a trick on me. Then I took a step forward and could make out the outline a little better. If I had to describe it, I would say it looked like a whispy cloud, translucent, moving slightly. Then, as I took another step forward, there was a huge flash of light in my face. Instantly blinded, I could make out almost a human form in the split second that my eyes functioned."

Contessa shook her head, "You're kidding."

"I wish I was," I said. "The weird thing was, the apparition completely disappeared. It was only a second until my sight started to come back, but it disappeared without a trace. I tell you, it really freaked me out. I went over to the wall and turned on the light and then searched the room. The only thing that was different was a slight wisp of smoke or some kind of vapor. I didn't know what to think. I still don't. I searched the whole main room and went over the bathroom with a fine toothed comb. No sign of anything and no visible way that anything could have escaped. There is only one tiny window at the top of the bathroom. Certainly not big enough for a human to get away. I know the front door didn't open. I even looked under the bed."

"You're scaring me, Trace. I don't like ghost stories. Are you sure you just weren't imagining something?"

"I've rolled this over in my mind a hundred times. The freaky thing was that blue topaz disappeared out of the left front pocket of my pants, which were on the chair at the side of the bed."

"So you are saying whatever it was reached into your pants pocket right in this chair next to the bed? That is crazy. I've always heard rumors about ghosts here. People would say they heard noises or saw something in the dark, but nothing like this."

"Believe me, I had a hard time getting back to sleep. I spent the rest of the night with one eye open. There was no more noises or anything except for one tell tail sign."

"What's that? Don't tell me it was blood or some cryptic marking?"

"Nothing sinister like that. It was just the faint smell of rose water, which led me to believe it might have been Alice or her sister. I asked the woman who runs the hotel in the morning, and she said the girls were in the staff room all night."

Contessa grimaced, "Now you are really freaking me out. You know they say ghosts sometimes have a sweet odor to them."

"I didn't know that. Well, I just smelled the silver tray and topaz, and it has a faint smell of rose water."

"Oh no. Are you sure you aren't making this all up Trace?"

"Take a whiff yourself."

Contessa bent down and smelled the tray. I could hear an audible gasp.

"Oh, that is so scary, Trace. There is a faint sweet smell there for sure."

"Well, you don't have to stay in the room if you don't want to."

"I'm a big girl, but that doesn't mean I'm not a little panicked. I just hope it doesn't come back."

"I think we both need to get some sleep. Tomorrow is going to be a long day."

She nodded, "So how are we going to work this since it sounds like you sleep with your clothes off. I've got a jogging suit in my suitcase that I can wear. We need to get you somewhat comfortable."

"Tell you what. Do you have some scissors in your bag? If you want to cut off the other leg of these jeans, I'll just wear them as shorts."

"Coming right up."

Over the next few minutes, Contessa took some time and cleaned up my burn, reset the bandage and cut off my other pant leg. I took off my work shirt and got down to my just my tee shirt. She then removed my splint and shoe and took a look at my ankle. She said, "Talk about black and blue, I hope this doesn't hurt as bad as it looks. You need to stay off of your foot for a few days."

I laughed, "Probably not going happen, nurse Contessa. I'll do my best, and yes, it does hurt like hell. I put a lot of miles on it today. That last hill out of the police car was the worst. Surprised I was able to walk at all. I guess it's probably just adrenaline."

"You'll know in the morning, but for now I think we both need to get some sleep. I'm going to go change and set the cot up."

With that, she took her suitcase into the bathroom. Emerging a few minutes later she was dressed in a white and pink jogging suit which showed off her fit and trim figure. I quipped, "Wow, it's a good thing you aren't downstairs with those wolves in that outfit. They would eat you alive."

She replied, "You can only imagine the whistles and cat calls. Thanks for saving me again, Mr. Armstrong."

"You're welcome. Can you help me with these covers. This drafty room will probably require a sheet. Last night it got rather cool in here."

"Sure, stand up on your good leg and I'll pull down this old bedspread."

As I stood up, I put one hand on her shoulder to steady myself on my good foot. The soft cotton of her top and the hint of her perfume was certainly enticing. After she had pulled down the covers, she turned, and we faced each other for a few seconds. I murmured, "You probably saved my life today. Thanks for trusting me and taking care of my burns."

She hugged me softly, "You certainly saved your cousin Mark's life today. Now we've got to get some sleep. Get settled here. I'm going to setup that cot and turn out the light."

I sat back on the bed, and she helped me pull my legs up. After covering me partially with the sheet, she walked over near the door to set the wooden cot up. As she went to open it, we both heard a big crack. The old wood frame had cracked in half."

After a muffled expletive, she said, "I'm going to have to go back to the front office and get another one."

"No, you're not. It's after one in the morning. It's too late to deal with that now. Just turn out the light and climb in the other side of the bed."

She didn't argue but just turned the light off, pulled off her shoes and crawled in the other side. Pulling up the sheet on her side she moved over near me. I could feel her hand softly on my shoulder as she whispered, "Good night Mr. Armstrong."

"Good night," I replied.

I was so dead from the day that I just closed my eyes, adjusting to the fact there was a beautiful woman next to me, but it was like we were two little kids on a sleepover. We started making small talk for a minute and then we slowly fell asleep.

Crack... I was woken straight up in bed. Contessa was jarred awake too.

"What was that?" she asked.

"I think it is the swamp cooler door which is timed to go off around one thirty A.M."

"I hope you are right. Are you sure it's not that ghost you were talking about?"

I raised up on my elbow and looked out across the main room, my eyes getting used to the dim light.

"I don't see anything. I'm sure it's just the cooler. Let's go back to sleep."

Contessa snuggled up next to me, "I'm scared Trace. That sounded like it was closer than the roof. I've got this strange feeling that someone is in here."

Lowering my head to the pillow, I replied, "It's just your imagination. I shouldn't have told you that story. Let's go back to sleep."

She raised up on one arm, her body now against mine and looked across the room. "I'm really scared Trace. It just feels like something is in the room."

I raised my head again and looked out. Nothing but a dim glow from the moonlight seeping around the curtains on the back wall.

Suddenly Contessa gripped my arm and sat up a little more. "Is that something moving over by the wall?"

My eyes strained again. In the darkness there appeared to be a wispy apparition slowly coming towards the bed. Before I could say anything, Contessa tensed and the ghost or apparition rushed at the bed. All of a sudden there was a tremendous flash of light. We were both momentarily blinded. Contessa's nails dug into my arm as she screamed...

As my eyes came back into focus, it was gone.

CHAPTER 34

Flinging the sheet off, I moved my legs to the side of the bed and tried to stand to see if I could see the apparition. The brutality of the day had taken its toll. My right foot cramped, and my left ankle was toast. I fell back on the bed in massive pain. Contessa had worked her way across the bed and jumped down to help me up. She turned on the lamp on the nightstand next to the bed. In her hand, she held the large blue topaz.

In a rather angry voice, she said, "Whatever that thing was, it didn't get the jewel this time. That's one of the scariest visions I've ever had. It was coming right at us. What the hell was that, Trace?"

"I wish I knew Contessa," I said. "Once the bright light flashes, it completely disappears into thin air."

"I see what you mean about the wispy smoke. Can you see it?"

"It's just like it was the first time. Very faint. Do you notice the slight odor of rose water?"

"I do. I'm going to turn on the ceiling light. Let's see if we can make out anything."

Walking over to the door, she hit the wall switch. The dim glow from the ceiling lights gave a better view of the room. There was nothing different or out of place from a few minutes before. Contessa's suitcase was on the chair next to the nightstand, while my coveralls and newly cut jean pant leg were folded on the dresser across the room.

Sitting on the side of the bed, I said, "My legs are toast. Can you check the bathroom? Last time there wasn't any sign of a disturbance."

"I don't know, Trace. I'm really freaked out now. I want to get as far away from this room as possible."

"I don't blame you, but it's so late we don't have much choice but to stay in here. Tell you what. Help me stand and I'll limp with you into the bathroom."

"All right, but do you have a flashlight? It's dark in there, and I don't remember where the old light switch was."

"My keys are in the front pocket of the coveralls. There's a penlight on the keychain."

She pulled the keys out of the pocket, helped me stand, and we headed towards the back of the room. The bathroom was directly behind the wall where the headboard of the bed was. Taking it slow, she turned on the penlight and shown it into the darkness of the washroom. The door was slightly open, and the beam played back and forth over the old tile floor. Propping myself against the door jam, she reached in with her left hand to feel for the light switch. I couldn't resist. I let out a slight "ayee", which made her jump about a half mile.

"Don't scare me, Trace. You're not funny. Just for that, you can put your bum leg to work and turn it on yourself."

She stepped back, with an apprehension that a wild animal was about to spring from the room. Limping and jumping with my right leg, I reached around the door jam with my left arm and felt for the switch. Something coarse rubbed against the back of my hand. I quickly pulled my arm back, only to realize it was a towel on one of the towel racks. Reaching in again, I successfully found the switch and turned it on. I pushed the door open with my bum foot and concluded that it was the same as the night before.

I said, "It's empty, just like before. Whatever that was just disappeared into a thin smoky mist."

"Trace, I have never believed in ghosts or supernatural things, but this is turning my stomach into knots."

"Take a look for yourself. There is no sign of anything."

Hesitating, she walked slowly into the room, "Where in the hell did it go? I know it didn't go out the front door, and there is no sign of it here."

"If you look up at the ceiling in the bathroom, you can see that small window to the outside, but no way could anything human get out of that."

Nodding in agreement, she said, "What about the wall behind the window curtain outside the bathroom door?"

"You can check it, but it's just a waist high window that goes almost to the ceiling and a short wall underneath covered in wainscoting."

"Hand me the light, there has got to be an explanation."

"Here it is, but I don't see how anything could get out there."

Contessa took the little flashlight and opened the old full-length curtains. Shining the light back and forth on the window and wall behind, she just shook her head. "I don't get it, Trace. That thing had proportions about the size of a person, at least as I could make it out in the dark. How could it completely disappear?"

"It's either supernatural, or there is some other explanation, one of which eludes my tired brain at one thirty in the morning. Let's go back to sleep. I can't stand much longer."

"All right, but you better let me snuggle with you, Mister. As I said before, I'm really freaked."

With her help, I got back into bed. Turning off the room light, she climbed in and laid right next to me. I reached up and turned off the side table light. The room was back into darkness.

In a soft voice, I said, "I don't think I've ever been in a bed with a beautiful woman under circumstances like this. Is that you shaking?"

"I'm about ready to run out that freaking door and scream at the top of my lungs."

"That's how I felt the first night I stayed here."

"Just going to bury my head into your shoulder if you don't mind."

"No problem, we'll fight it off together if it comes back. Let's get some sleep."

Holding on to me, I could feel her head on my shoulder. It had been a long time since I had been with a woman overnight like this. My girlfriend Janet was thousands of miles away in New York. Here I was sleeping with an attractive Latin woman, who had probably saved my life. We had just experienced something so unimaginable yet something so unbelievable, that I don't know anyone who would believe us. Would Janet understand this situation? I didn't know, but in a few minutes, we were both sound asleep. I was so dead that I slept soundly for what seemed like hours until I awoke from a dream. A dream that ended in a huge flash of light. As I opened my eyes, I couldn't tell if I was dreaming or if the thing was back again.

CHAPTER 35

I hate it when I wake up, and can't tell if I have been dreaming or if I'm waking up to reality. The flash I had just experienced was probably just the end of a dream. Opening my eyes wide, I looked over at the nightstand. The alarm clock said 5 am. Contessa appeared to be sound asleep, but I propped myself up on my left arm and looked out across the room. It was very dark, but the first rays of morning sunlight had made their way around the thick curtain, giving me a slightly better view than before.

Everything looked as it did before and I couldn't tell if there was any smoke or vapor in the air given the darkness. Turning the light on would surely wake Contessa. Eyes closed, I just pulled up the sheet and fell back asleep. At seven later that morning, I re-awoke. Contessa was up and making coffee. Rolling out of the bed, I tried to gingerly stand up. My burn was tolerable, but my left ankle was still a significant problem.

Contessa noticed me and said, "Whoa Mister, you should stay off of that until you need to walk."

Protesting, I said, "What I need is a shower to get all this Fallbrook dirt and grime off of me. So Nurse, what do you suggest with this burn?"

"Well, you have a couple of options. You can rough it out tough guy, pull the bandage off and just go for it. You'll probably die standing up and risk the chance of infection. Otherwise, you can cover your leg and bandage with a plastic bag and shower away. I would suggest the second option."

"So where am I going to get a plastic bag?"

"I actually may have a cleaner bag in my suitcase that you can use. Let's see if we can get you fixed up."

In the next few minutes, Contessa helped me get into the bathroom. I sat on the side of the tub, and then she wrapped my leg up. She helped me stand and step into the tub and the closed the bathroom door behind her as she left. Taking my shorts off, I showered, toweled off and put a loose pair of jeans on. Contessa helped me with my ankle brace and then she changed into a pair of slacks and a white cotton top. Repacking her suitcase, we locked up and headed down for breakfast, closing the old wooden door behind us. I made sure to put the Topaz in my front pocket.

As we took seats in the restaurant, the waitress owner, Madeline took our orders. Soon we were enjoying a couple of three egg omelets. Looking up, I said, "You know Contessa, I could get used to all this attention. I have no idea how I would have managed without you. They must love you at the hospital."

"I do medical care like this all the time, but I have to say, Mr. Armstrong, you are the best-looking specimen I've had in a long time. It's too bad you have a girlfriend. I might not have kept my hands off of you last night."

Blushing a little, I said, "I'm not sure if I still have a girlfriend. She's back in New York trying to get divorced from a very controlling husband. I'm really worried that things may not be going well. Just the tone of her voice the last time we talked has me concerned."

"Are you guys close?"

"The relationship has been going well. She does my books for me as a PI. We just got back from Paris a few months ago where we both were almost killed. Be real honest with you, I'm madly in love with Janet, but we can't move forward until she gets divorced."

"Sounds like a problem."

"Actually a real issue for her. Her husband lives in New York, works for the IRS and is a cheatn' SOB, sleeping around almost every night. She's got two kids out here in Sloan Beach and lives in a little cottage near the coast. If the divorce goes through, she may lose the house. The husband is a real slime-ball, and I have no doubt he'll pull something."

"No wonder you're worried, Trace. Many women will choose a roof over their head instead of a guy, even if he looks like you."

"That's what worries me. I don't exactly have a mansion she can move into. Time will tell. I have to call her tonight and see how she is doing. Last time we talked it didn't sound right. So how about you Contessa, must be kind of tough living alone out in the country."

"I don't mind living outside of town, but it is lonely at times. I've just buried my head in my work and odd jobs for the last few years. Since Jorge died, I've got into cooking and baking. The hospital pays the bills, but my real passion is to open a restaurant someday. When Jorge and I lived in Belize, we used to work extensively with the tourists, or touristas as we called them. I learned to speak English real well after a few years. We lived in the little beach town of Placencia. Jorge ran a scuba diving boat, and I had a little tourist bar and grill. He took the visitors out diving and then brought them back for lunch or dinner. Great business. I had so many great Latin and Caribbean recipes, such as lime drenched fajitas, avocado filled chicken tacos, and fry jack. My customer's loved me."

"Sounds delicious and a good life in paradise. So what happened?"

"Jorge got an offer to work for an American deep-sea diving company. Paid real good money and came with automatic green cards to the U.S. We talked about it for a few weeks and he decided to go. He sold the boat and headed to the Texas Gulf for training. Unfortunately, with the unbelievable pay came great danger, working on offshore oil rigs. I got our affairs settled, sold off the bar, and moved to Galveston six months later. He was renting a small apartment, primarily to store his stuff, since he was out on the rigs most of the time. I moved into the apartment, but within days, the bad news had come in. The ship he was piloting had sunk in rough seas after one of the Gulf hurricanes. I never saw him again."

"Wow, that's tough. Living in a new country, and your husband dies before you even got to meet up."

"It was really hard, but the company did have good insurance, and I got a payout. Jorge had some relatives in San Diego, California that ran a Mexican restaurant, so I moved out here. I worked in their restaurant called La Chabola, part time while I got some training as a nursing assistant at a career college. I ended up seeing an ad for a job at the Fallbrook Hospital for a nurse assistant, and I got hired on there about three years ago. Picked up the little house off De Luz for a good price with some of the proceeds from Jorge's estate, but most of it is put away for my own restaurant, someday."

"So how did you meet my Uncle Paul?"

"I met him through the Farmer's Market in town. You probably noticed the avocado and citrus trees on the back few acres of his property. Since I like to cook, I'm always looking for exotic varieties of fruits and vegetables. Paul and his wife Catarina had planted a half dozen unique varieties of citrus and avocado, usually found in Latin America. Catarina ran a little booth at the Farmer's Market on Sundays, selling and trading exotic delicacies for restaurants and chefs. She was part of a statewide group of farmers and growers that imported and exported fruits and vegetables."

"I remember that my cousin said she was originally from Portugal."

"Pretty exotic lady. I met her when she was delivering some limes and large avocados to La Chabola when I worked there. First time I went to the Fallbrook market after moving here I recognized her. We became good friends, and she helped me set up some accounts baking pies and other bakery products for restaurants in the area. With some of the varietals that she offered, I have been able to build a name for myself with some more exotic fruit pies. It's not a restaurant yet, but it has helped me gain exposure."

As we finished up breakfast, Madeline came by and left a check. Contessa asked her nonchalantly, "Is this hotel haunted?"

Madeline responded, "I've heard all sorts of rumors over the years, but I've never actually seen anything myself. Something spook you?"

Contessa replied, "Probably nothing, just a flash of light."

Madeline said, "Usually the reports are more of a noise or presence in the room. Hey, you never know. This place is over eighty years old. All sorts of things have occurred here."

I paid the bill and looked at my watch. It was just turning eight. Contessa said, "Can you follow me out to my place so I can drop my truck off. We have an hour before we need to be at the library to meet the deputies, and I'd like to check on my house. When I came into town last night, the word was that De Luz would be reopened this morning."

"Sure. Let's walk by the room and check on things, and then head out the back door."

We walked down the hall, I opened the large door and looked in. It appeared that the maid had been by and made the bed. Looked undisturbed. Closing the door, we walked out to the old Mercedes.

Contessa said, "What a beautiful German ride Mr. Armstrong. I'm looking forward to my trip back. My truck is over in the next row. I'll meet you at my house."

"See you in a few minutes."

She pulled out first, and I followed her to DeLuz. The road block had come down, and there didn't appear to be any smoke in the distance. A mile or so later I pulled behind her into her drive. The porch light was still on. Standing on the front porch, she invited me in. "Everything looks OK," she said walking into the kitchen. "How about I make some fresh guacamole and some salsa to take along. There is a bag of chips in the pantry. I have a feeling this meeting will take awhile, especially if they have inspected the residence."

"No doubt," I replied. Standing at the sink with a cutting board, she asked, "Can you grab the box of avocados out of the fridge?"

I held up a small box that had the name Hass on it. I replied, "Is this what you want?"

"Sure is. Have you ever made guacamole before, Trace?"

"No, can't say that I have."

"Hand me that knife. Let me show you how to prepare the avocado to mash up. First you have to slice it in half."

Pulling out a beautiful specimen, she put it on the cutting board. She said, "The avocados have a large seed in the middle, so it's best if you slice it all the way around from the outside and just pull the halves apart. That way the seed just falls out." Running the knife around deftly with the speed of an accomplished chef, she put the knife down and then pulled the halves apart. She let out a huge scream, as a large blue diamond fell on the cutting board.

CHAPTER 36

"What in the hell is this?" I asked, as we both stood there stunned. A large light blue gemstone was lying on the cutting board. Instinctually I picked it up and walked over to the window. A quick drag across the glass told me this was no Topaz. It was an enormous diamond. Worth hundreds of thousands of dollars, or more.

Contessa picked it up and held it up to the light, "It looks flawless. How did it get in an avocado?"

"It didn't just get in an avocado, it was deliberately put there, and someone willing to kill is looking for it."

Picking up the Avocado halves I asked, "Where did these avocados come from?"

She replied, "These are from the Fallbrook Farmer's Market. I swap six-count boxes once a month there with a vendor from the San Diego area. I pick up a box or two from your uncle and then swap them out with this other vendor's variety. Been doing it for Paul since his wife died. Paul would always have them set out for me, and I would pick them up and do the swap while I was at the market event, usually on the first Sunday of the month. When you and Mark were over yesterday, I passed along a box I had picked up last week along with the pie that I gave to Mark and Debbi."

"So how can you tell between the different avocado varieties?"

She held up the box, "It's right here on the label. One is Hass; the other is Hess." Suddenly her eyes got big, "Oh my God, Trace, I put the wrong box in the bag with the pie yesterday. In fact, I probably took over the wrong variety last week. I bet I took over the Hass Avocados that I picked up from your Uncle Paul and actually returned them. The ones in this box are the Hess variety that should have gone over to him."

"How could that happen? Don't they have different labels?"

"I just noticed that the boxes from San Diego now have the same triangular label from the California Avocado Board on one end of the box as the ones that Paul uses. The difference is the variety tag on the other end. The San Diego boxes never had that CAB label before. I just saw the familiar label and delivered them without another thought."

"We know that Mark said his attacker wanted to know where a large diamond was. I would bet that this light blue beauty was what they were looking for. Let's extrapolate this a little further. Sounds like avocados and possibly other fruit are some kind of a delivery vehicle for expensive gems. I bet this is why someone killed Uncle Paul. Whoever he was delivering this box to last week, found a Blue Topaz instead of a blue diamond in the avocado. People dealing with that type of jewels don't usually mess around. Probably killed him on the spot."

Contessa nodded. "You're probably right. Probably our creeper friend or an accomplice in town did him in and dragged his body over to the old hotel. I bet they left the Topaz in his pocket as a sign."

"Since we had seen numerous footprints, I bet that large creeper guy was waiting in Uncle Paul's house when we got back from your house yesterday. I remember seeing Debbi take in the bag with the pie and fruit when we got out of the truck."

Shaking her head, Contessa replied, "Your uncle had a large cooler in his back room where he kept the citrus and avocados that he harvested. I bet the goon was waiting there. Once he saw Debbi come in with the avocado box, he probably hit her over the head. Then he did the same to Mark and you. Now he had the box, so he set fire to the house to cover his tracks. Unfortunately, he goes outside, cuts open the fruit and doesn't find the diamond. That's when he drags Mark out, figuring he would know where the diamond was."

Nodding I said, "That's why he was hog-tied in the back of his truck and then dropped down a cliff. He took him to a remote location, questioned him, and when he didn't know where it was it was out the back and down the hill. Then they dumped the truck. A diamond this size might get one of us killed if anyone finds out that we have it. The perp is still out there. I would hazard a guess that this stone has a famous name attached to it."

Contessa held the jewel up to the sunlight, "It's not only a large diamond but the light blue color would make it all the more valuable."

I replied,"I guess the million dollar question is, did my uncle know about this or was he just delivering boxes of avocados?"

"Wow Trace, that opens up a whole bunch of questions. Your uncle always seemed like an honest man, but he was intimately involved in the rare gem business for many years."

"More questions than answers at this point," I said. I think we should keep quiet about this at this stage until we figure out who the players are."

She nodded and said, "It's almost nine o'clock. We better head back to the library and meet up with Mark and the sheriff. So what do we do with this blue beauty?"

"We can't leave it here. Not with the creeper and who knows who at large. In fact, I don't think it will be safe for you to stay here for a few days. Let's bring along the whole box and examine them later. For now, the jewels go in the safest place that I know."

"So where is that, Mr. Armstrong?"

"In the soles of my shoes."

"What? You're crazy. Both of those stones are over an inch long. How will you walk?"

"Allow me to show you my specially modified Oxfords." I pulled off one of my shoes, lifted out one of the insoles, and opened a small hinged door that opened into the hollow heel of the black work shoe.

With a surprised look, Contessa said, "I've never seen anything like that before."

"It's an old private eye trick. No one will ever think to look there. I've carried keys, bullets, notes and now even jewels in the shallow depths of a work shoe sole. One jewel in each shoe."

"Right out of James Bond," she quipped. "Q would be proud."

"Let's get out of here before we end up on the most wanted list."

Picking up the remainder of the avocados, she followed me out and locked up her house, making sure to turn off the porch light. Picking up her suitcase from her truck, she jumped in the Mercedes. I backed out and headed towards town. Just as we turned the first curve, a Fallbrook Police car passed us by on the left. Looking in the rearview mirror, I could see it pull into Contessa's driveway and park right behind her truck. Two guys emerged and went up to the front door. Our timing couldn't have been better.

CHAPTER 37

"Wow, that was close," I said, my eyes turning back to the road ahead. The old Mercedes accelerated briskly towards town, as I shifted to third. Contessa, focusing on the view behind, cried, "I can't believe those bastards are at my house again."

"I'm just glad we missed them. The thought of spending time in their slimy jail makes my skin crawl."

"The idea of them standing on my front porch is making me ill, she said. They treated me so badly last night. Pushed me around. Relentlessly asking about you."

"What imaginative story did you give them?"

Her tone turned to one of anger, "I certainly didn't reveal your real name, Trace. Just pretended that you were a craftsman, working on some odd jobs on my house. Your coveralls fit the story. I heard you use the name Bill Tracy when you were being roughed up, so I used that."

"Good tie in. Not sure what their deal is. No one in town seems to trust them. They left my uncle dead on the floor of the abandoned section of the old hotel. Took them a day according to Alice at the hotel to have anyone come for it."

Settling back in her seat, she said, "It's a small outfit, six local guys, a couple of cars, and a small storefront off Main. One guy's wife runs the front desk. Small jail out back. Tied in with the mayor and the city council. Good ol' boys. It was a lot better when the town used the North County Sheriff."

"Sounds like a power trip. Total control of things. When they put me in the car last night they roughed me up, threw me in the backseat, didn't read me my rights or anything."

Contessa nodded, "They don't like strangers, that's for sure."

"Think they might be involved in any way with the jewel we found?"

"Not sure, Trace. There are a couple of bad actors there for sure, especially the guys that picked you up last night. The rest just seem like they are in it for a paycheck and free donuts."

"I need to do a little undercover investigation later with them. For now, we need to play things low key with the sheriffs' department? Let's not say anything about the jewels or the body we saw at the house. We'll just cover the basic facts of the fire. Let's find out what they know."

"Are you sure, Trace? Why not just give them the jewel and mention the ring. That will take us out of the picture. We can go back home. Back to normal."

"I wish it was that easy. I'm sorry that I've dragged you this far into this, Contessa, but we've got too many loose ends. We know of one dead body, not to mention my cousin almost died and I was left for dead. We find a million dollar jewel in your house. If you go home now, you might be the next victim. I can't let you do that. Believe me, as a private investigator, I work with law enforcement, but I also know that they can't always protect me or my clients."

"Are you saying I'm one of your clients?"

"You've become a good friend. Someone I can trust. Someone who probably saved my life. Someone that I need to protect."

"I don't know, Trace. The more I hang around you, the more bad things happen. I need to go to work today. I'm not a P.I.; I'm a nurse. I don't like the police at my house."

"I know how you feel. You probably wished I never showed up at your door."

"You're more right than you know. Maybe you should just pull over now, let me out. You see the police. I'll walk home. I'm freakn' out. I don't want to go any deeper into your family problems. I don't want those bastards going through my house."

The car became quiet over the purr of the German engine. The conversation wasn't going well. It's funny how quickly fear manifests itself. People do irrational things. Make spur of the moment decisions. If I let Contessa out, I knew it wouldn't end well. Too many players in a small town.

We were coming to the city limits. Mission Boulevard just ahead. I slowed and pulled over to the side of the road. Pulling the parking brake up, I rested my hand on Contessa's leg. Looking her in the eye, I said, "Over the last day, I've seen two sides of you, Contessa. I saw the fear on your face as we met the ghost. I saw the tears when you saw the body in the fire." Raising my voice slightly, I continued, "But I've also seen an amazingly strong spirit in you. The nurse who wasn't afraid to look at my burns or my twisted legs. The spirit that helped you fight off a rogue Fallbrook cop and drove miles in total darkness with a stranger on a dirt road. Right now, I need that strong spirit more than anything. There is an evil out there that I need to confront, but I'm helpless to go this alone. My leg is toast; I can barely walk. You are an amazing person, Contessa, and I need your help. Mark and Debbi need your help."

Turning slowly, she paused. I couldn't tell what she was thinking. After a minute, she said, "You're right, Trace. I'm letting fear make me very selfish. You almost died more than once yesterday." Squeezing my arm, she said, "Mark and Debbi do need my help. Your Uncle Paul was a good friend. Put the car in gear and let's go. I'll call in sick. Let's get to the bottom of this."

In a few minutes, we pulled up to the sheriff substation office next to the library. Contessa held my door as I pulled my braced leg out. The burn rubbed against my pant leg, but soon I was standing again. We walked slowly into the office. There was one deputy named Pete there that invited us to sit down at a large desk. He brought us coffee and sat across from us. He said he was waiting for my cousin, but he would brief us quickly on what they had found so far. Before he could speak again, Contessa looked at him and said, "We found a jewel..."

CHAPTER 38

I couldn't believe what Contessa just said about finding a jewel. Instantly I thought about the gems hidden in the soles of my shoes. If the deputy was made aware of their location, I would certainly go to jail for grand theft. No questions asked. No explanations. No vain attempts to say we found it in an avocado. No one and I mean no one would believe that cockeyed story. Even seeing it with my own eyes, I could hardly believe it. No, I was about to be sent off for a long time.

Contessa glanced my way, smiled, and continued, "Sir, we found a jewel in the burned house. We went back there last night before you came and I saw a square diamond ring, a wedding ring, belonging to Mark's wife. It wasn't just on the ground but located on a very burned finger. I had seen her ring earlier in the day. I just thought you should know before Mark gets here. I wasn't sure if you had a chance to check the fire scene."

I regained my wits. Contessa didn't do me in. On the contrary, she sought to head off a very tense scene when Mark arrived. She didn't want to be the one relaying the bad news.

Deputy Pete was very consoling, "I'm sorry you had to see that, Contessa, but our investigators did confirm that there was at least one body in the remains of the house. As you mentioned, there was identifying jewelry on the body that would lead us to believe that this was a woman, middle aged, approximately five foot seven inches high. Because of the intensity of the fire and the structural collapse, along with animal scavenging, the remains are in bad shape. From the preliminary information you gave us last night and relayed through your friend Martino, we have determined three things so far. One, the fire was set externally to the house. An accelerator agent was found on the property. Two, the accelerator was rigged to create an explosion of the on-site propane tank, which did ignite and subsequently exploded during the fire. Three, the property owner's son, was extensively restrained with duct tape, blindfolded, and released from the back of a pickup truck down a 120-foot cliff, where he sustained extensive injuries and was left for dead in a creek bed at the bottom."

I nodded, "That is what we know at this point, sir. Not sure of any motive, but Mark can fill you in better than we can."

Deputy Pete said, "We'll be interviewing Mark separately when he can talk to determine his story and timeline. He is currently still at the hospital. Currently, we don't have any identifiable suspects or motives. I will be meeting with each one of you separately over the next hour and taking individual statements. As long as your stories collaborate, you'll be free to go, but we will need you to remain available for additional questioning over the next week."

Contessa seemed somewhat nervous, and I wasn't exactly keen on individual testimony, but we didn't have much choice. I was selected to go first. Pete took me into an inner interrogation room and asked me to sit down at a small table. There were no windows, and the door was locked behind him.

He asked, "Tell me about yesterday's events from the time you met with Mark in the afternoon."

With a little nervous energy I replied, "I was just visiting, preparing for my Uncle's funeral this week. Mark, Debbi and I talked with Contessa about his dad's last days yesterday afternoon at her house. This was before the fire started, but we still know very little. When we returned to my Uncle's house, Debbi took in a pie and some groceries that Contessa had given us to the house. Mark and I were in the work shed at the back of the property. It was really hot, and he went in to get a beer. I was out in the shed and then entered the house after fifteen minutes when Mark didn't return. Opening the kitchen door, I saw Mark lying on the floor just inside the living room. I was then hit over the head with a heavy object, and I blacked out. When I awoke, the house was fully engulfed in flame. I escaped from the burning structure with some pretty extensive burns and ran out back. When the propane tank exploded, it set off a massive brush fire."

I spent the next five minutes covering the rest of my journey through the canyon, getting on the bike and meeting up with Contessa. The deputy looked over his notes and followed down an outline. "That's the basics I have in my notes. Do you have any idea who might have done this or a motive?"

This is where I needed to be careful. Don't say anything unnecessary. Silence is golden. I've been in too many situations like this that have gone wrong. Very wrong. As a former detective with the Highway Patrol, I was often on the other side of the desk. I knew the typical questions. I knew the tactics. Twist the stories, ask leading questions. Thankfully since Martino was initially involved, we started out with a much greater sense of trust than most people would have.

Nodding at Pete, I responded to his question, "Only thing I can say that we noticed was some massive footprints, both in the shed and around the house. Size eighteen or so, huge with a German branding on the sole. Probably military boots would be my guess. From the size, I would imagine a pretty big man. Whoever it was must have lifted Mark's body into his truck. No lightweight could have pulled this off. Motive, not sure. Possibly robbery. My uncle was involved in the gem trade. That's about all I know."

For the next fifteen minutes I filled in some minor details, and he wrote down contact and location information. I was relieved when he let me stand up and walk out of the room. He then called in Contessa. Mark evidently was still at the hospital. Now I was alone in the front office. Time to do some thinking, and preparing... for the worst.

As a private investigator, I almost always have a shaky relationship with law enforcement. They like to control access and information. As an investigator, it's my job to gain as much data as I can. As a former cop, I know the realities on both sides. I don't necessarily want to withhold information, but I know only too well how evidence is used. In this case, finding the diamond was a major breakthrough. The problem was, we had no idea where the diamond had come from or who was involved. If we turned it in now, one of us would certainly be suspect. A gemstone like that doesn't just show up. Someone had to have stolen it, and there was certainly a person or organization missing it. I had seen for certain that there was at least one person willing to kill for it. My uncle and my cousin's wife were now deceased, and Mark and I were left for dead.

Contessa and my uncle were certainly in the trafficking flow of the jewel. It wouldn't be long before the next person in line was traced down. It became clear that we all were still in danger. It also was clear, at least for the perpetrators involved, that the dead should stay dead. Whoever did this should still think that Mark and I were dead. Mark, Contessa and I needed to disappear.

After 30 minutes had passed, Contessa and Deputy Pete came out of the room. Contessa looked beat, with perspiration apparent on her forehead. It was do or die time. Pete called me over to the table for a meeting. He said, "Thank you for answering our questions. You all have been through a major ordeal. Unfortunately, your cousin is not doing well. One of the deputies talked with him this morning at the hospital. He had a major breakdown after hearing about finding the body in the fire. My deputy had to call in help from the staff. He is suffering terribly from the bites, exposure, physical trauma and now the mental anguish. He's almost incoherent. I'm going to instruct deputy Chris to have him held over for at least a day for further observation at the hospital."

I spoke up, "He didn't look good last night. Thanks for setting that up. I'll take care of the family situation later." I went on, "As a former investigator, Pete, can I ask you a favor? Since we have no idea who did this or how many people may be involved, could you release some preliminary information to the local paper that two bodies were found in the fire and that they are believed to be Mark and Debbi Armstrong.

That is what the perp would expect the police to say. The fire inspectors would have found my burned body and concluded it was probably Mark's. It would also be a good idea to leave Mark's truck down the canyon for a few days until the case firms up. We don't want them to know that Mark has been found."

Pete nodded, "I'll see what I can do. I do agree it would be safer for all involved if the status quo went unchanged, at least in the mind of the public. I'll make sure that Mark is put in a private room at the hospital and listed with an alias. With the location of his truck, it will be necessary to bring in special tow equipment. We'll wait a few days to arrange to remove it."

"Good, that will give us all some breathing room. I do have another thing that I need to talk to you about."

"Go for it," He replied.

"I've only been in town a few days and have had a couple of run-ins with the local Fallbrook Police. Both encounters have been unprofessional. From what I've seen, I don't trust any of them. I understand they only have jurisdiction in the actual city limits of Fallbrook. I think it would be best if this information we just shared with you was not shared with them."

Pete smiled, "You have no idea how bad that relationship is, Trace. Even though our jurisdictions overlap, they treat us very poorly. Lots of politics in town. Two of those idiots have sketchy backgrounds and have had a number of run-ins with our guys. We try and stay out of town as much as possible. I'll tell you this. We are each on a different radio frequency, but we also share a joint county frequency that we usually communicate on. I'll try to keep things "in-house" for a few days and on our internal blotter, but I can't promise anything. Radio transmissions can be picked up by police scanners. As far as what has happened so far, they were just broadcast on our NC Sheriff channel."

Contessa spoke up, "Pete, do you think it is safe for me to go home or should I make other arrangements?"

Pete shook his head, "While I can't tell you what to do, Contessa, I'll tell you this. Where you live, it takes us on average at least twenty minutes to send a car. De Luz Road is over twenty miles long. With a killer on the loose, it would be best if you can stay with a relative or someone else. We only have a car through the area once a day."

"I'll help her out, Pete," I said. There is no way she is going back home till we get an idea who the perp is. How can I stay in touch with you?"

"Here is the NC dispatch number. Just ask for me. Shirley is the day operator. She'll know where I am. Please check in with me daily for the next week. We can use your help, Trace. Martino said you were one of the best. I usually don't like PIs, but Martino vouches for you. With all the crap that has gone down over the past two days, you're lucky to be alive. Please stay that way."

"I plan to," I said with a smile.

I told the deputy to tell Mark I would visit him at the hospital. Contessa and I walked back out to the Mercedes. I let her in the passenger side and started the car. As the motor roared to life, she turned and said, "Trace, I have a confession to make..."

CHAPTER 39

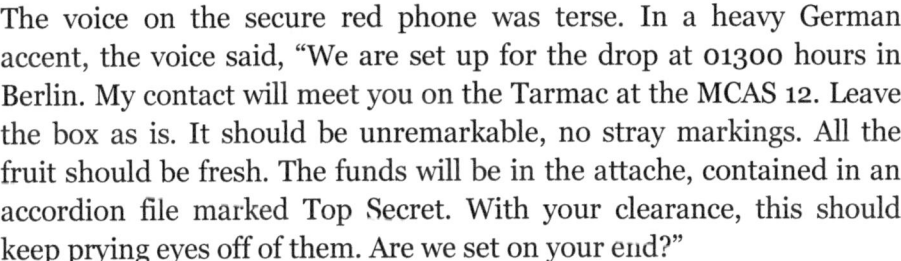

The voice on the secure red phone was terse. In a heavy German accent, the voice said, "We are set up for the drop at 01300 hours in Berlin. My contact will meet you on the Tarmac at the MCAS 12. Leave the box as is. It should be unremarkable, no stray markings. All the fruit should be fresh. The funds will be in the attache, contained in an accordion file marked Top Secret. With your clearance, this should keep prying eyes off of them. Are we set on your end?"

The colonel replied, "I am expecting delivery later today. Unfortunately, we had a courier succumb along the way. I have two replacements securing the merchandise. My flight from Pendleton leaves 0100 Friday morning."

"Has the original item been replaced?"

"Matched almost perfectly."

"Good, do not contact me again unless you are unable to deliver. I cannot guarantee a clear line without notice."

"Will do."

The line went dead. The colonel put the red phone back in its cradle and walked back to his desk. As he sat down, the door opened to his office. His secretary brought in his morning coffee and newspaper. He sat back, took a long sip and then almost choked. Right there on the front page was a picture of the Armstrong House. The headline read, De Luz house burns, two family members feared dead.

CHAPTER 40

Sometimes as a detective, you have to stop and take account of the situation. You can't go forward, without going backward first. For me, the last two days had been a blur. Here I was sitting in a borrowed car, albeit a nice one, hanging out with a woman I barely knew. I had a jewel in the heel of my shoe that was probably worth millions but had death written all over it. Somehow a calm came over me. Maybe it was just wishful thinking, or maybe it was the sometimes crazy woman sitting beside me, who had helped me recover from a horrific fire when any sane person would have turned me in to the cops.

As the engine purred, Contessa said, "I have a confession to make, Trace. When we were coming over here, I kept saying to myself that I ought to tell the cops everything that I knew. Spill the beans. Tell them about the Fallbrook Police, the boxes of avocados and that you had an enormous diamond in your shoe. For some reason, I didn't. I played along. Maybe it's because I've had an incredible time as your sidekick the last day and a half. I've been scared to death half the time when I wasn't in nurse mode or realizing I was laying in bed with a real handsome man.

I laughed, "I was kinda thinking the same thing. Trust is hard to come by in this business. I'll admit; I wasn't sure if I was going to get out of that office just now. Thank you. Besides hanging out with a beautiful woman like you can only improve my stature."

Smiling, she said, "So what do we do now, Mr. Armstrong. I called in sick today, and you have a large diamond we need to talk about."

"Let's get out of town," I said. There's a little Mexican restaurant in the neighboring city of Bonsall that I passed on the way up here. I didn't get any of that guacamole you were making earlier, so an early lunch sounds good to me. Have you ever been there?"

"I know it well. My friend Maria owns the place. I make batches of Mexican pastries for them once in a while. They have a quiet booth in the back where we can talk. You got a pen and paper in this thing?"

"Check in the glove box. Should be a pen and a small notebook."

I accelerated down Mission Blvd, trying to leave the encroaching town of 30,000 behind, if only for an hour or so. The two-lane road twisted through dry brown foothills, dotted with ancient Oak trees that were stronger than the many fires that had attacked them. I felt somehow akin to them, having survived yesterday's blaze. As the valley widened out, we were soon in the little berg of Bonsall, home to many small ranches and tree orchards.

El Rancho restaurant was set off on a frontage road. I parked around back, out of sight of the main drag. Entering, Contessa talked with Maria for a minute, and she led us to a table way in the back. Set up for four, we had enough room to spread out. On the table were large paper place-mats. I turned one over and pulled out the notepad and pen. Maria brought us some chips and guacamole and took our orders. The taco and enchilada plate fit the bill for me along with a couple of DosEquis beers to share.

Contessa sat across from me and turned the placemat sideways. Taking a pen out, I said, "Let's list out what we know so far, starting with the most obvious."

She said, "The elephant in the room is the diamond, obviously. It was contained in a box of Hess Avocados. I picked those up from the Fallbrook Farmers Market last week, the day before your Uncle Paul died."

"Was there a particular person you purchased them from?" I asked.

"We just do a trade. I usually have a couple of boxes of the Hass variety from Paul that I deliver, and pick up two Hess type from Max."

"Is it always the same person?"

"Most times it is Max or one of his kids. This time, Max mentioned that this batch was a special one that Paul had special ordered and that he needed it right away."

Nodding, I said, "So we can assume that Max has some knowledge of the transaction, whether or not he knew the contents."

"Correct. I've been picking things up from him since Paul's wife Catarina died. She used to handle deliveries for Paul."

"If something like a diamond was in one of these it seems like he would pick them up himself," I said.

"Paul got arrested for a DUI a while back and had a suspended license. He started having a problem with alcohol after Catarina died. At 68, he was a mess behind the wheel. In addition to drinking, he also had cataracts which damaged his eyesight and made it hard for his detail gem work that made him so popular. I was happy to pick them up. He paid me pretty well for odd jobs. I'm sure he trusted me a lot more than himself when it came to driving to town."

"So who is Max and where does he come from?"

"Seems to be an old friend of your uncle. He's based in San Diego down near the border. Last name is Heineman. Originally from the Chech Republic. Slight accent. Specializes in exotic items for the European community in the San Diego area. Certain kinds of fruit and avocados are the main items your uncle provided. A lot of specialized citrus. The coastal climate isn't conducive to their growth."

"So we have a long time friend of Paul's that trades fruits and vegetables through the Farmer's Markets. Seems legitimate. We are talking small batches, right?"

She nodded, "Really just a sideline. Never more than a few boxes. Mainly for some of the high-end restaurants in Hillcrest and Downtown."

Taking a pen in my hand, I replied, "Let's plot this out. So we know that the Avocado that contained the diamond came through Max from San Diego. It was delivered to you to give to Paul. So where would the fruit go from there?"

Contessa thought for a second, "Not sure exactly. Paul's main avocado business on his property is handled by a large conglomerate. Kind of a land rental agreement. They plant the trees and do the harvesting, and Paul gets paid. Paul's specialty business consists of a few dozen custom trees. More of a hobby than a real business. Most trading was done with the Farmer's Market people. However, I remember Paul had a few connections at a bar in Fallbrook. Military guys. Officer class. I remember him taking a box or two down there when I dropped him off. Out of Camp Pendleton. Probably for guys on the base or maybe officers at other bases. Paul had some very rare varieties. There are some real exotic chefs at the officer level that would love these varietals."

I laughed, "Talk about uncommon varieties, avocados that grow gems inside are really rare."

Resting my pen at a pivot point for a moment, I thought through the situation. Was this a one time deal, or had this been done before? Was Paul personally involved? What exactly did he know? The thought of my Uncle being part of a gem smuggling operation was a little disconcerting. I didn't know him or my cousin very well, but they always seemed above board.

I drew a circle with the pen, indicating the city of Fallbrook. Glancing at Contessa, I said, "So where was the diamond going from here? This thing has got to be hotter than hell. I'm not sure yet where it came from, but I would sure like to know where it was supposed to go."

Lifting her head, Contessa said, "I remember one of the guys who met Paul. I don't recall his name, but I do remember Paul calling him Colonel as he walked in the bar."

CHAPTER 41

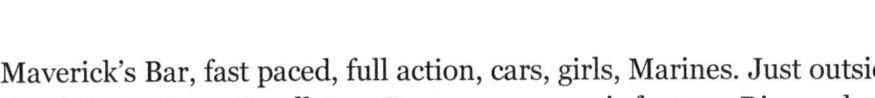

Maverick's Bar, fast paced, full action, cars, girls, Marines. Just outside North Gate, Camp Pendleton. Every young man's fantasy. Rice rockets, Porsche's, Mustangs, and Corvettes said it all. The place where everything happened in Fallbrook.

Like a scene out of the movie, Top Gun, Maverick's was a place where military life met civilian reality. This wasn't a dive bar; recruits need not apply. Officers only. Fast, hot, expensive.

One man ruled the officer class. The colonel had earned his reputation. Purple heart, tough looks, and one hell of a pilot. Colonel Rainer was what every Marine recruit wanted to be.

What the colonel wanted, the colonel got. No questions, no excuses.

So when the two men in uniform came up empty handed, action was required. Time was of the essence. Twenty-four hours or death. One box, one jewel, or hell itself would surely overtake life.

The two clowns in uniform had one choice, one option, one target. A small house on De Luz Road. The next link in the chain. Their last option. Or it was lights out... forever.

CHAPTER 42

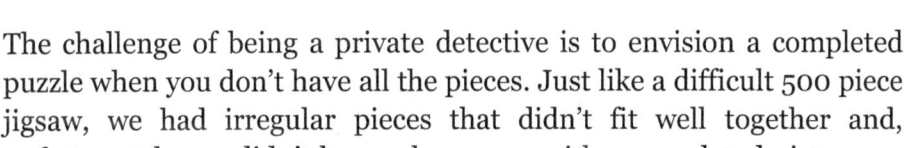

The challenge of being a private detective is to envision a completed puzzle when you don't have all the pieces. Just like a difficult 500 piece jigsaw, we had irregular pieces that didn't fit well together and, unfortunately, we didn't have a box cover with a completed picture on it to go by. However, a pattern was starting to emerge with the pieces we had.

Sitting in the back of the El Rancho Restaurant, Contessa and I were out of sight of the regular patrons. Finishing up lunch, I paid our bill and told Maria we would be working on a private project for a few minutes. She nodded approval and said she would not seat anyone nearby. As she left, I removed my shoes, undid the interior latches and removed the jewels. Putting the condiments and menu rack to the side of the table to block and view of what we were doing, I laid the stones together on one of the menu papers. Both over an inch long, their appearances were uncannily similar. The color and luminance were almost identical.

Contessa was amazed, "I can't believe how similar they are, Trace. Someone did a fantastic job on the copy."

I replied, "That's what my uncle was famous for. He made replica jewelry, using softer and substandard stones. From what my cousin was telling me, Fallbrook has small mines with quartz, topaz, and other crystalline stones. Paul mastered the art of the copy. Unlike cheap costume jewelry, his stones and settings were almost indistinguishable from the originals."

Contessa held the stones up to the light, "Absolutely incredible. So how in the heck did two people like us take possession of these two identical stones?"

"By total accident, I'm sure. The key is the large diamond. A stone as big as this one would only be found in a handful of places; probably a private collection or a museum. The other is an ingenious imposter stone, much lower quality, but enough of a lookalike to fool the uninitiated eye. While it wouldn't fool a gemologist, collector or even a run of the mill jewel thief, it might be close enough to avert suspicion for a short time in a display case, where you weren't able to hold it or examine it carefully."

"So what you are saying is that your uncle was involved in a two-way street. He made imposter jewelry, and provided the sub quality stones for a thief or other person that would replace the original with a fake."

I nodded, "I'm sure it wasn't his primary business, but think about it Contessa, this whole trafficking scheme is brilliant. You find a jewel you want to steal. You have Paul create a flawless copy, and then you ship them back and forth using something so mundane and familiar as fruits and vegetables that everyone consumes. No one would suspect anything."

An excitement came over Contessa's face. She said, "It's even better than that, Trace. As someone who immigrated from another country, I know how hard it is to get across borders with luggage and any type of jewelry. Customs agents are ruthless. Having a jewel like this in your suitcase would be suicide. Fruits and vegetables are brought in and shipped internationally all the time. Putting the jewel into an avocado is exceptionally clever. The huge interior seed is very dense. By hollowing it out, you would be able to get the fruit easily through an x-ray machine without detection."

"You're right," I said. "Paul evidently was a middleman. We know that you picked up the avocados from Max. So we know the next person down the chain source. Whether he was the thief or not is to be determined. For a thief, the avocado container gives a hands off delivery method and a deniable vehicle of transport in case they are caught. There may be people in this transport scheme that have no idea what they have in their possession."

"Someone unsuspecting like me," she said with a frown. "That stinkn' fruit could have got me killed."

"No kidding," I said. "We need to be very aware of what we are up against. The players in this puzzle may not know all the characters involved. It may have been setup that way on purpose. For example, whoever killed Paul, may not have any idea that you picked up the avocados for him."

"That person may be the same one who set the fire and killed Debbi and almost you and Mark."

"I think you are on to something. Whoever set the fire had torn the house and the shed up, looking for something. I originally thought it was jewels or money. But think about it, they left a box of minor jewels under the floorboards. If it was a box of avocados, where would they look for them?"

Contessa said, "Paul had a cooler in the back bedroom closet. It kept the fruit cool, but not near as cold as a refrigerator. I usually dropped off the boxes there when I did his cleaning. In fact, I had dropped off two boxes the week Paul died." All of a sudden a flow of tears came to her eyes, "My mistake with the boxes probably cost Paul his life. How could I have been so stupid."

I touched her arm, "Please don't be so hard on yourself. It sounds like the labels changed on the boxes you picked up. In any case, you had nothing to do with what happened. Let's think through this. Explain to me how the timetable works for the Farmer's Markets."

Her eyes seemed to brighten, "Fallbrook has two market days per week. There is one on Tuesday nights in town and another on Sunday morning. Both of these are held off of Main on a little side street which completely closes down. They have a lot of items and the market is about a block long."

I responded, "Sounds like a major town event."

"Actually quite big," she said. "Since there is a lot of agriculture in the area most of the local vendors and food trucks are at both events. Some remote vendors like Max come on both days, but the Sunday event is usually the largest. Since the market is on my way home from the hospital, I would pick up fruit on Tuesdays, drop it off at Pauls. I then would usually spend an hour or two helping him make dinner, clean up the dishes, and then do a light house cleaning. If he had items to go to the market, I would take them with me. I bake on Sunday mornings and deliver my pies, cakes, and other desserts along with his fruit to the Farmers Market in the afternoon before the vendors and restaurant people take off. We've been doing it this way for almost two years now."

"So you picked up two boxes of Avocados from Max on Tuesday night on your way home. One box contains the diamond . You put them in Paul's cooler. Paul has two boxes in there that are ready to go. One box contains the imposter stone. Not realizing the labels had changed, you picked up the ones with the diamond instead of the imposter as you leave. Paul delivers the phony box and things don't go well."

Contessa was in tears again, "Sounds about right. But then it gets real crazy. On Sunday, when you and your cousin came by, I find out that your uncle is dead. I've got two boxes of your uncle's Avocados to take to the Market. By the time we get done with our meeting, it's too late to go to the Sunday Market. Avocados have a limited shelf life. So they don't go to waste, I give one of the boxes to Mark along with a pie to take with him. I figured I would just keep the other box, which just happened to have the diamond in it."

"Oh man," I said, "You unknowingly hand Mark the item the perp at Paul's house was looking for. We get back there, Mark and I go to the shed, while Debbi takes the pie and avocados into the house and puts them in the cooler. The perp is probably in the house, most likely in the back bedroom. Debbi walks right into him. The rest is pretty easy to figure out. Debbi is dealt with, then as Mark walks in, he is hit over the head. He's on the floor as I walk in. The perp knocks me out. The perp now has the avocado box. He sets the house on fire to cover his tracks and get rid of witnesses."

Contessa was a wreck of guilt. Shaking her head she steadied and said, "I can't believe the luck on this. Let's continue this out, Trace. The way I see it he figures the house is isolated, and it will be some time before the fire department comes. The perp cuts open the fruit to make sure he has the diamond, only to find only plain fruit. He then goes back in and pulls Mark out of the house, the only one who might know where the diamond is. Tying him up and blindfolding him with duct tape, he puts him in the back of his own truck and drives off. Then pulling over on that isolated part of De Luz, he questions him. Not finding what he wants, he dumps the body over that long cliff and then pushes the truck over another cliff about a half mile down the road."

Nodding, I said, "Sounds logical. The fire burns the evidence. With no vehicle there, the fire department probably thinks it has been set by vagrants. It will be days or weeks until Mark's truck and body are found."

Contessa said, "So the perp is still out there somewhere without a diamond."

I nodded, "Probably madder than hell."

"No doubt," she said.

Standing on my good leg, I said, "It's time to flush out this perp."

"How are we going to do that?"

"We are going to set a trap... and use you as bait."

CHAPTER 43

"Mr. Armstrong, I've gone along with a lot of your crap in the last two days, putting my life on the line, but you are not using me for bait. What do I look like, a worm?"

"I'm sorry, Tessa, but we need to smoke this guy out, and you are the natural person to do it."

"So now you decide to call me Tessa... Mr. Armstrong, only my friends call me that. And I'm not putting my life on the line again for some stupid diamond that has nothing to do with me."

"I'm afraid, Tessa," I smiled, "that you are involved in this a lot deeper than I am. In fact, you really need me as a friend right now. Your adversaries know a lot about you, but nothing about me. They know where you live and probably know where you work. You can go to the police, but they already told you they can't protect you 24-7."

A slight smile came over her face, "So is this some kind of a protection racket you are offering Mr. Armstrong? Do you offer any guarantees?"

"Only if you let me call you Tessa."

"So are you saying you are a friend of mine?"

"A really good friend. One with benefits."

She laughed, "And what might those benefits be?"

"Well to start it offers round the clock protection till we catch the perp. It also includes a guy who is grateful for all you have done for him. Fixed his ankle, soothed his burns, and even made a diamond laced guacamole. One that is willing to put his life on the line for you. A friend like that is hard to find."

"But would this friend give me a hug when I need one. Like right now?"

"You better believe it," I said, opening my arms.

We stood there for a moment in a tight hug. Then she said, "Let's go, William Tracy Armstrong or should I say... friend."

Nodding, I said, "Let's do it."

"So how do we go about it?"

"Let's clean up here and find a thrift store."

"A thrift shop? What?"

"You'll see. We need to move up the chain to Maverick's Bar. Need to find the colonel. But we can't just have Trace and Tessa barge into a bar unprepared. We need a little misdirection."

"I like the sound of that. In fact, you can call me Miss Direction."

"All right Miss, let me just put the treasure back in my shoes and we can go."

Tessa said, "There is a large thrift store in Vista, a few miles down the road. They should have just about anything you need."

Within a few minutes drive, we were in a large strip mall. As we entered the huge store, I told her, "I need to look like off-duty military. You need to look like my wife or girlfriend. Think of the movie Top Gun."

"OK... Check out this rack, Trace. All military. Take your pick. Here's a fatigue shirt. Wow, a cool leather jacket."

"Those will work. How about a leather jacket for you?"

Looking on another rack she came up with a rather tight fitting one. "I like this one. Makes me look fast. Like I'm riding on the back of your motorcycle going a hundred and ten."

"Damn, woman, you look Indy car fast. You can ride in my Mercedes any time you wish. Let's finish off the look with some cool aviator sunglasses."

Picking up a pair, she slid them on my face. "Put on that Jacket, unzipped," she said. "Wow... just like you came off the flight line. Now we need some fast pilot call name for you."

"How about "Ghost," after what we saw last night. You never know when we might need to disappear."

"Ghost it is," she said laughing. "I like a guy who is transparent."

In ten minutes we were transformed. From civilian to off-duty military in a flash and for under fifty bucks. As a detective, I love thrift stores. We hopped back in the car and headed out.

"Let's go back to the hotel for a little while," I said. "I need to make some phone calls and prep for what we are going to do tonight."

"And what is it exactly that we are going to do?"

"We are going to offer the colonel a free gift at your house."

"Why my house?"

"Because the perp will be going there anyway."

"What? How do you know that?"

"It just makes sense. We saw the cops there this morning. You are the next link in the chain. We need to exploit that to our advantage."

"I'd rather leave my house out of it."

"I know you would, but it is what it is. You do have insurance don't you?"

"Yes, but I don't want to have to use it. What do you think will happen?"

"Not sure. We don't know the players... yet."

The conversation went quiet. In fifteen minutes we were back at the hotel. I parked behind the building, out of sight of the main road. Walking in the back door, we were soon back in my room. The bed was made, but everything else looked like it did in the morning when we left. I opened the drapes to let some light in. Standing in front of the mirror on the dresser, I tried different looks with the new clothes that we had purchased.

"What do you think, Tessa? Is the jacket better with a fatigue shirt or just a tee shirt?

"It's over 80 degrees outside, Trace. The tee is much better. Jeans are probably the way to go. Less formal. Try on the glasses."

The look was entirely believable, especially in the lower light of a bar. "Try on your jacket," I said.

She put it on, looked in the mirror, but shook her head. "Won't do," she said tartly. She went over to her suitcase, picked out a different top and disappeared into the bathroom. In a couple of minutes, she came back out. Her hair was pulled tightly back into a ponytail as she stood again in front of the mirror. The new top was much tighter and lower cut. The jacket accentuated her slim figure. She had applied red lipstick and eye shadow. The whole look was incredible.

"Holy Moly, you are going to have guys all over you, Tessa."

"You don't look bad yourself, Trace... er I mean Ghost."

"It's almost three; I need to make some phone calls. We need to get to the bar about 5 pm."

Tessa nodded, "Good, I'm going to get some shut eye for about an hour."

While Tessa napped, I called Martino. I got his answering machine and left him an underlying message about what had happened over the last 24 hours. I let him know that I would try him later that night. Then I put in a call to Janet, using my phone card, back in New York. There was no answer, so I left a short nondescript message, letting her know that I hoped that things were going well.

While Tessa slept, I walked up to the front desk. Talking with the owner, I let her know that I was expecting a couple of messages and that I would appreciate it if anyone was looking for me, that they not give out my room number. She agreed.

When I got back, Tessa was up. Visibly nervous, she paced back and forth.

"I don't know if I can pull this off, Trace. I'm just a conservative nurse, not a fast riding biker chick."

"Don't worry, the conversation should be short. What I do need to know is there any place on your street where we can watch your house without being seen?"

"The house next door is vacant right now. The owners are away on a European vacation. The key is hidden in their electrical box. We can hold up there if needed. I keep an eye on it while they are gone."

"Perfect. How about a place to hide the car?"

"There is an ivy-covered chain link fence between the property. We can pull the Benz into their driveway. With all the trees and bushes, you wouldn't be able to see it."

"The next question is critical. When my uncle went into town to go to Maverick's, what time did he go?

She thought for a second, "I know he usually went after seven and many times would return after midnight. When he lost his license, at first he took a taxi, and then he snuck out with his truck, staying on the back streets. The only reason I know is a friend of mine at the hospital would see him coming and going when he worked the night shift. He was aware that I often took care of him and was worried about him getting home, especially in that old truck."

"So we can guess that the "Colonel" would come in after seven."

"Pretty safe bet. The Pendleton guys get off work, have dinner and then come over for drinking. It can get pretty rowdy after nine or so. Once the alcohol starts flowing, it gets deafening."

"So here is the plan. We go in just after they open at 5. I leave a message for the colonel and then we hang out at your neighbor's house. If the bait works, we should see some activity at your home before dark."

"Trace, I don't like this. I don't want people trashing my house. Shouldn't we involve the sheriff?"

"Believe me Tessa, I would bring them into the story in a minute if I knew we could trust them. We don't know the players. By entering the known turf of my uncle, hopefully we can draw them out."

"So if they do come out, then what?"

"We play it by ear. We see who comes and what they do. Your neighbor has a phone don't they?"

"Sure, but then what?"

"We just call in the sheriff and catch them red handed."

"All right, smart guy. You make it sound so easy. I don't like it, but I also would like to get back to normal."

"Before we go, can you call the hospital and check on my cousin? I hope he's doing OK. Check and see if we can talk with him. I'd like to know a couple of things."

"Sure, give me a minute."

Tessa made the call and found that Mark was given a sedative and put on an IV drip.

Tessa said, "His vitals are better. They may release him tomorrow. For tonight, he's out like a light."

"Oh well, probably for the best," I said.

Looking at my watch, it was now after four. "Where is the bar exactly?"

"It's off Ammunition Drive, near the North Gate. There is a shopping center down the street where you can park."

Giving her a high five, I said, "Let's roll, Tessa."

She slapped me back, straightened her jacket, and we headed out. A few minutes in the car and we were in the shopping center. It was now or never.

Walking down the sidewalk, I said, "Attitude on."

We walked up, and I opened the wooden door to let her go first. The bar was almost empty as our eyes adjusted. There were a couple of guys at the bar and two more at one of the tables. Walking up to the bar, I said to the bartender, "When will the colonel be in?"

The guy looked at me and then over to Tessa. "Who wants to know?"

"Names Tracy, Bill Tracy. But the colonel knows me as Ghost."

"Who's the woman?" he asked.

"Tessa. A friend of mine. She's cool."

"Well Ghost, he usually rolls in after seven. What you need?"

"I've got something he's looking for," I said.

Eyes around the bar were now on us.

The bartender said, "What might that be?"

"He got the wrong delivery the other day. I've got the proper merchandise now."

Why don't you just give it to me?"

"I don't have it yet. He can pick it up at eight. Out on De Luz Rd. 247 De Luz. First house on the frontage road."

"What am I, a messenger service?"

"Just let him know. There might be a couple of bucks in it for you."

I threw a twenty down on the bar. I turned to leave.

I felt a hand on my shoulder. Big ugly dude had stood up from the bar. Spun me around. "Why don't you just give it to me right now," he said with a drunken smile.

I pushed him back. He stumbled some and then grabbed my collar, "Hand it over asshole."

Tessa looked at the fat menace and said in a loud voice, "Hey asswipe my Heckler and Koch says Back Off." With that, she reached into her jacket and pulled out the handle of a gun. The big man's grip instantly released. We walked out the door.

CHAPTER 44

"Let's get the hell out of here while we still can," I said as we exited quickly out of the bar.

"Agreed," said Tessa. "This old pellet gun comes in handy sometimes."

"Pellet gun... you sure had me fooled and that big guy too. When did you put that in your jacket?"

"When I was getting dressed. I've been in enough situations like that that I know it speaks loud. Real loud. The fact that it happens to look like a true H&K makes it all the better."

"Have you ever had to fire it?" I asked.

"Not in a long time... thankfully. Last time was in Belize. Really drunk guy came after me. One shot to the balls was all it took. His voice was a couple octaves higher for a while."

"So how did we do in there?" I asked.

"Believable, Ghost. With the jacket, patches, and your attitude, you nailed it."

"Now we get to see if we get a response. Keep an eye out behind us. Make sure we aren't being followed."

Tessa said, "Let's cut through the back door of the supermarket. Anyone following will have a hard time navigating those tight aisles without being seen. We don't want any of those guys to know what we are driving. Not like we are driving a nondescript Chevy or Ford."

"Great idea. A half dozen ears were listening to us in there. Time will tell who has a connection with the big guy. We should get to your neighbor's house right away. Get the car out of sight. I'm guessing the Colonel has some underlings."

After a coordinated maze through the store, we exited out the front. The blue Mercedes gleamed in the early evening sun as we got back in.

"How's the leg, Trace? That was a lot of walking. That limp seems to be almost gone."

"Tightening that brace for me before we left helped. The burn still hurts like hell, but with all the adrenaline I hardly noticed it. However, if something hits it, all bets are off. Pushing the clutch pedal is a challenge. Just as long as I don't have to run, I'll be OK."

"Good," she said. As your nurse, I don't want you falling off the wagon."

I revved the car slowly through the gears on Mission and soon we were turning left onto De Luz. The housing tracts disappeared, and Tessa's frontage road soon appeared on the right. Running Parallel to De Luz on the right side, the road was about a quarter mile long, with about a dozen half acre lots on the right. Thankfully the whole area had a lot of bushes and trees which hid most of the homes in a long cluster of green foliage.

Passing the first house, which was Tessa's, I backed into her neighbors driveway, pulling about 50 feet back, hiding the car completely from passersby on the road. Not knowing what to expect, I wanted to make sure we had a clear exit path. The front of the house had an old split rail fence along the street, with a large grassy yard behind it. The main driveway was 100 feet long, ending at the unattached garage. Up towards the street was a circular drive which ended in a second driveway on the other side of the yard. Gave me a little more confidence of a quick exit.

Leaving the car unlocked, we entered her neighbor's house with the help of a hidden key. The neighbors weren't due back for another week, so we had the house all to ourselves.

"So is there a place in this house where we might have a view of your house and driveway?" I asked.

Tessa responded, "The dining room should fit the bill. It's high enough and back far enough to have a view through the bushes. We can set up high chairs from the bar to give us a little better vantage point through the side window."

"OK, good. How about if we have to get into your yard. Is there a way to do that without going all the way up to the street?"

"There is about a six-inch space between the front chain link fence and the block wall. The block goes all the way back to the garage. I have been known to fit through that at times, but it is tight. With that leg of yours, you may have a problem."

"Good, we may have to get closer depending on the situation."

"Like what type of situation. I'm not liking this, Trace."

"We need to be able to see and hear what's going on. You can stay behind if you want to."

"And leave you with that bum leg... no way."

"Is there a way into your house without going through the front door?"

"There is a back door from the kitchen. Leads out to the garage. You can see that entry from the front door. There is also a side door that was added to the back bedroom when the previous owner rented out a room. You can see it from this side of the house. Small steps lead up to it. Separate lock and key. Interior door has a deadbolt on it to lock it off from the rest of the house. If I'm going over there, that would be the best way in. But I don't like that idea."

"What's in that room?" I asked. "Can we maneuver?"

"It's a storage area, but we should be able to move around OK."

"Last question. Do you have a gun?"

"Only the pellet gun. Not much range. Certainly wouldn't kill someone."

"So under no circumstances will we try and engage the enemy... whoever they are."

"I like that, Mr. Armstrong. Best thing you've said all night. Military guys are usually pretty good shots."

So now we sit and wait.

****

At 7 pm the evening shadows were long. Tessa and I sat high, looking through the side window of the neighbor's dining room. In the distance headlights came around the sweeping corner of De Luz Road. The car slowed and then turned into Tessa's driveway. It was an old Crown Vic with the logo of the Fallbrook Police on the side. Two guys got out and walked up the drive to the house. I walked over to the dining room window and slid it open on its tracks silently so we could hope to hear any conversation. Sitting back from the window so we wouldn't be seen, it was quickly apparent that these were the same two cops that had given me a ride the night before. The big guy named Patrick. His sidekick named Raditz. Big and little. Or should I say... Enormous and little. I could see the big man step on the porch followed by the other guy. They knocked loudly, "Anyone home?" they barked. I could hear Patrick say, "Do you think that Nurse bitch is back from work yet?"

Raditz replied, "Her truck is still the same place it was this morning. She isn't here. Lights are off. Probably working one of those long shifts."

"Good," said the big guy, "Break the door in. Got to find that box that the Colonel wants."

Tessa stood and exclaimed, "Those bastards are breaking into my house. The nerve."

Nodding, I said, "Just be glad you aren't there."

In the distance, we could hear breaking glass and a huge smash as Patrick put his huge foot on the door frame. Whap.. we could hear it slap back as it flew open. They were in Tessa's house. Lights came on, and we could see shadows going past the side window of the front bedroom.

Tessa said, "They probably won't be able to get into the back bedroom without going around. That interior door is unyielding and has a key lock both sides."

Sure enough, after a few minutes, Raditz came out the front door and went around to the side door. Pulling his gun out, he cracked the window pane and reached in to release the lock. He rumbled around for a few minutes, and then he yelled out, "Nothing here. The interior door is locked with a key. I'll come back around."

We could see him march back around. Just then there was another pair of headlights approaching. An open wheel jeep pulled up behind the Crown Vic. A huge guy jumped out. Probably over 6 foot 7, he walked up to the house. In a strong, deep voice he said, "You assholes here?"

Raditz voice replied, "In the kitchen, Colonel."

So now the colonel himself was in the house. He had taken the bait. And true to form, he had showed up a half hour early, preceded by his stooges from the Fallbrook PD. Unfortunately, as he walked in he slammed the front door. The conversations became muffled. I felt like just calling the sheriff's office, but we didn't have anything on them yet. They could certainly explain away why they were there. Looking at Tessa, I said, "Unfortunately, we are going to have to go over there if we hope to hear their conversation. You up for it?"

She shook her head, "Are you sure you just can't call the sheriff detective we talked with this morning?"

If we show up with the sheriff, those assholes would have us in jail faster than you can say lying son-of-a-bitch. Remember, the sheriff's department has a hands-off relationship with them. This house is technically in Fallbrook and their jurisdiction."

"Agreed, and now that we know they are involved, we would probably be in a lot of danger."

"How about calling your friend, Martino?"

"Too far away. Besides, he often works late. I'll touch base with him later."

"How about calling 911?"

"No use. The call would be routed to their dispatch."

"Shit, Trace, I don't want to go over there, but we need to know what is going on."

I said, "It's getting dark now. The shadows will cover our tracks. Let's just go over to that side room. The Fallbrook guys already searched it.

The outside door is wide open. If we are quiet, we should be OK. You just want me to go by myself?"

Shaking her head, she said sternly, "Let's go. We're wasting time."

With that, we walked quietly out the front door of the neighbors house, behind the Mercedes to the opening in the fence. It took us a minute to get through, especially with my brace catching on the chain link. Thankfully the darkness had taken over, now that the sun was behind the hills. With just a few steps we were climbing the stairs to the side room. Walking in, the room was very dark. Tessa guided the way. She propped herself by the side of the interior door; I took the other side. We could hear the voices clearly now.

Hearing the refrigerator door open, we heard Colonel say, "This is what I'm looking for you idiots. A box of freaking avocados. How hard was it for you to find this and bring it to me."

Raditz said, "We looked all over. Lots of boxes but none like this. We brought you the box of gems. Isn't that what you are looking for?"

The colonel raised his voice, "I'm looking for a diamond. Get me a knife and I'll show you where it is."

We could hear the rustling of drawers and the clink of silverware.

"Patrick, you fat ass, you take the knife like this and slice each one open. Watch."

We could hear the knife hit the counter repeatedly. One, two, three...

The colonel yelled, "Five down, the stone better be in this one or you guys are dead. What the hell am I paying you for?"

The knife rang out, and there was silence for a moment. It was apparent that no stone was there. We could hear things being slammed around. Then the colonel said, "Well look at this ... avocado pieces in the sink. It looks like you two have already found our diamond."

Raditz pleaded, "No way sir, we just got here. Look those pieces have turned brown."

The colonel said, "You expect me to believe that? Empty your pockets."

Clinking could be heard as change hit the floor. "Nothing there you sons of bitches. Go outside and open your car. You probably have the stone hidden there."

"No sir," Patrick yelled. "We don't have your diamond."

"You lying son-of-a-bitch. Get outside and open your car."

We could hear the front door slam open. To see what was going on, Tessa and I exited the room and peered around the side of the house. The front doors of the car were open. The colonel pulled all the contents out of the glove box. Then he had the guys open the trunk.

"That stone better be here. Pull out that spare tire."

We could hear clinking as the jack was loosened and the spare tire removed.

"Still nothing," said the colonel. "Lift the carpeting."

The colonel then just let out a huge yell. He backed up, pulled a revolver from his pocket and fired two shots. Pop-pop. Two cops dead. He then hoisted the bodies in the trunk, pulled the car keys out, and slammed the lid.

Looking at Tessa, I murmured, "Holy shit, Go, let's get in the car and get far away from here. That bastard is crazy."

She started to run in the darkness. I turned to run back to the fence, but I tripped over a sprinkler head and let out a yelp as my burned leg hit the ground. The colonel searched in the darkness for the noise and then saw my limp form getting back up. He yelled out, "Who are you?"

I started to run as fast as my bum leg would carry me. Looking back, the flash of a gun firing lit up the darkness as a bullet ricocheted off the block wall in front of me. Now I needed to become very small. Six inches small.

CHAPTER 45

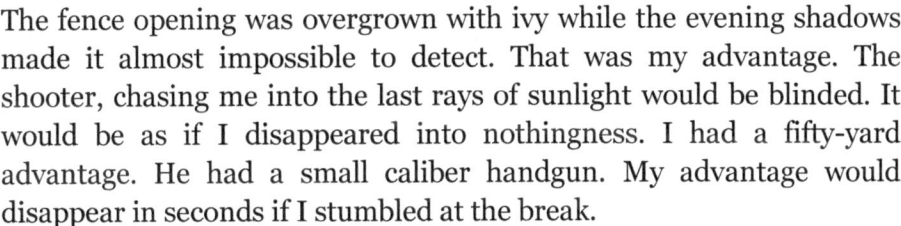

The fence opening was overgrown with ivy while the evening shadows made it almost impossible to detect. That was my advantage. The shooter, chasing me into the last rays of sunlight would be blinded. It would be as if I disappeared into nothingness. I had a fifty-yard advantage. He had a small caliber handgun. My advantage would disappear in seconds if I stumbled at the break.

Reaching the slim six-inch corridor to freedom, I had two choices; Lead with the bum leg or follow. Coming through before, I had entered with my good leg while my braced leg trailed. The brace had hung up on the chain link, stopping me cold. This time, I would lead with it. Facing the edge of the block wall, I thrust my left leg through. It hit solid ground. Sucking my gut in, I turned my head to view the Mercedes. It was six feet away. Tessa was entering the passenger side. With my hands on both sides of the wall edge, I swung my body through in one complete motion.

Another flash of light, caught in the corner of my eye, meant another bullet was coming my way, but I could hear it hit the side of the wall. Miss. Safety lay ahead if I could just make the door of the Benz. Twisting on my bad ankle, I swung my good leg around. Six steps and the door was opened. In a blur, I had entered the low-slung coupe. Key in hand, the engine fired, the clutch engaged and the car sped forward. Turning on the headlights, I hit the street and turned right, heading out of town down a long and dark De Luz Road.

It didn't take long for the colonel to realize what was happening. Doubling back, he got in his open cabin Jeep and took off after us. Revving through the gears, I had made some great headway, but soon his headlights were behind us. We had the advantage on the curves; he had the benefit of adrenaline. With two cops dead, everything was lost, if he didn't catch us.

The last futile rays of sunshine were dissolving into the darkness. De Luz is a dark and lonely road at night, and even with the high beams on, it was hard to see very far ahead. Colonel Rainer had the advantage, having driven this road with the military many times before. As I slowed for a big sweeper, I saw a flash behind in my mirror and heard the ping of a bullet off of the sheet metal. Handguns are notoriously inefficient weapons at much distance. His skill with firearms was apparent with his accuracy in hitting a moving vehicle.

Tessa yelled out, "I heard that one hit, Trace. What are we going to do?"

My heart pounding, I replied, "I'm going to try and stay ahead of him. Do you still have that pellet gun with you?"

She said, "It's in my jacket pocket, but it's got no range. I'm not sticking my head out with that."

"Best thing then is to keep your head down," I yelled over the screaming engine. "How far does this road go?"

"It winds around for over twenty miles before it exits into Temecula. No safe place to pull off."

"Shit, that bastard has the advantage. All he has to do is knock us from behind on one of these curves."

"Drive like you stole it then, Trace."

Just then the headlights came closer as we neared a sharp turn. Another bullet pinged off the car. Tessa ducked down, almost into my lap.

"Trace," she yelled, "is this a gun under the seat?"

"I forgot. Yes, it is. It's a nine millimeter Beretta. The FBI agents gun."

Reaching under my seat, she pulled it out and said, "Heavy sucker."

As the car rolled around another corner, I glanced over at it. "Looks like it has a clip in it. Do you know how to undo the safety?"

"Yes, it's right here."

"Good, undo it and pull the slide back to put a bullet in the chamber."

I could hear it click, "Now it's ready to go." I said. "Have you ever fired a gun like this before?"

"No, just small caliber stuff."

"Nine millimeters have a wicked kick. You'll need two hands."

"OK, what should I do?"

"No way will you be able to aim it backward. Don't even try. The kick will snap your wrist, and you'll lose it."

"Are you going to stop?"

"No way. He is too good a shot. Is there a straight part of the road ahead?

"About a mile up, just before the bridge over the river. There is a passing lane."

"OK, I'm going to slow a little to let him get right behind us. Then I'll quickly pull to the left and hit the brake slightly. The surprise will put us right next to him. You'll need to be ready. Aim for his torso. Bigger target."

"So I'm going to shoot the guy?"

"It's either him or us. We'll only have a second until he can react."

Nervously she said, "I've never shot anyone before. I don't like this Trace."

"You saw what he did to those cops. No hesitation. You're our best hope."

"Why don't I duck and you fire the gun?"

"Too much kick and I won't be able to aim. Sure miss."

"All right, you talked me into shit again. The passing lane is just ahead."

"Lower your window. Get ready. Both hands on the gun. When he is beside us, put both arms out, brace them on the window sill, and pull the trigger multiple times. His body is out in the open. Fire for his torso."

As we climbed a little grade, I could see the long straight road ahead. The jeep was about fifty feet behind. Downshifting to third gear, I slowed the car slightly. The taillights were now on our bumper. Suddenly there was a smash as he hit us from behind. Tessa screamed.

"Get ready," I said, accelerating slightly. Looking ahead the large metal bridge was in view. I'm going to count down from three.

Three

Two

One

I turned the wheel left and hit the brakes slightly. The jeep was now right beside us. The colonel had his gun in his right hand. Before he could react, I yelled, "NOW."

One loud blast, then two, then three.

Tessa screamed, "I missed."

The colonel had ducked his head.

"Fire again," I screamed.

Looking up, the bridge was just ahead.

The colonel moved his right arm in front of his body. He squeezed the trigger and fired at us.

As I saw the flash of his gunfire, I turned the wheel of the Mercedes hard to the right. There was a massive explosion of sparks. I hit the Jeep solidly with the wheel, as Tessa's gun fired again.

In my side vision, I could see the Jeep veer slightly right. It went over the concrete curb leading to the bridge, and the vehicle was sent violently right as the curb caught the front wheels.

The next second was a blur as I watched the Jeep hit the bridge railing and go airborne off the side of the concrete embankment and crash somewhere below in the darkness.

As I slowed to a stop, I looked over at Tessa.

She had a stream of blood running down her forehead.

CHAPTER 46

"Damn good driving, mister. You probably saved our lives with that move," she said.

"Did you know you have blood running down your forehead?" I asked.

"Really." Rubbing her hand on her hairline, she said, "Ow, the bullet must have grazed my head. The guy was a good shot."

"No kidding, thought we were goners with that right to left move. I saw the muzzle flash and just reacted. Thankfully this old Benz is heavier than it looks."

Tessa held the gun in front of her, "You weren't kidding about the gun. This Beretta is a bitch to shoot. Don't know if I hit him or not. Everything happened so fast."

Nodding, I said, "Did you see that Jeep sail? Not sure if anyone could survive that?"

"Doubt it," she said. "Between the bullet and the hard landing, he's probably in hell where he belongs. But we ought to check. "

Parking on the side of the road on the bridge, we both got out. It was fully dark now. De Luz has no street lights, but there was a sliver of a moon. About 30 feet below we could barely make out the shape of the jeep. There appeared to be no movement.

"Let's go back to your neighbor's house and call the sheriff. With two dead cops, a whole bunch of people will be out on this one. The fact that their car is in your driveway automatically implicates you, unfortunately."

"Agreed. I'm just glad I wasn't there alone. Bad as this has been, your help probably saved my life. Appears that any witnesses were taken out. One thing for sure, no way in hell do I want to stay there tonight. In fact, I don't know if I ever want to go back there."

"Don't blame you. Hard to say how they will react to this whole episode. We've got bullet holes in Mercedes, but I don't know if we have any eye witnesses. If they find his gun, that will go a long ways to proving what we say is true."

"How do we play this?" she asked.

"Just tell them what happened tonight. Keep the diamond and the bar scene out of it. We don't know the actual thief yet or who the intended buyer was. We just happened to stumble in the middle of this mess and still may be targeted."

"How long is this mess going to go on?

"Hopefully not much longer. I do want to check a couple of things before the cops come tonight. Let's get back to your neighbor's house and make the call."

Within ten minutes, we were pulling back into Tessa's neighbors' yard. She went into their living room, while I walked back over to her house. The car and the yard looked just like it did before. Evidently the other neighbors down the block had not heard the commotion. Walking across the grass, I looked down at the gravel driveway. Right where the jeep was parked, bright as day in the muddy dirt next to the lawn was a number of footprints. Footprints from a German Panzer boot. Just like the prints we found outside of my uncles' house.

****

Staying on the grass, I walked around the back of Tessa's property. Didn't want to disturb the crime scene so I stayed outside. Looking in the kitchen window, I saw avocado pieces and a box strewn all over the floor and counter. They were definitely after the box of avocados. I felt pretty confident that we had found our perps that had torched my uncle's house. Footprints, hired labor, avocados. It all fit.

I returned to Tessa's neighbor's house. She had called work and arranged for another day off from work. She said, "Mark should be able to come home tomorrow afternoon. His vitals are looking better, but they have him on an antibiotic drip, so he doesn't get an infection from all the bites. It appeared that he had teeth marks from a coyote, so he'll need to get checked for rabies."

I replied, "The rabies tests are the worst. I had to go through one of those with the Highway Patrol. Dog bite, no rabies shot. I never want to do that again."

Looking over at her, I put my hand on her shoulder. "Are you ready for this call? Can't guarantee what's going to happen. While I know you didn't have anything to do with this, having people break into your house looking for something may make you a suspect. I suggest we play this very low key. We don't mention anything about a diamond. We may have to backtrack later, but I would feel a lot better if we see if we can find out more about the actual robbery and get Martino involved before revealing or turning in the diamond."

She nodded. "After all this, I don't want to go to jail on top of it."

I reiterated, "Just be aware that law enforcement gets real crazy when one of their own is shot. I know. I used to be one. With two guys down, your house will be a media circus."

"Make the call, Trace. But I have one favor. Can I stay with you tonight at the hotel? That is, if I'm not in jail."

"No problem. In fact, I wouldn't have it any other way. I don't want to let you out of my sight until we're sure this is over.

I picked up the phone and called it in, dialing the direct dispatch line that connected to Deputy Pete. I gave him a quick overview. Within minutes, we had sheriff cruisers from all over North County on the street in front of Tessa's. Soon there was an ambulance and a coroner's wagon. TV vans then pulled up as the bodies were removed from the car. The whole area was lit up like a sound stage.

Another group of deputies drove down De Luz to the bridge. Deputy

Pete came in his cruiser and met with us next door. He had a couple of detectives inspect the Mercedes, take pictures and remove bullet fragments. We went inside and went through the usual interrogation procedure. At first with individual statements and then together.

Just then Pete's walkie talkie went off. Attempted carjacking on De Luz Road...

CHAPTER 47

As the 9-millimeter bullet ripped through his left shoulder, Rainer fired across his chest with his right hand. The 22 caliber gun kicked violently, shooting high and causing him to lose grip. The old Mercedes erupted across his lane, crashing hard into the jeep's front fender, ripping the steering wheel out of his left hand. The next few seconds were like a slow-motion movie. His vehicle veered past the outer curb of the river bridge, causing the left front wheel to turn to the right violently. Before he could react, the jeep was airborne over the side of the embankment, sailing slowly downward into blackness. All was quiet for a split second before the vehicle slammed into the cliff, once, twice, and then all forward movement was forcefully stopped by a large boulder.

Ejected forward, the colonel's chest hit the steering wheel, his head violently smashing into the windshield. Death averted by a very stiff shoulder belt. As the open cab vehicle came to rest in the shallow water of the river bed, Rainer was still for a long minute. Regaining consciousness, overwhelming waves of pain engulfed him. Blood gushed from his shoulder wound and dripped from numerous facial cuts. Unfastening the seat belt, he tried to move. He could barely breathe, the agony of broken ribs. He sat in abject darkness, the front of the jeep completely demolished. In the distance, he heard the sound of the Mercedes driving away.

Assessing his situation, he had only one goal in mind. To get back to the police car, with the dead cops in the trunk. If they were found, the game was over. Dump the car, dump the bodies, his alibi as an upstanding Colonel of the United States Marines would be strong.

First task: Stop the bleeding. Standing slowly along the shallow bank of the river, he removed his blood drenched camo shirt, and felt the wound. In and Out. Top of the left shoulder. Lucky. He removed a first aid kit from under the seat and unwound a roll of gauze bandage. Winding the stretchy material under his armpit and tightly over his shoulder, he secured the bandage with strong tape. Bleeding slowed.

He rinsed his shirt in the river, rung it out, and put it back on, feeling cold in the night air. Picking up his leather jacket that had piled behind the passenger seat, he put it on slowly, the intense pain of his shoulder offset with the warmth of the soft material. First problem solved.

Now he needed a weapon. The 22 had flown from his hand during the crash and landed somewhere in the river. Futile to try and find it in the dim moonlight. He had a stored weapon in the back. 9mm military issue Glock. Opening the rear hatch, he secured the gun and found stored ammunition in a side compartment. Loading the bullets into the clip, he tested the action. Ready to go. Second problem solved.

Now he faced a thirty-foot climb to the road. Testing his battered legs, he took slow, shaky steps forward in the darkness. Painful, but still able to walk, his eyes adjusted to the moonlit night. He saw that it would be better to walk along the river bank and under the bridge. There was a maintenance walkway on the other side. Climbing the dirt access path he was soon on the side of De Luz Rd, headed back towards the house and the police car. Third problem, solved.

Now he needed a way to get there before law enforcement could arrive. He thought to himself. The assholes in the Mercedes will certainly go back to the house where they started from. Call the sheriff. Expect me to be dead. I need to kill them, take the Fallbrook car and dump it. But how to get there in time?

The answer came around the corner right then. A man in a Buick was driving from Temecula to Fallbrook. The colonel walked out into the middle of De Luz and waved the car down. Rainer walked up to the driver's window and motioned him to put it down. As the window clicked down, the man asked, "What's going on?"

Pulling the Glock from his back pocket, the colonel aimed it at the man's face and said, "Out of the car, now."

The man looked surprised and went to open the door. In a quick move, he pushed the door out hard while hitting the gas. As the car roared forward, the door hit Rainer in the knees, knocking him to the pavement. Instinctually, he rolled on his stomach and fired at the Buick. The bullet hit the rear window, shattering it, but the car continued down the road.

Maybe the next one will be better.

He continued walking down the road. Very little traffic at night. Each minute that ticked off lowered his chances of success. His thinking became muddled.

Maybe I should go the other way. Back to the base. Go over the back fence, off De Luz. Get a night flight to Europe before the shit hits the fan. Disappear. Best way to do that would be to stop a car going either way. Need to go five miles North. Get over the parameter fence. Use call box on the base. Midnight flight. Executive clearance.

The colonel decided that whatever way a car approached, he would stop it. Decision made. Shoot first, ask questions later. He walked toward town for over five minutes in the darkness, staying to the side of the road in the shadows. In the distance from town came a pair of headlights. Out of sight behind a tree, the colonel put the gun in his back waistband. As the lights neared, he walked slowly out into the road, putting his left hand up to stop the car. There were two people inside the white sedan. Two would have to die.

As the car pulled up closer, it suddenly stopped, and the doors flung open. Shit—undercover cops. Two guns were aimed directly at him. "Put up your hands, sheriff's department." the driver yelled.

The element of surprise was now necessary. Be smart, play dumb. "What's going on?" Rainer yelled back.

"Put up your hands. I'm not going to ask you again."

Rainer acted like he couldn't hear them. "What did you say?"

The deputy on the passenger side ventured out from behind the door, handcuffs in one hand, gun in the other. He shouted, "Put your hands in the air. Don't move."

Rainer put a hand up to his left ear, acting like he couldn't hear. "What?"

The guy from the passenger side approached carefully, gun drawn, yelling now, "I said, hands in the air."

Rainer played dumb. "What was that? Did you say on the ground?" With that, he got down on one knee.

The deputy walked closer, as Rainer got down on his other knee. Rainer said, "I'm getting down."

The cop said, "Freeze right there."

Rainer again put his hand up to his ear."What? I don't understand. Did you say facedown?" He then pretended to get down on his left hand, as his right hand went behind his waist, grabbed his gun, and brought the gun up into a firing position as he rolled on the ground to the right. He started firing in the direction of the closest deputy as he rolled over again in the glow of the headlights. One bullet hit the cop in the leg causing great pain. The driver's side deputy started firing, but the fast moving Colonel made a hard target. Rainer rolled and then popped an elbow up to fire at the other cop. Bullets from the Glock smashed into the driver's door. Surprised by the sudden move the driver's side deputy ducked. Rainer jumped to his feet and started to run across the road to the safety of darkness in the trees.

He almost made it.

The avocado truck coming at high speed around the corner didn't even see him as the colonel was pitched high into the air.

Lights out.

CHAPTER 48

Tessa's house was a media and police circus. After about 90 minutes, Pete met with us privately. He said, "The two Fallbrook cops were killed with small caliber gunshots to the back of the head, just like you described. The bullets appeared to match the 22 caliber slugs removed from the Mercedes trunk. The detectives called in from the bridge on De Luz. They have a high powered tow truck on the way, but they did find the jeep and photograph it. Blood was all over the interior, but the driver survived.

Tessa spoke up, "Oh no, you mean the colonel still roams the earth? How could that be?" Tessa pointed to the graze wound on her forehead, "That guy almost killed Trace and me tonight. You can see where this blood is; he didn't miss by much. I'm not going to sleep well until that killer is dealt with."

Pete replied, "It appears that his seat belt saved him. His giant size and muscular build probably didn't hurt. Unfortunately for him, he didn't survive a shoot out with our deputies."

"What? He's dead?" I asked.

"He tried to carjack our undercover car. That's after he had unsuccessfully attempted to carjack a soldier who happened to be driving along De Luz tonight. Bad luck on his part. Had he picked another car, he might have got away.

Tessa spoke up, "I'm feeling better already."

Unfortunately, he shot one of our deputies in the leg. He'll be OK. Pulled an old deaf trick on our guys. Smart guy, until he ran in front of a speeding avocado truck coming around the corner. Put his lights out forever.

I shook my head at the irony of that. I said, "That's a shame about your deputy. That guy was ruthless. No conscience. I did notice the bootprints from the colonel on the driveway tonight appear to be the same as at my uncle's house. We seem to have fleshed out three perps. Two cops involved and one Marine Colonel. I'd heard bad things about the Fallbrook cops, but tonight confirmed it."

Pete said, "Our detectives are working on a motive, but it appears to have something to do with precious gems, possibly diamonds. Not surprised about the Fallbrook guys. Too many bad run ins with them. Nothing worse than dirty cops. Surprising about the colonel. We've notified military police. Can't believe someone of his rank would be involved."

I said, "He probably got involved because of the incompetence of the Fallbrook guys. Something went wrong, and he went berserk." Pete stood up. "Tonight I'm going to let you get some sleep, but we need you to stay in the area for additional questioning. I'll let you take your car, but we may need it back for further testing. I suggest you stay someplace secure."

I replied, "I'm currently at the Fallbrook Hotel. How is that?"

Pete smiled, "Some investigators on this case are staying there. With their cars out front, it should be pretty safe."

The night was a blur. Car chase, interrogation, and now we had to find a place to eat. I was completely beat. Tessa was a mess. She could only watch as detectives searched her house for clues to a double murder. Somewhat depressed, she said, "My house will never be the same. Thankfully the cops died outside. What a complete mess. All thanks to you Mr. Armstrong." She said facetiously.

I cracked a weak smile, "I'm just glad you're still alive, Tessa. When I saw that blood on your forehead, I thought it was over. I say we get the hell out of here, before something else happens, or some other detective wants more information. Trying to explain that gun under the seat was a bear. I thought for certain I was going to jail. Thankfully the FBI guy that owns the car has a concealed carry permit. We just happened to take advantage of it. That short call to Martino saved the day. He vouched for me and Robert, the car owner."

Tessa said, "Martino was great. Without his testimony, we'd both be behind bars."

"He's saved my ass more times than you know." I said. "He picked me up when I was down a few years ago. I had turned my life to shit. He's one of those guys that really cares about other people. Took me in, saved my life."

"Speaking of saving someone's life, I'm so glad you told me to brace my arms against the door sill. That gun has one nasty kick. Can only imagine what would have happened if I tried to shoot it one handed like we see in the movies. Total B.S."

Nodding, I said, "You're one hell of a good shot under pressure. Unfortunately, the cops have that gun now."

"I'm rather pissed myself. They took my pellet gun too. At least we don't have to worry about the colonel anymore."

"I say we get out of here, head over to the hotel, grab a late dinner, and get some sleep."

****

Dinner at the Fallbrook Hotel was good. Madeline, the owner, had made a spectacular Tri Tip. For being the owner, cook and part time waitress, she was doing a fantastic job. She mentioned there were a couple of messages for me at the front desk. It was apparent by the haircuts that law enforcement was present. The clock on the wall said 11 pm. Time to call it a day.

As we walked by the front desk, Alice poked her head out of the bar, "A couple of messages for you, Trace. One that might make you real happy." Handing me an envelope, she turned to walk back into the bar. "Present company excluded," she said with a wink and disappeared.

Tessa tugged my arm, "What was that supposed to mean?"

"Probably a message from my girlfriend Janet," I said. "Maybe she made progress on the divorce."

Tessa stopped dead in her tracks, "Should I get my own room? I don't want to put you in a bad light. You know how people talk."

"I'm not letting you out of my sight until that killer is caught. Janet of all people would understand."

"I hope you're right. Good news, I'm too tired to jump your bones anyway. One long day."

"Agreed," I smiled.

Back in my room, Nurse Tessa took over. Pulling down my sock, she said, "I told you to stay off this foot. Now your limp is back. Tomorrow you're staying off of it."

"Yes mother," I teased.

I pulled my jeans down, and she unwrapped my bandage. "The burn is healing nicely. I'll redress it. You should probably put your cutoffs on. Keep pressure off of it."

"Tee shirt and cutoffs it is," I cried, taking off the leather jacket and hanging it on a coat tree by the door. "We made a believable team at the bar today. All eyes were on you, Tessa. That jacket does you good."

"Well, "Ghost," you played the part perfectly. Even Tom Cruise couldn't have done it better."

"I'm just glad you had your weapon of choice with you. You'd make a damn good cop. This Heckler and Koch says..."

She said, "I need to get to get cleaned up and get to bed. Do you have an extra tee shirt? I'm running out of clothes. I only packed for one night."

"Sure, they're a little long, but don't you dare go running down the hall in one or people will certainly talk."

Opening my suitcase, I handed her the last one. "I was only planning to stay until tomorrow. We need to get this wrapped up."

"No arguments from me. By the way, did you open that message from the front desk?"

"No, not yet. I'm afraid to."

"Do you want me to open it?"

"No, I'll do it while you are getting cleaned up. If I'm in tears when you get back, you'll know what happened."

She picked up the tee shirt and walked into the bathroom. I opened the envelope. One short message was from Martino. Said he would call tonight. The other was from Janet. It was rather short. It just said, Made progress, flying home this evening. Call me at the office tomorrow.

I didn't know whether to cheer or cry. Probably didn't want to leave personal information with the clerk. I didn't blame her, but at least it sounded somewhat encouraging. Tessa came out of the bathroom dressed in my shirt. Baggy on her. Not flattering at all. I took off my shoes, diamond and all, and put them right beside the night stand. Someone would have to walk past me to get to them.

Walking to the other side of the bed she said, "Lights out, mister. I feel like I'm dressed in a shopping bag. So how was the message?"

"OK," I said, turning out the bedside lamp. "Said she is flying home tonight. Call her tomorrow. Progress."

"You don't sound happy. What do you think?"

"I'm hoping that it was short because of having to talk with the desk clerk, but I'm not sure. I believe she is frustrated. I know I am."

She reached over with her hand. Softly she said, "Thanks for running that guy off the road, Trace. Messed up his aim."

I propped myself up on one arm, reached over and kissed her on the forehead. "I'm just glad you don't have a big head like me."

She kissed me back softly, "Janet is a lucky woman. I hope she realizes that."

I sighed and laid back, staring at the dark ceiling.

Soon we were both asleep. Dreams of fast driving took over.

As my dream got intense, I was suddenly awakened. Tessa was shaking my arm, "Trace, wake up. There was that noise again."

Looking over at the alarm clock, It was a few minutes after one. I murmured, "Is that the same noise as last night?"

"I think so. Sounded like metal on metal."

Propping myself up, I pulled back the sheet and put my feet on the floor. I said softly, "I'm going to stand up this time and move out into the middle of the floor. If that thing comes at me, I'll be ready."

She sat up behind me, "Be careful. This is scary."

The room was really dark, but I could make out the dim moonlight around the outer edges of the long curtain. The room seemed to get cold, and I had the sense of some type of presence. I took a step toward the curtain. It almost sounded like something breathing. I was getting freaked out, but I held my ground. Suddenly in the darkness, there was something glowing right in my face. Tessa screamed.

I reached out in front of me with both hands. Something cold ran over my arm. Multiple flashes of light blinded me. It was like the whole room was on fire, yet frozen at the same time. It was like hell itself had opened up. I moved my arms again as my sight cleared. Nothing. Tessa reached and turned on the light. A wisp of smoke was all that remained.

CHAPTER 49

I'm a realist. I don't usually believe in things I can't see, especially when people talk about the supernatural. I don't believe in ghosts, werewolves, or vampires. They just seem like total fantasy to me. Yet here I stood in a dimly lit room staring at a wisp of smoke that was alive, just a few seconds before. I felt its cold presence on my arms. It certainly didn't feel human. People are warm and soft. This thing, whatever it was, felt cold and hard. The scary thing about this whole episode was the fact it was right in my face. It seemed to have a human form, but the face or whatever it was, seemed ghostly white.

Tessa got up from the bed and stood next to me. She was shaking slightly as she put her hand on my shoulder. "What the hell was that, Trace? I could feel its cold presence before it appeared again. This time, the light was so bright, it was almost like it exploded. In that flash, I could swear it had a human form, yet I couldn't make out any detail."

"It was right in my face this time," I said. "And the freaky thing was, it touched me this time. Right on my arm. Cold as ice. From the side of the bed, where did you see the form at when the flash appeared?"

"I saw it right in front of you. Almost like a mist. Just for a split second."

"It completely blinded me this time. I still see spots in front of my eyes."

Tessa nodded, "It seemed like the light came from all over. Almost like it exploded."

"So in your flash, could you make out any shape or form?" I asked. "In my vision, it seemed to have curves like a human. Possibly female."

Tessa pondered for a moment. "Remember when you were a kid and played ghost by putting a sheet over yourself? This wasn't like that. With a sheet the lines were straight. This was different. More human."

"Let's take another look around the room."

I turned on the ceiling light and the light on the dresser. We walked the room from front to back. Pulled open the curtains. Nothing. Tessa got down on her hands and knees. She said, "Nothing under the bed, but there is a faint smell of rose water again."

Walking to the front door, I opened it. No sign of any activity.

I said, "Nothing out in the hall. I'm glad you're here, Tessa. I would be going insane by this time without you. At least you saw the same thing that I did."

"Sorry, I'm not much help, but that is one freaky spirit. I want to get the hell out of here, but I can't go home. I feel like I can't go anywhere, Trace. Feel my hand, I'm still shaking."

"Today will be a better day, I promise. For now, we don't have much choice. You're going to need some sleep. You got your house to deal with."

"Agreed," she said. "I'm going to try to sleep again. Good night, Trace."

Looking down, I felt relieved to see my shoes next to the night stand. At least the ghost didn't get those. With that, she crawled back into bed. I could feel her hand on my back. It was still shaking slightly, and I knew it wasn't because she was cold.

****

Sleep came fitfully, but finally morning came. We both showered and dressed. Down to our last clean clothes, I put on some Khakis and a sports shirt, Tessa had on jeans and a knit top. Looking at my watch, it said seven am, too early to call Janet at the office. Tessa used the phone to call in and check on Mark. He was still out, so it was uncertain if he would be able to go home today or not.

"Let's get some breakfast," I said. "Then I want to drive out to my uncles' house. A couple of questions have been bugging me. I think all the law enforcement will be at your place. You can check in if you want to as we drive by."

"I'd rather not. No offense, but hanging out with cops is not my idea of a great time. I've had to take another vacation day. I'd rather do something fun. Let's go to your uncle's house and then get out of town for a few hours. You ever been to Old Town Temecula?"

"Not for a long time. Great little Mexican Cantina there as I remember. Sounds like a great place for lunch. Sandia Creek Rd off De Luz is a shortcut. Tacos and a Margarita sound good to me. Maybe some guacamole, without diamonds in it."

"Perfect," she replied.

After breakfast, I checked in at the front desk. No more messages. Making sure I still had a reservation for the night ahead, we walked out the back door, and I retrieved the old Mercedes that was parked near one of the undercover cars. Looking at it in the daylight showed two small bullet holes. One in the side, the other in the trunk. A scrape mark on the right side where I had hit the Jeep. Nothing that some Bondo and paint couldn't fix.

The drive to my uncle's house was uneventful. As we drove past Tessa's place, all was now quiet, but there was yellow crime scene tape all around the house. The front door was still ajar. A sheriff's car was in the driveway. Tessa said, "At least they have someone watching over it. Pete told me to call in at 9 am this morning. I'll do that after your uncles' place."

"I can't imagine how you feel right now. All your possessions fair game." I replied.

"Just glad I keep a clean house. I don't have many valuables. Not until that box of avocados showed up, at least."

My uncle's house was on the right up ahead. I had planned to park up the road, but the cops or someone had repaired the wooden driveway bridge over the drainage ditch. Pulling in, the original gate and lock were gone. Removing some yellow tape draped across the entrance, I proceeded down the drive. Around the curve of the hill the burned out remains of the house and shed were on the right. Everything tagged with little markers; the whole home area had yellow tape around it. The smell of smoke was strong. Instead of parking in the usual spot, I turned to the left. The avocado and citrus groves started on the clearing and continued up the hill. There was a small access road that went a short ways into the avocado grove. I pulled in there to hopefully keep the car out of sight if the police or someone should show up.

We both got out, the morning sun warming things up. "I want to check out a couple of items in the daylight," I said. "The first is the footprints that we saw."

Tessa said, "It appears they have sifted through the whole house. There are tags all over it."

"I'm sure the coroner has removed the body. The remains of the roof have been moved. I hope this isn't too emotional for you."

"I'm numb, Trace. Last night about sent me over the edge. I think I'm cried out for awhile."

As we walked around the edge of the house area, there were all sorts of footprints now. From the firefighters to the police, there had been a lot of people in the area over the past two days. Coming to the concrete walkway that indicated where the front door of the house had been, I looked down and walked slowly. As we got further away from the house, I found a clear boot print that had been there before. "Tessa, here is a clear impression," I said. "It looks just like the one I saw last night."

She bent down, "Yep, same Panzer style boot. Clear insignia on the sole. I would say it was the same person."

I followed the path of the prints as best I could until they disappeared altogether. "Look here Tessa, the prints stop next to these tire tracks." I said. "This must be where they loaded Mark into the truck. You can see shuffling."

"There are a bunch of other prints here too," She said.

"Hard to tell if these other prints are previous to the arrival of the fire and police. But at least we have a pretty good confirmation that the colonel was here or maybe another military guy like him."

"These prints are huge, Trace. I doubt you'll find many other guys as big as he is. Look at this print next to your shoe. It's like two inches longer."

"Wow, what a difference. Makes me look like a midget in comparison and I'm five foot eleven."

"So we have a good idea who did this and a possible track covering motive."

"The prints are pretty clear, but I have a couple of other nagging questions."

"Like what?"

"For one, we were in Paul's house and also his shed. We found a small box of tools, a workbench torn out from the wall, and he had a cooler in the house. But where did he actually work on the gems? The shed had some minor tools, but nothing a pro would use."

"Good question, Trace. I just figured he had moved everything into the shed at the back of the house."

"What do you mean moved?"

"When his wife died a couple of years ago he scaled back his business since he had a hard time driving. He used to have a shop and storefront in town where he did his work and sold low-cost jewelry. When he closed the shop, I just figured he moved everything into the work shed. I never came out here. This was his domain. I just helped him in the house."

"So the question is, where did everything go? Was there a workroom in the house? I don't remember seeing anything?"

"Nope. Just a regular three bedroom ranch house. One was the Master where he slept; the other was converted into a den where he watched TV and the back room had an extra bed for guests and had the cooler in the closet area."

"Do you think he sold them?" I asked.

"It's possible, but he still had me delivering things."

"Mark and Debbi said they found a box of semi-precious stones under the floor boards in the living room. Someone else had broken in and raised a few of the boards but evidently didn't search long enough. They did a better search and found the small box. How big was his workshop?"

"Quite a few tools. Full storefront."

"So is there anyplace else on the property where he might have stored them?"

"Not really. He has a small shed with gardening tools at the back of his fruit orchard, up here by the hill. But that wouldn't be big enough for much. I saw him out there once, and it was just a small workbench with some pruning shears and fertilizer."

"Can you show it to me?"

"Sure, it's just past the spot where we parked."

We walked back to the car, and Tessa showed me the footpath leading up to it. It was just a lean-to against the hillside. Green and made of wood, it had a pull handle on the outside. Opening the door, it was just like Tessa had described. Just a large wooden shed with a workbench.

"Wow, total dead end here. Like you said, some shears and fertilizer."

Tessa nodded, "Just some old fertilizer. Probably real old from the look of it."

I bent down carefully and took a look. The date was from the 70's. Wow.

"That stuff had been here a long time. But there is something strange about this shed. Did you notice the footprints on the floor? They continue under the workbench. Like someone has walked there before."

"Let me look." She said. "You're right. Unless your Uncle Paul had really long legs, someone has left footprints there. How can that be?"

"Not sure, but this bench would have to be moved out of the way to walk through there."

"Check this out, Trace. The edge of the bench is hinged."

"Wow. Let me try lifting the other side."

With a hard pull, the workbench came loose from the wall on the side.

"Look at this Tessa," I said excitedly. "The bench pivots right up. Let me lift it all the way."

The bench went up, and I was able to prop it against the left side wall of the shed. Now that the bench was out of the way, there was a small handle revealed on the back wall.

"Trace, is that a handle?"

"Looks like it. Let me pull on it."

I tried pulling backward. Nothing happened.

"It's stuck," I said.

Tessa gave it a try, "Maybe it slides instead of pulls?" With a sharp side motion, the back wall of the shed moved to one side, revealing a long dark tunnel behind it.

"It looks like a mine shaft," I said.

"You game to explore?" she asked.

"Sure, let me pull out my penlight,"

With my little flashlight in hand, we headed back. After we had got back about fifteen feet, we came to a solid metal door and enclosure. There was a lock on the handle, and it wouldn't turn. I tried pushing on the door with my shoulder; it would not budge. The door and enclosure looked like they had been there for decades. Everything was thick with rust. Now what to do?

Something clicked in my memory.

"Tessa, when Mark and I were searching the other shed, we found a key taped to the underside of the toolbox tray. I put it on my keychain for safekeeping. Kind of looks like a small skeleton key. Here, hold my light."

I put the key in the lock and tried turning it, but the mechanism was frozen. I tried the key different ways. Suddenly as I was applying a sideways pressure, it gave a slight bit. Trying again, it made a sound like sliding rusted metal, and slowly the latch opened. Pushing the door, my little one cell light led us into the darkness. We had found the entrance to a mine. Just inside was a huge workbench full of tools. We had found Uncle Paul's private workspace.

CHAPTER 50

The tunnel we discovered appeared to be a mine of some sort. It was tall enough to stand in and reinforced with sturdy timbers. About six feet across, it seemed to have been created decades earlier. Musty cold air greeted us as we walked in. The work area was to the left, just inside the door. In the dim light from the entrance behind us, I saw three long worktops installed between support timbers and backed up to the tunnel wall. There appeared to be metal conduit running along the ceiling, indicating that there had been electricity at one time.

Tessa spoke up, "This is amazing Trace. Almost entirely hidden from the outside world. In the few years that I've known your uncle, I had no idea this was here."

"This is beginning to answer a lot of the questions that I've had with my uncle's family and past. By the look of these timbers, this has quite a history."

We walked along the edge of the worktops; Tessa said, "Is this a light switch?"

"Give it a try," I replied.

Instantly, the entire work area was flooded with light from above. The tables contained power equipment, storage containers, and an extensive array of hand and power tools.

"Tessa exclaimed, "Wow, this is more extensive than Paul's shop in town. More permanent."

"It's interesting," I said, "that the larger equipment seems ancient, but the smaller hand tools are almost new. This work area appears to have been here for years, but the hand tools indicate that he moved his shop items here recently."

Tessa picked up a small box. "Here is a sapphire ring that looks ready for delivery. Looks like a retail setting. This is what I remember about Paul's shop. He had a glass display case with many items like this." Laughing, she said, "Look at the end label, Gold plate ring, green quartz. One classy fake. It looks like the real thing."

I walked past the last workbench and saw a dark metal cabinet in the next space between timbers. Opening the door, I said, "Wow... score. There is a lot of expensive items here. Looks like an old store safe you would find in a jewelry store."

Tessa pulled out a small tray from one of the shelves inside, "This is a display holder for a dozen rings. I wonder if these are real or impressive fakes?"

"Probably fakes, as the door is open and has a flimsy latch. Check this other cabinet next to it. It is made of much heavier steel and has a heavy lock mechanism. The good stuff must be stored here."

"Is it open?"

I pulled the latch, "Surprisingly yes it is." I said as the door revealed different styles of containers. A few of the boxes contained finished jewelry, but most of the contents were raw stones, blank rings, and an assortment of metal attachments. "This is a jewelers working case with raw materials."

Tessa walked past me to the next opening, "Check this Trace, an actual small safe cemented into the wall. Heavy combination lock. Must be the precious stones. Unfortunately, it is locked."

"All we need now is the combination," I mused.

"Good luck on that. That combination was probably stored in your uncle's memory."

"Or maybe it is a combination of those numbers that were scrawled on the bottom of the work tray in the tool box in the shed. I wrote those down on a back of one of my business cards."

Opening my wallet, I searched through for the card, "Hmm, four numbers listed. Let me spend a minute on this and see if I have any success. 24-13-5-10 was the way they were listed."

Trying the numbers in order did not work. I tried a couple of other substitutions. No luck.

Tessa said, "Did you try them backwards? Everything for the last two days seems like the complete opposite of what we thought."

"Let me try that," I said. A few clicks later, I said, "Still no luck."

"Just our stupid luck. Like this whole case one step forward, two steps back. Now what?"

With a smirk, I said, "We try what you just said. Roll the first number initially and do the other three backwards."

24-10-5-13... Click.

Tessa shook her head, "Oh my gosh, you sarcastic genius, you figured it out. What's in there?"

I showed my penlight on the interior. There were small jewelry boxes and a larger avocado box. I pulled a couple of small boxes and the large avocado box and put them on the workbench under the bright lights.

Opening one of the smaller boxes revealed a large sapphire, uncut. Another had a ruby looking jewel. "This is the real stuff." I said, "These must be worth a fortune, and probably a lot more once they are cut."

"What's in the Avocado box?" asked Tessa.

"Let me pull off the lid."

Struggling a little, the cover finally gave way.

"Oh my God," cried Tessa as she viewed inside. "It's stacks of money."

"And not just any domination, these are thousand dollar bills in clusters. And check this out, there are layers here separated by a false cardboard bottom."

"So that's how they moved the money," she said. "I kept wondering how the players got paid."

"Yes," I cried. "Now everything is starting to make sense. Jewels in fruit was ingenious, but it didn't make much sense for paper bills. But false bottoms on these avocado boxes allows the money to move with the fruit. And check this out. The money is tightly stacked together with no spaces so it would x-ray as just a thick piece of cardboard. You could probably move fifty or a hundred bills at a time with no risk."

Putting her hand on my arm, she asked, "Did you have any idea that your uncle was involved in this type of thing?"

"Jewelry possibly, but not money. No wonder people have been dying. Imagine how much money you could transport in a standard fruit transport truck. They often carry hundreds or even thousands of the half dozen size boxes."

"Think about this, Trace. All you would have to have is one or two boxes among those hundreds to pay off just about anyone. A needle in a haystack situation. When a truck like this goes over the border, they don't x-ray every box. The usually pick one or two at random."

"Amazing transport method," I said. "I wonder what other surprises are in here? We've found jewels both fake and real. A whole set of production tools and now money to finance the whole operation."

Taking a step back, I surveyed the whole mine. It continued into the darkness deep into the hillside for some distance. I tried to take it all in. Walking back up to the safe, I picked up some little individual boxes of assorted gems. Then I noticed a small black journal on the side of the safe on the top of one of the larger jewel boxes. Opening it, I said, "Look at this Tessa. It's a detailed journal of everything that Paul had been working on. Item names, contacts, dates, monetary amounts, and a running total."

We put it on the workbench. Tessa said, "This book goes back years. Different contacts, different destinations. Look at this page, this must be the current diamond. See how it is described.

SD History Museum investigate 5-86
BI Arrives 8-88
Survey room
Safe Replica created
8-20-88 transfer with 50 to MX
8-21-88 Substitution
8-25-88 acquired BI arrives
8–27-88 Transfer to CR

8-30-88 Arrives Berlin
9-10-88 CR delivers 200
9-12-88 50 transfer to MX with CZ

Looking over Tessa's shoulder, I said, "No wonder the book was locked up. Totally incriminating trail. Sounds like this whole thing was started over two years ago."

"Check this Trace, the delivery is supposed to take place this Friday. In Berlin. Delivered by CR. Must be Colonel Rainer."

"No wonder he was willing to kill. Probably has a military flight out on Wednesday or Thursday."

Tessa nodded, "But what I don't understand is the small amounts of cash to the participants. A diamond as big as the BI, whatever that stands for, has got to be worth millions. So who gets the big payout?"

"Good question," I said. "Maybe the colonel? Maybe more money to come later?"

"Man, I wouldn't do it for that. I'm not putting my life on the line for fifty or a hundred grand."

"But Tessa, look at how many pages there are in this little black book. Other dates, other jewels. Gone on for years. Look at all the checkmarks. Deals were done. Maybe the idea is not to get greedy. Just be a loyal delivery boy. Looking at the avocado boxes, it would be relatively easy to transport fifty or maybe even one hundred grand in the hidden areas, but anything more would be precarious."

"Maybe so, but it just seems off to me. And who is CZ on the last entry? Someone we haven't run into yet?"

"CZ is a mystery. Not sure. Initials for someone. I want to check out the rest of the safe and explore the back of the mine."

Tessa nodded, "While you do that, I'm going to look further through his journal. Maybe another reference to a CZ?"

With my penlight, I looked through the safe some more, opening some of the larger boxes. My battery was going dead so it was hard to make out markings and names but there was a wide variety of beautiful gems, some cut and some uncut. My light just about flickered out, so I just felt around at the back of the safe. Cardboard boxes, plastic trays, a metal box of some type. Thoughts were running through my head. How long had this been going on? What was this mine all about? How long was it? Where did it go? I decided to find out.

With the last dim light of my penlight, I started walking back into the mine. It appeared that it was about thirty feet into the hill when the shaft turned to the left. It was following the curvature of the hill. As I got deeper into the mine, the curve of the tunnel hid the light of the benches from behind. The mine got darker and darker, my penlight finally failing. In almost total darkness, I decided to turn back. The tunnel probably went at least a quarter mile. It was probably a quartz, topaz or possibly even an old gold mine. The walls were dug out long ago.

As I came back up to the workbenches, I wanted to take another look in the safe. I put my hand deep inside. I called out to Tessa, "My light went out before I got to the end."

She didn't reply, but a deep female voice filled the Tunnel with a statement? "Give me the diamond or she dies."

Looking up, a darkly dressed woman in a ski mask stepped out from behind a timber, her arm around Tessa, covering her mouth. A gun pointed at the side of her head.

CHAPTER 51

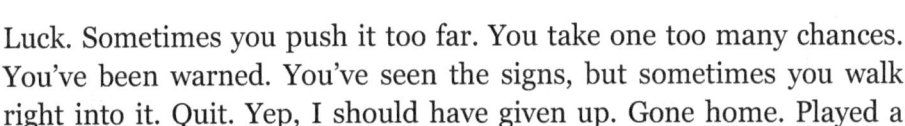

Luck. Sometimes you push it too far. You take one too many chances. You've been warned. You've seen the signs, but sometimes you walk right into it. Quit. Yep, I should have given up. Gone home. Played a different game, a different tune. Woulda, shouldas.

But as a private detective, there is no going back, no reset, no do-overs.

Deal with it Trace.

Right in front of me was a strong, powerful woman, dark hair, ski mask, with her gloved hand around the mouth of Tessa. A woman that didn't deserve to be here. One pull of the trigger and her life would be taken. Not fair.

However, in every situation like this, there are wants and needs. The strong woman somehow knew about the diamond that I possessed, and probably needed it. Her future probably depended on it. I needed to know who she was, and how she found out where we were.

Negotiation is an art of wants, needs, and possessions. Currently, the woman held most of the cards. She had a gun, Tessa, and a bad attitude. The woman in her grip was a bargaining chip. She needed a diamond first; then she could kill us both. I needed to improve my odds.

It's funny how your mind works when you face odds like this. First it's blank. Then remorse. Then action. Split second decisions.

I had two advantages. First, my right arm and half my body were in total darkness behind a large metal cabinet. I had an element of surprise. The second advantage was I had my hand on a large metal object in the safe. Not sure what it was. My mind said, God, please let it be useful. It's funny how God comes into the picture at times like this. I guess I like God better than luck. In that slow motion split second of thought, my right hand moved small boxes out of the way. The object was metal and seemed to be heavy. I pulled it towards me. My hand felt the shape. It was a gun. My faith just increased, exponentially.

Now my odds were better. Moving slightly to the right behind the cabinet, I transferred the gun to my left hand as I felt for the safety. Off. The feel was an H&K. Small caliber. 22. This meant one thing. Head shot only. Good news, the recoil would be small. I had a chance with my left hand. But would the gun work?

"Where is the diamond?" the woman yelled. Tessa screamed as she pushed the gun hard against her temple.

"Let the woman go," I said firmly. "There is now a gun pointed at your forehead." Raising my left arm, I said, "This is between you and me." Now was the time my mind thought through my options. Priority, get Tessa to safety. I thought about just shooting her in the head, but left handed would be tricky at best. Unfortunately, as soon as she heard my voice, she moved behind Tessa. Clear shot gone.

"Give me the diamond, you both walk." She said calmly.

"Who are you?" I asked.

"An old friend of Paul. I know all about the diamond."

"Let her walk first, and then we negotiate."

"How about I torture her first, then I torture you until you cry for mercy?"

"The police are right behind us," I lied. "You lose."

Pushing the metal door behind her closed with her boot, she said, "Now it doesn't matter."

Negotiating with hostages is never pretty. Many times someone dies. I was at a disadvantage now. Sure the woman might not get the diamond, but Tessa would indeed die.

Wants and needs. Possessions.

I possessed the diamond, but it meant nothing to me. I wasn't going to sell it. In fact, the longer it was in my possession, the worse my life had been. The diamond did mean something to the woman, however. It involved millions of dollars.

The woman had Tessa as her possession. She was a bargaining chip, human shield, but also a liability. Hostages are always difficult. Tessa did mean something to me. At this point she was everything. If anything happened to her, I would not be able to forgive myself. She had guided my steps, healed my wounds, and saved my life.

Trading possessions are difficult.

If I gave her the diamond, or even let her know where it was, it would certainly mean death to one or both of us. However, if she had to let Tessa go to gain possession, we might have a successful transaction. Might was the keyword here.

The diamond was in my shoe, not a location that lent itself to quick retrieval. The woman did not know it was there, which was to my advantage. To my right was a safe. It contained assorted jewels. I had seen a green sapphire, a red ruby; but what I needed was a blue diamond.

With my left hand holding the gun, my left eye on Tessa, I reached into the safe with my right hand. I felt three closed boxes. One by one I would need to inspect the labels. Would one contain a diamond? I needed to buy time.

"Let's work this out," I yelled.

Box one in my right hand. Side view, Amethyst, no.

She yelled back, "What do you suggest?"

Box two in my hand. Side view, White Topaz, looks like a diamond, wrong color.

"I trade the diamond for your hostage."

Box three in my hand. Side view, Ice Blue CZ, what the heck is an Ice Blue CZ?

"Give me the diamond, I let her go."

Box three. Lid off. In my hand. Side view, looks like a blue diamond.

What is a CZ? Worth a try.

"I'm going to put the diamond on the floor and push it out. You'll need to let the hostage go."

Holding the gun steady, I dropped the box to the floor, lid off, no description.

"Alright," she said.

"Let her go, now," I screamed.

She released her grip on her mouth. Lowering her right hand to her shoulder, she pushed her slightly forward. I pushed the box a few inches forward with my left foot. We were now six feet apart.

"Push it over here asshole," she said firmly.

"Let her go, and I will." I replied.

Pushing her a little further forward, she ducked her head behind Tessa. At five foot seven she was just an inch taller. No shot.

"Come on, asshole. Let's get this over with." She scowled.

Diversion and luck was now needed. Arm on her shoulder, she wouldn't be able to snap her neck. I looked at Tessa, made eye contact, and nodded my head slightly as I winked. This would be it. Hopefully she would know my signal. Right hand ready.

With a swift tap with my left foot, the box went sliding across the floor, as I screamed, "Duck Tessa." Having read my signal, she dropped her legs and ducked her head. My right hand came across as I stepped out from behind the cabinet, the gun firing as my right hand steadied my shot.

Dead accurate.

Tessa screamed with pain as she gripped her shoulder.

The bitch had ducked.

The woman's gun fired at me, clipping my arm as I ducked back to the right. The pain intense.

Now her strong right arm held Tessa tight around her torso as she bent down to retrieve the jewel with her left. No shot. Within seconds, she had the jewel and still had Tessa. She pulled her back up the tunnel as she said, "Before I kill her, I need to make sure this is real."

She pushed her over to the first workbench. Transferring the gun to her right hand, she kept me covered as he slid the jewel against the metal tabletop.

"Thank you asshole for giving me the real thing. Now you get to watch your girlfriend die. She transferred the gun to her left hand, and pulled Tessa upright. Putting the gun to her temple, she counted down. Tessa screamed. The bitch was hidden behind her. I had no shot.

Three,

Two,

One,

A gun pushed into my back.

"Drop the weapon. The game is over."

I dropped the pistol.

The deep voice yelled over to the woman holding Tessa, "I've got him, you can let her go."

CHAPTER 52

Tessa stood there in shock, still screaming. Her life spared by someone from the darkness. I went to turn around but was greeted by a loud voice behind me. The gun behind me pushed forward, "Get over there next to Contessa," the voice barked. It sounded somehow familiar. I took a few steps forward and reached out for Tessa. We embraced for a second and then I turned around to face our captors. With the stark light of the workbenches in the background, I could just see silhouettes of two people, both wearing ski masks and baseball hats. Both appeared female, each with guns pointed at us. One reached down and picked up the gun I had dropped. The strong woman held up the diamond and said, "You almost lost your life for this Ice Blue Demon, Contessa. We will take it off your hands."

The strong woman took off her hat and mask. A strange look came over Tessa's face, almost in shock, like she had seen a ghost. Her eyes clearing in the dim light, she said, "Catarina? Is that you? I thought you were dead."

"I am dead, as far as you are concerned," the woman said. "I just came back to relieve you of this little gem."

Tessa shook her head, "But how? I don't understand. I went to your funeral."

"So did my husband Paul and a lot of other people. Put it this way. I'm a good swimmer. There are definite advantages to being dead."

The one that Tessa had referred to as Catarina spoke again, her voice directed at me. "You've caused us lots of problems over the past two days, Mr. Armstrong. First, you refused to die. And then you hook up with this woman, who somehow intercepted the delivery of the diamond. Now you must be dealt with."

Trying to get a better view of our captors, I moved slightly to one side. Catarina was a strongly built latin woman, probably in her late fifties. Dark short hair, small scar on her left cheek. The other person spoke, voice deep, dressed all in black. "Well, we meet again, Trace. Last time I saw you, you were lying face down on the floor of your uncle's house."

"Who are you?" I cried, still not sure of the voice.

The silhouette moved to the side, into the light. A hand reached up, removing the hat, mask and sunglasses.

"Recognize me now?"

It was Debbi, Mark's wife.

Utterly shocked, I said, "Debbi? But we saw your burnt body in the fire. What in the hell is going on here?"

Using her normal voice now, she said. "That's what we wanted you to believe, Trace. One of our local homeless druggies provided a nice cadaver that played the part of me nicely."

Thinking back to what happened at Paul's house, I knew I had to play this close to the vest. I wasn't sure if she knew that Mark survived and was in the hospital. "So what happened to Mark? I asked. "Is he with you? We didn't see the second body."

"He has been dealt with," Debbi said. "We had to pull him out of the house when the diamond wasn't in the box we brought over from Contessa's. Unfortunately for us, he didn't know where it was."

Tessa was shaking her head, "How could you do this Debbi? How could you kill your husband?"

Debbi smiled, "It's real easy. He didn't want to come with us. The same reluctance as his father?"

Catarina spoke up, "We couldn't have any loose ends. That's

business. He is rotting away in a swamp, certainly dead by now."

Nodding at Tessa, I motioned with my eyes to play along.

Shaking my head, I asked, "I don't understand any of this Catarina. What's this all about?

"You have to understand the private jewelry business," she said. "This project was planned out over two years ago. We knew the Ice Blue Diamond would be coming to San Diego on a museum tour. We set players in place. Someone to steal the jewel and someone to buy it. Paul and I were the intermediaries. Unfortunately, he wanted to play it safe. He brought in his old military friend, the colonel, to handle the selling end. I had contacts in South America who were willing to pay full price. The stupid bastard was willing to take 200k for it. Going price is over three million."

"So I take it you had a falling out," I said.

"You have to understand the situation. This is a very dangerous occupation. Total trust is required. Any mess up along the way and people go to jail, or as you have seen, they die. When you add another intermediary like the colonel, you increase the risk exponentially."

"So you had a connection in South America. Why didn't he want to use that?

"He said there were Cartel connections. He didn't trust my direct buyer."

"So I take it you didn't trust the colonel?" I said.

"Would you? Saw he shot a couple of cops on the news last night. He is a take no prisoners type of guy. In this business, friends can be liabilities. When money is on the line, trust is better than friendship. In fact, I would rather deal with a known criminal who knows the rules than a friend, any day."

"So you just decided to disappear."

"Better than getting shot by Colonel Rainer. No trust whatsoever. Guy was on a power trip. Had Paul wrapped around his finger. I just went over the side of the boat while everyone was asleep or passed out. Then I swam to a waiting craft that took me to Mexico. Biding my time in Acapulco since then."

Tessa spoke up, "So how long has this operation been going on?"

"Paul has been involved since the 60's. I met him as a Latin America connection years ago. When his first wife died, I came to the states. Marriage to him provided a visa and green card. Love was secondary. We made great business partners, but lousy lovers."

I spoke up, "So how long has this mine been here, Catarina?"

"Probably a turn of the century quartz mine," she said. "Paul purchased the abandoned lot in the 50's. Built the house, and then covered the hillside with fruit and avocado orchards."

"So who came up with the gems in fruit idea?" I asked.

Catarina smiled, "Pretty clever, huh. Paul tested both citrus and avocado. Avocados work really well with their large seed. We've used them for years. Works great across the border."

Tessa was shaking her head, "So how did Debbi get involved?"

Catarina said, "Pretty simple actually. I've known Debbi for years. American connection. Real estate jewelry thief. As a realtor, she has total access to a lot of expensive homes. Jewelry theft is easy when you have someone like Paul to make replica stones. Tour the house, make the exchange. Nobody even knows the stone is gone. Once I decided to disappear off the fishing boat, I had a hard time getting across the border. I couldn't use my old ID. So I contacted Debbi. Offered to bring her into the ice blue plan."

Debbi gave a sarcastic laugh, "Your cousin Mark didn't have a chance, Trace. I put on the old charm and had him in the palm of my hand in no time. A little alcohol and a trip to Vegas and we were married."

Scratching my head, I said. "So what went wrong with your best-laid plan?"

Debbi said, "It was the whole problem of bringing Contessa in. When Paul got the DUI, and his sight started going, he began having you, Contessa, make the Farmer's Market pickups. Another player added to the process. Evidently you found out about the avocado setup or somehow got the boxes mixed up."

"And," Catarina said, "Paul decided to drive into Fallbrook himself and make the trade with the colonel the Tuesday night you picked up the box from the Farmer's Market. We had the whole house fire cover-up ready to go the next day. The woman cadaver, Mark and Paul would be setup in the house and the colonel would get the blame."

"How in the heck did you plan to do that?" I asked.

Debbi would meet with Mark and Paul in the house and knock them out like she eventually did on Sunday. A hypo with veterinary tranquilizer works well and leaves no trace."

Shaking my head, I said. "So that's how you did it? I know I was knocked out cold, but my head only hurt a little when I woke up. But what I don't understand about this whole thing was how you were going to implicate the colonel?"

"Really simple. I'm surprised you haven't figured it out yet."

"What did you do Debbi, invite him over with your sexual prowess?"

"Nothing that complicated."

"Then what? He was definitely at the house. We saw the footprints."

"That's what I wanted you to think."

Raising one of her feet, she had on a huge German Panzer boot.

"Oh shit. I should have seen that. You had me completely believing that the colonel was there."

"My whole size eight shoe fits snug in these size eighteens. Makes it real easy to walk completely anonymous. None of my footprints at all."

These revelations rattled my head. The colonel was a known entity. Military trained, ruthless, and an excellent shot. These two women, an unknown quantity. One thing for sure, they weren't going to let us walk out of here. In fact, seeing what they almost did to Tessa, I had no doubt what their plans were for us.

Listening for the last few minutes, it became apparent the most ruthless of the duo was Debbi. She stalked my cousin, and was ready to burn him to a crisp with the flick of a match in a house that included my uncle. She almost burned me to death on Sunday. Thankfully, the vet tranquilizer hadn't lasted any longer.

Catarina now seemed to be in control. Tessa and I had no weapons, while both women were armed with serious handguns. Catarina knew how to hit a target. Think, Trace, Think.

Stall, ask questions, draw them out.

Looking at Catarina, I said, "So how did you get the avocados to keep from spoiling once you opened them up for the jewels? Once air hits the fruit, it turns brown."

"Simple, we do it while they are still attached to the tree. Natural healing takes over. Within an hour, the wound is sealed over. A diamond this large can be a problem, so we used a flexible funnel to install them after we drilled a hole with an expanding bit to hollow out the large seed. Paul perfected it."

"One thing just occurred to me, Catarina," I asked. "With everyone in the family dead, who gets the life insurance money, if there is any?"

Cat laughed, "So you figured out the rest of our plan, Trace. A few years down the road, everything settles out, and the proceeds go to a trust account for an imaginary niece in South America. Identification is so easy to alter down there. Difficult to say if the diamond or the cumulative insurance will net us more. You can be sure that the two of us are worth more dead, than alive."

Tessa shook her head. "No wonder you wanted your husband dead, Debbi. What an evil bitch."

Debbi paced nervously, and finally said, "Are we going to sit here chatting all day, Cat? We need to deal with them and get to the border. You know I hate this damn town. If I ever see another avocado, I think I'll puke. Our entry visas to Mexico Sur are only good through tomorrow."

"What are you going to do with us?" Tessa asked nervously.

Debbi smiled, "I'm going to do what Cat should have done earlier. Bullet right through the brain. You stupid bitch have caused me more grief over the last few days than anyone else in my life. Taking the diamond was genius. We didn't know you knew anything about it. Too bad you came back here today. That old Mercedes gave you away."

I spoke up, "So if you saw the Benz, how did you get in here?"

"Simple." Debbie said. "We knew you were staying at the Fallbrook Hotel. Just waited and watched this morning. Followed the Mercedes here. Parked the rental car down the street. Cat saw the shed opened out front. She went in that way. Waited for an opportunity. I went in through the other entrance on the back side of the hill. Hidden down in one of the old aqueducts. Cat had one of Paul's old keys. I just crawled in there, walked down the tunnel and saw what was happening. You almost walked into us with that stupid penlight. You're lucky it went out when it did."

Catarina spoke up. "Instead of shooting them, I say we just let them rot in here, that way if we should need them again, they will still be alive... for a day or two. Besides, the thought of them dying of thirst or hunger is much more creative than dying instantly."

Debbie shook her head, "What if they start screaming? Won't someone hear them?"

Catarina said, "No one for miles. Both entrances are secure heavy metal doors with sturdy locks. We just make sure to manually lock them outside and close the shed door. It will be years before anyone finds their bones."

"Ohh, I like that," Debbi said. And if someone does find them, the colonel will get blamed."

Perfect, said Catarina. "Debbi, get that box of money on the counter and those box of gems in the safe. The rest of the stuff is crap."

Catarina looked at me, "Thank you for opening the safe, Armstrong. Paul changed the combination every few months. I had no idea what it was."

The two women put their hats back on along with sunglasses. With their guns pointed at us, Catarina said, "Back into the mine, you two."

I walked backward a few yards, Tessa followed.

"Grab me that combo lock on the wall, Debbi," Contessa barked.

Opening the metal front door with the inner latch, they started to walk out slowly, facing backward, guns still aimed at us. I thought about charging them, but I didn't want to get shot. My arm was already bleeding from a nasty flesh wound.

As Catarina pulled the door to a close, she yelled around the opening, "At least you'll die in each others arms."

I could hear Debbi laughing, "Give her a goodnight kiss for me..."

The door slammed shut. The lock clicked.

CHAPTER 53

It's times like this that you see displayed on soap operas. What would happen if you were stranded on a mountain with no chance of escape? No one coming. Ever. Man, woman. Would you rip each others clothes off and have mad passionate sex and slowly die in each others arms or would something else happen? TV always made this out as some romantic interlude.

Reality was, it was the last thing on our minds. It was a hot summer morning. Temperatures in the high eighties. No water, no food. Neither of us were prepared for this.

I put my arm around Tessa. She was in tears. "What are we going to do now?" she screamed. I tried to calm her. I said softly, "We'll get out of here. The car is still outside. Someone will find us."

She buried her head in my shoulder, "How could those women be so evil, Trace? I know both of them. I never imagined being killed for a stupid diamond. Debbi is ruthless. She left you for dead and dumped her husband's body over a cliff. How can this be happening?

I responded, "Large sums of money distort reality. In law enforcement, we see it all the time. People fight over thousands or even hundreds of dollars. Families break up, divorces happen, people cheat each other. When you raise the stakes to millions, consequences increase. People die. No wonder that jewel is called the Ice Blue Demon. Way too much blood on it."

"But why us? We had nothing to do with it."

"Because it passed through our hands. With something like this, no one is safe."

"Thankfully the blood diamond is long gone now. But how do we get out of here?"

"My first thought is to explore the other end of the tunnel. Quarter mile long, ending in a drainage ditch, according to Catarina. The problem is, the tunnel is pitch black. It must turn at one spot. Otherwise, we would have a hint of light. Thankfully we still have electricity.

"Maybe we can find a flashlight in here? Lots of tools on those benches."

"Let's take a look," I said, trying to deflect the mood of the moment.

Inspecting the benches, we looked in some of the drawers and under the table. I didn't want to tell Tessa the real diamond was still in my shoe. Catarina and Debbi evidently got a man made diamond called a CZ, or Cubic Zirconia. That is the description that was listed on the box label of the jewel I had pulled from the safe. Almost as hard as a real diamond, but worth only a fraction as much. This must have been the CZ that was to replace the real Ice Blue Diamond that was listed in Paul's little book. Probably needed a final cut. Locked away in the safe, waiting for the arrival of the real diamond to be modified. Most CZ's are white. Somehow this one had a blue tint.

Tessa opened one of the drawers with some of the newer tools from the Fallbrook shop. Right dead in the middle was a four cell metal flashlight. She lifted it out and slid the switch. A bright beam was emitted from the end. She said, "Alleluia, Trace, let's explore this puppy. You lead the way. Here take the light."

She handed me the light, and we set off down the tunnel. As we got past the safe, the whole tunnel looked like it had had little use. There were spider webs and dark dust on everything. The floor was just dirt mixed with a little gravel.

"I'm surprised we didn't hear those women approaching," I said.

"Enough gravel here to make some noise."

"I wondered about that too," said Tessa. "But we were so interested in the work area we didn't notice them."

"Check this out Tessa," I said, pointing the light at the dirt floor. "One set of size eighteen German Panzer boot tracks. I would never have guessed that Debbi, of all people, would be wearing them. Totally threw me off."

"Hmmm, I wonder if the police took a mold of the print if they would match up?"

"Good question but they certainly look close enough to fool the average private detective. I sure was fooled."

As we walked along the tunnel, we came to a left turn, evidently following the curvature of the hill. As we went around the corner, the backlight behind us disappeared. "I'm going to put out the light Tessa. See if we can make out the end of the tunnel."

Turning the light off, everything went pitch black. As our eyes adjusted, there was a little sliver of light way off in the distance. I put the light back on, and we proceeded. In a few minutes, the tunnel turned again, and there was a solid metal door right ahead, much smaller than the front door. You would have to crawl through it. On the right side was a latch.

"With my brace, that's a tough reach," I said.

Tessa bent down on her knees. "I'll give it a go. Light is coming from the outside, Freedom a foot away." Crawling forward, she pushed down hard on the latch. "Stuck solid. There is a keyhole. You still got that skeleton key?"

"Right here." I pulled the key from my pocket.

Lying on her side for more leverage, she inserted the key in the lock. "Not the right one. Doesn't engage."

"Just our luck. Any idea where this leads?"

"Light is coming in around the hinges. Let me see if I can see anything." Moving forward, she put her eye near the rusty upper pivot. "Pinhole view. Concrete drain. Just like Catarina said."

"Hear anything? I think this may be near De Luz Road."

"Hang on a sec." Turning her head, she put her ear up to the hinge.

"Car in the distance. We're probably on the hillside overlooking the road."

"Anyone ever walk on De Luz?"

"Not often. I can't see the road from here. Door leads to the culvert."

"Damn, probably not worth yelling. . ."

"I'll give it a try for good measure." She turned to face the door and yelled 'help' in a loud voice. No response. "Other than straining my vocal chords, I don't think that is a solution." She crawled back, kicked the door for good measure, and stood up in the dim glow of the door joints.

I said, "What are you thinking?"

She smiled. "That I need a donut."

"A donut? At a time like this?"

"You asked. Yes, that's what I'm thinking. I'm hungry, and I've missed my daily donut for the last two days."

"Daily donut? What the hell, Tessa. You look too fit to have a donut habit."

"I cook. I make pies, cakes, and sweet treats. You can't make sweets all the time without partaking. I have a daily donut on the way to work. Sorry, I'm in withdrawal. And I'll let you know I have a good donut every day. I don't mess around. No little donut's, mister. I go all the way. I am craving a huge cinnamon roll right now."

"That does sound good; I'll admit. But how do you stay so thin?"

"I also have a jogging habit. Couple miles a day. I jog so I can eat. Simple. So how about you? What are you thinking?"

"Other than getting the hell out of here and buying you a donut, I'm thirsty. It's got to be eighty degrees already."

Tessa nodded, "I'm dying of thirst too.

"Any other thoughts?"

"Are you a praying man, Trace?"

"I used to be. My ex-wife took me to church every weekend. After I found her in bed with the youth pastor, I kinda lost faith."

"Wow, it would be hard after that."

"How about you, Tessa?"

"I pray with my patients at times at the hospital, especially when they are really sick or have a terminal disease. I've seen God work miracles when things seem hopeless."

"Maybe you can say a prayer for us now. I'm so thirsty. Would love it if God could turn this rock into wine."

"Wouldn't that be nice, but that's really asking for a miracle. Maybe just for someone to find us."

"I'll take that, but wine would be really good right now."

We held hands and Tessa prayed for our situation. I even said a few words. It had been years since I talked to God. After a couple of minutes, we opened our eyes.

Unfortunately, things were just as bleak as they were before.

I said sarcastically, "Man, I wish I was in Maverick's Bar. I'm getting so thirsty. To think I used to have a drinking problem a few years back. Man what I would give for one of those bottles of wine that I used to hide in the back of my pantry. I remember Martino finding a case that I'd hidden. He called me out on it, but right now, I'd drink it straight down. Even cheap wine would do."

Tessa's eyes brightened as she snapped her fingers. "You may be on to something, Trace."

"What do you mean?"

"Think about your uncle. He must have worked in this tunnel a lot. What did he have at the end?"

"Not sure what you mean."

"What I mean is your uncle had a drinking problem. He drank at the bar, but I'll bet he drank out here too. All we need to do is find his stash."

"You're right. But what makes you think he would drink here?"

"Don't doubt a nurses intuition. I see it all the time. Guys coming in stone drunk and the wife has no idea where the booze is. The question is, where would your uncle hide the alcohol out here?"

"Why would he hide it when it was only himself?"

"Old habit. His wife used to be out here with him."

"Makes sense. If it were me, I'd hide it in front near the work area. As a former party drunk, I can tell you I would want it where I could sip it."

"Exactly, Trace. Let's run up and check. No use standing around in the dark."

I laughed, "Maybe you can jog up front. Get ready for that donut."

"I would, but I got to help 'Limpy' along."

"Maybe it would be a good idea to conserve our energy in case we have an extended stay."

"Don't get off on that pessimistic crap. You promised me a donut. I'm holding you to that."

"OK, OK... you run ahead. I'll drag myself along."

Walking, it took about five minutes to get from the back of the tunnel to the front. Thankfully, after our eyes adjusted, there was just enough light to see a few yards ahead. The big problem area was the turn halfway through. The timbers narrowed somewhat for a few feet; the ceiling dropped, and the metal conduit started. The main tunnel was about six feet high. Tall enough for me to walk upright. My head scraped slightly at the turn.

As I came into the lighted area, I could see Tessa rooting at the bottom of one of the cabinets.

"Any luck?" I asked.

"There are a couple of tall cardboard boxes at the back of this one. Can you help me?"

"Sure."

"Here, let me drag this out. You open it."

As I tore into the cover, I said, "Box of old tools."

"Here's another, looks like the first,"

"More tools," I said.

Standing up, she said, "Let's check the front cabinet."

Rooting in this one, she pulled an empty box out, "Nothing in that one. A different one behind it."

This one rattled as she pulled on it. I thought to myself, *Maybe God does answer prayer. . .* As it came into the light, I said, "Bingo. A small case of wine, conveniently hidden behind an empty box. You are a genius, Tessa. . . Whatever your middle name is."

"Marie, Tessa Marie Castillo. So what do we have here?"

"Six bottles of wine, Tessa Marie. Let me pull one out. 'Fallbrook

Winery.' Local stuff. Merlot."

"Well it isn't donuts, but it will keep us alive and happy for a day or two." Excited, I said, "I say we open one right now. I'm dying of thirst."

"Before we party, let's clear this workbench off."

"Always the practical nurse." I smiled. There were a couple of stools where we could sit at the bench. After we had wiped things down, we took a seat on stools at one of the worktables.

"Pop that sucker open," Tessa cried.

Shaking my head, I said, "Um... how? I don't have a corkscrew."

"You men are never prepared, and my shoulder bag is in your car. Look in the drawers."

"Here is something we can use," I said. "A large screwdriver."

Within minutes of pushing and pulling, trial and error, I had the cork removed. I passed the bottle over to her, "A toast to one of the bravest nurses that I know."

Picking it up, she took a deep swig, "Oh my God, that is good. Best wine I've ever had. Remind me to thank the Fallbrook vintners."

"I actually know who they are," I chuckled. "The family that runs the hotel own the winery. I had a glass of their wine the first night I was here, but I bet this tastes better." I took a big swig. "Wow, amazing."

For the next couple of minutes, we passed the bottle back and forth. Soon, we were a little happier.

Tessa said, "That was better than a donut. Now we need to figure out how to get out of here."

Nodding, I said, "I don't want the party to be over, but you're right. How do we get out of here?"

Reality came quickly. I cleared off more space on one of the worktops and opened the little book to a blank page. Picking up a pen, I said, "We've got a quarter mile tunnel. Both ends with metal locked doors. The front door is hidden behind a workshed. With the door and shed in place, sound will not travel very far. The Mercedes is out front but hidden in the grove. Eventually, people will come looking for us."

"That could take days or even weeks, Trace. That grove is thick, and we only happened to see the footprints leading here."

"If someone does find the workshed, I think our voices would carry that far."

"But they have to find it, Trace. It's way in the back of the grove. If they locate the car, good chance they might locate the shed."

"That is one solution. We know the house out front is an active crime scene. But is there a reason to search back here?"

Tessa frowned. "Not sure. They don't know what we know."

"So what are other possible options?"

Tessa scribbled a picture on the sheet. "We could set a fire by the other exit. Smoke may attract someone."

"Interesting idea, except we might get smoked out. Dying by smoke inhalation is not my idea of a way to die."

"We could try it up here by this front door. Just use a small piece of cardboard from one of these boxes."

I'm game," I said. "I even have a few matches in my wallet."

Tessa wadded up some cardboard. We stood by the front door, and I lit it up. It started smoking. "Wow, the smoke is not going out the door. It's going into the tunnel. Let's follow this along."

I kept the flame going as we slowly walked through the tunnel. The smoke kept going inward. "This is probably exiting out the other end of the tunnel," I said. "Maybe we can attract someone."

We kept walking slowly, and the internal air draft kept the smoke going inward. As we turned the corner midway through the tunnel, something strange happened. The smoke went straight up.

"Look at that Tessa, instead of going to the other end of the tunnel it is going up to the ceiling." In the light of the cardboard flames, the top of the tunnel here was covered in old plywood. Over to one side, I could see the metal electrical conduit go up into the plywood. Reaching up, I pushed on the wood. It raised slightly. Handing the burning cardboard to Tessa, I pushed the plywood to one side. All of a sudden the whole sheet of plywood fell to the floor. Looking up in the light of the flames was a vertical shaft with a crude ladder. The smoke went straight up. The central vent. Maybe, like the smoke, an exit to freedom. When in doubt, look up.

CHAPTER 54

A stairway to heaven just opened up above us. A little over two feet in diameter, it was just big enough for one person to climb. Whether it would lead to the promised land, or just promise more frustration was to be seen, but there it was. It consisted of a ladder made crudely out of 2x4 lumber, tacked onto the side of the vent chamber. It appeared to go at least twenty or thirty feet up.

Tessa looked up, "Pretty narrow chamber. With that leg of yours, I think I ought to be the one to venture up here."

"As much as I want to bust out of here, you're right. My ankle hurts just looking at that climb. I'll grab one of the stools and the flashlight."

"Get a hammer too. Who knows what we'll find at the top."

Making a quick trip back to the work areas, I rounded up a stool, flashlight, and a claw hammer. I also found an old baseball hat in one of the cabinets. With any crime scene, experience told me, wipe down any surfaces for fingerprints. Should we get to freedom, having anonymity would be an advantage. With a rag, I went over all common areas that might contain a print, including the wine bottle.

With the stool in place, I put a cloth on top to keep our footprints from being visible. While my shoes had smooth soles, and Tessa had casual tennis shoes, not leaving behind easy identifiers would be key.

Tessa noticed my action and asked, "What's with the rag?"

"Just covering our tracks. Think about it. We just had two dead women come through here. Is anyone going to believe they came to life?"

"Good point, Trace. I did notice they both were wearing gloves. Didn't make sense until I thought it through. If they exit the country, there will be no confirmation. Our word against... what? They left no prints."

"That's why I wiped all smooth surfaces down. Better safe than sorry. As an ex-cop, I always put myself in law enforcement shoes. If a detective were to come through here, what would they find?"

"A lot of us and nothing of them."

"Yep. Certainly wouldn't want to go to jail for the deeds of imaginary dead women."

Tessa shook her head, "Let's stop imagining getting out of here and give it a go."

I placed the stool under the vent. Shining the light up the chamber, I said, "That ladder is pretty rickety. You may want to brace with your arms and body as you climb."

"Give me that hat. That should deflect any rats or mice on the way up."

"That's a pleasant thought, not to mention spiders and other bugs."

"Shut up. I may be a nurse and all, but I still hate spiders. I'll make sure to send all that vermin down to you below. You'll need to boost me up and then hand me the flashlight. Hang that hammer on one of my belt loops. This is one time that I wish I had long sleeves on."

As she stood on the stool, she could reach the first rung easily. I tucked the hammer in one of her back belt loops.

"Grab my legs and give me a boost," she said.

"Here goes." With that, she was off and climbing. I stood to one side of the shaft as she stepped higher. Loose dirt and rock came tumbling down, just missing my head.

"How you doing?" I yelled.

"This ladder is ancient. Hope it holds."

With that, I heard one of the rungs break through along with a curse.

Dirt, rock and old wood fell.

"You OK?" I yelled.

"About lost the flashlight on that one. I do see light above."

As her voice got harder to hear, more debris fell.

"I heard a distant whoop of joy, "I'm at the top. Looks like a wire vent plate and a latch. Here goes."

I could hear metal on metal. "This thing is rusted, but I'm making progress."

I yelled, "Great news."

Just then I heard her scream. "Arrrgghh"

I yelled up, "You OK?"

"There are gopher holes all around up here. Just met one face to face."

More banging and pinging.

"Any luck?"

Three loud taps.

"Not sure."

Three more taps

"Think of donuts." I quipped.

I could hear her laugh, "Here's one for a cinnamon roll."

Smack, smack, sproing.

"I'm through. Freedom," she yelled down. "Can you get on the ladder?"

"I'll give it a go. Otherwise, you'll have to come around front."

"They padlocked it, remember."

"Damn, I forgot. OK, here goes."

Plodding my way up on the stool with my good leg, I was high enough that I could reach to the second rung. With difficulty, I pulled myself up until my right knee hit the first rung. Then it was pull up with my arms, rest my knee, one step at a time. Everything hurt, especially my left leg and where the bullet grazed my arm, but this was my way to freedom. Slowly but surely, one step at a time, I made the thirty-foot climb. Reaching the top, Tessa helped pull me out into the middle of an avocado grove."

She helped me up on my good leg. I said, "Freedom and fresh air. I wondered if we would ever make it out of there. No one would ever know this mine vent was here. It's flush with the ground. Looks like an irrigation cover."

Nodding, Tessa said, "What a brilliant hiding place, Trace. Check this out. The electrical box that powers the sprinkler controls for the grove splits off right here. The conduit drops into the dirt next to the vent."

"So the electricity for the grove also powers the mine. No one would ever notice."

Tessa hugged me again, "We made it out of another bind, and you owe me at least a donut, but since I pulled you out of this mess, I'm going for lunch."

"Coming right up. Let's get back down to the car. I need to get Martino involved in this. Another jewel, and two women who are both supposed to be dead, and somehow we have to explain to Mark that his wife had tried to kill him. Kick some of those avocado leaves over the vent so it won't be seen."

"Covered. No one would know anyone was here. Let's go to the donut shop on Main. It has a pay phone and a little room off to the side. Good place to meet."

We made our way back down the grove on the hill until we got down to the Mercedes. The rest of the property still deserted. We were soon on our way.

. . .

Goody's Donuts was a cute but small wooden post-war house, converted to a proper business, Just off the corner of Main and Fallbrook avenues, it boasted a large sign, a few hard to get parking spaces, and three picnic tables out front under a huge pepper tree. One of the outside windows was converted into a to-go window, but most business was conducted inside. The aroma of coffee and sugar-laden donuts greeted us as pulled into the lot.

"Park around back under those large trees, out of sight." Tessa said. "I know the owner."

"Good idea. This blue sports car is like a billboard, advertising its intrinsic beauty with color and chrome. Best not to attract attention."

"Agreed. Now that I have my shoulder bag back, I've got sunglasses again. With them I can be here, hidden in plain sight, feeling safer. Not that I don't want to be seen with you, Trace, but it seems like this town has eyes in every crack and crevice."

Pulling a ten dollar bill from my wallet, I said, "Get what you want. I'm going to use the pay phone out back to call Martino. I'll take one of those huge cinnamon rolls."

She nodded, "I'll be in the side room. The place is quiet now. Can't believe it's almost noon."

Dialing home, I caught Martino in the shop.

Picking up, he said, "What's up?"

"Too much to explain on the phone. Can you break away and drive up to Fallbrook? About an hour's drive."

"Busy day, man. Kawasaki overhaul. Can't it wait?"

"Sorry man, but we had a couple of women come back from the dead. They left Tessa and I for dead. "

"What?"

"We just escaped from an underground hellhole. Lucky to be talking to you. Need your help. . . Bad.

"Where are you?"

"Donut Shop, Main and Fallbrook."

"Hey, you know that no self-respecting law enforcement guy can pass up a donut shop. Be there soon."

Martino was that kind of guy. Not a lot of questions. Just action. I walked back into the shop and sat with Tessa for a few minutes.

"Martino's on his way." I said. "Hopefully, he can help us make sense of things."

Tessa held out her arm, "In the meantime, there is something you need to do. You need to call that girlfriend of yours."

"Oh man, In all the death defying commotion, I forgot about that. She'll probably be pissed, but I know she's got a million things going, just back from New York and all."

"I know I'm pissed. You told her 9 am. It's afternoon. Get on the phone. You can have your donut when you get back."

Smiling I said, "Alright, alright. . . It's one pm. She should be back from lunch."

Walking out back to the phone again, I dialed. Janet picked up first ring, "Hey Janet, this is Trace." I said.

"About time," she cried. "I thought you died or something."

"Almost. Crazy things going on here in Fallbrook."

"Can we talk later today? I got a meeting coming up in ten minutes with two important clients. Short story, the divorce is started. Not pretty, but started. Sounds like a lot on your end too."

"Dead perp, two dead cops, and a whole lot more. Martino is on his way up here to help me out."

"Wow, sorry Trace, I can't talk now. Got to get this meeting setup. Sounds like we have a whole lot to discuss."

"OK, I'll call you later today."

"Sounds good. Oh, by the way, a large envelope came to you by courier. Fallbrook return address. Says urgent on the front. Want me to open it?"

"Please. Not sure what it might be?"

I could hear rustling as she tore the envelope open. She said, "Looks like photographs. Let me turn them over."

There was a pause for a second; then her voice went very loud. "What in the hell are you doing in Fallbrook, asshole? I can't believe this shit. There are three large 8x10 black and white photos of you. One in bed with some gal, half dressed in a skimpy top. Here's another. Looks like a naked gal in a neglige and you are trying to grab her breasts, that other gal in the bed behind her. Another looks like it was taken by the naked gal herself. I can see her hand reaching for your bare chest."

"What are you talking about, Janet. I know nothing. . ."

"You know nothing? The note in the envelope says you can send $500 to get the negatives."

"What?"

"Don't ever bother calling me again, you total friggin asshole. You can't explain your way out of this one. I go back to New York to move on with our relationship, and this is what you do? Go to hell, Armstrong."

Click!

My head spun. Then it came to me. Now I knew what the ghost and flashing light in the hotel room was. . . Blackmail.

CHAPTER 55

In the flash of a second, everything made sense. The bright light in the hotel room was the flash of a camera. The wisp of smoke was the burn of the flashbulb. The ghost was a real woman, scantily dressed. How she got in the room and how she disappeared remained a mystery.

Janet and I had been through a lot, but this was different. Trust was broken. Simple explanations would not overcome explicit photos. Explaining Tessa in bed with me would be difficult. Explaining a bare-chested woman might be near impossible. I needed help. To think of losing a healthy relationship over a blackmail attempt made me furious.

Walking back into the donut shop, Tessa could read my face. "Not good," she said as I sat across from her. "What happened?"

"It's all your fault," I said.

"My fault? How so?"

"The photos on Janet's desk have you lying in bed behind me. Your skimpy jogging suit top didn't help."

"What? What in the hell are you talking about?"

"That's what I asked, right before she hung up on me. The ghost with the bare breasts sent her over the edge."

"Ghost. . . Bare breasts. . . Trace Armstrong, start at the beginning."

It seems that a large envelope arrived for me at my office today. Janet helps run my business, so I had her open it. It contained three photos. One of you behind me on the bed. One of me reaching out for a scantily clad woman with uncovered breasts, and the last, taken by the ghost itself, of its female hand, reaching out for my bare chest."

"How. . . You mean. . . "

"Yep, the ghost was real, and that bright flash of light was a flash bulb on a camera. Three nights, three flashes, three pictures. Hell, they only want $500 for the negatives."

"Oh my God, Trace, I thought I'd seen it all with you, but this is just crazy. I'd say you were nuts, but I saw it with my own eyes. How in the hell did that woman get in the room, and more important, how did she get out?"

"I've got lots of questions about this, but the most important is how do I explain this to Janet? She is unbelievably pissed right now."

Shaking her head, she said, "I'll tell you this, don't let much time go by. If I were Janet, I'd be in orbit about now."

"Believe me, she is. But. . . Got to put my P. I. hat on. You have a pen and paper in that shoulder bag of yours? Write these questions down."

"Go ahead."

"One, does the hotel know about this? Two, how did they get in and out? Three, How did they get the photos to my office so quick?"

Tessa thought for a second, "The hotel would have to have some relationship with this person. Whether it was intended or not is another question."

"I haven't seen the pictures, but we might have a better idea if we can get some type of description. The photos were eight by tens. Black and white. Sounds like a pro to me."

"That large size would indicate a pro for sure. Black and white means a local darkroom. They had to develop them overnight and then deliver them. We have a large room at the hospital for x-rays. Developer, equipment, darkroom. I'd say it indicates a professional photographer."

Nodding, I said, "Given the time and delivery, they wouldn't be able to send out for lab development and get them back that soon. A one-hour photo place does 4x6 color prints in an hour, but not enlargements."

"So who takes photos on a regular basis at a hotel?"

"Wedding photographers. Special event photographers—dinners, retirements, and graduations. With a hotel like the Fallbrook that has been around a long time, there are probably dozens of regional photographers that use it on a regular basis."

"But who would the hotel recommend for a party or dinner on short notice? If we find that out, we can probably reduce our list extensively."

"I say we test the waters later this afternoon. Let's see if we can hire someone to take photos of us at the hotel. Since I'm still staying there, I bet the front desk can accommodate us."

Tessa stood up. "In the meantime, I have an idea," she said. "How about if Nurse Contessa calls Janet for you. I'll pretend I'm calling from the hospital. Want to check on your burns."

"At this point, Tessa, I'm game for just about anything. Last she said, she would never talk to me again."

"Us women are like that, aren't we? Give me your number. I'll use my nurse charm and directness."

"She is pretty direct herself. Office manager. Lots of experience with deadbeats."

"Tell you what. Money on the table. Five dollars says I can get through to her."

"You're on," I sighed.

We both walked outside to the pay phone. Janet had about thirty minutes to have cooled down. Probably out of her meeting by now. Tessa picked up the receiver, "What's Janet's last name?"

"Johnson. The business name is Sloan Business Management."

"OK, You dial, I'll talk. You can listen in."

I dialed the phone. In three rings, I could hear a rather exasperated Janet answer the phone.

"Sloan Management, Janet speaking."

Tessa said, "This is Contessa from the Fallbrook Hospital. I'm trying to reach Trace Armstrong ."

"He isn't here, can I take a message?"

"I'm calling about his burn scan. It's important that I talk to him soon."

"He has been out of the office for a few days. I'm his office manager. Is he in trouble?"

"He was burned badly in a house fire. Can barely walk on a damaged ankle. There is a risk of infection if we don't redress the burn."

"Last I talked to him, he was staying at the Fallbrook Hotel."

"I treated him there, the last two days. He's in lots of pain."

"He called earlier today. Not sure where he is now?"

"Are you Janet Johnson, by chance? He has you listed as 'Girlfriend' on the contact card."

"Yes, I am."

"If you hear from him, he needs to check in as soon as possible."

"I'll let him know."

"By the way, you must be one lucky lady. All he talked about was you since he got burned. Worried about you being gone."

"Just got back last night. Long tiring trip."

"He is gonna need your help when he gets back. Tough patient. After the house fire, he was involved in a shootout. Two cops died."

"What? He mentioned something about the cops."

"He just got a contact wound but a big scare."

"Oh man."

"Last time he checked in this morning, Trace was waiting for his friend Martino to get here. Do you know Martino?"

"Trace's roommate. Nice guy. Law enforcement."

"Hopefully, Trace can get things wrapped up when he gets here. On top of everything else, we got some kind of blackmail photo scheme going on at the hotel."

"What? How do you know that?"

"Cause Trace told me that you received pictures earlier today, and I'm in the background."

Janet's voice raised on the phone... "What—who are you? You're the gal in the bed? Now you're getting me really pissed."

"I know it looks bad, but we have to figure out who the other woman is. This lady appeared in Trace's hotel room the last three nights after midnight. Like a ghost. Flash of light. Disappeared into a wisp of smoke."

"You expect me to believe this ghost crap? That woman was naked. What were you doing, partying all night? What the hell are you doing in Trace's room?"

"Janet, you have to believe me. I know you want to hang up on me. We had a killer on the loose. Car chase, shootout. Trace saved my life."

"I'm just furious right now. I come back from a husband trying to screw me over and now this shit."

"Trace needs your help now. He's in the other room. He needs a description of the other woman in the photos. Please don't hang up."

There was a long pause. "Alright, put him on,"

Tessa nodded for me to delay a minute and then pick up the phone. I said, "Janet, please listen. We've got some kind of photo scam going on at this hotel."

"No kidding. How could you have a naked woman in your room and think it was a ghost? I don't understand?"

"We are trying to get to the bottom of this. To explain everything that has gone on for the last three days would take me hours. But bottom line, I need to know what the woman looks like so we may have a clue who we are dealing with."

I could hear her fussing with the envelope on her desk. She said, "Unfortunately, the face and body are covered with lace. Pictures are in black and white. Light colored hair, shoulder length. Ample chest."

"What does the note say?"

"For negatives, send five hundred dollars in cash to P.O. Box 1550, Fallbrook."

"Can I ask a big favor?"

"I'm not in the mood for favors about now."

"Can you drive up in the morning and bring the photos? I need your help to get to the bottom of this. Need to get this solved before leaving town."

"I don't know. These pictures are incriminating." Another pause. "I can probably come early, before work. All I can say is you better have a good explanation for all of this."

"You know I love you, Janet. We've been through too much for me to let this kind of crap break us apart."

"There are two things I know, Trace Armstrong. I love you a lot. The other is the woman in the bed behind you is drop dead gorgeous. Nurse or not, you better have a good explanation, or I'll set fire to your good leg."

CHAPTER 56

I hung up the phone. As we walked back to our table, I said, "I owe you big time for that conversation. You're one hell of a motivator. How did you know what to say?"

"That's what I do for a living. Do you think people like being in a hospital, being peeked and poked? No way. They fight me every inch of the road. It's my job to make sure they go through with the necessary procedure or operation. Pain and significant discomfort are usually involved. Your girlfriend was easy compared to some of the tough guys that come in. The tougher they are on the outside, the bigger the wimp they are when they are lying in a hospital bed. Believe me, it's not just these baby blues that gets them to cooperate, I guide them to a decision by limiting their options. Give them an easy route and a tough one. When I eliminate the usual excuses they most always comply."

"You had me sold. Now all we need to do is tell Martino a believable story when he gets here."

Tessa nodded, "From what you say, he's a trustworthy guy. I say we level with him. Hopefully, he'll know how to proceed."

"We need to get you back to normal. Having your house in limbo is crazy."

"It would be nice to sleep in my own bed, even with all the

commotion," she said. "Now that we know there was a live person taking pictures in your hotel room, I think you'd like to be somewhere normal too."

"No kidding. That lumpy old mattress at home sounds pretty good right now. After we get done with Martino, I'd like you to help me do a little more sleuthing at the hotel. . . That is if you're up for it."

"A little Ghostbuster's action? I'm definitely up for it."

"The big question is, how did this woman get in my room, and an even bigger question, how did she escape in the blink of an eye?"

"That old hotel certainly has it's share of secrets. Lots of ghost stories. I want to open the blind and take a good look."

"I bet we find something, now that we know about the pictures. Think about it, Tessa, whoever sent the pictures wanted the pictures to be at my given address when I returned. My guess is that the person has access to the room schedule."

Nodding, she said, "Makes sense. They obviously have some access to the hotel. I like your idea of having pictures taken. I have a hunch the perp is nearby."

****

The rumble of a large Kawasaki motorcycle filled the air. Glancing out the window, I saw Martino dismounting from a large police bike in the parking lot. Martino is a lanky guy, half Japanese, half Hispanic, about 5-8. The scrappy kind of guy you'd imagine teaching a karate class.

Sticking my head out the door, I motioned him inside. Introducing him, I said, "Tessa and I have been through a lot over the last two days. I don't want to waste your time. I need to make sure that her life gets back to normal. No more death threats, assassination attempts, etcetera."

Martino sat across from me. Passing over a police folder, he said, "I agree. Good news on the colonel. They recovered a small caliber handgun from the accident scene. Found under the wrecked jeep. A preliminary report says ballistics match the bullets that killed the two

Fallbrook cops. That matches your story and will certainly lower your suspect score. Also found an enormous amount of blood in the vehicle. Military police are working on it from their end."

"Let's draw this out on paper," I said. "I want to get you up to speed on what we know at this point." Turning over one of the sheets of paper, I pulled out a pen. Over the next five minutes, Tessa and I drew out a timeline on a sheet of paper, complete with characters and motives of the original jewel theft. From museum theft to the farmers market, all the way up to delivery to the colonel, the plot was straight forward.

Martino traced the line with his finger, "Makes perfect sense. You've got a quiet museum theft, a jewel replacement to allay suspicion from an intermediary trafficker. This person delivers the real gem to the colonel, who has an overseas buyer. The process is reversed to get paid. Regular setup in the jewel theft business. Imposter jewels are not uncommon. The avocado scheme is unique and brilliant. Would have never guessed that. So what went wrong?"

"From what we understand, my uncle inadvertently delivered an imposter stone to the colonel."

Tessa spoke up, "I mixed up the boxes from the farmer's market by mistake. Paul took the one that was supposed to go back down to the thief."

"Uh oh," said Martino. "I imagine that didn't end so well."

Tessa put her head down, tears welling up, "Not at all."

I replied, "From what we understand, the colonel discovered the imposter stone. He was livid and had a couple of dirty Fallbrook cops rough him up after the drop trying to determine where the real stone was. My uncle was drunk, had no idea about the mixup. The police went a little too far, and my uncle fell backward. He ended up hitting his head and died. They left his body in the abandoned part of the old hotel."

Martino shook his head. "So now everything is up in the air."

"Exactly. He sends the cops over to my uncle's house the next day to try and find the diamond. They tear everything up in the shed and in the house, but they don't find an avocado box or the jewel. They report back, empty handed. In the meantime, my uncle's house is set on fire."

"I see the writing on the wall," Martino said. "The house fire covers their tracks. Colonel then sends the guys to Tessa's place. The next link in the chain."

"Evidently the cops or the colonel knew about Tessa," I said. "He sent the police over to search the place in the morning. They didn't find anything. He then met them over there at night. We overheard the commotion. He found another box of avocados, but no diamond. He accused the cops of taking it. Lots of arguing. He then had them open their car and trunk. Nothing found. Two shots later those guys were in the trunk and dead. He saw us, the chase ensued, and he ended up off the side of the bridge."

"I still have the scar from that one," Tessa mused, as she pointed to her forehead.

"Yikes, that is one close call. So at this point, we have a lot of conjecture and overheard conversation. Avocados and avocado boxes. We still don't know if the diamond exists and the colonel is now dead. Is that about it?"

Tessa glanced at me nervously, not knowing how to proceed. I spoke up, "I need to level with you, Martino, we did find the diamond."

"What. . . Where was it?"

"It was in a different box of avocados. We discovered it by accident when Tessa went to make some guacamole, yesterday morning."

"You found the diamond? So what did you do with it? Did you tell the sheriff?"

"Long story. I'll explain in a minute. No, we didn't tell the sheriff. With all the commotion, we would be prime suspects if we had it."

"OK, so you found the diamond in an avocado. Then what?"

"That made everything click. The story started to unfold. Now we had an idea what was going on and how they were trafficking the gems. Then we just asked the question, where would the diamond go from Paul? That's when Tessa mentioned Colonel Rainer Jackson. We knew my uncle died in town after being in a bar."

Tessa said, "Paul used to talk about seeing the colonel at Maverick's Bar. We just put two and two together."

I quipped, "I got the great idea to see if the colonel was involved. We just went to the bar yesterday afternoon and left a message for him."

"What kind of strange message did you leave?"

"Just to meet us at Tessa's address on De Luz at 8 pm. That we had something of his. Something that he lost."

"Are you crazy, Trace? So you called this guy out?"

"Hey, I figured if he wasn't involved he'd just put it off as a hoax. Sure enough, he showed up, but not until his two Fallbrook cop friends ransacked Tessa's place the hour before."

"So what are you guys doing all this time?"

"We were hiding out at Tessa's next door neighbor's house."

"You are nuts, Armstrong. Go on—"

"Probably, but we had to know what was going on. Who the players were. The sheriff told us point blank that they only had one car through the area per day. If Tessa had gone home yesterday, she probably wouldn't be sitting here now."

"So don't tell me, let me guess. You snuck over to Tessa's house while the guys were trashing it."

"You know me too well, Martino. Went in the back room. Overheard everything."

"So what happened next."

"Once the colonel shot the cops, we realized how crazy he was. We ran for it. Didn't expect violence like that at all. I tripped over a sprinkler, and he caught wind of us. Took a couple of pot shots. We took off in the Mercedes. Next thing I know, he is chasing us in his Jeep."

Martino said, "So you guys have a shootout and end up running the colonel off the road. He survives and is killed later in a shootout with sheriff deputies. I take it you still have the diamond?"

"I'll explain about the diamond in a minute. However, we now know someone was impersonating the colonel. Short story. He's didn't start the house fire."

"How do you know that? Was it the cops?"

"No, but we know who did."

Glancing up, he said, "Go on."

301

"Two dead women set it."

"What? Say that slower. . . Two dead women set the fire. . . How can that be?"

"They came back from the dead," Tessa said. "I know what you are thinking. We're crazy. We both thought we were crazy when we saw who it was."

"OK, you've peaked my interest. Who might these mystery ladies be?"

"I need to start at the beginning again. Otherwise, it won't make sense."

"Go ahead, " he said, shaking his head.

"Tessa and I thought the whole jewel theft story was over and done with this morning. We knew the colonel was dead. Most of the pieces fit, but there were a few things that just didn't seem right. When we had overheard the cops talking, some things just didn't add up. I decided to go over to my uncle's place and look around. The main thing was I couldn't figure out where he actually did his jewelry work."

Tessa smiled, "I told Trace about a little gardening shed up in the avocado grove behind his uncle's place. That is the only other structure on the property."

I continued, "We took a look inside. It was just an old shed, full of fertilizer, gardening tools, and footprints that led to a wall."

"What? Footprints into a wall?"

"That's what we said. With a little investigation, we found the rickety old shed was actually the entrance to an old mine."

"You've got to be kidding?"

"Nope, the back panel of the shed slid to one side revealing a locked metal door. Long story short, we found my uncle's hidden workshop, equipped with electricity, heavy duty tools and lots of assorted gemstones."

Martino seemed incredulous, "So there is more to this story than meets the eye."

"Actually, quite a bit more. Tessa and I looked around and discovered my uncle's journal, complete with notes about many different jewel theft transactions including this one. This robbery was actually planned over two years ago."

"The hidden life and workshop of Uncle Paul Armstrong."

"You got it. The work area has florescent lights, a safe and two work cabinets. I decided to take a walk back into the mine. It is about a quarter mile long. Ancient. After exploring, I came back up front, only to find Mark's stepmom, Catarina, with a gun pointed at Tessa's head."

"Catarina. How could that be? Didn't she die a few years ago?

That's what she wanted everyone to think."

What happened then?"

"We had a negotiation. She wanted the diamond; I wanted Tessa. Thankfully I had found a gun in the safe. We had a standoff. Even though she is 5-7, she hid behind Tessa. I didn't have a clear shot.

Martino shook his head, "Man, negotiations with hostages don't usually go well."

This one didn't. I put the diamond on the floor and pushed it halfway to her, hoping to get a clear shot. Short story, she ended up with the diamond and was just about to end Tessa's life, when a mystery person came from the back of the cave and put a gun to my back."

"So who was that?"

Glancing his way, I said, "My cousin's wife, Debbi."

"What? How could that be? Debbi died in the fire."

Nodding, I said, "That's what they wanted everyone to believe. They conveniently set up a cadaver to take the place of Debbi in the house fire. Catarina had been in hiding in Mexico for the last two years."

Shaking his head in disbelief, he said, "You've gone all crazy on me. Now you've got women coming back from the dead."

"Believe me, Martino, these two women had the perfect plot to hijack the diamond and completely throw suspicion to the colonel." I overlaid the plot by Debbi and Catarina to seize the jewel and explained how they had set things up.

Martino took a pen to the plot line on the paper. "So if I hear you right, we have two women, one who has been presumed dead for two years, come in and hijack the theft process. They had planned to take the avocado box with the diamond in it, set fire to your uncle's house with your uncle, your cousin and a cadaver in it. To the outside world, this is a tragic accident. It is setup to look like a propane tank explosion. Debbi is presumed dead. The women go over the border to Mexico and places south. They sell the diamond for millions and live happily ever after."

"As crazy as that sounds, that is the basic plot," I said. "Oh and you can add a life insurance scam on top of that."

Tessa said, "Everything was going according to plan until Uncle Paul died. They had to change parameters. Debbi had called me and asked if I still had a box of avocados. I said I did. I actually had two boxes. On Sunday when Debbi, Trace and Mark came by, I sent over just one box of avocados. Unfortunately for them, it didn't have the diamond in it. When they got back to Paul's house, Debbi knocked out her husband and Trace with vet tranquilizer, set a parameter fire, and was ready to go with Catarina. It was then that they discovered the diamond was not in the box. The women dragged Mark out of the fire, hog-tied him with duct tape, and tried to find out what had happened to the diamond. He didn't know anything, so they dumped his body and his truck off of De Luz Road."

Martino jotted down some notes on the drawing. "So we had three people looking for this diamond the last two days."

"Yep. What we found out was, Catarina had a key to the lock on the metal door at the other end of the mine. When they saw us enter the front, Catarina came in the front, Debbi came in the back. Debbi watched the gem transaction from the darkness. Once Catarina had the diamond and had tested its hardness, I got the gun in my back.

"So then what?"

"They locked the tunnel doors and left us for dead."

"So why didn't they shoot you too?"

"Probably in case something went wrong."

Tessa spoke up, "Actually Debbi wanted to shoot me in the head. Catarina said she would rather see us die slowly. No one would ever know we were there."

"So how did you get out? You're sitting here now."

Tessa said, "They didn't realize there was a vent shaft. Thankfully that led to freedom."

Martino asked, "So I take it they are on their way to South America with the Ice Blue Diamond."

Tessa said, "Unfortunately, they got the stone. Supposedly going to sell it for over two million dollars."

As Tessa was talking with Martino, I secretly slipped off my right shoe. Undoing the inner chamber, I picked out the diamond with two fingers. I said, "They got what they thought was the Ice Blue Diamond. Here is the real one." Tessa gasped as I dropped the actual Ice Blue on the table in front of them.

CHAPTER 57

"Oh my God, Trace Armstrong, get that death diamond away from me," Tessa screamed. "I had no idea you still had it."

Glancing at Martino, I said, "Can you do something with this? There is way too much blood and tears on this light blue jewel."

Martino shook his head, "So if this is the real diamond, what do the women have?"

I replied, "They have an Ice Blue Cubic Zirconia, specially designed for this transaction. Almost an identical copy according to Uncle Paul's journal. Unlike some of the lesser fakes, it has the hardness almost to match a diamond. It was supposed to go back to the museum to take the place of the real thing after a final sizing modification."

Martino asked, "Aren't CZ's white? How did he pull that off?"

"Radiation treatment, evidently," I said. It was in a box in the safe that had a nuclear radiation warning on it."

Martino pondered the situation for a moment, and then said, "Let me make a quick phone call." With that, he walked outside to the payphone.

I reached over for Tessa's hand. I said, "I had no idea how much crap we've been through the last couple of days till we wrote it down."

Tessa looked worried, "I hope Martino is not turning us in for jewel theft."

"Not a chance," I said. "He has a lot of connections. I imagine he is calling in some favors right now."

In about ten minutes, Martino walked into the back room. "Good news," he said. "I talked to Fred, one of my insurance company connections. He ran a query on the Indemnity database and found that the Ice Blue is insured by Fairmont Mutual. Fairmont is a company that I've worked with in the past as a consultant. Are you familiar with high-end jewelry insurance?"

Tessa and I both shook our heads. I said, "I know a little bit, working with law enforcement, but nothing concrete."

"When items of high value are insured, one of the problems that most clients, museums, and insurance companies dread is the threat of a security breach. If the news media were to get a whiff that this diamond had been stolen, insurance rates for all items in the museum would go up, public perception of the institution would go down, and private donations and consignments would dry up. It's worth a lot to keep total discretion in these matters. Insurance companies and institutions would much rather pay a suitable finders fee for the return of an item rather than prosecute or go public with the breach."

Nodding, I said, "So what you are saying is, the museum and possibly insurance representatives from Fairmont Mutual might be willing to pay for this diamonds return, as long as the transaction is kept quiet."

"Exactly. I mentioned to Fred that I might have an item of considerable value that might be available for restoration if compensation can be arranged for the individuals that found the item."

Tessa asked, "So this is like a quiet reward. As long as we don't go public we might receive a benefit."

Martino said, "As we sit here, I want to go over some things as an insurance consultant that I think you should consider as well as from a legal standpoint. If you are willing to keep this situation in confidence, I'm sure we can secure compensation for each one of you."

"I'm confident that you can count on me," I said. Tessa also replied in the affirmative.

"I have another question, "Do you know if your cousin Mark is aware of the mine at the back of your uncle's property?"

"I'm sure he doesn't. We spent the afternoon in the front work shed, and he didn't know any more about his dad's property than I did."

"Good. Here is what I recommend. As a private investigator, you are under no obligation to reveal your client's personal affairs. As a law enforcement professional, I would recommend that you allow the local agencies to investigate this matter thoroughly and let them come to their own conclusions. Currently, if you were to reveal the whereabouts of the mine and tell the story of the two women, you and your family may be liable for a host of perceived crimes. Since the women are currently out of the country, you would have no way to verify what you say is true. Since there are deaths involved, insurance investigators may also be involved. With the passing of the colonel, you'll have military investigators as well."

Tessa nodded, "So you are saying we should act like today never happened."

"Unless questioned specifically, I would recommend that you keep this conversation and events in confidence."

"I am certainly willing to do that, especially with the fact that my cousin will be dealing with the death of his wife," I said.

"I'll tell you this, Trace. The chances of Catarina and Debbi surviving the financial transaction of selling a valuable gem like the Ice Blue to a Cartel or other official is slim at best. It is probably best for everyone if things are left as they are."

Tessa said, "I will be checking in on Mark at the hospital this afternoon. Things are going to be very hard for a while. He doesn't need the added burden of knowing that his wife tried to kill him. This conversation doesn't leave this room."

Martino picked up the diamond, wrapped it in a napkin and put it in his pocket. Martino went over some details and made notes. "I will see that it is returned to its proper resting place. I'll be in touch about arranging compensation."

After a few minutes, we wrapped up our notes. Tessa and I said goodbye to Martino. I put my hand on her shoulder. "I don't like keeping secrets, but I do agree with Martino that we should just leave the investigation to the sheriff's department."

She smiled, "As a nurse, I have taken an oath of patient privacy and confidence. You can count on me. We certainly did nothing wrong. Your quick thinking probably saved my life more than once over the past few days."

"You certainly saved mine. My burn and my leg are feeling better. Let's go back over to the hotel and see about getting our pictures taken."

"Sounds good, Trace. Once we are done there, I'm going back home, check on everything, and then do an extended night shift at the hospital."

"Why would you want to do a night shift?"

"So I can get some sleep. The hospital has a great nap room. I also need to check on your cousin. The thought of sleeping in my house is still a little creepy."

"I can't say I blame you."

I sat back down for a second and pulled the blue topaz out of my left shoe.

"What's with that?" she asked.

"I'm not sure. It's certainly not the cursed diamond. Maybe I'll leave it in the room where I found it."

Tessa smiled, "Let's do something special with it. Let's have it be in the photo with us. Whoever was in your room will certainly recognize it."

CHAPTER 58

The old blue lady looked dingy in the afternoon haze. The Fallbrook Hotel had seen better days, better years, better clients. Like an old woman in a nursing home, waiting to die, it just sat there. The usual signs of hotel life gone. Yet as Tessa and I walked in the front door, a familiar and friendly voice greeted me, "Well if it isn't Trace Armstrong with a lovely lady," said Alice, from behind the front counter. "Haven't seen you around much."

"Hello Alice," I replied. "This town has been keeping us busy. This is my friend, Tessa. One of the locals from out on De Luz."

"Hello Tessa," she replied. "Weren't you here the other night after the fire? I remember those striking blue eyes of yours."

Tessa smiled, "Yep, one of the ones on the cot. Mr. Armstrong here saved me from the hordes in the parlor. Let me bunk in his room. You sure looked busy that night."

"Poured more beer and wine than we had in months. Profitable night. A few broken cots and some loud boys, but overall, I'd rather have some rowdies than the creaky silence of this old place most evenings."

"You folks still running the winery? I love some of your Pinot's."

"Barely, stuck here with the termites, tell ya the truth. Since dad died, everything has been hard. Probably have to sell the vineyard soon."

Tessa replied, "Why not sell this old place. I'm sure the real estate is worth a fortune."

"As I was telling Trace the other day, the city council has this place listed as a historic site, but there is no funding. Means we can't tear it down."

"What a shame," Tessa said. "You can't fix it; you can't get rid of it."

I spoke up, "Hey Alice, Tessa and I are thinking of getting some pictures taken. You got any photographers you would recommend?"

"You aren't getting married are you, Mr. Armstrong?"

I laughed. "Oh nothing like that," I said. "Just some friendly shots."

"There are three photographers in town that I'm aquatinted with. The first is Peggy, who does boudoir and fashion shots. Works out of her home. Know her from her many client and magazine shots out at the winery. Nelson Scott is a prominent wedding and business photographer off of main. Always booked up months in advance, but does excellent work. Then there is my mom's sister. She has a place just down the street. Greta's Photography and Magic she calls it."

"Photography and Magic? What's that about?"

"She's done weddings and events here at the hotel for years. Also a magician. Does a great show. Lots of parties in town."

Hmmm, I thought. A magician... someone who can disappear and reappear.

Tessa said, "Think Greta would be around this afternoon?"

"You might find her there. Weekends are her busy time, weddings and all. Does the darkroom work during the week."

"Where is her shop?", I asked.

"Just on the other side of the old cemetery. Go out the back door, turn left. Little old post war bungalow up the street. Sign in the window."

"Thanks," I said, as Tessa and I walked down the corridor. The shadows were getting long from the surrounding foothills as we exited the hotel, crossed the street and walked past the old cemetery. Just on the other side was a row of small bungalows. Many had been converted into businesses. There was a dentist, florist and right next to the cemetery was the little shop we were looking for. The house was craftsman style with a large covered porch, a center door, and good sized picture windows on each side. On the left side, stenciled across the glass was the arch logo that said, Greta's Photography. The right window said Magic Supplies and Lessons. Walking up to the door, I mentioned to Tessa, "Let's see if we get any reaction as we enter."

"If she was the one in your room, I expect something."

The walkway up to the house was neatly trimmed, the grass on each side freshly mowed. Walking up the steps, I opened the wooden door and walked up to the counter. We were greeted by a small 'ring bell for service' sign. With a decided ding, the curtain behind the counter moved, and a sharply dressed woman in a green dress appeared. She had rich golden hair, pulled back behind her ears. Her face was made up with deep mascara and brightly painted red lips, set off with a thick gold necklace.

With a slight European accent, she said, "Can I help you?"

I was watching her eyes, but it appeared that she did not recognize us. I said, "My friend and I are looking for someone to take a few portrait shots of us while we are in town."

The woman looked us over, and replied, "Are you engaged or getting married?"

Tessa said, "Not yet, just friends. We came into possession of a large gemstone and would like a portrait that includes it."

"Interesting request," the woman said. "I'm Greta by the way. How did you find me?"

I said, "Alice over at the hotel sent us. She told me you are her mom's sister."

"Excellent," she said. "I do a lot of photography for their clients. I'm headed out for a wedding rehearsal in about an hour, but I have a little time now. If you want simple studio shots, I can get those now and mail them to you. I'll just need a 50% deposit upfront."

Nodding approval, I said, "Do you have any package deals?"

She smiled, "If you are willing to pay in full upfront, I'll get you five 5x7 color shots for $50. An extra set will be $25."

Opening my wallet, I pulled out two twenties and a ten. "Sounds good. Where do you want us?"

"This way." Pushing back the curtain she took my money and led us back to a small studio with a dark blue backdrop.

"You say you want to highlight a gemstone. Are you talking about a ring?"

"No, just a large blue Topaz." I pulled the large blue gem from my pocket. "Do you have a silver tray or something to show it off?"

"Wow," she exclaimed. "That is some jewel. I do have a small black velvet tray that might work. Let's try putting the tray on top of a stool and have you stand on each side."

Turning on some house lights, she positioned a tall black stool in the center of a screen. Bringing out a small black sheet, she covered the stool and put the black tray on top. "Let's put the jewel in here and see if we can see it's brilliance."

Handing her the jewel she put it on the tray. "I don't like it," she said. "I think silver might be better. Let me get one out of the kitchen."

She returned in a minute with a tray almost identical to the one I had seen in the hotel. "Let's try this." Centering the jewel on the tray, she smiled. "Much better. Let's get the two of you to each side."

She put a 35mm camera on a tripod and setup a flash unit. "I'm going to turn down the lights a bit, so we don't get light distortion. Smile."

As Tessa and I stood next to each other, the flash unit went off numerous times. It felt like the bright flashes we had experienced in the hotel room. "A couple of different poses please," she said.

We looked at each other and put our hands behind the jewel. Nothing seemed out of the ordinary. If this lady was in my room, she was either one hell of an actress or for some reason didn't recognize us."

"Wow, those flashes are bright," I said.

"Lot's of candlepower," she said. "Let's me take wedding shots from far away."

In a couple of minutes, she finished up. She led us back to the front counter. "I've got to run to the rehearsal. My daughter will finish up with you. Fill out your address on this return envelope. You'll get your prints in about a week. Chelsea will be out in a minute. She is finishing up some work in the darkroom. Sorry, but I've got to go." Grabbing a coat, she yelled back, "Chelsea, customers at the front. They need a receipt."

I could hear a muffled, "OK, be there in a minute."

Greta walked out the door and headed down the street.

Tessa and I stood at the counter. Shaking my head, I said, "I don't think she's our photographer."

Tessa replied, "I don't think so either. Way too cool."

From behind the curtain came a small voice, "I'm coming."

The red cloth curtain opened, and a young woman came around. Thin, sandy hair. Looking up, she made eye contact with us. She froze for a second and then let out a huge scream. She turned and ran behind the curtain.

Tessa said, "That's her, almost certain."

I ran back behind the counter, flung open the curtain, only to see a door at the back of the shop slam closed. Tessa, who was now beside me, said, "Let's go get her."

CHAPTER 59

It's not often that I just start chasing a stranger, especially a stranger I've seen for less than a second. However, when someone reacts the way this young woman did, my mind went into overdrive. Matching up memories of a ghostly figure seen multiple times in my room at night, I knew we had our person. Now we just had to catch her.

Running to the door that had just slammed shut in front of us, Tessa wrenched it open, I took the lead and entered a dark passage. There were stairs that led downward into a very dim basement room. Stopping at the bottom of the stairs, we both stood still for a second, getting our bearings. In the quiet, we could hear footsteps leading away. My eyes started to adjust to blackness, the damp musty odor of mildew filling my nostrils.

"She is heading towards the hotel," Tessa said. "Can you see the door over on the far wall?"

I focused in that direction and could just make out the thin dark outline of a door. "Let's go," I said, running in that direction.

Tessa looked down at my foot. "Can you run?"

"I'm O.K. I don't want her out of our sight." My left leg with the brace hurt but my movement was getting better. While I couldn't go at my usual full pace, I was making pretty good progress. Tessa was beside me now, her athletic prowess apparent. She reached the door and pulled it open; The latch gave way as a cold, damp blast of air greeted us. Facing the dark tunnel, I asked, "You up for this?"

"Go for it, Trace. Don't let her get away."

We descended a few more stairs and started running in what appeared to be an old sewer or drainage tunnel. The ceiling was low, so we had to crouch down as we moved forward. The floor was wet and slimy, smelled of mold and decay. As we continued, there were openings in the ceiling at regular intervals, dim light seeping through the vents.

"Where do you think we are," I asked as we ran.

"Have to be under the old graveyard. Probably an old drain."

"Where does this lead, I wonder?"

"I guess we'll see," she said.

Our eyes had adjusted now, which made our forward movement faster. However, the woman we were chasing was a little shorter and certainly more familiar with the passage. I held up my hand for a second. "Let's stop and listen," I said. We were both breathing hard, but we could hear running steps in the distance.

"She's still up ahead. I don't want to lose her," she said.

Running again, we soon came to a wall, a passage going to the right and another sloping down to the left. "The right passage must lead to the hotel," I said.

"I hear steps in that direction."

We turned right in the dim light, the tunnel now rising slightly. "We must be getting near the hotel," I said. The vents above are gone."

The tunnel got very dark, light only coming from behind. Up ahead we could hear a door or access port open and close. "She must have exited the tunnel," Tessa said. "Keep your eyes open."

As the passage got darker, there was a small set of steps leading upward on the right. "I think this is where she went," I said. "There is an access door here. I'm going to try it."

I pushed upwards, "Feels like she put something heavy on top of the door. I can move it slightly, but whatever it is is really heavy."

Tessa said, "Let me in next to you. Let's both push at the same time."

As we pushed, the door moved a few inches. "OK Tessa, let's count this down and push... three, two, one, lift."

The door moved upward over a foot. I took another step up and put my shoulder into it. "One more time," I yelled. "Three, two, one, lift." This time, we could hear something heavy slide off to one side. I pushed the hatch open. Climbing up, I saw a couple of old sand bags off to the side.

"Two fifty pound cement bags. Damn heavy when it's over your head."

Tessa nodded, "Now where? It looks like we are in the sub-basement of the hotel. No sign of our young photographer."

The area we were in was expansive. The light was dim, but I could make out extensive pipes, vents, and short retaining walls. Unfortunately, the basement area here was only five feet high.

"Look Trace," Tessa said, "this is laid out just like the hotel. Each room above has a retaining wall on each side. Pipes and vents lead up to the bathroom and floor registers. The center hall is open, and the whole hotel has a brick retaining wall around the perimeter."

I responded, "Each room has a crudely painted number. Must correspond to the room numbers above."

Tessa was fascinated as she walked into one of the sub-areas on one of the rooms. "Check this out. There is a newer ladder on the back wall. Looks like it leads into the add-on at the back of the rooms for the new bathrooms. At the top of the ladder is an access panel. I'm going to push up on one."

Tessa pushed and heard the coarse sound of wood sliding on wood. The panel lifted up. Tessa raised her hand into the opening.

"Now I know how your ghost got into your room," she said. This panel is the wooden floor of the cabinet under the bathroom sink. Just move it up and you have three feet of access. Doors on the outside will keep you hidden until you exit into the room."

Looking up where she was, I said, "You're right. There appears to be a ladder in each room where they installed the new plumbing and sinks. Just lift the under sink access panel and you can get in. However, you're not going to get back out of that room without a lot of noise and hassle. Certainly not as fast as our ghost disappeared."

"True," she said. "Let's go down to your room. It was room seven as I remember."

We walked back out of the first room sub-basement to the long corridor. We both stood still for a minute. Silence, other that running water in the pipes above. I said, "Not sure where our friend went. Let's check out the underside of my room."

Walking down the under hotel corridor, the area above had huge pipes and vents running the length of the building. Tessa said, "I think this is it. Odd side of the corridor, four rooms down. Must be room seven."

"Yep," I said. "Here is the old spray painted number."

We crouched and walked to the back of the room; Tessa noted, "Same access ladder like the first room. Looks like it has been accessed recently. Splinters and wood dust of the floor."

"OK, so that is how she got in. . . How did she escape?" I sat on the dirt floor and in the dim light I looked at the floor joists above. There was a regular pattern. 16-inch joists, cross-braced at regular intervals.

"Tessa let out a whoop, "Look at this area. Footprints start here out of nowhere and lead to the corridor."

Glancing up at the hardwood floor above, the boards had been cut, spring hinged, and a latch had been added to one end. "This is it, " I said. "What a clever mechanism. Push once it pops down slightly. Push it again and it opens. Sixteen inches wide, two feet long. Just drop into the basement and the floor springs back up and pops silently into place."

I fiddled with the latch and pulled it open. The hinge was silent and created in such a way that the door moved slower than normal, so it wouldn't bang or make noise. I could see my room above.

Tessa said, "Wow, is that quiet. Look at the edges. There is a flat carpet seam all around."

"Genius," I said. Look at this. This thin flat seam goes under another thin flat seam above. From the room, you would never know that the carpet had been modified."

Tessa smiled. "I've heard about contraptions like this, but I've never seen one in person. Magicians use them all the time. The secret is they have to be undetectable and silent."

"Smooth and quiet," I replied. "I bet our photographers daughter is long gone. But now we know her secret. I wonder how many of these have been setup in this old place?"

"Let's look."

Walking up and down the corridor, it appeared that four of the odd numbered rooms had the trap doors installed.

"I see at least four, "I said. "But they don't look new at all. Someone set these up a long time ago."

"All in the family, I bet."

"No doubt. Let's run upstairs. I want to ask Alice a few questions."

"So how do we get there, Trace?"

"The hard way, I guess. Let's climb through the bathroom."

"How is that leg of yours doing?"

"Much better. The adrenaline must have kicked in."

In a few minutes, we were back in my room. I put one of the room lamps over the under sink floor opening so I would be able to determine if someone had come in while I was gone.

Tessa picked up the phone and called the hospital. "I got in on tonight's shift," she said. If you can drop me at home, I'll drive by myself."

"Will do, but I want to buy you an early dinner first. My treat in the dining room."

Locking up the room, we went up to the front desk. Alice was still there. I said, "I realize it's early, but can you make us a sandwich or two?"

"Mom's in the kitchen," she said. Turkey Tuesday. I'll have her bring you a couple of turkey sandwiches. Take a seat in the bar."

Tessa and I sat at the bar and Alice brought out a couple of steaming hot sandwiches. As she dropped them off, I said, "Tessa and I had our pictures taken by Greta today. Lovely lady. Noticed she had a daughter."

Alice came up close, "Her name is Chelsea. Works over here sometimes at the front desk. She's a little weird. She's been messed up since her dad went to prison. Her mother and father used to be professional magicians. Worked the hotel, hospitality circuit. Made lots of money. Probably noticed the magic sign on their window. Greta still does magic parties, but that's about it. Chelsea was always the one that was sawed in half or disappeared in the stage tricks. Her smaller size helped."

"What happened to her dad?" I asked.

"Embezzlement. We jokingly say, he made money disappear."

Tessa and I looked at each other.

"Like father, like daughter," I said.

CHAPTER 60

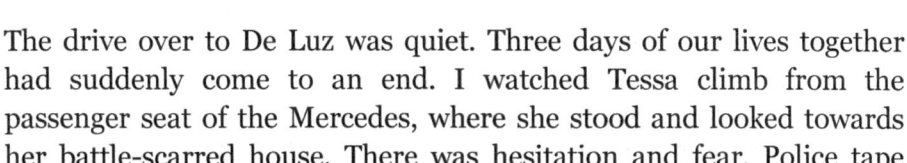

The drive over to De Luz was quiet. Three days of our lives together had suddenly come to an end. I watched Tessa climb from the passenger seat of the Mercedes, where she stood and looked towards her battle-scarred house. There was hesitation and fear. Police tape fluttered in the wind. Walking around the car, I stood next to her and whispered, "It will never be the same, will it?"

Turning slowly, she put her arm on my shoulder. "It's just a house, Trace. Houses can be sold, but what we shared over the past few days is something I will never forget. You saved my life. That house would have been my grave, but now it's just a broken reminder that there are a lot of greedy, self-serving people in this world. People that would take your life for an inch long jewel from hell."

She kissed me softly on the cheek and then turned to go. Stopping a few feet from me, she turned slowly back, her sharp blue eyes catching mine. She whispered, "It's not over, Mr. Armstrong. This isn't a fitting ending. I don't have words now, but I must go."

I could feel a tear in my eye. A woman who had taken care of me, saved me, and gone through the most horrific of circumstances was going away. I felt so many emotions at that moment. She had become a trusted friend, someone you could count on, through almost any circumstance. She had healed my wounds and given me strict instructions to get better, even though I somehow ignored them.

"We made a pretty good team, Tessa," I said. "I had no idea you were such a good detective."

"That we did, Trace. But if you expect me to quit my day job and join you. . ." She smiled. "I'll have to think about that. Tell you the truth, I enjoyed being your sidekick. One hell of an adventure."

"Even with the bullets, fire and caves?"

"We could leave those out next time," she laughed, "but the ghost hunting—now that was intriguing."

"You got a deal. I'll call you in the morning at the hospital. Let me know how Mark is doing. Hoping I can get a good nights sleep. Hopefully, our ghost was scared away."

"I'm just going to pick up a uniform, close the door behind me, and drive my truck to work. There will be plenty of time to deal with things here. I'm just not prepared to face them yet."

With that, she walked towards the house, opened the door, and turned on the porch light. As I got back in the Mercedes, I watched her walk out, get in her truck and back out of the drive. She wasn't kidding about her house. As her taillights disappeared down De Luz, I thought about the curvy road that had caused us so much trouble. It was long, desolate, and had so many hidden secrets. It now held a few more. . .

****

I was tired now, the afternoon blues taking over my mind. The Mercedes engine purred along as I shifted to third, long shadows creeping across De Luz. Put my finger on the power window switches, pushing both down at the same time. The hot, dusty air of summer swirled through the cockpit as I hit the radio button. B B King singing the blues and I was thinking of how much I was going to enjoy getting home. One more day in this town preceded by one more night in the lonely hotel, with sad expressions on the faces of the three women behind the counter. At least I could escape. Drive away. Sweet Alice was trapped, not even a break to see the sun. Her mom destined for the kitchen. I thought of doing them a favor, lighting a match and putting the wooden hotel prison to death for good. Not today.

I felt a pang of loneliness. Empty seat next to me. Tessa missing. Gone to work. Gone from my consciousness. Janet would be up in the morning. Not sure how that was going to go. But now I was just lonely. Late afternoon blues.

There are times in life when you should just be happy. Now was one of those. I was alive, for heaven's sake. Escaped a prison, escaped a fire, driving free down damn De Luz Road.

One thing came to mind. One stupid thing I could do that might change something in the universe. I guided the car into the hotel parking lot. Left the windows down. Walking briskly in through the front door and into the foyer. Alice was behind the front counter. I said nothing, just walked behind the counter and took her by the hand. "I'm taking you to heaven," I said as I led her to the front door.

"What? Where are you taking me, Mr. Armstrong?" she asked.

"Heaven," I replied again.

"I have to cover the front desk."

"Heaven can't wait," I said, leading her to the passenger side of the Mercedes. Opening the door, I had her sit in the seat. Walking around to the driver's side, I got in, fired the engine and said, "Close the door."

Surprisingly, she complied. Driving out of the parking lot, I headed south, out of town. There was no traffic in that direction. The clock on the dash said 5:15. She probably thought I was crazy, but she just asked a simple question, "What is heaven like?"

"You'll see in a few minutes," I replied. "For now, close your eyes, and imagine what heaven will be like. What do you see?"

"I see green trees, blue skies, and a shining city."

"Who is there?"

"Happy, smiling people."

"What do you hear?"

"Harps and soft music."

"What do you smell?"

"The aromas of fruit and good food."

"Good. Keep your eyes closed. We will be there momentarily."

I turned off De Luz and entered a small dirt road. The road was full of ruts and bumps which were a challenge for the low slung car. Pulling up on top of a small hill, I said, "Keep your eyes closed, Alice."

Getting out of the car, I walked around, opened her door. "I'm going to guide you to heaven. Keep your eyes closed for a minute longer."

"You're scaring me, Mr. Armstrong."

"Nothing to be afraid of, I promise. I want you to stand still now and turn this way. I guided her to the top of the hill. "Now open your eyes,"

"Oh my God, Trace Armstrong, it's our winery."

"From what you told me, this is heaven."

"You have no idea. My dad died down this hill in an accident. I've always wanted to make something of this. . . But the hotel. . ."

"The hotel is hell. This is heaven."

"But how? You can see that the area is full of weeds. The vines are dying."

I pulled the large blue topaz from my front pocket. "This is a symbolic start. I want you to have this. My uncle loved your wine. This will help pay for a first planting."

"But how do we start?"

"I have a couple of friends that can help you. For now, I just want you to take in the view. I want you to dream of heaven. Take in the aroma, listen to the birds, see the sunset."

"How can I pay you back?"

"I want to share a bottle of your first new vintage."

"What will we call it?"

"Blue Topaz."

****

I took Alice back to the hotel. Everything was quiet. Her little trip unnoticed.

"Thanks for going with me today, Alice," I said. "I just wanted to give you hope that there is life outside this dreaded hotel."

"When you said you were taking me to heaven, I didn't know what to think at first. But when you had me close my eyes, I pictured rolling hills, green trees, and friendly people. Fallbrook has always been known as the friendly village. When my family, the Whittingham's, came here in 1958, I was just two years old. My dad's vision was to recreate the joy and sense of community that this hotel represented when it was first constructed in the late 1880s. He took an enormous gamble rebuilding this old place. It was a complete wreck when he bought it. Sometimes I think it would have been better if it was just torn down in '58. The bulldozers were ready."

"I didn't realize it came that close to destruction."

"The heavy equipment was out front when he signed the papers. My dad is the son of a lumber baron out of the Northwest. Rebuilding an old wooden hotel just made sense for the family business. It took two years to renovate, with all sixty rooms being restored and each one having a bathroom added. The grounds were spruced up, and the grand old girl reopened to the public in 1960. Fallbrook became a destination again."

"The early years must have been exciting."

"Growing up, there were always parties and weddings. Famous people would come to town and visit. Movie stars came out from Hollywood. As a little girl, my twin sister and I always felt special. I have signed pictures from Bob Hope, Bing Crosby, and others. The Fallbrook, as it was known, was the center of town. Restaurants and shops along Main flourished from visitors all during the sixties. The railroad had a Fallbrook Special that came on the weekends. The train station was half a block away, bustling with eager guests and sightseers."

"So what happened to the glory days?"

"Everything was going well until they decided to remove the railroad tracks in the early seventies. You have to understand that Fallbrook has always been train-centric, but off the beaten path as far as road traffic. When the weekend trains went away, so did the town. Businesses left, restaurants closed, and the hotel fell into disrepair."

"But why take the tracks out?"

"When the tracks were first run in the 1880s they went all the way through the hills to Riverside, fifty miles north. But flooding on the

Margarita River kept washing them out. In the early 1900s the tracks through the river canyon were abandoned. The train was then rerouted to end in Fallbrook. My dad was a visionary. He always thought that new construction techniques would allow the original tracks to be rebuilt, and Fallbrook would be a central hub. The hotel would be the town centerpiece. He had plans to double or triple its size. He figured the inland valleys would eventually be filled with houses. Houses that would be built with family lumber."

"So I take it, someone's vision was different from your dads."

"In the 70's, passenger train travel went out of favor. State planners were focused on cars, cars and more cars. Interstate freeways and superhighways were built. The train tracks disappeared, and Highway 395 turned into eight-lane Interstate 15, twelve miles outside of town."

"So you were left with an expensive hotel to run, but very little traffic."

"Without the train, Fallbrook ceased to be a tourist destination. It became an agricultural area with olives, citrus, and avocados."

"So your dad, being the visionary that he was, decided to open a farm based business—a winery. This area has the perfect climate for grapes. Wine is a very profitable commodity. If you can't beat them, join them."

"Exactly," she said. "Unfortunately, he died doing what he loved, cultivating the grapes, and we are saddled with this termite infested 'historic' monstrosity. As you pointed out earlier, for me, being at the winery is heaven, this place is hell."

"Can you do me a favor?" I asked.

"Sure."

"Let's go in the bar for a minute. Pour two glasses of your best wine. Put it on my tab. I want to toast your future vintage."

She brought two glasses and filled them halfway with an estate blend Cabernet.

She put the blue topaz on the bar. We held our glasses up.

To the first blue topaz wine ever created. . .

Cheers!

CHAPTER 61

───────────〰───────────

The hotel was quiet Tuesday night. Many of the weekend guests had checked out. There were only a few people in the restaurant, certainly not enough to justify a dedicated establishment. My overnight stay was uneventful. No more ghosts in the room. I slept well, not having to worry about flashing lights or diamonds in my shoe. As morning dawned, I opened the curtains wide, letting in the morning sun. I took a look at where the trap door was on the carpet. Almost undetectable.

Looking around the room, I did notice something that I hadn't seen before. In one of the light sconces on the wall, one of the interior bulbs looked different. It wasn't currently lit. That's when I noticed that it was an electronic flash bulb. Evidently triggered by a wireless control on a camera, it would indeed give off a blinding light. That was how the side shots were taken. Funny I hadn't noticed it before.

Janet was going to meet me downstairs at eight. I packed up my items but decided not to check out until later. Calling over to the hospital, I caught Tessa for a moment. She said, "Hey Trace. I'm on floor duty now. I'll be off later this morning at 8:30. Your cousin Mark isn't doing so well. Multiple infections, his leg is messed up from his trip down the hill, and he has some pretty significant burns from the house fire. Not to mention losing his wife. We are going to keep him for another day or two."

"At least I know he is in good hands," I said. "I'm meeting Janet at eight. Not sure how that is going to go. I'm thinking of sending her to the photographer's shop."

"Good idea, get her involved. She'll come around."

"I think so. By the way, no ghosts last night. I got some sleep."

She laughed, "Good for you. I got some sleep too, but I'm worried about how it is going to be when I get home."

"Need some help? We should be around till noon?"

"Tell you what, if you are up for it, I'll treat both of you to breakfast at the Main Street Cafe at nine. They owe me some money for some pies. Great pancakes. I'd like another go with the gal at the photo shop."

"You got a deal."

I hung up and then made a call to another cousin who was involved with my uncle's funeral. Had her postpone the funeral for a couple of weeks and notify local relatives. Locking my room, I walked up front. Janet's 240Z was pulling into the drive. I decided it might be good to meet her at her car.

I walked up and helped her out, "Man it's good to see you, Janet," I said, giving her hug and embrace. Dressed in a tapered white top and khaki dress pants, her shoulder length amber hair looked shiny in the morning sun. Her deep mascara accented vivid green eyes.

"I missed you, Trace," she replied. "My ex-husband is a real ass. So glad to be home. At least I got the divorce started."

"Been crazy here too. Got a brace on my foot and a huge bandage on my leg, not to mention being shot at."

She smiled, "That's the detective I know. Always in trouble. So what's up this morning?"

"Have you eaten?"

"No, I figured I'd make you take me out somewhere."

"How about pancakes? Little cafe up the street. My friend Tessa said she would treat."

"Your friend Tessa? What if I don't want to eat with your friend Tessa?"

"I'd like you to meet her, Janet. She is just coming off the night shift at the hospital. Has a contact at the Main Street Cafe."

"She's the nurse I talked to yesterday. The one in the picture with you?"

"That's the one."

"The cute one. . ."

"The nurse one. . ."

"The really cute one. . ."

"The really nurse one. . . , " I laughed.

Janet gave me a smirk, "Alright mister, I'm only going to do this cause I'm hungry. You know I'm the jealous type."

I took Janet by the hand and led her up the parking lot towards Main. Soon we were outside the little restaurant bungalow. Entering the side door, the waitress sat us at a side table. Janet sat next to me. We both ordered coffee.

Looking up, I saw Tessa walk in the door. She was in an unflattering white nurses uniform. Her dark hair was pulled back into a pony tail, and her makeup was subtle. She looked OK, but certainly not like I had seen her before. Subdued was good for this meeting. I stood up. "Janet this is Tessa. She worked with my uncle and has been my nurse for the last couple of days."

Janet stood and said, "Nice to meet you. I guess you are a real nurse. Thought Trace might be lying to me."

"Yep, real nurse," Tessa said. "Your boyfriend is one hell of a difficult patient. First he's getting burned, then falls down a hill, and then he gets shot at. The worst thing is, he doesn't listen. I told him three times to stay off that ankle, but do you think he listens to me. . . No way. I hope you might have better luck."

"Better luck. I don't think so. Last time I went somewhere with him, we got shot at, and I ended up in the trunk of a car. Not my idea of a fun date."

Tessa pulled back her hair on her forehead, "I hang out with him, and I get a nice bullet scar on my noggin. I'd say he's a dangerous man."

"Dangerous man, " I laughed. "The guy that was chasing us was the dangerous man. Thankfully Tessa is a good shot."

Janet said, "It sounds like a crazy adventure. What exactly happened?"

We ordered breakfast. Then over the next ten minutes we told Janet about the fire, the colonel and the Fallbrook cops. The chill had gone away from the conversation. Tessa and Janet seemed to be getting along okay. I then explained what happened at Greta's Photography the day before.

I said, "After chasing the daughter yesterday, we found out how she was accessing the hotel and getting in and out of the guest rooms."

Tessa said, "There is a drainage tunnel that runs under the street and up to the hotel. She would gain access to the hotel subfloor area, then climb in under the sink and get into the bathroom. Then, standing in the middle of the bedroom, she would attract her prey with her wispy lace covering. When someone would walk towards her, she would blind them with a flash. The person suddenly can't see a thing. She drops through the trap door, into the basement area. All is left in the room is a whisp of smoke from the flash bulb and the subtle smell of rose water. Clever use of a photo flash."

"Wow." Janet said. "Then all she needs to do is develop the prints and set up the blackmail. If she has access to the register, she knows the names of the clients, their address, and possibly the company they work for."

I replied, "Depending on who is in the room, she has pictures of the client and any guests that they have. Many people might not want their spouses or employers seeing pictures like this."

Janet ran her eyes from me over to Tessa, "So Trace, you still haven't told me what Tessa was doing in your room?"

I said, "The first night was a fire, the second was the fact that they were stalking Tessa's house and had just shot up her place. We honestly didn't know who or what was going on."

Tessa spoke quietly, "I know the pictures don't look good, Janet, but I will tell you two things. One, nothing happened. And two, staying at the hotel saved my life. Had I been at home, I wouldn't be here now."

Janet said, "I'll be honest, Tessa, I'm the jealous type, but seeing the bullet scar on your forehead, I not only believe you but would have done the same thing myself."

Flagging the waitress to pay the bill, I said, "So now we need to smoke out this person for good. I suggest we send Janet in by herself to talk to Greta while Tessa and I hide out on the side of the house. If you can draw the daughter out, we'll block the front door and have a talk with her."

Janet replied, "How about this. I just walk into the shop, go to the front counter and offer to pay for the pictures that were sent in the envelope. If the mom knows about them, we know she is part of the deal. If not, I just say loudly that I'm going to drop the money at the PO Box. You guys are outside as I come out. If the daughter follows, we have a talk."

"Sounds like a plan," I said.

Finishing up at the restaurant, we walk down Main until we got to Oak Street, where Greta's shop was. Tessa and I held back as Janet walked in the front door. Standing out front, somewhat hidden by street trees, we watched through the window as Janet talked with Greta. We could see Greta shake her head as she viewed the pictures. Janet turned and asked loudly where the Post Office was so she could pay for the photos. As Janet walked out, she headed down the street towards Main. Within a minute, Chelsea walked out the door and down the front steps. Tessa and I stepped out from behind the trees. She glanced up. Startled, she turned and ran back into the house. Tessa ran after her, and I was right behind. As we entered the shop, Greta was standing at a desk to one side. Chelsea ran around the counter, through the curtain and right into a large cabinet. The door opened and closed. Tessa was right behind her. Stopping in front of the enclosure, she opened the wooden door. The cabinet was empty. As Greta walked in, I was right behind her. "What is this all about?" she asked. "Aren't you the folks who ordered pictures yesterday? They won't be done for a week."

Just then Janet walked back in carrying the envelope. I opened the envelope and pulled out one of the pictures. I said, "We want to talk to your daughter about these photos that she took over at the hotel. She wants $500 for them, and we need to pay her."

Greta thundered, "Chelsea's not here as you can see."

Tessa smiled, "Oh Chelsea is here all right. I happen to know how these magic cabinets work. If I just hit this hidden latch up here, the door will open just like this."

She hit a hidden latch, and the door opened, revealing a very squished Chelsea.

Janet said in a stern but calm voice, "Can we go out front and discuss this matter?"

Greta pulled Chelsea's arm and marched her out front. The three of us walked back out around the counter.

"What is this all about? What has my daughter got to do with any of it?"

I spoke up, "Well it seems after you had left yesterday, Chelsea saw us and led us on a wild goose chase underground, back to the hotel. We found out how she had taken these revealing shots over the past few nights, and we just want to pay her for her time."

Greta seemed dumbfounded, "Let me see one of those photos."

I pulled the one out showing the ghost from the side, "This is one of the most revealing ones. The person in that picture is your daughter."

Greta shook her head, "My daughter's chest is not that big. You've got the wrong person."

Janet walked back behind the curtain for a second and then returned. She had a plastic bustier and a lace shawl in her hand. "Well, Greta I think you'll find that when your daughter wears this bustier and shawl, she looks just like the ghost in the picture."

Greta looked at her daughter standing behind the counter, "What do you know about this?"

"Nothing," she said at first.

Suddenly her voice got very stern. She said, "Don't lie to me. What is this all about?"

Chelsea's eyes welled up, "I just did what I used to do for daddy when someone had a strange woman in their room. You know, the ones dressed all cute."

"What?" she yelled.

"He had me photo them in bed and act all spooky, like a ghost."

"When did you do this?"

"Before he went to prison. They would always send money in. He would pick it up at the post office. He always told me not to tell you. Said it was a secret. That he wanted to use the money to surprise you."

Chelsea appeared to be in her late teens. It became evident that she was employed in a blackmail scheme.

"So who delivered the pictures," I asked.

"I would send them by courier to the business address listed on the register of the hotel. Made sure to address it to the name on the log. We had a card that dad would put inside. He got lots of money for these pictures. He said not to send them in the regular mail. We could get in trouble if we did."

Greta said, "So what made you do this yourself?"

"I know you told me you were hurting for money since dad went away, so I thought I would do it again. It's kind of fun to see people get all scared. When I wore the bustier, dad got more money. He hooked it up, so the rooms had a second flash that worked with the camera. Sometimes I would put the camera on a stick like tripod, so I could take pictures of the ghost, like I did with you."

Greta was dumbfounded, "How did you get out of the rooms, Chelsea?"

"Just like we used to do on stage with the magic box. The rooms had silent trapdoors just like the stage did."

I asked, "Was there anyone at the hotel that knew about this?"

"I'm not sure," she said, "but I know dad gave mom's sister money sometimes after I played ghost."

The whole picture was now becoming more apparent. The young woman was being used by her father and possibly her aunt to take revealing photos. Prostitutes and others in the rooms with businessmen. Probably for years. Now that she was older, it was hard to tell how innocent she was, but she was certainly naive. Another hidden secret of the Fallbrook Hotel.

Greta said, "I'm sorry about all this. I'll make sure it doesn't happen again."

I asked, "Can you get us the negatives?"

Chelsea went into the dark room and picked them out.

Tessa said, "One more question, young lady. Why did you run yesterday when you saw us?"

Chelsea said, "Daddy always told me to run if anyone ever came here with the envelope of ghost pictures. He said that some people don't like ghosts and might try and hurt them. He was right, you chased me."

The three of us got ready to go, but I turned and asked Greta one last question. "Can you take a shot of all three of us and add it to the pictures you took yesterday?"

"Sure," she said. "It's the least I can do."

She had us line up in front of the blue background.

A trio of ghostbusters. . .

EPILOGUE

The three of us left the photo studio, smiling and probably a little bit concerned. We had uncovered the secret of the hotel ghost, one that was very convincing, even to a detective. Chelsea was probably lucky she had not been hurt in her escapades over the years. It was readily apparent why her dad was in prison.

We walked back to the hotel and went back to my room for one last perusal. I showed Janet how the trap door worked and showed Tessa the flash bulb in the wall sconce. Walking out, I motioned to Alice that I would be in touch. I handed her the door key. I motioned to Madeline behind the curtain to come out.

I said, "We just paid for some pictures taken in our room and you should ask your sister for a commission. Tell her Chelsea was like a ghost. We hardly knew she was there."

From the look on Madeline's face, it was obvious that she was in on the setup. She said, "I'm not sure what you mean Mr. Armstrong. We usually don't allow photographers in customers rooms."

I smiled, "Not to worry. I think it was just a figment of our imaginations. One second she was there, the next second she was gone. Thankfully Greta is sending us some new photos. Ones that are not over exposed."

I winked at her, letting her know we were onto her little scam. Walking out, we all left the hotel in separate cars and headed back to Tessa's house. Inside, the place was a wreck. The colonel and his cop cronies had pulled everything out of cabinets and thrown everything on the floor. The kitchen was strewn with soggy blackened avocado pieces.

Tessa looked around, tears in her eyes. "I've always loved Fallbrook, but this is difficult to take. Sure, my insurance will take care of it, but I don't think I'll ever feel safe here again."

Janet had a tear in her eye too, "No wonder you didn't want to come back here. What a mess and bad memory."

Tessa said, "I'm going to lock up and go back to work. I'm not ready to deal with this."

The three of us hugged, and I took one more look around. The Caribbean art on the walls was joyous, but everything else was dismal. We walked out, and I drove home.

* * * Three Months Later * * *

It was November now, the days were shorter, and Janet and I were off for a long weekend. Destination, Fallbrook. Her long distant divorce was moving along but seemed to have constant setbacks which frustrated her no end.

Tessa had invited us up. Seems she had taken on the care of my cousin, Mark Armstrong. She helped him get into rehab and had been there for him through two funerals. There was talk of an engagement. She had moved in with Mark, helping with his burns and getting him back on his feet.

Walking into Mark's house, Tessa said, "Three months ago I had a very big crush on a guy with the last name of Armstrong. Now I've got one that says he wants to marry me. I'm here today to tell you all that I'm going to say yes."

Mark said, "Tessa has changed my life. It's been tough over the last three months, rehab and all, but this is one nurse that really cares and is one hell of a cook. I miss my dad and miss my wife, but moving forward we will rebuild. At my dad's place, we bulldozed the house and shed and are going to expand the avocado and citrus groves. Insurance helped pay for the groves, and I was able to get a new truck. My old one is still down the side of the hill. Probably never be able to get it out of there."

Tessa said, "You probably heard I'm leaving the hospital. I'm going to set up a restaurant at the new winery in town. Remember Alice from the hotel. Well, she is running the place now. It's ironic, but the old Fallbrook Hotel will finally be torn down. It seems a fire that started in a wall sconce in room seven, burned half the place. No one was hurt, but it's too expensive to repair. Condos and businesses will take its place."

Mark said, "The Fallbrook Police Department has been disbanded after those two cops were shot. Now everything goes back to the North County Sheriff's Department. Can't say that anyone in town is sad about that."

Janet looked around the house and said, "I see that Tessa moved her cheerful Caribbean beach paintings over here. I just love those with the ocean blue background. Livens the place up."

I had taken back the 280 SL to my FBI friend. A little body work and some fresh paint made it better than new. Turns out the little South American battery bug was planted on the Benz by none other than Captain Kirkpatrick of the North County Sheriff's Department. Martino had taken the wayward bug and placed it on the police chief's private car. This led to a very embarrassing encounter as Mr. Kirkpatrick was found letting the air out of all the chief's tires. Oops.

I read in the paper that the Ice Blue Diamond had a new and spectacular exhibit space created at the San Diego History Museum. The whole museum has a new state of the art security system, set up curiously by a newly hired security consultant named Max.

As I walked out to the backyard, Tessa took me aside. "Martino's finder's fee helped with the restaurant. I can't wait to get started. Lots of avocado and citrus dishes, and my specialty diamond guacamole, served in a stunning clear crystal avocado dish."

Smiling, I said, "I invested part of my finders fee into the winery itself. Alice is promising me the first uncorking of a Blue Topaz Wine.

Part merlot with some blueberry overtones. Put some in a chilled glass." Reaching out for Tessa's hand, I said, "I'll invite you to our Ice Blue Reception."

ADDENDUM

———————◦◦◦———————

I would like to thank the kind people at the Fallbrook Historical Society for their help in researching the history of the Fallbrook, including the hotel, the police force, various mines, and the curvy and treacherous De Luz Road.

The Fallbrook (Ellis) Hotel depicted in this book was sadly torn down in 1958. The railroad tracks were removed in 1971. We can only imagine what Fallbrook would have been like had they restored the hotel and kept their railroad tracks in operation.

Fallbrook is an unincorporated community and has contracted with the San Diego County Sheriff's Department for police services for many years.

John Scot, 2016

ABOUT THE AUTHOR

John Scot is an author based in San Diego County. You can find out more about his books on his author page at http://johnscot.com.

John also writes non-fiction books and runs a popular blog. You can find out about his other books at http://johnwrichardson.com

John blogs at http://personalsuccesstoday.com

www.ingramcontent.com/pod-product-compliance
Lightning Source LLC
Chambersburg PA
CBHW062015170626
46813CB00001B/166